JOAN COLLINS

LINDEN PRESS/SIMON & SCHUSTER
New York · London · Toronto · Sydney · Tokyo · Singapore

Love &
Desire
& Hate

Linden Press
Simon & Schuster Building
Rockefeller Center
1230 Avenue of the Americas
New York, New York 10020

Originally published in Great Britain by Random Century Group,
20 Vauxhall Bridge Road, London SW1V 2SA
LINDEN PRESS/S & S and colophon are registered trademarks of
Simon & Schuster
Designed by Caroline Cunningham
Manufactured in the United States of America

Quality Printing and Binding by:
ARCATA Graphics/Kingsport
Press and Roller Streets
Kingsport, TN 37662 U.S.A.

For Robin
With all my love

They are not long, the weeping and the laughter
Love and desire and hate:
I think they have no portion in us after
We pass the gate.

ERNEST DOWSON *Vitae Summa Brevis*

Prologue

*T*he *Chief Inspector of the local police didn't like movie people at all. He* disliked them disrupting his happy playground of a town when they were shooting, and he hated it even more when one of them died.

There was only one thing worse than a death on location and that was two deaths; now there were three.

This last tragedy appeared to have been an accident. An old wooden cable car carrying the unfortunate man had crashed down to the rocky beach, killing him instantly. For the third time in as many months Chief Inspector Gomez had been awakened from an untroubled sleep to attend to the needs of this ill-assorted group of actors, producers and technicians, who now stood ashen-faced on the beach by the light of a sickly moon, the light Pacific breeze ruffling the chiffon and silk of the women's dresses.

He began by asking them some well-chosen questions.

The young *wunderkind* director, the first to have reached the body, told Gomez that without exception every member of the cast and crew had loathed the dead man—but:

The legendary leading lady protested that he had truly been a gentle man beneath his ruthless exterior.

The underaged, overly sexed ingénue kept repeating over and over,

"Death comes in threes," in her whispery French accent, while her spinster chaperone wept, feverishly wringing her hands.

The award-winning screenwriter blew her nose and latched on to the comforting arm of a young policeman, explaining to him exactly what she thought had happened, as the distinguished English character actor with the plummy voice announced that in his opinion the contraption had always been a death trap.

The dashingly handsome star said nothing, but he wondered where his mysterious fiancée had disappeared to.

Just as Gomez was deciding to send everyone away, a young police officer ran up and urgently whispered in his ear.

"One moment," the Chief Inspector called out. "One moment, please." Then he proceeded to speak quickly in a low voice.

He told his shocked and attentive audience that a preliminary examination of the cable car wreckage indicated that it had been no accident.

"It is murder," he said.

But of course one of them already knew that, because one of them had an excellent reason to kill.

As they stared at each other in stunned silence, no one noticed as the last of the amber beads which had been clutched in the dead man's hand rolled slowly into the warm sea.

Part One

Inès awoke in the Ritz Hotel beside a snoring Italian officer, with waves of pain shooting through her body. Outside the windows of the sumptuously decorated Louis XIV bedroom she could see the chestnut trees which were just beginning to blossom, and feel the cool spring breeze on her aching body. Inès adored Paris with a passion which could not be extinguished by the multiplying throng of Nazi uniforms continually parading up and down the streets, the constant ache in her belly from lack of food or the brutal men she had to serve.

She turned to look at the sleeping man next to her. By the skin on his body he appeared to be quite young, but his face, even in sleep, was cruel and insensitive, and his short bloated body bordered on the grotesque. She shivered with revulsion, remembering his so-called lovemaking last night with horror. *Merde*—what this monster had done to her.

She had met General Scrofo two days before in the Café Flore on the Left Bank, when she went to observe *la vie de bohème* which appeared on the surface to continue much the same as usual. Artists, writers and students still sat sipping drinks on spindly iron chairs outside the bustling cafés. There was always good conversation, laughter, and gentle plumes of cigarette smoke. Only the men in gray and green uniform who also sat sharing the friendly ambience indicated that Paris was an occupied city.

As Inès sipped her coffee, the hazy afternoon sunlight glinted on her golden hair, dappling her cheeks, emphasizing the bloom of her youth. Picasso was sitting at a nearby table surrounded by his usual group of sycophants and beautiful models, and his mesmerizing black eyes stared with an artist's interest in Inès' direction as he puffed on his yellow Gauloise while luxuriating in the adulation of his admirers. Inès felt she could understand the fascination that this middle-aged, balding man held for the young women with him—were it not for the more pressing attentions of the Italian at the next table, she would have answered his silent black-eyed call and joined his adoring coterie. But General Scrofo advanced on her in his heavily flirtatious manner, an appointment was made and the die cast.

The following evening she walked to her rendezvous with the General, from the boulevard Malesherbes, past the place de Wagram and across the river Seine. The boulevard Malesherbes, one of the longest streets in Paris wound past the *marché* at the Porte de Champerret, where the few remaining scraps of food and clothing were available.

Inès stopped for a sip of water from one of the bronze drinking fountains, the legacy of the English nobleman Sir Richard Wallace. Many Parisian streets boasted these charming yet functional sculptures. In the early 1870s, at the end of the Franco-Prussian War, Wallace had given them to the city which he loved, a token of his admiration for the bravery of its citizens in surviving the siege of the Prussian army. Inès hoped that in the 1940s the citizens of Paris would manage to survive the invasion of the Germans and Italians with equal courage.

Inès had been grateful for the water last night; the air was humid and dusty, and she was not looking forward to what awaited her. But it was her job—just a job. Yves always told her she must think of it only as that. Inès passed only a dozen or so cyclists and a few pedestrians on the boulevard. There were no cars for private citizens in Paris now. Only the sinister black Mercedeses of the Gestapo or the SS sped by, their darkened windows hiding the evil that lurked within.

Inès slowed her pace, thinking of all the enemy officers she and her friends had entertained at the Ritz and other Parisian hotels. Inès and Jeanette had often shared tricks together, joking hollowly about their profession, which was one of necessity. If they did not sell themselves, they had no other skills with which to survive. Yves told Inès he was unable to support her now. She was trapped in this life but made the best of it, hoping it would not last forever. When the war was over everything would change.

One day Yves informed her that Jeanette's body had been pulled from the Seine, brutally beaten. Inès was always aware that this could happen to her, too. The Nazis—and their allies, the Italians—were cruel, vicious men to whom whores were just toys to be used for whatever perversions they desired. Inès realized she was lucky to have escaped a similar fate.

Although Yves had forbidden it, Inès had gone to see Jeanette's body in the morgue, staring horrified at the once-pretty young girl, at the bruises that covered her bloated body, the deep cuts across her breasts and belly. Inès' heart beat faster with fear.

The night she died Jeanette had left the night club L'Éléphant Rose with a group of drunken Italians. Jeanette had wanted Inès to come with them, but Yves had a better trick for her that night and Inès always obeyed Yves. Even though he was a pimp, he was a kind man, with a wicked sense of humor, and she paid him the respect he deserved. Lucky for him she did, otherwise it could have been her broken body lying in the morgue. It was Russian roulette with these enemy monsters. The girls had to do whatever they desired, never sure when they would turn into sadistic beasts.

Inès was determined to survive this war, survive the Germans, the Italians, the rationing, the privations and, most of all, survive the indignities she suffered. She was going to make something of herself one day: what, though, she did not yet know.

As she entered the most beautiful of all Parisian squares she paused to admire the perfection of the octagonal place Vendôme. Honey-colored stone buildings were perfectly enhanced by the black and gilded enrichments of their balustrades and the gray-green of their sloping roofs. The stone gargoyles above the doorways of some of the buildings seemed to be jeering at her with their lolling tongues so she did not linger. Running lightly up the red-carpeted steps of the Ritz, she was directed to General Umberto Scrofo's suite by a contemptuous middle-aged concierge.

Although he had to serve Nazi generals, SS militia, Gestapo officers, majors, captains, and generals of Hitler's and Mussolini's armies with smiling servility, the concierge despised them all. Disapproval of Frenchwomen who fraternized with the enemy was all too visible on his craggy face as he watched the young prostitute going into the lift to the second floor and God only knows what degradation from General Scrofo. She was little more than a child. The concierge shrugged. It was none of his affair—he too knew the meaning of survival. These days it was every man, woman and child for themselves.

She was by no means the first underage girl whom he'd directed to Scrofo's quarters in the past two years. The thirty-year-old General liked nubile, Nordic-looking blondes, and this girl looked a suitable partner for tonight's revels.

"Come in, *cara*," said the General, surveying her with a cold smile. "And close the door." He was standing behind a marble-topped table and pouring pale amber liquid into a delicately fluted, gold-rimmed glass which, he had been assured by the most important *antiquaire* on the fabourg St.-Honoré, was from a set of glasses owned by Talleyrand himself. Inès noticed that many of the decanters on the table glittered in the soft peach lights, as only very expensive objects do, and her eyes opened wide with wonder as she took in the expensively furnished lavish room.

"Have some champagne," he commanded, taking in her slim figure, blue eyes and golden hair. Yes, she was as freshly beautiful and young as he remembered from their brief meeting in the café. Her face was devoid of makeup and she looked virginally innocent. He ran a thick tongue across his sweating upper lip and, putting his hand casually in his pocket, felt himself hardening.

She would do. She would do very nicely indeed. He had chosen well. Now he would play with her, taunt her, in the piquant way he liked best.

"What is your name, *cara?*" he asked in a reassuring tone, watching her look of appreciation as she sipped the vintage champagne.

"Inès Dessault, sir," she said, looking admiringly at an eighteenth-century ormolu-and-bronze clock on the ornately carved marble chimney-piece as it struck nine times.

"Inès, a pretty name for a pretty girl. Come over here, Inès, take off your coat, I won't bite you." He laughed softly. He loved to tell them that he wouldn't harm them. A trusting look would come over their silly little faces and he could see their bodies visibly relax. No matter that they knew that he and his allies—Hitler's Master Race—had seized their country, pillaging it for every piece of treasure which France possessed. No matter that they all knew of someone, somewhere, who had been taken away in the middle of the night to some unspeakable place. A sliver of kindness from the enemy, a flicker of feigned affection, and the idiots smirked like gullible puppets. Stupid. They were all stupid, the French. Men and women. They thought their culture was without equal, that their pictures, their sculptures, their boulevards, their architecture, were supreme. Arrogance was inbred in them. Herr Blondell, who each day supervised the collection and shipping of dozens of works of art to Germany, said that soon all that the Gallic fools would have left of their beloved culture would be their boulevards, their parks and their chestnut trees. All their priceless treasures—the furniture, the greatest artistry which the sixteenth, seventeenth and eighteenth centuries had to offer—the paintings, sculptures and objets d'art from Versailles, the Louvre and the Jeu de Paume, the accumulation of hundreds of years of collective genius, all would be gone. These riches would be secured in the Fatherland, owned by the Master Race—with the exception of a select little hoard which Umberto Scrofo was cunningly keeping for his own future, safely hidden in a cellar in the rue Flambeau.

Inès slipped her thin coat off thinner shoulders. The red silk dress was new, Yves had given it to her only last week. She didn't ask where he had found it, it had obviously been stolen, but it was of good quality and she recognized the couturier's label—Worth.

"Sit down, Inès Dessault," Scrofo instructed, gesturing towards a crystal bowl filled with a gritty-looking black substance unfamiliar to her. "Have some caviar."

Caviar! Inès had heard of it, but this was the first time she had ever seen it. The taste was strangely salty but not unpleasant, and she was always hungry these days. She wondered if she might be appearing too greedy, but the General didn't seem to care. She sat on the edge of a blue moiré bergère, eating hungrily. He certainly was a strange-looking creature, this officer. No more than five foot three, he had a wide squat body and an enormous, almost bald head which seemed out of all proportion. His uniform was thickly encrusted with medals and insignia, and he wore several rings on his stubby hands, which Inès did not think was quite correct for an officer. She saw the General's hand making circular motions in his pocket and smiled to herself. She knew that like so many enemy officers, he probably had a sexual problem. With the unforgettable atrocities which they witnessed at the front, the men often needed outlandish tricks to arouse them. A flash of thigh or breast was not enough. They needed titillation, stimulation, something to goad them to excitement. Yves had taught her how to do that, often practicing with her in his big soft bed. Yves ... whenever she thought of him, she was filled with love.

All her friends told her how lucky she was to have a pimp like Yves Moray—a man who loved her, even though he took her money. A man who never beat her, or abused her as so many of the other *maquereaux* did to their *poules de luxes*. A man whose warm kisses and caresses made up for the heartless and cold-blooded screwing which she endured from her clients. A man who made her laugh with his magic tricks both in and out of bed.

Deliberately, with ingenuous, practiced ease, Inès sat balanced on the edge of the bergère, her slender legs parted just enough to let the General see where her silk stocking tops ended and her slim white thighs began. She wore no panties and her stockings were secured with a pair of red satin garters, a flea-market bargain from last week.

She saw the General's eyes search for a more erotic sight, and she reached for the caviar, dipping her finger in it and sucking it slowly, her eyes never leaving his. Slowly she allowed her red skirt to slide up past her thighs so that Scrofo could see part of her golden mound. Nonchalantly, Inès dropped her other hand to the blond fuzz, touching herself gently, and saw the small bulge in his trousers become more pronounced. This was going to be a piece of cake. With luck she would be out of here in half an hour, off to L'Éléphant Rose, leaving this lout satiated and snoring happily. There she would be reunited with Yves and they would sit together giggling at poor old Gabrielle when she sang her latest songs to the idiotic Germans who drank each night until they were sick.

She moved her index finger rhythmically, becoming slightly aroused in spite of her lack of interest in the officer. Good. That would make it better with Yves tonight. She would tell him everything. Describe the reactions of the General staring in fascination at her sex under the red dress, laugh about the bulge throbbing in his trousers like a little mouse. She would tell him what it felt like when the General took her, and how she felt with him inside her. Yves would get tremendously aroused and he would possess her so violently, yet so passionately, that they would come together in a burst of rapture. She shuddered with expectation, feeling herself moisten with desire. Well, so much easier for this great brute to shove it in. Why doesn't he hurry up?

She smiled up at him sexily as Yves had taught her, then put a triangle of toast covered with caviar in her mouth, sucking it with relish while keeping her other hand busy.

He was ready now. She could tell. His breath was coming in shallow gasps, one hand fumbled with the buttons on his trousers; the other brought the glass to his lips, draining the last few drops.

"Go in there," he ordered huskily, gesturing towards the bedroom. "Get undressed, but leave your stockings and shoes on. Do you understand?"

Inès obeyed, feeling lighthearted. Soon it would be over. She had him hooked now.

She lay back on the cool linen sheets of the four-poster bed, admiring the blue-and-gold ceiling. A magnificent chandelier hung in the center, the cut crystals tinkling faintly in the breeze from the open windows. Her hands sensuously cupped her breasts as she continued to stimulate herself. It was, she had to admit, rather exciting, making love with the enemy. It was something that she would never admit to Yves, but when one of the more handsome German officers took her, if he was gentle, she would find herself responding to his moans of delight, and several times her orgasms had been almost genuine. But not tonight. Tonight she was saving her genuine passion for Yves. This Italian was a grotesque pig-faced creature. She must use her erotic expertise to finish him off quickly. But not too quickly, otherwise he might feel cheated and make her wait for an hour or two until he felt ready again.

Umberto entered the room, still wearing his uniform. His hands were behind his back, but his rigid penis was sticking out of his unbuttoned fly, and he looked so ridiculous that Inès had to stifle a giggle. Most men looked ridiculous with their cocks stuck straight out in that silly way. But Scrofo looked even more so because his organ was small, about the size of a ten-year-old boy's. This didn't seem to bother him though as he strutted into the bedroom, the cigar in his mouth almost twice the length of the thing sticking out of his trousers. He removed his trousers and shirt swiftly, then leaning against the Louis XIV commode next to the bed he gestured to Inès to start on him. She concentrated on Scrofo's small, stiff penis, imagining it to be Yves'. Her soft fingers stroked the stretched skin seductively, and she started to caress his wide white thighs, her mind far away.

The slashing pain as Umberto suddenly brought a whip down with stunning force onto her naked back was completely unexpected.

"Whore! French whore!" He laughed harshly as he cracked the whip against her shoulders with all his force, and Inès screamed in agony.

"Yell all you want, Mademoiselle. These walls are completely sound-proofed, and no one would come to rescue you even if they heard you. Suck me, bitch!" he commanded, his face a mask of sadistic pleasure as he slashed her again. Inès tried to obey, moving as best she could while he rained blows down on her, screaming obscenities.

"Sir, please *don't*," she begged, trying to move away from him. "You're hurting me."

"That's the idea," he leered. "I love hurting whores, especially French whores."

He grasped a fistful of Inès' long blond hair. "What are you?" he asked hoarsely, his eyes slits of brownish-black ice.

"Inès Dessault, sir," she whimpered softly.

"*What* are you, I said," he roared. "You know what you are, don't you, Inès?"

"Yes sir."

"Then tell me, slut. Go on, tell me what a whore you are."

"I'm a whore," she whispered as tears coursed down her cheeks. "I'm a—a—whore..." She hated herself, hated him, but she was thankful because the beating had stopped.

"Of course you are, Inès. You're a disgusting little slut—a horrible rotten creature, and this is what a whore like you deserves." He threw her roughly onto her stomach, forcing himself into her from behind with a moan of pleasure, his hands pulling her hair back so brutally she felt her neck would break.

Inès screamed as fresh pain engulfed her.

"Tell me again, slut." His breath was coming faster now as he held her around the neck by her hair. "Tell me what you are."

"I'm a whore," she whispered weakly, her tears raining on the pillow.

"Again," he demanded harshly, the stubble on his chin scraping her back. "Say it *again*, Inès. Tell me what you are, I like to hear you say it."

"A whore. I'm a whore," she wept.

"And a stupid one too," he sneered. Suddenly he stopped and she collapsed onto the mattress, sobbing with relief. She heard him opening a drawer, and raising her head from the pillow saw that he had removed a terrifying object from it.

"Roll over," he commanded harshly. "On your back, and open up those legs."

Eyes wide with fear, Inès obeyed, staring in horror as he strapped onto himself a rubber contraption shaped like a giant penis.

"No," she screamed. "Oh no, no—please don't—you can't." She tried to roll away but he grabbed her hair and in spite of her struggle started to force the hideous object inside her. She screamed but he clapped his hand over her mouth, hissing.

"If you don't shut up I'll ram this down your throat, and then you'll be a dead whore as well as a stupid one."

Pain came and went in great waves as Inés closed her eyes, praying for this excruciating suffering to end. She had never felt such agonizing degradation.

At last Scrofo's moans were becoming faster and Inès knew it must be ending. His hot breath scalded her shoulders and his saliva dripped onto her face.

"Yes, yes, you *whore!* You filthy French *cow*—you disgusting bitch. This is for *you*!" With a scream of satisfaction, the General gave a final vicious thrust, at the same time punching Inés in the face so violently that she lost consciousness.

He was born in Calabria, the toe of Italy, of a mother drunken and negligent and a father ignorant and weak, in the year before the outbreak of the First World War. It was a bitter winter night when Umberto Scrofo was pulled into the world. His mother had suffered agonizing labor for more than forty-eight hours before she was finally delivered of a child with a head out of all proportion to its tiny writhing body. The horrific ordeal and massive loss of blood left her only half alive.

Carlotta was barely twenty-three and the youngest of six children, all of them married and all with several children of their own. The already large family was growing fast, with many mouths to feed and precious little income with which to do it. The pitifully small amount of land which her father cultivated for vegetables had not only to feed his brood, but also to produce enough to sell at the market for necessities.

Carlotta never cared about her only child. Although it was no fault of his, he had injured her so badly during his birth that lovemaking was painfully uncomfortable for her afterward. Umberto's father loved his son, but as soon as the boy grew old enough to know which of the men on the farm was his father, Alberto was conscripted into the Italian army and the family did not see him for three years.

Carlotta called Umberto her little pig, her runt, and mocked him constantly. Full of resentment, she never forgave him for the pain he'd caused her, or for the loss of her sex life. She began to drink great quantities of rough wine all day long, and being an aggressive young woman, would often pick fights with anyone who cared to have one.

Sofia, Umberto's grandmother, also had little time to spare for the ugly boy with the huge head, and his cousins soon followed the example of their elders. By the time he was six Umberto was treated virtually as an outcast by the family, and was the butt of all their jokes.

At the age of seven, left in charge of his aunt's new baby girl, he decided to amuse himself one afternoon. He started sticking pins into the baby's bare bottom, never quite enough to draw blood, but enough to make the infant scream long and satisfyingly. This amused Umberto enormously, and he found that tormenting creatures smaller and weaker than himself gave him real pleasure. He once put a stray cat that he'd caught into a pot of water on the stove, watching it scream in agony as he boiled it to death. But he was discovered doing this, and Alberto pulled down his pants and thrashed him so soundly in front of the whole family that in the future he became more careful. Umberto was so humiliated by the incident that he allowed his sadistic impulses to lie dormant for several years.

At the age of twelve, while peeing with three of his male cousins in a field, the eldest, Pino, a strapping lad of seventeen, pointed to Umberto's penis and with peals of laughter screamed, "*Guarda* the little acorn! Cousin, your little *cazzo* hasn't grown a millimeter since you were seven. Hey, look at Benno here." He pointed to seven-year-old Benno, whose little penis pointed bravely into the ditch as he aimed his stream.

"Guarda, guarda!" Pino screamed with laughter, "Umberto's got the tiny little dick of a seven-year-old."

The other boys crowded around eagerly to peer at it, all of them proudly fingering their penises, which seemed to Umberto's eyes to be exceptionally long and thick. He cringed, and his cock cringed with him. It was very small indeed, but he hadn't really taken much notice of it before. Now it had become a thing of scorn, a freakish object for others to mock.

The boys soon told all the male members of the family of their discovery (the women would never have tolerated such vulgarity) and the news spread fast among the rest of the village men. Umberto Scrofo had a tiny penis the size of a bambino's, and they never let him forget it. The ignominy and shame remained with him always.

Its size had never increased. He tried excessive masturbation, as one of his kinder cousins helpfully suggested that this practice might help it grow, but that only made Umberto interested in girls and sex, which caused him even more frustration.

At sixteen he attempted to make love to the plain young daughter of a neighboring farmer. She was known to be easy and to "put out," but when she saw his childish equipment she started to rock with laughter, saying, "That's the most ridiculous excuse for a cock I've ever seen—it's no bigger than a thimble. I wouldn't even feel it inside me—take the pathetic little thing away, it's no good to any woman."

Poor Umberto. It wasn't until he was drafted into the Italian army in the spring of the following year that he began to come into his own. From then on—as promotion followed promotion—he never looked back, knowing that in time he would find a solution for his humiliating inadequacy.

2

Y ves Moray had found Inès when she was a weeping ten-year-old waif.
Thumb in mouth, dressed almost in rags, she was standing outside a shabby
block of flats where her prostitute mother had broken her neck by falling
drunkenly down the stairs.

Yves the Magician, as he was called, had known the mother, Marie, but
only slightly, since she was far too old to be in one of his *poules de luxe.*
A fleshy blonde, she was only thirty when she died, but already well past
her prime. The frightened girl, her mother's sole mourner at the burial,
was another story. She would be a rare beauty. Yves could see the potential
in her tangled honey-colored hair and in her innocent yet somehow carnal
slanting blue eyes. But her personality was cold, frightened, uncommuni-
cative. Little wonder. Marie had been short on maternal instincts, and Inès
had been left to fend for herself since she was a toddler. Yves took the
frightened girl under his protective wing, since there was no one else who
could do so, or would want to. He saw in her a kindred spirit for he too had
been orphaned as a child.

In the first weeks that Inés lived in the sanctuary of his house she never
smiled. Yves opened up his sorcerer's basket for her, fascinating her by his
sleight of hand with cards, his hocus-pocus with colored scarves, his skill
with the juggling of oranges. But the little girl would just sit there watching
him wide-eyed, sucking her thumb with a sad solemn expression.

One day Yves was smoking a cigarette and found the child's eyes fixed upon him as usual. "How about this one, Inès?" he said, and popping the lit cigarette inside his mouth with his tongue, he stared at her bug-eyed until two long streams of smoke issued from both ears.

At that Inès let out a shriek of pure laughter that didn't stop until tears ran down her face. Yves picked her up, hugged her tightly and from then on the ice was broken. Inès had smiled, and whenever her beloved Yves was near her she smiled a lot.

Yves was gentle and kind with Inès. He sent her to school, gave her warm clothes and enough food to eat, and loved bringing happiness to her sad little face. Within a year she was wildly infatuated with him, following him around whenever he was home like a devoted puppy, but he realized that Inès was really frightened of men. The only men she had ever known were the coarse oafs who had paid churlish court to her mother. Louts from back streets, they bought Marie's body for a few francs, often abusing her too. Many was the morning when Inès had awoken to the sound of her mother's whimpers as she examined the black eye or swollen lips that one of her "gentlemen" had given her. Eschewing Inès' timid offers of assistance, Marie would usually give the girl a cuff for her consideration.

Sometimes Marie would be lucky enough to land herself a "Mic," but usually he would be some heartless pimp from the alleys of Montmartre who would take all of Marie's earnings, spending it on whiskey, other women and scented hair pomade in exchange for the loveless lovemaking that he would provide for her.

As she got older, each of Marie's successive pimps seemed to become more avaricious, odious and unkind. Marie seemed to attract men who treated her badly and beat her, and often when they had drunk enough absinthe they liked to beat Inès too. The child grew to hate her mother and the vile men who punished them both, but there was little she could do about it.

At the time her mother died, Inès had never known a kind word from a man. She knew well what a pimp was and what he did. She saw how harshly they treated their women, and she knew in her childish heart that none of them was worth a sou. But Yves Moray proved a different customer altogether. Younger than the usual "*macrous*" that Marie had suffered, he had a roguish smiling face made even more appealing by a nose that turned up into a pair of curved nostrils which seemed to flare like a horse's whenever he laughed. His hair was pale brown, soft and curly, and when it was wet it clung to his head in tight Grecian curls. His eyes were a merry hazel, full of life and amusement, and when he laughed, which was often, they crinkled enchantingly. Inès used to stare at him covertly as she studied at the kitchen table at night. Some of his select stable of girls would sit adoringly at his feet while he regaled them with magic tricks, stroked them fondly like kittens and made them feel special and cherished. All of the girls worshiped Yves, not only for his kindness, amiable winning nature and impish smile, but for his fascinating conjuring act. He could juggle six oranges at a time without dropping one, as the girls whooped him on with cries of glee. He could do magical card tricks, making the ace of spades or the king of hearts disappear into thin air, and then "discovering" it under one of the girls' skirts. This would cause such shrieks of laughter that Inès would look up crossly from her housework, wishing that she was part of the enchanted circle at Yves' feet. He had all manner of bewitching tricks to enthrall his whores. For it was important to Yves to enthrall. Since the age of ten his childhood and early youth had been spent on the streets of Montmartre performing the conjuring tricks and magic he had learned at his father's knee. By the time he was seventeen girls flocked around him, mesmerized by his cheeky charm. It wasn't long before he gave up his life of street busking and let the girls take care of him. With Yves the Magician there was never a dull moment.

Soon he had cast a spell over the child Inès, and in her preadolescent way she tried to attract him. She wanted him to love her. Craved his affection. He was the father she had never known, the benign kindly laughing uncle she had always wanted, the lover she needed to captivate and make her own. But although Yves found her appealing, she was too young, so he made her wait for him for more than three years. Made her wait until she thought she would die for want of him. Made her wait as she sat sulkily in the front parlor of his house in the respectable Parisian suburb of Neuilly, listening while he made love to Francine or Olivia or Anna, or to any of the others. Sometimes she would eavesdrop on the sounds of his lovemaking, her ear against a thick tumbler pressed to the wall between their two bedrooms. Weeping bitterly, she listened to the sounds of the man she worshiped as he made love to other women, and sometimes she touched herself clumsily, finding a kind of relief.

Inès was precocious in both face and body. On her fourteenth birthday, standing before him rose-colored and golden, she stood on tiptoe to kiss his lips thanking him for the small presents he had bought for her.

She particularly loved a slender bracelet of amber and silver beads which he had found in an antique shop off the rue Jacob. As he fastened the filigree clasp around her slender wrist, he could almost smell the scent of musk emanating from her as she breathed. "Oh, thank you, Yves." The smile of an innocent Venus made her look even more seductive. "It is the most beautiful bracelet I have ever seen—I will never take it off. *Never*."

Inés was wearing her simple school uniform, a white blouse with a wide collar, a dark blue serge tunic, pleated, sturdy shoes and long woollen socks. Her hair fell halfway down her back, curling in delicate tendrils around her oval face. With her clear blue eyes and golden skin, she looked like one of Botticelli's angels. Yves was a man who truly appreciated women, even though he exploited them. He examined her: the seductive, knowing look on her face that predicted delights in store for him; her budding breasts, whose rose-tipped nipples were hardening under the blouse. The parted pale lips seemed aching to be kissed. His eyes narrowed as they met the shy gaze that told him what she desired. She was ripe, she was ready, it was time. Finally Yves the Magician allowed Inés, the teenage seductress, to conquer him.

They made love for hours in the warm, soft darkness of his bed. She knew how it was done—she had been in the room often enough when her mother had been at work.

Ever since Inès had reached the age of awareness—five or six—she had watched what Marie had done with her men. Some of them liked her mother's style so much that they came back week after week, for months, even years. So although Inès was technically a virgin, her mother had been an excellent teacher of the erotic arts. With a natural instinct as well as lessons learned from hours of observation, she gave Yves the most enthusiastic lovemaking that he had ever had. From that time on, Inès had shared Yves' bed nightly; he soon found himself entranced by this child with the gorgeous face, magical body and sexual tricks of an experienced courtesan, and he managed to teach her even more.

Six months later, with the advent of war, pandemonium ruled France. Several of Yves' regular girls fled Paris, and he had little choice but to put Inès to work. She started off at a nightclub owned by Gabrielle Printemps, L'Éléphant Rose.

As the daughter of a whore, Inès wasn't really too upset. Yves loved her, she worshiped him, and she didn't really care much about anything else. Being a professional prostitute was only a job. She didn't like it, she didn't dislike it. It was just the obvious and inevitable way of her life.

The men she slept with meant nothing; her mind was far away when they possessed her body. She knew they could never possess her heart because that belonged totally to Yves, her wonderful, magical Yves. She was his completely, and whatever other men did with her could make no difference to her devotion to Yves.

Their mutual passion was pure and strong, symbolized, Inès thought, by the shimmering amber-and-silver bracelet strands which encircled her wrist and represented the eternity of their love.

As the morning light began to flood into the bedroom Inès regained consciousness. Her head throbbed painfully. The linen sheets were encrusted with blood, her blood, and the pain all over her body was so intense that she wanted to weep. She had to escape from this loathsome creature who snored next to her, she had to get away immediately—but he had not paid her yet. No matter, she would take the money herself. God knows she'd earned it.

Please let him stay asleep, she thought as she crept from the bed, wincing in agony. His trousers lay on the floor where he had thrown them, next to the discarded whip and the disgusting false penis. She still ached from the numbing pain of it. Quickly she searched through his pockets but there was no money in them. Glancing at the snoring man, she tiptoed into the marble bathroom, where, in the full-length mirror, she saw her bruised and tear-stained face, her shoulders and breasts covered with welts and cuts, the dried blood on her thighs. Flinching in pain, she squatted over the bidet, washing herself with scented soap. It was then that she noticed the thick wad of francs lying by the side of the marble washbasin, next to his razor and toothbrush. There were a lot of notes, more than she usually made in a month. Should she just take what she was usually paid or all the money to make up for the atrocities Scrofo had done to her? "Take them all," she whispered to the reflection of the pale wounded girl who looked out sorrowfully from the mirror. "You deserve them, Inès."

Hastily she seized the banknotes, just as the Italian lurched into the room. Seeing what she was doing, he grabbed her hair and smashing her head against the marble wall with all his strength, screamed "A whore *and* a thief, huh? There's only one way to treat scum like you—give you more of what you had last night."

Inés saw with dread that he held that disgusting rubber object in his hand and that he was erect again. He forced her over to the washbasin, all the time mouthing his litany of filth. Oh, my God, he was going to do it again. He couldn't, he simply couldn't. It was unbearable.

"Please don't," she sobbed. "Please, please stop—you can't do this again. Please, you can't. I promise I'll come back when I'm better. I am in so much pain—such pain, look, I'm bleeding."

"Good." His grin revealed sharp yellow teeth and she could smell the reek of garlic and stale champagne, see that his eyes were bloodshot and wild. "The way *you* want it, I only do with *proper* women," he gloated. "Italian women, *good* girls, ladies, not French harlots like you. I only do it like *this* with *scum*." He bent her over the basin, and his small penis, stabbed into her with the dull pain of a blunt knife. "We will do it like *this*—and then we will do it again with *this*," and he brandished the repulsive plaything in front of her. "My little rubber friend. You like him, Inès, don't you? I know you liked him last night."

"No!" screamed Inès. "No! Please!" As if in a dream, her eyes suddenly focused on an old-fashioned cut-throat razor which was lying open on the marble counter. Without thinking, the terror and pain so excruciating, she picked up the razor and lashed out blindly behind her. She heard the General scream in anguish and then a great crash as he fell to the floor. Inès gasped when she turned and saw what she had done. The blade had sliced across his throat as cleanly as a seamstress cuts into a length of cloth. Blood bubbled from the wound and his eyes rolled back in his head. There was no doubt that he was dying. Ghastly rasping sounds issued from his throat even though his tiny penis still stood lewdly erect, like some defiant flagpole. Stricken into immobility, she watched as his huge bald head, spattered with the blood that pumped from his throat, lolled sideways onto the floor.

Inès gazed at the dead man, panic-stricken. She had killed an Italian officer of the occupation. What on earth was she going to do?

Frozen with fear, Inès didn't know how long she stood staring at Umberto Scrofo as blood poured from his neck and mouth onto the shining marble tiles. In the mirror, she saw a terrified girl whose blond hair hung over her face in matted snarls, whose eyes were wild and who had blood on her hands. She had to get out.

It was seven o'clock. How long before one of the General's aides would call for him? He was bound to have army matters, maneuvers, something to do, he was an important part of the war machine. He had told her that at the café. Her mind raced with possibilities. She could just leave, after she dressed in the red frock and shabby coat which she had worn the previous night. The concierge had barely looked at her when she arrived. He wouldn't remember her—would he?

Her fingers rubbed her chafed wrists, raw from Scrofo's brutal treatment, and she ran them under the warm tap water. Then with a shock she realized that her lucky bracelet was missing. Fear made her limbs tremble uncontrollably as she rushed into the bedroom, throwing back the bloodied sheets, searching desperately for her precious beads. The bracelet—her talisman—anyone who knew her would instantly recognize the fine strings of amber and silver beads which she always wore. If they discovered the bracelet, it would only be a question of how long before they found her. In a frenzy she dropped to the floor, crawling about on hands and knees, but the bracelet wasn't there. Tears rolled down her face, stinging her cut lips, her bruised cheeks. Then she remembered: she hadn't been wearing it last night! The clasp was loose and Yves had promised to take it to be mended. Thank God, oh, thank God.

Back in the bathroom she grabbed the wad of notes—they were well paid, these Italians—then ran back to the bedroom and flung on her clothes. She had retrieved everything except one red garter. So what? Every whore in Paris wore red garters. They couldn't possibly trace her with that—could they?

She shoved the other garter and her stockings into a pocket and cautiously opened the suite door, looking down the deserted corridor. Her heart beating painfully, she tiptoed down the passage towards the back stairs, hoping to find the staff entrance. As she crept down she heard laughter and a door opening, and hid herself around a bend in the stairway as several chambermaids came chattering down the long hall to begin their shifts. Entering a changing room in shabby dresses, they emerged in starched blue-and-white uniforms, and sped off to begin their work.

Inès' heartbeat was so loud that she imagined the chattering girls might hear it. She wondered what sort of security the hotel would have at the back entrance. Would they, like many hotels, have guards who must check the staff out for possible theft after every shift? Would the employees have to carry identity cards which proved they worked there? It was almost more of a risk than to leave by the front entrance—nevertheless it was a decision she must make.

She looked at her wristwatch, another present from Yves. It was nearly seven-thirty, over half an hour since she had sliced the razor across the General's throat. She shuddered at the thought of how the authorities would punish her if they ever caught her. Execution would be the least painful death she could expect for someone of her age and looks. They would no doubt inflict on her the most sophisticated tortures, after the inevitable multiple rapes. Death would be a blessing. No, she was determined that this would not be her fate, this was not the way she had envisaged her life. In spite of her past, in spite of the ignominy of her profession, Inès possessed innate pride and belief in herself. She was determined to escape. The stream of arriving girls had now slowed to a trickle. Two more exhausted, gamine-faced young women, little more than children, arrived, then there was a lull; it was now or never.

Mustering all her courage, Inès strode purposefully into the small room in which the maids changed. None of the girls even looked at her, so busy were they dressing and gossiping. Keeping her head down, she moved along to the last shabby overcoat hanging on the row of hooks. Below each hook was a locked wood-and-wire netting cage in which the girls kept their handbags and walking shoes. Their identity cards would, no doubt, be in those handbags.

Inès put on the tattered overcoat, which was too long for her. There was a flimsy scarf in the pocket, and thankfully she tied it around her matted hair. All she needed now was another girl's identity papers. Stealthily she pulled at several of the little hatches on the wire cages, but they were all securely locked. Never mind, she had her coat and scarf, and most important of all, she had courage. Tightening the belt on the overcoat, she followed two chattering chambermaids who were going off shift. They clattered down granite steps to a small foyer inside the door leading to the rue Cambon. A Ritz security guard sat at his desk, cigarette drooping from a tired mouth. Behind him stood a Nazi officer staring at the wall with a look of deep melancholy.

Hans Meyer was usually one of the most zealous and thorough of guards. This morning, however, his mind was elsewhere. The previous night he had received a letter from his fiancée in the Fatherland: she had fallen in love with his own father—a widower for many years—and they would be married by the time Hans received the letter. She was very sorry, of course, wartime stress and all that, but *c'est la vie*, and she hoped Hans would try to understand. He had been so full of rage that he had drunk himself into a stupor and was now suffering the worst hangover of his life. He took no notice of the prattling maids who were emptying their handbags onto the trestle table for the guard to examine. His father! His beautiful twenty-two-year-old flaxen-haired Fräulein was going to marry his bald-headed sixty-year-old father. Between bouts of nausea, he plotted his revenge, totally ignoring the guard's cursory examination of the girls' belongings.

Inès emptied her handbag onto the table and the guard halfheartedly flicked through its meager contents. Lipstick, mirror, comb, a door key, a few francs. The wad of two thousand francs was well hidden in her shoe.

"Okay, you can go," said the guard. "Next."

Praying the German soldier would not question her lopsided walk, Inès bundled her possessions back into her bag and strode out into the golden Parisian sunshine.

Free! She was free. But how long could it last?

That spring of 1943 the Gestapo seemed to be everywhere in Paris, and they were a sinister sight. They lurked in black Mercedeses wearing heavy leather overcoats, with the dreaded swastika emblazoned on their sleeves. They smoked harsh cigarettes, looking with dead eyes at everyone who passed.

They always pounced at night. Small groups of men, their cold eyes insensitive to human suffering, sometimes accompanied by ferocious Alsatian dogs straining at their leashes, would come to their victims' homes without warning. The dogs could root out "enemies of the Reich" hidden anywhere—in cellars, cupboards, even concealed behind walls.

Every night the Gestapo discovered groups of hidden Jews, herding them into trucks to be sent to God knows where. All French Jews had to wear badges, on which JUIF was printed in yellow letters, and none of them ever knew when they could expect to hear the dreaded sound of barking Alsatians, the staccato rap of the SS at their front doors. Every Jew lived in fear, but all of them did their best to disguise it.

Polished leather jackboots glistening, gray uniforms bristling with insignia, the long, dark shadow of the Third Reich fell across the entire Jewish population of France that spring. But although every patriotic citizen detested the sight of the enemy soldiers, with true French spirit they tried to live as normally as possible. The Nazi soldiers, their coarse faces framed by ugly helmets, leather straps tight under their chins, were ruthless, completely without mercy. They had been trained a long time in Germany for this moment and they treated the French nation with undisguised contempt.

Agathe Guinzberg had spent the last of her teenage years hiding in a basement in Montparnasse. The house was owned by Gabrielle Printemps who also owned L'Éléphant Rose, the club next door, a favorite haunt of enemy officers and their floozies.

Gabrielle lived with her grandfather, mother and crippled eighteen-year-old brother, Gilbert. By chance, that particular evening when the Gestapo arrived to arrest the Jewish Guinzberg family, Agathe was at the Printemps' house, reading to Gilbert. When the Printemps family saw what was happening across the street, they made Agathe hide down in their basement. Peeping through lace curtains, Gabrielle saw Agathe's family pushed unceremoniously into the back of a truck. There were three little girls under twelve, two boys of about fifteen and sixteen, and their mother and father. The commandant didn't seem to realize that he should be taking a family of eight *Juden* off to await deportation to the camps. He was weary. This was the fourteenth family they had "collected" that night. He knew that there should be several children, and indeed there were, so that was that, he had filled his quota for the night, now he could go off and enjoy himself.

The truck took the Guinzbergs, with all the other Jewish families to a makeshift camp outside Paris. There they joined several hundred other families and were soon put on a train to Buchenwald, from where none would ever be heard of again.

Hidden in the Printemps' cellar, eighteen-year-old Agathe slowly learned to adapt to living alone among the spiders and the cockroaches; with the mildew and the stench of drains; with the rats, the mice and the unspeakable horrors of her fertile imagination. She had been given a supply of candles but was told to use them sparingly. Her only substantial meal was delivered by Gabrielle in the morning, when the last drunken footsteps of the enemy echoed down the cobblestone streets. Only then did Agathe allow herself to light a candle, eat her food and spend the next few precious hours reading in the recesses of her tomb. Occasionally a brief note from Gabrielle accompanied the food—the latest news of the war, good or bad, or perhaps a concerned query about her welfare. Gabrielle was terrified to the point of paranoia about talking to Agathe. She believed that walls—even floors—had ears, and consequently kept conversation to a minimum. Agathe was able to wash only once a week, when Gabrielle would send down a basin of lukewarm water, and soon her clothes hung on her sparse body in filthy tatters. Whenever her head itched so much that she could hardly stand it, she would pick the lice from her scalp, cracking their bodies between her thumbnails like peanuts.

Agathe's mind began to inhabit a world of its own as each day drifted into endless night. There was darkness all the time except for the blessed candles; it was bitterly cold and damp; but at least she had some comfort—the books.

If her body suffered from lack of nourishment, her mind did not. Gabrielle's grandfather had been a bookseller who specialized in rare books, and the cellar was crammed with leather-bound volumes of Balzac, Molière, Racine and Victor Hugo; poems by Byron, Shelley, Voltaire, Baudelaire and Robert Browning; and escapist adventure stories by Alexandre Dumas and Rider Haggard—all piled high in the damp cellar. Better mildew on the precious volumes, Grandfather had said, than for them to fall into the hands of the Germans. Throughout her numberless lonely nights, Agathe read hundreds of books as she prayed for the occupation to end.

Agathe had studied ballet since she was a child—her ambition was to be a prima ballerina. To retain her sanity, she would often practice, whirling and bending frenziedly in the darkness, humming the music of *Swan Lake* and *Giselle*, her mind full of the glory that could be hers when she was released from captivity. Unable to count the days to her freedom, for she had no idea when it would be, she was a prisoner without parole—a jailbird with no end to her sentence.

Gabrielle had given Agathe her own rosary and crucifix when she first went into the cellar. Despite being Jewish, Agathe took comfort in the amber beads, constantly caressing them, praying for her deliverance.

Sometimes she scribbled plaintive notes to Gabrielle: "How much longer will the war last?" The reply would always be the same: "Not much longer, child, I hope. Have faith, we are all praying for it to end soon."

Every night Agathe heard the raucous laughter of German and Italian officers who patronized the nightclub next door, the shrill, high-pitched shrieks of their young whores, and Gabrielle's husky voice singing to them. As rats and cockroaches scurried around her feet, and her body shook with the cold, she began to learn the true meaning of hatred.

Early one evening before the club had opened, the Gestapo came to the house for a routine search. While Gabrielle and her family were being questioned, two Alsatians sniffed around the bedrooms, the front parlor and the kitchen. Agathe could hear the sound of boots clattering above her, and froze. The cellar opening was covered by a sheet of metal set into the floor of the scullery, camouflaged by cracked linoleum. Agathe trembled on her filthy bedding in the blackness beneath them, but remained undiscovered because the dogs were far more interested in the appetizing scent of meat in the larder, and barked enthusiastically.

Whenever Gabrielle passed a platoon of soldiers in the street she shuddered and looked away. Each time she took a plate of food down to Agathe, she wondered fearfully how long it would be before the girl was discovered and Gabrielle's own family were persecuted for hiding her. But as the months and then the years passed, she began to realize that Agathe had been forgotten by the Nazis; she no longer existed.

As the Jewish population continued to be systematically exterminated, as the hunger pangs of France grew more severe, the French Resistance worked on.

Maurice Grimaud was the best forger in France, the unrivaled expert in counterfeiting identity papers and passports. A highly valued member of the Resistance, he fraternized at L'Éléphant Rose several times a week, playing the jovial drunk, the buffoon, making the hated enemy laugh. The Germans enjoyed his idiotic antics, encouraging him to sit at their tables to joke with them. Since liquor loosened tongues, he picked up enormous amounts of information which was invaluable to the Resistance.

Maurice was a man of so many faces who had so many hiding places that the Gestapo were never able to track him down because they had no idea who he really was. He was a master of disguise, an expert in calligraphy and counterfeiting, and his efforts on behalf of the French Underground were legendary. He had nine lives and had not yet lost one.

He was a generous old friend of Gabrielle's. She was becoming extremely worried about Agathe, and decided to talk to Maurice about the girl. The last time Gabrielle had shone a torch on Agathe's face, she could hardly believe what she saw. Agathe was wasting away to nothing, her hair had turned lint white, her face was so thin that her cheekbones stuck out like pieces of jagged glass, and the deep hollows around her eyes were those of a forty-five-year-old woman. Her appearance had changed so radically that Gabrielle decided that, with new identity papers, she could be released from the cellar. No one would ever recognize her. Gabrielle also thought that if the girl died—and with Agathe looking so frail and ill this was not a remote possibility—getting rid of the body would be a great problem. Besides which, Gabrielle needed someone to work behind the cash desk at her club. Agathe could work for what she ate, and sleep on a cot in the parlor.

Thanks to Maurice, Agathe soon possessed an authentic-looking set of identity papers, passport, birth certificate and even a complete set of school reports going right back to kindergarten. They were masterpieces of his art and Maurice was proud of them.

When Agathe was finally helped out of the cellar and took a few falterings steps into the backyard, the faint autumnal sun was such a shock to her system that she fainted. She weighed barely ninety pounds. Her skin was as pale as mountain snow and her black hair had turned completely white. She looked so different from the plump, laughing teenager who had disappeared nearly two years ago, that even the neighbors who had known her before gave her no glance of recognition.

In the following months Agathe sat silently behind the cash register at L'Éléphant Rose, watching the Germans and the Italians fraternize, observing how they abused the French whores. Her hatred for every one of them grew like a cancer in her weakened body.

Traitors. Those girls, so young and pretty, were despicable traitors who betrayed their country and their people by consorting with the enemy. She hated all the Frenchwomen who hung over the soldiers and officers, laughing with them, fondling their bodies, kissing their cruel lips. No one ever gave *her* a second glance and Agathe realized bitterly that her prettiness was gone forever. Although she was just twenty she looked fifty, and though she ate heartily her body remained almost skeletal. Silently each night she sat in the tiny glass-walled booth at the back of the nightclub, to all intents and purposes immersed in the accounts. Her silver hair and pale skin glowed spectrally in the dim lighting and she constantly fingered her rosary as she simmered with a quiet but consuming rage and a desperate desire for revenge.

*"**Y**ou did what?" Yves' eyes narrowed and the color drained from his* face.

"*Chérie,* it is *not* possible. Why did you have to *kill him?* What he did couldn't have been *that* terrible, surely?"

"It was, Yves, it was torture. You have no idea of the pain and the horrible things he did." Inès tried to control her hysteria, sipping at the whiskey which a rabbit-faced waitress at L'Éléphant Rose had brought her. "I *had* to do it, Yves—I had to, he would have killed me if I hadn't, he threatened to kill me. I know he would have—I know." Tears streamed down her cheeks.

Gabrielle, with a murmur of sympathy, passed her a handkerchief. *Merde,* what slime these men are, she thought. She had seen the bruises and cuts on Inès' body and looked pityingly at the girl who, in her grief, looked little more than a child.

They were sitting in a dimly lit back booth of L'Éléphant Rose. Although it was eight-thirty in the morning, the club had only just closed. Yves' brain raced with the problems they all now faced. Whatever Inès had done, no accusing finger must ever be allowed to point at the club. It was much too valuable to them all and too many lives would be put at risk. Even though most of its habitués were the enemy, the club was still one of the most important cores of the Resistance in Paris. The enemy must never know that the killer of an Italian officer had in any way been assisted by *le Maquis.*

"Thank God you met him in the café and not here," Yves said. "Did anyone see you with him? Anyone at all?"

"No, no, I don't think so—he was sitting at a table alone—it all happened quite quickly. He knew very well what I was when he picked me up. I was wearing that low-cut green dress. We only spoke for a moment or two before he propositioned me. And told me to meet him last night at the Ritz." She started to cry again and Gabrielle poured her another shot of whiskey. "I should've gone and sat with Picasso," sobbed Inès. "He smiled at me too."

"Shut up, Inès," snapped Yves. "The concierge last night—do you think he saw you?"

"I can't remember." Inès did her best to recall the events of twelve hours ago, which already seemed like an eternity. "I don't think he looked up at me when I asked for Scrofo's room number—but you never know with concierges, do you?" More tears ran down her face and her shoulders heaved with sobs. Gabrielle squeezed her hand sympathetically.

"No, I suppose you never do." Yves' voice was grim. "But since you *did* speak to the concierge, the Gestapo are sure to question him. There are probably no more than two or three hundred blond teenaged prostitutes in Paris. It's only a matter of time before they trace you, line you up for the concierge to identify—and then accuse you. Don't forget, they will find fingerprints."

"Yes—yes, of course," Inès groaned. *Why* hadn't she thought to clean the marble surfaces of the bathroom, the handle of the razor, the champagne glass? It was too much to think about. She felt dizzy and nauseous. All she wanted was to sleep in the safety of Yves' arms. She wanted him to stroke her hair, comfort her, tell her that everything was going to be all right, promise that he would take care of her, as he always had done.

"Come. We must go to see Maurice right away," Yves said decisively. "We have no time to lose."

After four days the scandal and gossip about the murderous attack on the Italian General began to die down. No suspect had been found, and the concierge at the hotel had a conveniently patriotic memory block about the prostitute whom he had seen going up to Scrofo's room. No one else had seen Inès at the Ritz that night, and there were simply no clues as to the identity of who had slashed the General's throat.

While Yves and Maurice decided what to do with her, Inès was hidden in the same cellar where Agathe had lived for so long. When Gabrielle came down to cut and dye her long blond hair, she told Inès that plans and arrangements were under way to smuggle her over to England.

"He was a complete bastard, that Italian General. I heard about him," Gabrielle said as she fluffed up Inès' newly dyed shoulder-length dark hair.

"You would not *believe* the disgusting things he did with some of the girls." Her voice was full of bitterness. "They say that *he* was the one who killed Jeanette. Everyone who knew him, even his so-called friends in the army, seems happy that he's gone. I think you did us all a big favor, *chérie*."

"When will Yves get me out of here, Gabrielle?" Inès said plaintively. "I'm so lonely and frightened. There are hundreds of spiders and rats and cockroaches. I have the most terrible nightmares—I keep on seeing Scrofo's face—I just can't sleep. I'm scared." Inès began to cry, but Gabrielle grabbed her hair, bringing the girl's face close to hers.

"Listen, little girl," she whispered fiercely, "you are very lucky. *Whatever* that swine did to you, you *are* a whore, and it's your *profession* to serve and satisfy men, even pigs like him."

Inès winced as Gabrielle continued: "We are all risking our lives every day for you, you ungrateful, selfish child. And as for being frightened, we had to keep Agathe down here for nearly two years, and she never complained. You're lucky to have a man like Yves who loves you—even if he is only a pimp," Gabrielle told her. "Not many little whores are so lucky. And to let you know how *really* lucky you are, my friend Maurice has been working day and night for you on your identity papers. Tonight—" she leaned forward—"tonight, you have a nice surprise coming, and you don't deserve it."

"Hmmm, good. Excellent. Very convincing."

Yves admired the worn French passport, the set of bound school reports dating back over ten years and the ragged identity card with Inès' photograph. They were all made out in the name of Inès Juillard, and they appeared completely authentic.

"From now on, that will be your name," Yves told her. "You must forget that Inès Dessault ever existed. She is gone forever."

They had been cycling through the leafy country lanes of Normandy towards the coast of Calais, where they were to meet their contact. Now they were lying under a huge chestnut tree and the afternoon sun dappled Inès' dark brown hair with highlights of burnished gold. They felt almost safe while they ate their frugal sandwiches and drank from a bottle of rough red wine. In the distance they could see some farmers toiling in the fields, and it seemed that country life was going on much as usual.

Inès leaned forward to kiss Yves. He wore scruffy peasant clothes, with his hair cropped and a three-day stubble on his cheeks, but his magnetism stirred her more than ever.

"Yves," she whispered, her tongue tracing his lips, "Oh, Yves darling, I love you so much." Her hands caressed him inside the coarse cloth of his shirt as his lips hungrily responded to her delicate kisses. She stretched out like a cat on the soft grass surrendering herself to his touch.

Danger made their coupling sweeter. The smell of the sweet crushed grass mixed in her nostrils with the scent of Yves, the warm familiar smell which Inès loved beyond all others.

Their bodies fused, fueling each other's fire. This man was the only person in the world Inès had ever truly loved, and she knew she could never love another.

Too soon he looked at his watch, saying briskly, "It's three o'clock, *chérie*—we must go or we will never be in Calais by eleven."

He spoke almost lovingly to Inès, although he knew he had never compeletly loved anyone in his life. He had decided that it was necessary that he accompany her to England, for if the Italians ever discovered who had murdered Umberto Scrofo, life for those who had anything to do with Inès would become very unpleasant indeed. Like the Gestapo, they were not particular about whom they tortured, or how they did it, and a murderess's pimp could expect no mercy from Mussolini's men.

An old blue-and-white rowboat was waiting for them in a small cove down the coast from Calais, exactly where the Resistance had said it would be. In it were three men who were also, for one reason or another, being smuggled out of France by the partisans.

As Inès sat hunched in the tiny craft, watching the French coast recede, she breathed the fresh sea air gratefully, feeling more free than she had for days. The four men rowed vigorously. It was a fine, spring night with little wind and few cross-currents, so they made the crossing in good time. Four hours later Inès blinked in wonder as she saw the magnificent chalk cliffs of Dover appear, dimly lit by weak moonlight.

As soon as the boat beached, the men hauled it quickly up onto the pebbles, covering it with fishing nets and clumps of seaweed and waited for their contact to arrive. As they had been told to expect, a man cautiously approached them through the darkness, mumbling a few words of welcome. The contact handed them a brown paper parcel which contained five English ration books made out in fictitious names, identity cards and some crumpled pound notes. There was also a timetable for the local trains, and four different addresses in England.

Inès and Yves eagerly peered at their own particular address:

Madame Josette Pichon
17 Shepherd Market
London W1

"Shepherd Market." Inès rolled the name on her tongue, savoring the Englishness of it. "How pretty it sounds. Oh Yves, do you think there will be lambs and chickens and a maypole with ribbons on it in the middle of the village square?"

"Hardly, *chérie.*" Yves chuckled at Inès' naïveté. "England is suffering in this war almost as badly as France. Night after night German planes bomb London to hell and back. From what I've heard, Shepherd Market is right in the center of everything. We'd probably have been safer in Paris."

"I don't care where I am, *chéri,*" Inès sparkled, "as long as I'm with you, Yves. That's all I want."

6

"*Oh, dammit, not again,*" *Phoebe mumbled to herself. She had just* crawled into bed, shattered after another long night of toil at the Windmill Theatre, where "We never close" was the famous motto. "Not another bloody air raid. Will it *never* end?"

Half asleep, she pulled on her warm dressing gown and fluffy sheepskin slippers. Carrying a Thermos of hot tea and a bag which contained her worldly essentials and went everywhere with her, she staggered down seven flights of stairs into the scant comfort of the crowded air-raid shelter.

Along with the other occupants of her block of flats she tried in vain to doze while the sound of exploding bombs echoed through the darkened and shuddering shelter, babies cried and children whimpered with fear. As soon as the All Clear had sounded, the weary group picked up the bits and pieces of their lives and ventured shakily back to their flats . . . until the next night.

Phoebe sighed with exhausted relief as she let herself in, and throwing herself onto the bed slept the dreamless sleep of the innocent. She had survived yet another night of Luftwaffe air raids, yet another night of earth-shattering, deafening noises as the anti-aircraft guns blazed and the German bombs blitzed the city to hell.

In the morning she listened to the BBC as the solemn tones of Alvar

Lidell broadcast the extent of the damage to the city. Over seventy buildings had been partially or completely destroyed, fifty-two civilians killed and more than twice that number injured. His voice was grave as he recited the death toll, and Phoebe switched off the wireless. She couldn't bear to hear such bad, sad news.

After patiently queuing in her local teashop for a cup of strong tea and a sticky bun with some scant raisins in it, she picked her way fastidiously down Great Portland Street towards the West End. The streets were covered with shrapnel and debris, but thankfully none of the buildings that she passed had collapsed. Most of the bombing had been concentrated near the river, from where she could see a tall gray pall of smoke rising above the chimneypots of Oxford Circus.

Phoebe's natural exuberance managed to flourish even in war-torn London. At twenty-three she had the robust curves, creamy skin and willful red hair inherited from her forebears—stalwart country men and women from the north of England, not afraid of hard work and deprivation. Hardy British stock, they had all been survivors, and she was going to survive this bloody war, even make the best of it. She wasn't going to allow herself to get depressed. She had a job to do at the Windmill Theatre: to entertain the boys—the boys in blue, the boys in khaki, the boys in green, even the boys in white. They were all on leave, all with weary, jaundiced eyes that spoke of dreadful war experiences—which their raucous laughter belied. The showgirls would give seven performances today, as they did every day. They would change their costumes no less than forty-nine times—seven changes in each show—and some of them would even bare their breasts for the soldiers to gawk at.

Phoebe's thick Cuban heels clacked down Regent Street, daintily avoiding the street cleaners who were trying to sweep up "Jerry's garbage." In spite of the nightly air raids, Piccadilly Circus was always a hive of festive activity. The statue of Eros, God of Love, had been removed from the center of Piccadilly to a safe haven. Allied military men of every nationality milled about in a maelstrom of color and movement, and dozens of young women mingled on the pavement, chatting to them animatedly. There was a carnival atmosphere in Piccadilly Circus, a desperate gaiety on the faces of the crowds as if to say that the war could not affect them.

No matter that for many servicemen leave was over tomorrow, and they were off to fight in North Africa or Burma or Salerno. It was party time all the time in London, especially in the West End and particularly at the Windmill Theatre.

Phoebe walked past Lyons Corner House, where two long queues stood waiting patiently for it to open, and hurried up Shaftesbury Avenue.

Entering the stage door, she stopped as she saw one of the best-looking

young men that she had ever laid eyes on, talking animatedly to the stage
doorkeeper. Thick, dark brown hair in unruly waves, jet black curved
eyebrows, a handsome, slightly saturnine face, and a nose and cheekbones which were almost a living replica of Antinous, the youth so beloved
of the Emperor Hadrian. Navy blue eyes met hers briefly, then turned away
without the remotest flicker of interest as he continued chatting to the old
man.

The stranger was dressed in a gray Prince of Wales checked three-piece
suit, a pale blue shirt and an extravagant tie. A light gray homburg was
tipped rakishly over his eyes as he leaned toward the doorman, charm
oozing from every pore.

"But look here, old chap, just tell the boss that I've had *years* of experience in variety. Manchester Hippodrome, Gaiety Theatre, Liverpool, the
Alhambra in Brighton. I've topped the bill at all of them. And," he whispered conspiratorially, "I've got the best repertoire of blue jokes this side
of Blackpool Pier—I've had 'em rolling in the aisles, old chap, everywhere.
Here." He handed the disinterested man a typewritten résumé which was
glued to the back of an eight-by-ten smiling photograph of himself. "What's
your name, old chap, by the way?"

"Fred," said the doorman unsmilingly.

"Julian Brooks is my name—comedy's my game." Julian gave Fred the
benefit of a smashing smile with a perfect set of even teeth, framed by a
small, beautifully trimmed Ronald Colman moustache.

"Why aren't you in the army then?" asked Fred, looking suspiciously at
the photograph which the young man was waving at him.

"Flat feet, old boy. Not very honorable, but there we are."

Phoebe felt a tingle of excitement as her eyes connected again with the
stranger's for a fraction of a second.

"That's why I'm so anxious to do my bit for our boys, old chap. I've got
comedy routines that will have 'em splitting their sides. They'll go back to
fighting Jerry with a big smile on their faces—and so full of piss and
vinegar, the Hun will run like rabbits." He smiled engagingly, but to no
avail. His charm fell on stony ground with the stage doorkeeper.

"Nah, sorry, mate." Fred pushed the photograph back at him. "We're not
'irin' anyone, guvnor's orders, and even if we wus—I ain't the one wot does
it, so piss off—and go peddle yourself somewhere else." He picked up the
Daily Mirror, immersing himself in Jane's cartoon exploits, leaving Julian
standing there in disappointed frustration.

Phoebe stepped forward. Mustn't let this one get away—handsome, still
young, obviously not about to be posted to foreign parts, to become can-
non fodder like some of her ex-lovers had been stupid enought to do.

"Hello, I'm Phoebe Bryer," she gushed, holding out a well-manicured hand. "I work here. May I help you?"

"You most certainly may." Julian looked at the tumbling Titian curls, fresh complexion, sparkling eyes and luscious curves. What a cutie this one was, he thought, a delectable dish indeed. Sending out availability signals, too. Perfect.

"I think you just might be able to help me, Miss Bryer," he said, his Royal Academy of Dramatic Art accent smooth as silk and twice as seductive. "Perhaps you would allow me the honor of buying you a delicious cup of tea and a sticky bun at the little coffee shop on Shaftesbury Avenue?" He looked her up and down with the requisite amount of lust and Phoebe felt her cheeks start to tingle.

"It would have to be after the next show," she said excitedly. Not again, Phoebe, said her warning conscience. It's much too soon after Jamie—whoa, my dear, slow down. She gave Julian a sweet but saucy smile. "We break at noon, but only for half an hour, I'm afraid, so you'd better be on time."

"Wonderful. I'll meet you here on the dot. Okay?" He smiled again, and she noticed the dimple in his chin.

"Okay," said Phoebe with a maidenly blush. "I won't be late."

Fred put down his newspaper and, with a meaningful look at the clock, announced, "Curtain's up in fifteen minutes, duckie, and from the look of yer, you'll need all that time to put yer slap on." He gave Julian a baleful glare and snorted, "Time to move orf the premises, laddie, let the little lady get to work," and buried his face in his tabloid again.

"Noon, then, it's a date." Julian winked at Phoebe and, tipping his hat rakishly, left her with a waft of Brylcreem in her nostrils and romance in her heart.

7

Julian Brooks had been packed off to a prep school on the south coast of England at the age of eight. He had been short for his age, and, being an only child, was shy and nervous around other children.

Amid the hustle and bustle of Victoria Station he clutched his much-loved teddy bear tightly, weeping quietly as his mother, fair and pretty under her aigrette-feathered hat, bestowed a dry peck on his wet cheek, and bade him a fond farewell for the duration of the three-month autumn term.

In the railway carriage with five other sniffling eight-year-olds all trying to control their misery, an equally sad Julian gazed unseeingly at the damp Sussex countryside while the train sped on.

With the exception of his austere mother, women were rather a mystery to Julian. His father had been killed at Arras in 1917, two months before Julian was born, and his mother and nanny had taken sole charge of him since his birth. He had been deprived of the companionship of an adult male and was terrified at the idea of living with over a hundred other boys. He wanted to be with his mother and his beloved nanny; he had dreaded going away to boarding school.

But school turned out to be much better than he'd expected. He found he could head off the teasing the boys gave him because of his lack of stature by making jokes about his height, sometimes even drawing attention to his lack of inches before they did and sending himself up about it. Soon he progressed to imitations—Charlie Chaplin, W. C. Fields, Buster Keaton, Harold Lloyd—regaling the dormitory each night with his impressions of these and other favorite stars, making his classmates laugh so loudly that Matron would bang on the door, issuing fierce threats.

When he was thirteen he was sent off to Eton College, where much against his will he developed a passion for Wilson Minor, who occupied the room next to his. Because of his strikingly beautiful face Julian was soon nicknamed "Looks" Brooks by the older prefects, a nickname which would stay with him for the rest of his life. He became much in demand as a "fag," running errands, picking up jars of Marmite or honey from the village stores and delivering notes from the prefects to boys in other houses. Some of these boys of seventeen or eighteen made no secret of their desire to have Looks Brooks for themselves, but Julian always deflected their passes with a quip or a one-liner. He was popular in the rooms of the older boys at night, where he would happily perform turns from the cinema and music hall, and regale them with his vast repertoire of filthy jokes.

One hot day in June, Simon Gray, a tall, eighteen-year-old senior boy in Julian's house, who had been making unsuccessful passes at Julian for some time, sent him off to deliver a note to his current lover.

The boy's house was over two miles away, an exhausting run on a boiling hot afternoon. On the way, Julian sat down for a rest in the shade of a great Dutch elm, fanning himself with the envelope which soon came unstuck in the heat. Curiosity never having really killed the cat, he opened it, reading, to his horror: "Darling boy, isn't Looks Brooks *divine!* And I've been having him regularly for the past six months! Maybe when we meet next Tuesday, we can both have him *together* . . . Eternally mad for you, Simon."

Julian's heart jumped and he could feel a deep flush spreading over his face and neck. That he could be discussed like a tart or a piece of meat came as an ugly shock. He and Wilson Minor always referred disparagingly to boys who "did it" with each other as poofs or queers. That he should be thought of as "one of those" was infuriating.

Wilson was as blond, blue-eyed and delicately skinned as Julian was dark, heavy-lidded and exotic-looking. They had, of course, experimented sexually with each other, as most boys had at English public schools. The odd, unspoken fumble or mutual masturbation when too much beer or Pimm's had been drunk was never to be discussed by the light of day. But a poof? Him? Julian Looks Brooks—never in a million years! He would rather die than have people think that of him.

Twenty minutes later, as Simon's lover read his note, Julian saw a look of sly interest creep across his face. Licking his lips, the prefect examined the boy from head to toe with lascivious eyes, which made Julian's face blush the color of poppies. Sauntering to his desk, the prefect penned a quick reply to his paramour. Julian naturally read it on the way home: "He is certainly divine, darling, but I'd much rather have you. Next Tuesday *comme toujours*—eternally yours!"

Julian started worrying about his feelings towards his best friend. Although not exactly platonic, they never spoke of their mutual attraction or their love for each other; it was a "manly relationship," but one that now, obviously, had to end or Julian would be thought of as a poof. He couldn't bear that, not to mention the fact that the shame would probably kill his mother.

From then on, Julian became the most sports-mad boy at school and even more of a clown. Although he adored Wilson, he felt that these feelings were wrong, so he ended the relationship abruptly, much to Wilson's shock. Every holiday he arranged to spend with boys whom he knew had sisters and female cousins, and at fourteen he started on his magical primrose path of the seduction of the fairer sex. Since he suddenly grew several inches in height between the ages of fourteen and fifteen, he had little difficulty in persuading even the most virginal of damsels to allow him at least a discreet kiss. From then on, such was his sex appeal and charm that it was usually easy to persuade them to go even further.

When Julian was twenty he had the distinction of being not only the most handsome boy at the Royal Academy of Dramatic Art, but also the finest actor, easily the most popular student, and the man who had the most success with women.

At twenty-one he went into a repertory company where he deliberately and systematically seduced every female in the company whether she was young or old, pretty or pretty ugly.

He loved sex. He liked to prove himself, adored feeling his masculinity conquering the weaker sex. He learned everything he possibly could about women. Seducing them was too easy. His looks were so arresting that with just a little smooth chat any chickie could be cajoled into the feathers before she even knew what was happening. Julian excelled at the super-fuck. He flew his conquests to the moon and back again on a surging sea of sexual rapture which none of them had ever experienced before. He was a true Don Juan, the peerless romantic Romeo, Casanova in corduroy trousers. Irresistible to women, he would go to any lengths to ignite them, to make them his forever.

Phoebe had little difficulty in arranging an audition for Julian. After all, her uncle was one of the Vivienne Van Damm's major shareholders. (Indeed, this was how she had obtained her own job, despite having limited experience in singing or dancing.) The Windmill Theatre was short on smart young comics with a clever patter and genuinely good jokes. The servicemen, who all loved to watch the long-legged, full-bosomed Windmill Girls dance, preen and posture, also wanted to hear raunchy, dirty, close-to-the-knuckle humor, delivered by someone who wasn't their father's age.

Julian was extremely funny. His repertoire of jokes ranged from droll, dry, almost too subtle humor to those which were so incredibly and disgustingly filthy that some of the younger soldiers were quite shocked.

Julian and Phoebe lost no time in slipping between the sheets together. Phoebe was considered fast. At twenty-three she had enjoyed at least a dozen affairs and she was uninhibited and natural in her lovemaking. Men were to be toyed with, to be enjoyed, and Phoebe enjoyed them well and often.

As for Julian, he soon realized he had fallen into a pot of honey. Although his chosen profession was acting, he had not had a legitimate theater role since leaving Maidstone Rep. Despite this he was convinced, as indeed was Phoebe, that his day as a leading man would eventually dawn. Until then he was happy to be the resident comedian at the Windmill Theatre all day and to share Phoebe's cozy bed all night. He allowed her to think that he had fallen in love with her. He knew that was what all girls wanted to believe, although he himself had never managed to fall in love with anyone for longer than a week. He had happily fucked his way through RADA and rep, and although now apparently settled, he still managed discreetly to seduce almost all girls at the Windmill while living with Phoebe. This was further tribute to his palpable sex appeal, spellbinding charm and expert manipulation of the female sex.

Everyone thought Phoebe was the perfect mate for Julian. They shared a similar sense of humor, and possessed huge ambition. When Phoebe suspected Julian of bedding her friends and co-workers, she wasn't prone to bouts of jealous nagging like his previous girlfriends. She just looked the other way, pretending not to see. Her mother had given her that piece of valuable advice. Their lovemaking was a source of delight and, despite the war, they enjoyed their life together immensely.

Yes, they were a good couple, well suited. Everyone said so. Julian should marry her.

8

*H*e was hungry, terribly hungry, but Nikolas couldn't remember when
he hadn't been hungry. His body was pitifully thin, the flesh drawn tightly
across his olive-skinned cheekbones, his stomach was concave and his ribs
showed through his shabby shirt.

He was standing on a parched grassy hill high up on the island of Hydra
while the black-robed priest droned on. The sea was a dark blue mirror,
and the Peleponnese Mountains of the Greek mainland just a smoky haze
in the distance. The body of the last of his baby sisters was being laid to rest
in her pathetic grave. His mother leaned heavily on him, her thin frame
draped in black, her eyes reddened by endless tears.

But Nikolas Stanopolis would not cry. At sixteen he was the head of the
family. It had been less than a year since his father had been executed along
with eight other Greek fishermen who had been accused of aiding and
abetting the partisans in the mountains. Nikolas would never forget that
terrible day.

Down in the port where a few fishing boats bobbed lazily, pulling gently
at their moorings, he had watched a group of men in the center of the
square being savagely beaten with rifle butts until their faces turned to
pulp. The entire population of Hydra had been forced to watch and then
see them shot. What made the event even more horrible was that the Italian

soldiers who had carried out this atrocity and many others seemed to derive brutal satisfaction from seeing these wretched men die. The soldiers joked with each other, laughing as their prisoners screamed in agony.

Silently, in a ragged circle, the population of Hydra had stood watching. There were three hundred or so black-shawled women, the young almost indistinguishable from the old, so wizened and weak were they from lack of food and the cruel deprivations of the island's occupation. A few puny children scampered about, even the horrors of war powerless to suppress their antics. A dozen adolescents stood transfixed with horror, and a handful of toothless old people shook their wrinkled heads as they watched yet another execution with a stoicism born of longevity and passive resistance.

Nikolas had clasped his arms around his mother, trying to give her support and comfort as she leaned against him, burdened with grief. His mother was thirty-four but looked more like sixty—worn out with fear and the torment of watching her children suffer and die. At her breast was the youngest of her brood, a little girl who weighed no more than twelve pounds though she was nearly a year old. The nourishment she received from Melina's shriveled breasts would not be enough to sustain her for much longer.

There was hardly any food left in the village. No goats, no pigs, not even any donkeys—the villagers survived only on what they were allowed to forage from the sea.

Within a year, Nikolas' last brother and sister would die slowly and painfully, along with almost a third of the island's children.

The Hydriots were a simple but proud race, used to hard work, and their island had given them a good living for several hundred years. Such was the determination and resilience of its inhabitants that Hydra was the only Greek island which had never before fallen to an enemy. Even the Turks had found it impossible to conquer a hundred years earlier.

The Germans had stolen all the available food to feed their armies fighting in the Afrika Korps. Crops were seized, sheep and goats slaughtered, olive groves and orchards laid waste. The Nazis had battles to fight, and little or no feeling for starving women and children.

When the Germans left in 1941 the Italian army came to garrison Hydra. As it was considered a backwater post—it was eleven miles long and sparsely populated—the dregs of the Italian arm were sent. Louts from Sicily and Naples who could barely read before the war issued orders, made rules and used their tyrannical power to instill more terror in the islanders than the Germans had ever done.

Benito Mussolini was their revered leader and their idol. No matter that he was so self-conscious about his puny height that he insisted in all official photographs that he be photographed from below; every halfwit in the Italian army blindly worshiped Il Duce.

Nikolas' thoughts of his father's terrible death were interrupted by a chilling shriek from his mother. Her baby's pathetic little coffin was placed in the grave and she slid to the ground in a spasm of grief. Melina's worry beads slipped from her feeble grasp as the priest gravely offered her a shovel to sprinkle the first spadeful of dry earth onto the tiny driftwood box.

Wailing in sympathy, three women helped the weeping Melina back to her feet. The priest's voice droned on, ignoring the women's sobs. He had become so conditioned to grief that he was almost immune to the agony of his starving villagers. He couldn't count the number of children he had buried in the past two years. The poor Stanopolis woman had lost four, as well as her husband. But at least she still had the boy, and at sixteen, although painfully thin, he was tall and had the resiliency of youth. At least Melina had someone to depend on: recognizing the look of defiance in his face, the priest felt instinctively that the boy would survive. He brought the simple service to a close, and watched as his congregation shuffled wearily away.

Almost doubled up with grief, Melina, escorted by the three women and Nikolas, slowly made her way to the sanctuary of the cool stone walls of her little hilltop house. The small group of mourners climbed the steep cobblestone steps of the narrow winding street, and one by one entered the shuttered darkness of the Stanopolis house. The women fussed over Melina while Nikolas went to his room, his eyes prickling with the stinging tears he had tried so desperately not to allow his mother to see.

Opening up the chipped blue shutters, oblivious to the beauty of the olive and almond trees which grew outside his window, he thought of vengeance. Vengeance on the Germans, vengeance on the Italians. But most of all, vengeance on the commanding officer of the Italian garrison, the fat pig who now ruled Hydra without justice and without mercy, and whom the locals called "Gourouni."

Nikolas fidgeted fiercely with his mother's translucent yellow worry beads, which he'd picked up at the graveside, passing them back and forth between his fingers. He leaned out to gaze at the highest point of the island, where all the glorious eighteenth-century mansions stood, built by rich shipowners. Gourouni had chosen the most beautiful and imposing of them to be his official residence.

He was the undoubted cause of the recent crop of executions, the cause of the deaths of Nikolas' father, his brothers and sisters. Nikolas thought him filthy, depraved, corrupt scum, a travesty of Mussolini. All of the villagers silently mocked the squat fat figure as he preened and postured in his ludicrous musical-comedy uniforms thickly encrusted with gold braid, glinting with stolen medals.

In his exquisite neoclassical villa, set in lush gardens of grape, olive and pine trees, was the plunder from a dozen of the wealthiest Hydriot mansions, and from the fabled temples of the surrounding islands of Spetsai and Aegina. Rare paintings, tapestries, sculptures and eighteenth-century furniture which would hardly have been out of place in Versailles filled the villa, which he proudly believed to be the finest in all Greece. Some of the luckiest villagers were employed as gardeners, cooks and housemaids.

Elektra Makopolis was one of the latter. Exactly the same age as Nikolas, she had lived next door to him all their lives. Occasionally she managed to smuggle a loaf of bread or some fruit or cooked meat out of the Commander's fortress. She would share anything she pilfered with the Stanopolis family, as there was no one left of her own. Her father had been deported to a labor camp by the Germans, and soon afterward her mother had starved to death. A young Italian lieutenant with a grain of sympathy in his heart heard about the wretched girl's predicament and found her a job in "the Palace" where she worked hard polishing marble, cleaning furniture and scrubbing floors. Everything Elektra knew about the Palace she had described to Nikolas in minute detail. Every atrocity which she saw committed by Gourouni she reported to him . . .

There was a faint tap at his bedroom door and Elektra appeared.

"Nikolas," she whispered, "I've brought you some cake and hot coffee."

Coffee! How had she managed to find coffee? Nikolas didn't want to ask. She had stolen it from Gourouni's villa, knowing full well the penalty if she were ever found out. He swallowed the bitter liquid and wolfed down the delicious honey cake greedily.

The two of them leaned out of the window and Elektra ran a hand through Nikolas' untidy curls. He tried to muster a smile. He loved her and she loved him. It was all very simple. Both their families had known for years that one day they would be united by the marriage of Nikolas and Elektra, and now it was inevitable that it would happen.

"He showed a movie last night," whispered Elektra. "Some of us sneaked into the projection booth to watch it. Oh, Nikolas!" Her lovely young face glowed with excitement. "It was so wonderful—you cannot believe what an exciting film it was. American, of course, with a wonderful little girl with ringlets who sang and danced. She was tiny, maybe six or seven years old—but so clever, and so pretty. I wish you could have seen it, Nikolas, you would have loved it—I know how much you love movies."

Nikolas was passionate about films. Before the war, he had gone to the open-air cinema to watch his idols. He was mesmerized by the brilliance of film directors like Alfred Hitchcock and John Ford, and he studied their techniques, returning time after time to see their work.

But there were no longer any film performances for the villagers. Now the only place movies were shown was up at the Palace where Gourouni somehow always managed to procure the latest offerings from Hollywood.

Elektra looked at Nikolas. His eyes were riveted on the Commander's citadel: it seemed to glow with a fiery light as the late-afternoon sun reddened its white marble walls to the color of blood, and the hated Italian flag flapped gently in the faint breeze.

They both thought of the toadlike creature who now inhabited the house. A sadist who regularly sent innocents to their deaths, who tortured men for pleasure, all the while accumulating the spoils of war.

"He's probably busy stuffing his ugly face." Nikolas' voice was full of hatred. "Guzzling meat and wine, thinking about which movie he'll show tonight. He's a murdering monster. He shouldn't be allowed to live."

"Nikolas, guess who made the film?" Elektra tried to change the subject. Whenever Nikolas started talking about Gourouni, it was difficult to get him to stop. He seemed to have an obsession about the man. "My American uncle, you remember him? The one who went to America years ago, before we were born—the one who has done so well." Her face beamed with pride. In the past, her mother had often talked of her eldest brother, the brash young man who was always so ambitious, so determined to leave Greece, to succeed in the new country, and who had finally triumphed there.

"Spyros!" she said proudly. "Spyros Makopolis. I recognized his name at the beginning of the film. It was in *huge* letters—'Produced by Spyros Makopolis.' Isn't that wonderful?" Her smile was radiant. "He's from Hydra, Nikolas, and he produces films in Hollywood." She leaned towards him, fingers gently stroking his face. "If he can do it, Nikolas—so can you."

"One day—if ever this war is over—we will both go to Hollywood and I will make such wonderful films that the whole world will want to see them," said Nikolas bitterly. "But not before that sadistic pig is dead." His voice rose in passionate rage and he looked again towards the mansion and thought of the destruction of Gourouni, and how only fools underestimated the pride of the Greeks.

It had been a convivial evening. The film, the latest offering from the MCCP studio, was excellent, and the female star was a ravishing creature, blonde and ripe, who looked no more than eighteen. Both the Commander and his aide-de-camp, Major Volpi, found her so appealing that thoughts of her juicy charms lingered pleasurably.

The wine had been excellent. A Château-Lafite '29, two cases of which had been discovered last week in the cellar of one of the Hydriot mansions.

The Commander stretched and yawned as he unbuttoned the gold buttons of his skintight blue uniform. He admired his reflection in the narrow eighteenth-century gilded mirror which was hung on his dressing room wall in the most flattering light. He was a *bella figura*, no doubt about that. His resemblance to his idol Mussolini seemed to be increasing, particularly now that he had completely shaved his head and always copied Il Duce's latest uniforms in the most painstaking detail. The one he now wore was impressive, of the finest gabardine, one of many made for him by a good Greek tailor on the island.

Never mind that the uniform he should be wearing as Commander of Hyra was a drab gray. The stupid villagers knew no better, and as for his soldiers, with the exception of Volpi, whose palms were more than well greased with silver, they were a bunch of dolts.

The Commander undid the heavy gold buckle of his wide leather belt, then took off his jacket and shirt and tossed them onto a brocade-covered Jacobean bergère.

The dim peach lamp on the armoire illuminated his face and torso with a soft flattering glow. He smiled at his reflection admiringly, his small eyes almost disappearing into the pads of fat surrounding them. The bald bullet head, sensual lips and strong chin were pleasing to him, as were the hirsute barrel chest and thickly muscled forearms.

The only thing about his physical appearance that didn't please him was the thick keloid scar that traversed the base of his Adam's apple in a clean three-inch line. He always attempted to conceal it with his high-necked uniforms. The rumor on Hydra was that someone had tried to kill him, that he had hovered between life and death in a Parisian hospital for several weeks, and only the attentions of the finest throat specialist in France had saved his life and his larynx. Now he could talk only in a harsh, rasping whisper, which further added to his terrifying demeanor.

He fingered the scar gingerly. They had never found the girl who had slashed his throat with his own razor and left him for dead on the cold marble floor of his bathroom.

He had survived that bitch's murderous attempt only by overwhelming physical strength and will to live. But even though the throat surgeon had done a brilliant job in saving both his life and his voice, Umberto Scrofo would never be satisfied until he found the girl who had almost killed him, and paid her back a thousand times over for her crime.

9

Nikolas leaned his head against the whitewashed stone wall of the tiny balcony and sobbed. His beloved mother, the last family link he had left, was dying, withered by starvation, her heart broken.

Melina lay on her bed, weakly fingering her rosary, mumbling over and over again the names of her dead husband and children. She had simply lost the will to live. The light had gone out of her warm brown eyes, leaving them expressionless and dead, and she weighed less than ninety pounds. She had even refused to eat the small fish which Nikolas had managed to catch by spending some fourteen soul-destroying hours in his boat. Two of the village women attended her, their faces stoic masks of suffering.

Nikolas was in total despair, his mind numbed by misery and privation. All he could do was pray that his mother wouldn't die. He went back into his room and opened the drawer next to his bed. From beneath a meager pile of shirts and socks, he took out his knife. It was in a brown leather sheath, shiny and new. He had found it yesterday as he was cleaning his nets on the beach. One of the soldiers had obviously dropped it, and Nikolas had quickly put it in his pocket, hoping he was unobserved.

Now he slowly pulled the shining blade out of the holder and watched the dying moon's reflection shimmer on the polished steel. He ran a thumb gingerly down the cutting edge, feeling the sharpness of it. How he would love to plunge this blade into Gourouni's fat stomach and wrench it until his entrails spilled onto the ground like a gutted fish's.

Nikolas knew he would take great satisfaction in watching that sadistic swine wriggle in his death agonies. He imagined the Italian's face contorted in agony, pleading for help, but he was interrupted in his fantasy by the sound of his mother weakly calling his name. Quickly replacing the knife in its hiding place he ran downstairs to kiss her and to bid her a tender good-bye. It was time to fish now, to catch the only sustenance left for them.

He strode purposefully down to the harbor, his thoughts still full of Gourouni.

Although it was not yet five in the morning there was a bustle of activity in the tiny fishing port. Nine or ten fishermen, all either under sixteen or over sixty-five, were carefully arranging their yellow and cream nets in the bows of their boats, preparing their lines for today's catch. The bare bulbs in Dimitri's beach bar glowed yellow, giving a jaundiced look to the hard faces of the Italian guards who lounged about, paying no attention to the fishermen, thinking only of when their watches would end. Some looked so drunk that there was little chance of their protecting anything, should the Allies have picked that moment to invade Hydra. But there was no likelihood of that. The Allies had no strategic interest at all in the remote little island. Dimitri gave Nikolas a friendly *"Yassou"* as he poured him a small cup of thick, sweet coffee and pushed a tiny piece of honeyed baklava across the counter. The boy drank and ate gratefully, pleased that Dimitri always managed to have coffee and cake in his bar. In return, he hoped to bring Dimitri some *pompano,* red mullet or sea bass, although the fish had not been jumping recently. Even at the nearby islands of Mykonos, Spetsai and Poros, it was as if all sea life knew there was a war on and wanted no part of it.

Dimitri leaned conspiratorially towards Nikolas, with a glance at one of the snoring Italians.

"I listened to the wireless last night," he whispered, making a great show of wiping some glasses with a grubby rag. "It's going to all be over soon, Nikolas, very, very soon."

One of the sleeping soldiers gave a loud snore which made Nikolas jump nervously.

"They say it's only a matter of weeks before the war is over. And they say that the Allies will win for sure. They've really got the Boche going now."

The boy drained the dregs of his coffee. "It's incredible news, Dimitri, I hope it's true."

"It's true," whispered Dimitri excitedly. "Believe me, Nikolas, it's true. The Allies have got these pigs on the run. Keep your fingers crossed,

Nikolas—maybe this time next week we'll be free, we'll have our island back again."

Nikolas nodded his thanks to Dmitri with an excited conspiratorial smile, and set off to fish, feeling more lighthearted than he had for months. Soon the war would be over. Soon the Hydriots would be rid of their murdering oppressors and it would be time for the villagers to forget. But Nikolas knew he could never forget his hatred for the Commander.

Umberto Scrofo read the terse orders on an official paper which had arrived during the night by messenger from his commanding officer.

Propped up in his ornately carved Venetian bed between the finest linen sheets to be found in all Greece, he was surrounded by old master paintings of erotic scenes. A richly colored tapestry had been draped carelessly over an elaborate Henri Jacob daybed against one wall, and a set of four magnificent sculptures—which might have been by the hand of Michelangelo himself—lurked in the shadows of the four corners of the room.

But this particular morning Scrofo derived none of his usual pleasure from any of them.

As soon as he read the message he leaped furiously from his bed onto the pale Aubusson carpet, mouthing profanities at the hapless officer who had brought him both the message and his chamberpot. He aimed into the delicately painted receptacle, held in the trembling hands of the young lieutenant, while launching into another wildly vituperative verbal attack. The scar on his neck throbbed as it always did whenever he was angry. He bounced around in his short silk nightshirt so much that the unfortunate youth could barely manage to keep the pot under the General's Lilliputian organ.

Barking out orders in his rasping voice, Scrofo darted about his bedroom, flinging objects into gaping leather bags which had miraculously appeared, wrapping precious artifacts and bronzes in thick velvet cloths, helped by a handful of clumsy gray-uniformed soldiers.

The message received that morning had galvanized him into a vindictive rampage. So he was supposed to evacuate the island immediately, was he? And leave behind all the priceless booty which he had so painstakingly collected? He would see about that! He wasn't going to leave any of his treasures on this pitiful excuse of an island.

Squeezing into a black uniform which had grown too tight with the many months of excess, and pinning on as many medals as time permitted, he clattered down the marble staircase in his high tight boots.

"I want every last one of the islanders here at once," he barked in his strained croaking voice to Major Volpi. "Go into the village and round them all up now. Every man, woman and child. *Now*."

"Very well, sir," said Volpi, saluting smartly while privately thinking what an oaf this Commander was. But who was he to cast stones? Before the war he had been in prison for murder; now he was a favored citizen, a much admired soldier.

"The sick ones too?" he inquired.

"Every one of them," snarled Scrofo. "Every single one of the inhabitants."

He paced feverishly around the magnificent villa appraising the pictures, statues and furniture which filled it, taking mental stock. It seemed to him that his plunder was smiling at him in a most pleasing way, bathed as it was in the gentle morning sunshine. Peerless treasures of only the highest quality—all his, all stolen. His dream had been eventually to take his treasures back to Italy, and once ensconced there he would become a respectable *antiquaire*, selling beautiful things to collectors and competing with the best art dealers of London, New York and Paris. That dream would now be shattered unless he could get everything packed, crated and transported down the three hundred or so cobbled steps to the harbor at once. His plan was to load them onto a hidden yacht, sail over to Albania, and from there, on to Italy. He would take only four trusted accomplices with him, whose pockets had already been well lined with gold bullion. And he was well prepared. Up from the cellar came the soldiers carrying wooden crates, cartons and great quantities of packing materials. At once his troops set to work, wrapping and crating the pictures and sculptures as fast as they could.

Soon the villagers arrived. Small children, old men and frail women were divided into makeshift working groups to pack up Gourouni's loot.

Melina had been pulled from her sickbed by a posse of soldiers. Now, almost too weak to walk, helped by the devoted Elektra, she was commanded by Volpi to wrap a collection of exquisite enamel-and-gold Fabergé eggs. Even in their weakened and dazed state, the women were stunned by the beauty of the jeweled snuffboxes, the richly gilded and inlaid furniture, the brilliant colors of the eighteenth-century paintings and the golden flesh tones of the Rembrandts.

Melina's eyes were so clouded that she could hardly see. Her hands were trembling so much that it was practically impossible for her to hold onto anything. The soldiers moved among the women, yelling at them, giving them a sharp punch if they didn't seem to be working fast enough. The frightened children had been given the task of crating up Scrofo's collection of extremely rare first editions of Dante, Goethe, Shakespeare and Tolstoy, and the little ones stumbled about with frightened eyes as they tried to handle the precious volumes without damaging them.

Suddenly with a startled cry, Melina let slip a crystal egg encrusted with seed pearls and precious stones. With a noise like a gunshot the priceless treasure shattered on the marble floor.

Everyone stopped what they were doing, to stare at the wretched woman, but Melina's eyes were so glazed with despair and fever that she felt no fear as the dreaded Gourouni approached her.

"Do you see what you've done, you stupid idiot!" he rasped, his face scarlet with fury. "Idiot. *Idiot! IDIOT!*" He cracked his pistol down on her skull with the full force of his rage. Melina felt no pain as blood coursed down her waxen face. She felt nothing as she lay in a crumpled heap and the enraged Scrofo rained blow after blow on her face and head as he screamed abuse.

"Back to work," Scrofo screeched as terrified children ran crying to hide under their mothers' skirts. "Back to work or you'll suffer the same fate. And no one had better break anything else."

Some of the villagers crossed themselves while several people moaned quietly or openly wept. Quietly Elektra asked permission to remove Melina's body and Volpi nodded a curt affirmative. She wrapped the pitiful, wasted shape in her long black shawl and two other women helped her to take Melina out into the bright sunshine, where with tear-stained faces they laid her gently down in the cobbled courtyard.

When Nikolas returned to the harbor at sundown he was pleased with his catch. It was the best for a long time—almost half a kilo of whitebait, several red mullet and a couple of plump pompano. They would have a feast tonight. Dmitri was sure to give him some olive oil and some potatoes and tomatoes, maybe even a small bottle of wine, in exchange for a few fish. He, Elektra and his mother could then celebrate the imminent end of their island's occupation.

As he hauled his boat up the pebbled beach, a weeping black-shawled Elektra, her long hair ruffled by the breeze, ran to him and threw herself into his arms.

"Nikolas, oh, Nikolas, I'm so sorry."

"Sorry—for what? What is it, Elektra?" He was suddenly apprehensive. Elektra was usually a strong, resilient girl. Toughened by the harsh life of the island, she retained an innate gentleness which inspired devotion in all who knew her.

Sobbing quietly into Nikolas' shoulder, she told him of his mother's death.

Nikolas' face hardened. He had known his mother could not survive much longer, but the war was nearly over—surely then she would have recovered? He tried hard not to weep. He would never forgive Gourouni for this—never.

"Where are all the soldiers now?" he asked harshly.

"Gone. Every last one of them. They sailed this afternoon. We burned their flag when they left," she told him. "All of their flags."

"Did the bastards murder anyone else before they left?" Nikolas asked as Dmitri came out of his bar bringing him a glass of brandy.

Dmitri put his arms around Nikolas, trying to comfort the boy whom he loved like a son.

"No," Elektra said gently, her hand stroking Nikolas' cheek. "No one else. Oh Nikolas I'm so sorry."

Nikolas drained his brandy, the unfamiliar burning sensation fueling him with unaccustomed power. Seeing the forlorn faces of his friends, he was filled with such anger that his fury almost had a life of its own. He needed to kill. He wanted to plunge his knife into the Italian pigs, killing them all, but especially he wanted to put his hands around the throat of that diabolical Commander and squeeze the life out of him. He wanted to watch him die before his eyes. Wanted to hear his slug-like lips beg for mercy. As he felt the knife in his pocket, Nikolas knew he had the power of death in his fingers and knew too that his hatred would eventually give him strength to do what he had to do.

"One day—one day—one day," he muttered harshly, fingering at his mother's beads furiously as though they were the tendons of his enemy's neck. "I'll kill him if it's the last thing I do in my life. I shall find that murdering bastard and make him suffer more than he ever dreamed possible. By the time I have finished with Commander Umberto Scrofo, he'll be begging me to kill him, I swear it."

10

*I*nès *was perfectly content living in London, although she missed Paris.*
The tiny flat in Shepherd Market on the top floor of an old Georgian house
was cozy, and its leaded-glass windows trapped every ray of the pale London sunshine. Often she sat on the window seat, looking out over the tops
of the plane trees in Green Park, her mind far away, thinking about Paris.
Were the Gestapo still searching for her? Nightmares about the dead Italian
General still disturbed her sleep, but Yves' arms were always there in the
night to soothe her fears when she would wake screaming and drenched
in sweat, and in the morning he would make her laugh again with some of
his magic tricks.

Yves kept up with news of the French occupation through the newspapers and wireless while Inès devoted herself to mastering the English
language and keeping house for him. She would spend her mornings
trying to buy food with ration books which allowed them only the barest
essentials. Casseroles were hard to make with four ounces of meat, and it
was impossible even for a French girl to make an omelet for two with just
one egg.

Yves had contacted some of the names he'd been given, intent on building himself a new life in London. He was often out all day, while Inès
listened to the wireless and sang as she cleaned and dusted the flat, rel-

ishing her new domestic role. For the first time in her life, she was living a normal existence and she worshiped Yves more than ever.

She struck up a friendship with Stella Bates, a redheaded girl who lived on the floor below. Often they would shop together, carrying their string bags in search of groceries, sugar, butter or jam—all commodities in short supply and for which coupons from their ration books were necessary. Stella regaled Inès with amusing stories of her life. She was a successful prostitute, with few qualms about her profession. A couple of years older than Inès, she had an attractive body and a flaming halo of red hair which ensured that she rarely spent her evenings alone. She was also very funny, and even Yves was amused by her cockney repartee.

He had recently brought up the matter of Inès' returning to "work," a subject she hated to discuss. She didn't want to be a prostitute anymore. Her intense love for Yves made the thought of being with another man an anathema, and the experience in Paris was still far too vivid. But Yves was becoming more insistent. Money was always short, they had rent to pay. He couldn't make enough on the black market to keep them both, and he wasn't qualified for anything but menial work or his clever tricks.

"I'm not a good enough magician for the music halls, *chérie,*" he laughed. "It's up to you to start making some money for us." But Inès resisted, hoping against hope that Yves would get some sort of job, maybe even marry her, so that they could continue this proper life that she was relishing so much.

Eventually Yves convinced her that she must become the breadwinner or they would both starve. So she confided most of her life story to Stella, without mentioning that she had killed a man. Stella gave her sage advice.

"It's time to stop trollin' the streets, darlin', you're *much* too classy for that. I've got a really nice, exclusive clientele now, duckie—references only—so, just give me the word and I'll fix you up with one of my classy titled gents. No kinky stuff, I promise you."

Inès grimaced, but Yves was hungry and demanding. She had no choice but to become a whore again. But at least this time it would be with English gentlemen, not enemy louts.

London was swarming with servicemen of all nationalities and a party mood prevailed. Even though the Blitz continued as the German bombs hit their targets with monotonous regularity, London's nightclubs still had a carnival atmosphere which made people forget that a war was going on. The favorite haunt of partygoers, the Café de Paris, had sustained a direct hit the previous year, killing at least forty revelers, but the wartime festivities continued unabated.

The following night Stella invited Inès to go to a nightclub with her. "I've got a date with a very nice gent an' a couple of friends of 'is, and they're anxious to make whoopee, luv—so come with us, we'll have a lovely time, I promise."

Inès reluctantly told Yves, who insisted that she go.

"You must start working, *chérie*," he said heatedly. "We need the money. You know we do."

"I know," said Inès gloomily. "Oh, Yves, how much longer will I have to do this? I hate it. I hate it more and more."

"Not much longer, *chérie*." Yves smiled, stroking her luxuriant hair and nuzzling her neck in the way that always gave her excited shivers. "When the war is over we will be able to go back to Paris, I will get a job there, I promise you, and you can stop this life. Now be a good girl and get some good clients tonight."

After dressing carefully in her one good black dress with a wide belt which accentuated her narrow waist, Inès stood balanced on the tiny kitchen table while Stella first painted her bare legs with dark pancake foundation and then carefully drew a line down the back of her calves with a stub of eyebrow pencil.

"There," chuckled the redhead when she'd finished, pleased with her handiwork. "Now duckie, if you can get a hold of one of these Yanks tonight you won't 'ave to do this anymore—it'll be nylons, nylons, nylons all over the bleedin' place, not to mention chockies and cigarettes and all sorts of lovely goodies. But tonight we concentrate on the toffs."

"OK," said Inès gloomly. "You're the boss Stella."

The Bagatelle was in a gala mood, packed with revelers. As Inès followed Stella she admired the baroque decor of the fashionable nightclub.

A wide red-carpeted staircase swept grandly into the bar, the walls of which were covered in great golden mirrors. On scarlet velvet chairs dozens of well-dressed vivacious young women sat engrossed in conversation and flirtation with a variety of men, many in uniform, some in black tie. Paul Adams' band was playing the catchy current hit tune, "I Left My Heart at the Stage Door Canteen," and Inès felt her pulse beat faster to the rhythm of the music. She was suddenly quite excited to be on the town again. Her months in London had given her a passable command of English, which she was eager to practice, and in spite of her trepidation about the evening the animated atmosphere started to whet her appetite for a good time.

Stella's date was an educated, jovial titled man in his thirties, up from Shropshire and determined to paint the town red. Champagne flowed, as did his jokes, which Inès found mostly incomprehensible but which had Stella bent double with hilarity. The club was dark and smoky and the tiny lights with their pink pleated shades on each table cast a flattering glow on everyone's face.

Stella was in top form, her cockney humor fired by the atmosphere, trading wisecracks with Lord Worthington, whispering to Inès that he was a real live lord. " 'E's in some top position at the Foreign Office, a real toff," she said when he went to greet some friends who had just arrived.

"And bloody generous 'e is, too, luv—gave me a tenner extra last night, and sent me over a pound of bacon and a pair of nylons this morning—look!"

Proudly she extended her slender legs for Inès to admire the new nylon stockings.

"Ssh, 'ere 'e comes," warned Stella as Lord Worthington returned with two younger men in tow.

"I've brought over a couple of chums, my dear. I hope you don't mind if they join us—Charlie and Benjie. Introduce your friend, will you, old girl? I'm off for a pee."

Charlie, who was short and plump, turned out to be the Honorable Charles Brougham, and Benjie, who was tall and skinny, was Viscount Benjamin Spencer-Monckton. The two young men ensconced themselves on either side of Inès, both seemingly spellbound by her cleavage.

"What a splendid accent you have," murmured Charles, his hand brushing against her knee, his eyes on her breasts.

"Yes, it's absolutely spiffing. French, are you?" breathed Benjie.

"Yes." Inès smiled demurely, not altogether displeased by the young men's interest in her. Lord Worthington had now returned and was howling with laughter at another of Stella's bawdy jokes. Inès thought her two titled admirers were not bad-looking in a bland English way, attentive and well mannered, even though both were quite drunk. They were infinitely preferable to the portly pomposity of Lord Worthington.

"Would you care to dance?" Benjie asked as the band began "Moonlight Becomes You."

"I'd love to," Inès smiled. "I haven't danced in a very long time."

As they wended their way through the throng of swaying bodies, Inès suddenly stopped dead in her tracks, an all too familiar fear gripping her. She shook her head as if to dismiss the hallucination. Surely it couldn't be? It simply couldn't. Benjie was pushing her politely to move on, and she edged past the man's table with mounting dread.

Cold black eyes met hers for an instant, and she froze again. How could he be here in the Bagatelle in London when almost a year ago in Paris she had killed him? What was Umberto Scrofo doing in London? An Italian general from Mussolini's army sitting at a ringside table as bold as brass, with a bottle of champagne in front of him and flanked by two blond hookers. It was impossible.

But there was no mistaking the tiny vicious eyes, that huge bald head, the cruel mouth. Mesmerized, she stood before his table unable to move a muscle. The man's eyes caressed her body for a second, then swiveled back to the two blondes, and Inès was swept into the middle of the packed dance floor, trembling violently as Benjie took her in his arms.

"Are you all right, old thing?" he asked solicitously. "You're shaking like a leaf. You look like you've just seen a ghost."

"I think I have," Inès whispered, holding on to him tightly, willing her heart to stop beating so wildly. She looked over again at the table where she thought she'd spotted Scrofo. A fat, bald man was sitting there, shoulder to shoulder with two buxom blondes, but it certainly wasn't Umberto Scrofo, of that she was now absolutely positive. She laughed out loud, a great burst of hysterical relieved laughter. How stupid she was, what a silly fool, with her over fertile imagination. Of course it couldn't have been Scrofo—he was dead. But in those horrific dreams which haunted her subconscious so many nights, he was very much alive. She could still clearly recall every last detail of the grotesque Italian, and just glimpsing a man with similar features or a similar shape was enough to plunge her into a turmoil of fear and anxiety. Inès knew very well that her imagination had always been too vivid for her own good, and she breathed a great sigh of relief that it had been no more than her fancy which had conjured him up. Scrofo was dead and gone—forever—and that was that.

As Inès' waves of panic subsided and the orchestra started to play the romantic "Bewitched, Bothered and Bewildered," she decided to concentrate her attentions on Benjie's erect penis which was begging for notice as it prodded insistently against her thigh. She smiled up at him, slyly acknowledging it, and his pale, almost transparent gray eyes, fringed with sandy lashes, looked away from her shyly as he blushed.

Poor bashful man, she thought sympathetically. He was obviously unused to being in such close proximity to a woman. To make him feel more at ease she rested her head lightly on his shoulder and placed her hand gently on the back of his neck as the romantic music washed over them. She started singing, "I'm wild again—beguiled again, a simpering, whimpering child again—bewitched, bothered and bewildered am I."

Benjie's breathing became more erratic, and as the dance ended, he bent his sandy head to hers, whispering self-consciously, "May I see you again, Inès? I know it's a bit of an imposition because you've probably got a boyfriend and all that, but I do find you terribly attractive."

Inès smiled. He was titled and rich, personable, from a good family. Yves had been telling her for weeks that she had to start work again. This young man seemed kind, and cultured. If she had to continue her career as a prostitute, she could do a great deal worse than become the mistress of Viscount Benjamin Spencer-Monckton. After all, there was a war on.

Even though the war was at its harshest peak and nightly blitzes devastated London, Benjie took Inès on a social whirl such as she had never known before. Although he must have known she was a professional, he treated her like a girlfriend whom he wanted to woo. His manners were impeccable, and Inès became caught up in the time of her life.

The night after they met he took her to a film at the Odeon Leicester Square and then next door to his favorite nightclub, the 400, where he seemed to know everyone, and everyone knew him. The intimate private club was jammed with young aristocrats and society figures. Some of the men were in uniform, some in black tie, a few of the more conservative even wore white tie. They were a high-spirited, jolly crowd bent on merrymaking, and Benjie and Inès moved from group to group as he introduced her to his friends. They were so young, these men, Inès thought. Babies, some of them. No one could see there was any fear or trepidation in the men's hearts by their behavior. The abandoned pleasure-seeking and frantic revelry made each night like a New Year's Eve spree. Many of the young people at the 400 seemed madly in love, and there was a great deal of petting and smooching on the congested dance floor.

"More people get engaged here than anywhere else in London," Benjie shouted to Inès, a twinkle in his pale eyes, as they danced to the music from the new Broadway musical *Carousel.*

Benjie's elusive hardness started to poke again at Inès' thigh, and she smiled up at him as she sang seductively, "If I loved you, words wouldn't come in an easy way."

"Lovely," breathed Benjie, holding her so close that his protuberance almost made her wince. "You have a lovely voice, Inès, in fact everything about you is lovely."

"Thank you," she smiled. "You are very sweet, Benjie."

The following night he took her to dinner at the Gay Hussar in Greek Street, then to the Berkeley, where they danced the night away to Ian Stevens and his peppy music. As usual the place was swarming with pleasure-seekers of every nationality. The band played many of Inès' favorite tunes, and she hummed and sang them to an enraptured Benjie. He particularly liked her version of "This Is a Lovely Way to Spend an Evening," and insisted that the band play it several times.

Afterward they walked home through Berkeley Square as the birds were singing their morning song and the soft fingers of dawn were creeping across the plane trees.

"Tomorrow?" he asked softly as they arrived at Shepherd Market.

"Yes," she whispered, wondering when and if he was ever going to kiss her.

"We'll go to the Savoy with Charles and his girlfriend, Henrietta," said Benjie. "Black tie. I'll pick you up at eight." With a dry kiss on her cheek he tipped his hat and walked away off towards Curzon Street.

"Well," asked Yves sleepily from the bed as she came into his room. "Has it happened yet?"

"Not yet," sighed Inès, flopping onto the bed and into her lover's warm arms. "Not yet, *chéri*. He's English, this may take a little more time than usual. I think he needs to get to know me first."

"Hmph," snorted Yves. "He better hurry up. It's all right for you being wined and dined every night, but this poor Frenchman is starving to death. Oh, *mon Dieu,* I would *kill* for a steaming cup of *café au lait* with three teaspoonfuls of sugar, and a hot croissant dripping with raspberry jam."

"You'll just have to live on love," teased Inès, kissing his lips. "Until I break down Benjie's British reserve, love will have to do, my darling."

Inès was running out of evening clothes. Indeed she was running out of any clothes at all. Her clothes cupboard, like their food cupboard, was practically bare, and she had so far worn the same secondhand black dress on every date with Benjie. In desperation she asked Stella if she could borrow something, and the girl threw open her wardrobe door for her friend.

"Whatever you like, luv—take anyfink." She smiled generously. "We're about the same size—'cept I'm a few inches shorter an' a bit more flashy than you luv."

That was an understatement, thought Inès. Stella's wardrobe was crammed with brightly colored frocks decorated with all manner of beads, buttons and bows.

"What about this?" Inès reached into the darker recesses of the cupboard and pulled out a pale gray crêpe dress, the bodice trimmed with gunmetal bugle beads.

"Ooh, that was me mum's!" shrilled Stella. " 'Er only good frock it was, she got it from a lady she did a good turn for. It's a bit too drab for me, dearie. It would look good on you though. So you can 'ave it—it's a present."

"Oh, Stella, *thank* you," cried Inès. "You're the best friend I've ever had in the whole world."

Inès tried on the dress. It was the first full-length gown she had ever worn, and it accentuated her height and slim, curved hips. Bias-cut, with short puffed sleeves, the skirt ended in a fan-tailed pleat which Inès almost tripped over as she tried to walk across the room.

"You'll 'ave to practice with that, luv," laughed Stella. "You'll look a bit of a burk if you come a cropper on the dance floor in front of all those la-di-das. You need some matching shoes too. C'mon, let's go to Dolcis. For seventeen and six you can get a nice pair dyed to match—it'll look such a lovely outfit then, an' I'll teach you how to walk with the train."

"But I haven't *got* seventeen and six," wailed Inès. "Stella, I don't have more than a few shillings."

"I'll treat you to the shoes." Her friend grinned. "I've 'ad a very good month, dear, thanks to the Hon. Charlie Boy—you can do the same for me, dear, if I ever go through a dull period. Look out, Oxford Street—'ere we come."

Inès had enough clothes coupons in her ration book for the shoes which Stella bought, and enough coupons left over for at least two more dresses. She had only bought a few things since arriving in England, but although she had the precious coupons she had no cash.

After their shopping trip Stella came to Inès' flat to inspect the contents of her wardrobe.

"Oh, dearie me, duckie, you'll never be successful on the game wearin' that little lot," she said disparagingly, flicking through Inès' meager supply of clothes. "Tell you what, as soon as the Hon. Benjie manages to get his noble pecker up, we'll go on a little shopping spree, you and I—at least Yves can get you some clothing coupons on the market, can't 'e?"

Inès nodded.

"Good," said the redhead. "Never forget, Inès my friend, money maketh the man, but clothes, my dear, most definitely maketh the girl."

They dined at the Savoy Grill amid soft lights and the soothing melodic sounds of Carrol Gibbons' Orchestra. Like everywhere in London it was packed with eager diners and even more eager dancers. The five-course menu was delicious and Inès wished she could smuggle some leftovers to take to Yves.

"Damn good spread for five bob, don't you think, Charlie?" asked Benjie.

"Absolutely spiffing, old boy. Soup—fish—meat—sweet—savory, excellent, just as it should be. Let's order a bottle of claret, shall we?"

Inès looked around. She felt ill at ease with Henrietta, a debutante from a titled family who had merely sniffed when introduced to Inès, looking her up and down rudely before turning her head dismissively. Inès had blushed. She wondered if Charlie had told Henrietta that she was a tart. She hoped not, but Henrietta seemed to avoid any kind of conversation with her, hanging on the two men's every word.

They were on the fish course when the air-raid siren went off. Its harsh, familiar sound caused a sudden silence in the room. Almost at once their waiter was at the table.

"Won't you please follow me, ladies and gentlemen," he said in a smoothly assured voice. "Your dinner will not be interrupted, I promise you."

Bemused, Inès followed the waiter down several flights of stairs. The entire roomful of people trooped in an orderly manner to the basement, where almost a facsimile of the Grill Room met their eyes. Dozens of tables were laid with sparkling white cloths and highly polished knives and forks. They were ushered to their table where their dinner and the dancing continued as if nothing had happened, until the All Clear sounded and everyone went back upstairs to the Grill.

"Is this normal?" Inès asked Benjie.

"Oh, yes, my dear," he said airily. "The Savoy is completely organized so that if the bloody Blitz interrupts their sacred dinnertime, they have everything prepared to continue business as usual in the basement. Good idea, what?"

"Absolutely spiffing," smiled Inès.

The following week went by in a haze of nightclubs, bars, theatres and restaurants. Inès was taken by Benjie to the Milroy Club in Mayfair, where they listened to the melodic piano playing of Tim Clayton, and to the Orchid Room in Brook Street, where the maitre d'hôtel, Jerry Marco, greeted Benjie like a long-lost brother. He insisted they try a new drink from New York called the Bronx. It was a potent mixture of gin, orange juice and Curaçao, and Inès drank so many of them that she found herself getting almost too forward with Benjie. He drew away from her swiftly and she realized he needed to make the first move.

"I think I'll stick to champagne or white ladies in the future," she groaned to an impatient Yves the next morning, giving him one of the rolls she had smuggled out of the restaurant.

"I don't care what you drink, chéri, as long as you make some money soon," he sighed. "This poor macrou has an ache in his belly that only a good meal will dispel."

"I'm trying," said Inès. "I'm really trying, Yves."

A few nights later Benjie took her back to the Bagatelle again with

Charlie and Stella. Edmundo Ros was playing torrid Latin American music and the sexy beat excited both girls.

"C'mon, let's do the conga," yelled Stella excitedly, grabbing Charlie's hand and leading him onto the packed dance floor.

"Come on, Benjie, let's do it too," said Inès, trying to pull the young viscount up.

But Benjie was too embarrassed and inhibited to attempt the conga, even though several of his friends were part of the long line that wound through the club whooping and shrieking. He was drinking pink gins dripping with angostura and occasionally he would put a match to the mixture, watching with childlike glee as it ignited.

"Whew, that was a good one," exclaimed Stella, out of breath and laughing as she came back to the table, her red hair in disarray and her lips bare of their usual scarlet slash. She leaned towards Inès conspiratorially as she reapplied her lipstick with a heavy hand.

"It's a whoopsee-do and up to the chandelier with *that* one, dearie!" She gestured towards Charlie, who had a satisfied expression on his face as he adjusted his trousers.

"What do you mean?" asked Inès.

"I mean, dear, 'es like the bleedin' Eiffel Tower in 'is private parts. Ready, steady, *and go*—whoa—whoa—I won't 'ave to work too 'ard tonight, luv, I guarantee—it'll be an easy bit of goosey-gander. 'Ow're you doing with yours, ducks? 'As 'e 'ad the 'orn yet?"

Inès shook her head regretfully and looked at Benjie. Was he ever going to make a move? A week had gone by without any sort of pass. It was definitely time for her to try to seduce him before Yves wasted away to nothing. If Benjie wasn't going to play, maybe she should look around for someone else. There were plenty of available-looking men around, a lot of cute young Americans too. It shouldn't be too difficult to find one who wanted her, they all seemed to give her the eye and wolf whistles whenever she walked by. Yes, maybe she should go off with one of these good-looking Yanks. At least she'd get paid, and probably even get some nylon stockings, and tins of fruit, too, if she picked a generous one. But she decided to give Benjie one more chance.

After they left the Bagatelle she realized that Benjie was quite drunk. Hailing a taxi, she bundled him into it.

"Shepherd Market," she told the driver. "And quickly, please."

In her flat, in the bedroom next to the one she and Yves usually shared, she threw herself on him with excited cries and appropriate moans, and eventually succeeded in getting his clothes off him, and into bed. Once there, however, she immediately realized that he might have a few sexual problems. He seemed not able to rise to the occasion.

"Oh, dear, naughty thing—where's he gone?" giggled Benjie, pink with embarrassment. "He was certainly there on the dance floor the other night. Why is Willie being such a bad boy?"

"Don't worry," soothed Inès, applying expert pressure to the limpness lying crumpled forlornly against his thigh. "Willie will be back, I guarantee you."

"I say, that's wonderful," said Benjie a few moments later, a twitch betraying the return of his amorous appetite. "I rather like that!"

"Thank you, *Monsieur,*" Inès smiled, working diligently with delicate expertise. "We aim to please."

"Go on," whispered Benjie hoarsely, "don't stop, Inès—it's awfully good." But unfortunately, with the exception of that one tiny initial spasm, the viscount's noble cock remained sadly flaccid.

"Don't worry, *chéri.*" Inès was all sweetness and understanding. "I will take care of it—just relax. Don't do anything, Benjie, just enjoy this." Yves had shown her how to turn clients on when this happened—as it so often did.

There were several traditional methods of arousing a limp cock, and Inès decided she would try them all. After all, if Viscount Spencer-Monckton was to be an important client she had to please him. Enough to get a good remuneration. Maybe if she was really good she'd get a tenner. First she attempted the ice in mouth then the hot-water method. This succeeded only in making Benjie squirm and giggle like a ten-year-old, and diminished his manhood even more. She then gave him the ever popular ice-cream-cone treat. Although genuine ice cream was a rare commodity in wartime London, Inès improvised with a few ounces of her precious jam ration. But it was all to no avail. Benjie's cock was so soft, so shriveled with terror that it seemed to want to go to ground in his scrotum.

"He's a naughty little fellow," sighed Benjie, mortified. "Maybe you should smack his bottie."

Ah, a clue at last, Inès thought and leaping into action she commanded in a menancing tone, "Turn over, Benjie."

He eagerly obeyed and his pink skin started to redden as Inès began smacking his small, tight buttocks.

He murmured into the pillow, his cultured voice sounding as high-pitched as a five-year-old's, "I've been *so, so* naughty, Nanny, *such a bad boy.*"

"Then the naughty boy must be spanked," Inès said sternly, biting her lip to stop her giggles.

"Ooh no, Nanny," cried Benjie, "you can't spank me—it'll hurt."

"Oh, but I can," said Inès gruffly. "Like this, you bad boy. You naughty, naughty little boy."

Harder and harder she pummeled him, his moans of delight muffled by the pillow, his writhing bottom proof of his growing excitement.

"You are a wicked, terrible creature," she admonished, slapping away at his skinny shanks. "Nasty little boys must be punished." Slap—slap—slap. "They must be beaten until they beg for mercy."

"Punish me—oh—*please,* Nanny," Benjie groaned in ecstasy. "Oh, Nursie, tell me what a bad boy Benjie has been."

"Bad boy—boy *méchant, petit garçon.*"

Inès' palms stung, and her breath came in gasps. She was desperately trying to stop laughing. But then she started to become strangely excited herself. She had rarely inflicted pain on a client before, and suddenly she was finding it exhilarating. She picked up Yves' ivory shoehorn from the bedside table, and rained a series of sharp blows with it on Benjie's now scarlet bottom.

"Ooh, ooh, Nanny, you punish me so well," groaned the naughty boy. "But now I'm going to punish *you* with my big nasty sticking-out stick, Nanny dear, so turn over, it's Benjie's turn now." With that he rolled over, confronting Inès with an enormous smile and a matching penis.

"Lie down now, Nanny, quietly," Benjie whispered authoritatively. "Don't let Mummy hear what I'm doing—you must keep quiet. You've been such a *naughty* Nanny that now Benjie must punish you with this."

With that he thrust into Inès, riding her with joyful, throaty cries while his pale patrician face with its refined features contorted in ecstasy.

"That's right, Nanny, you deserve this. Benjie's got you where he wants you now, and you—you—you better not tell—Mummy or Daddy, oooh—ahhh!"

Half an hour later, after a glass of vintage port and some digestive biscuits which Yves had managed to find, the viscount was ready again. This time Inès improved her dialogue, finding acting talents which she never thought she possessed as she embellished the bad-little-boy/naughty-nanny scenario. Benjie was in seventh heaven, and Inès found herself feeling curiously maternal towards him, even somewhat protective. When he left at dawn he put a pile of crisp white five-pound notes on the dresser and Inès was delighted.

After stocking up on essentials to feed the hungry Yves, she and Stella took Oxford Street by storm. She had twenty pounds and enough clothing coupons for four new dresses.

"Gor blimey, luv, he's bleedin' generous for an 'onorable," said Stella enviously. "Twenty-five quid 'e gave you?"

Inès nodded.

"Your you-know-what-twat must be lined with gold, duckie, that's all I can say," snickered Stella as they admired the dresses in the windows of Bourne & Hollingsworth. "Lord Worthington only gives me a tenner, and the Hon. Charlie the same. Whatever did you do to get twenty-five quid?"

Inès said nothing, changing the subject as she spotted a dress she liked in the window. "Ooh, look, Stella—it's lovely, is it not?" She was admiring a dark brown satin frock with a sweetheart neckline edged with pink silk. It had a large pink bow at the daring décolletage, three-quarter-length sleeves with a little bow at each elbow, and an intricately draped skirt.

"Mmm," Stella sniffed disparagingly at it. "It's a bit drab for my taste, ducks, but I s'pose it would look good with your 'air."

"What's the price?" Inès peered at the tag.

"Thirty-seven and ninepence," said Stella. "That's a bit of all right—it won't break our little bank. C'mon, ducks, let's get you glamorous."

After they had bought the brown dress, and then a black one, and another pair of shoes, and some new earrings, Inès started to feel frugal, but Stella was insistent. She liked Inès and enjoyed helping her.

"We've got to do somefink about yer boat race," she said, dragging a reluctant Inès down Regent Street towards Swan & Edgar in Piccadilly Circus.

"My what?" asked Inès, almost colliding with a handsome City gentleman who tipped his hat, smiling at her charming figure laden with packages.

"Yer boat race, dearie—yer face."

"What's wrong with my face?" asked Inès defensively.

"Look, duckie, I always call a spade a spade—well almost always," said Stella. "Frankly, ducks, you're gettin' a bit too long in the tooth to go around with the scrubbed virgin look."

"I'm just eighteen," said Inès indignantly.

"I know, I know, and I'm King George's auntie," said Stella. "It don't matter 'ow old you are, dear—the bloom's startin' to go orf—you know what I mean? You've been on the game for four years now since you was fourteen, so it's time to tart yourself up—get a nice sparkling new look. 'Ere, now get a load of that—ain't they pretty."

They stopped at the cosmetics counter in Swan & Edgar, one of the few places that still sold bits of makeup in London. A long queue of eager young women craned their necks eagerly to look at the desirable, hard-to-obtain articles, and Inès looked into the glass showcase full of lipsticks and rouge pots with excitement.

"Do you think it will suit me?" she asked anxiously after she had parted with a precious half crown for one scarlet lipstick which smelled of candle wax, and a small pot of brick-colored rouge. The makeup was rationed, one to each customer, but some of the girls, after making their purchases, quickly slipped to the back of the queue again to buy some more.

"You'll look the Queen of bleedin' Sheba by the time I've shown you what to do," Stella smiled. "We need one more thing now."

"What's that?" asked Inès as Stella hustled her down Piccadilly towards St. James's Street.

" 'Ere we are," Stella said proudly, as they arrived at the exclusive gentlemen's bootmaker, Lobb. "By appointment to 'is bleedin' Majesty 'imself—come on, Inès."

Inside the shop she pointed to a tin of black boot polish displayed discreetly on the polished oak counter.

"We'll 'ave one of those," she told the salesman who looked them up and down disdainfully. Two obvious tarts if he ever saw one, although the dark one was sexy in a foreign sort of way.

Inès gave the man sevenpence for the boot polish, and the two women rushed home giggling like schoolgirls. Stella was going to give Inès a lesson in makeup.

"Now you're the dark and sultry sort," Stella told her. "Me, I'm the outdoor type, with a talent for indoor games!" She opened the tin of shoepolish and began to paint it around Inès' pale blue eyes with a little brush. "Now no peeking." She doused Inès' face with white powder, dabbed a generous amount of lipstick on her pale lips, and stroked her cheekbones lightly with rouge. She fiddled with her long hair with curling irons for half an hour, and then allowed Inès to look.

"An' *voilà, chéri,* or whatever you say in Froggie land," exclaimed Stella triumphantly. "*La grande transformation*—Cinderella into Hedy Lamarr."

Inès looked at herself in amazement. The woman who stared back at her in the cracked dressing table mirror looked like a Hollywood vamp. Dark red lips in a pale, almost translucent skin, contrasted brilliantly with her light blue eyes. They glowed with a sultry sparkle, the heavy shadowing of black boot polish exaggerating their luster and depth to great effect. Her dark hair was parted in the middle and fell to each side of her face in asymmetrical waves and curls.

"*Mon Dieu,* is that me?" breathed Inès.

"You bet it is, dearie," chuckled Stella. "And I'll tell you somefink for nuffink. When the Hon. Viscount Benjie sees you tonight, dearie, 'is little wee willie winkie is going to get as 'ard as a bit of Brighton rock. He'll be N-S-I-T tonight, I betcha."

"What does that mean?"

"Not Safe In Taxis, dearie," sniggered Stella. "Now throw some of this over yourself tonight, luvie." She handed Inès a small bottle of perfume in a distinctive geometrical bottle.

"Chanel Number Five," whispered Inès reverently. "Where did you get this, Stella?"

"Never you mind, luv, never you mind," said Stella mysteriously. "All I know, duckie, is that once old Viscount Benjie-poo gets a whiff of this, 'is dickery-dickery will be up 'igher than a bleedin' barrage balloon."

"His what?" laughed Inès.

"Dickery *dock,* dearie," said Stella in mock exasperation. "It's rhymin' slang, see. Don'cha know what dickery dickery dock means?"

"Oh, yes, I get it." Inès smiled. "Okay, Stella, I think I'm ready to go to the rub-a-dub-dub tonight."

"You're learnin', girl, you're learnin'."

Soon Inès had Benjie and several of his society friends totally under her spell, and her career as one of London's most beautiful and successful courtesans was well and truly launched.

Inès entertained her viscount three times a week. He preferred to visit her in the evening after dining at his club.

She hardly saw Yves except on weekends when her bluebloods returned to their country estates from London. Yves was pleased with the money she was now making, and she saved up her own sexual thrills, or at least most of them, for weekends with him. Although she did occasionally become aroused by some of her clients, Yves was her man, their sex life was as torrid as ever, and he still made her laugh like no one else could.

Inès was happy. The money rolled in, enabling them to afford more luxuries from the black market. Her clients occasionally brought her expensive presents and always treated her like a lady when they were not treating her like a nanny. She loved Yves and he seemed to love her. Everything was almost too good to be true.

Since clothes coupons were hard to come by and Yves had found several bolts of beautiful prewar fabric, Inès decided to learn to sew. Yves bought her a secondhand sewing machine and she quickly learned to love dressmaking. Although fashion magazines were hard to come by, Inès went to the cinema often, and she would copy the gorgeous clothes the Hollywood glamour queens wore. She particularly liked the gowns Esther Williams wore in *A Guy Named Joe,* and Lana Turner's in *Slightly Dangerous.* She gave the first dress she made—a floral print in shades of cyclamen and dark blue—to Stella.

"You're a real chum, you know that, duckie," the redhead said, her eyes shining gratefully. "No one's ever given me anything before, unless I've 'ad to give out to get it—if you know what I mean. Thanks, Inès, I really appreciate it."

Inès smiled. Stella was the first real girlfriend she had ever had, and she valued the friendship tremendously.

"Oh, by the way, duckie, I've been meaning to ask you this." Stella was admiring her reflection in the new dress. "You are taking care of yourself, aren't you?"

"What do you mean?"

"Against the old you-know-what. Against falling in the family way—you're doing something, aren't you?"

"Well, not really." Inès started to blush. "Yves always has said I'm too young to get pregnant so I just cross my fingers—"

"You little fool." Stella was cross now. "Yves is even more of a bloody burk than I thought. Right, my girl, I'm making an appointment with Dr. Wright in Weymouth Street first thing tomorrow. We're getting you fitted with a good old Dutch cap."

When one or the other of them was not entertaining clients, Stella and Inès were inseparable.

Inès taught the redhead how to sew on her old Singer machine, and the two women spent many afternoons devouring fashion magazines, searching for new styles to copy.

Under Stella's tutelage Inès learned the intricacies of cosmetic witchery. How to put up her hair with three pins and a lick of glue, and where to find the precious dye to keep her blond hair the dark brunette that she now preferred. She learned jokes and songs, for Stella was a cheery soul who liked a sing-along with the wireless. Stella knew all the popular songs of the day, and taught Inès the lyrics to most of them. She also taught her how to do the conga, the rhumba, the jitterbug and even the Lambeth walk, and they practiced them together to Stella's old gramophone with girlish squeals of laughter.

The two of them often went to the cinemas in Leicester Square to see the Hollywood musicals that were being churned out of the studios to fulfill the needs of a public which craved light entertainment.

Sometimes they window-shopped together in Oxford Street and Bond Street, admiring the expensive things that were far beyond their means.

Inès was thrilled to have a female companion in London. Since Jeanette had been murdered she had had no one with whom to share confidences and dreams. She simply adored having a best friend. Stella was like a kind older sister to her and made life much more fun.

But after a time, Inès' close and sisterly relationship with Stella seemed to cool. Suddenly Stella never had time anymore for their shopping trips or for the intimate chats on personal philosophy and life which had become so important to Inès.

Stella had told Inès that she was terribly busy with her afternoon clients, and since Inès' clients visited mostly at night, they gradually started to drift apart.

"Yves, Yves, darling," Inès called excitedly as she opened the front door of their flat. "I'm home."

She was happy. A naughty weekend at the Viscount's country house with plenty of giggles and spanking had ended abruptly when a telegram arrived, announcing that his dragon of a mother was returning home a day early from a trip to their Scottish estate. It had thrown him into a complete tizzy. Frantically, Benjie bundled Inès into his Bentley, drove her to Godalming station and put her on the London train with a cursory peck on the cheek and a thick wad of clean white fivers in her bag.

She hummed to herself as she walked into the hall of the flat. It was only two o'clock on a Sunday, and the beautiful summer afternoon stretched ahead for her and her lover.

"*Chéri!*" she cried, dropping her suitcase and running through the small drawing room towards his bedroom. "I'm home. Get up, lazybones. I've had a reprieve from his lordship, isn't that a—" Her voice trailed off as she opened the bedroom door, to see the two of them curled up together, asleep like kittens in a basket.

She couldn't see the girl's face, only the long, carrot-red hair which fanned out over Inès' favorite antique linen pillowcase; that pale freckled arm thrown possessively across the muscular shoulders of her man. Inès stomach churned and her legs started to buckle.

Her loud intake of breath stirred them into sleepy wakefulness.

"Oh, my Gawd," Stella muttered glumly, picking up a transparent black chiffon robe. "Christ all bloody mighty. Sorry, luv, you know 'ow it is, I'm reelly sorry." She disappeared into the bathroom and Inès heard the sound of water running. She felt as if a fist had thudded against her heart, smashing it to pieces.

Yves lit a cigarette with a great show of indifference. It dangled from his lips as he stared at Inès dispassionately, both arms behind his head, the smoke rising into his curly brown hair. His hazel eyes were narrowed, giving her no clue to his feelings as he said, "Why didn't you tell me you were coming home?"

"I thought you loved me, Yves," she said, her voice choked with tears.

"How could you do this? And with Stella—my best friend—how *could* you?"

"*Chérie,* I did love you—I did. I *do* love you." He dragged at his cigarette, searching for words. "I love you like a—friend—like a sister . . . like my own daughter."

"What are you saying?" Inès was stunned. "What we do together, Yves, is hardly what a brother usually does with his sister."

"I know. I know. Look, Inès, I have to be honest. I know you'll understand, but things happen. *C'est la vie,* I suppose." His voice was low and sincere. He evinced no sign of guilt, no pang of remorse; he seemed cool, and too collected.

Inès sank slowly into the armchair at the foot of their bed, staring into the face of the only man she had ever loved, her broken heart fluttering wildly. She felt sickened.

"I know this is hard for you, Inès, but four years is a very long time for a man like me to be with one woman. I think I've taught you a lot, and I love you, *chérie,* but I must admit my love has been more . . . more—well, paternal, lately."

"No!" cried Inès. "No. Yves, it's not true—what are you saying?"

"I'm leaving you," he said flatly. "I must. I was going to tell you next week—I'm going back to Paris. I want to go back." He paused, taking a deep drag on his Gauloise. "And I'm taking Stella."

"Stella? You're going with *Stella?*" Inès could barely speak from the shock and pain. "*Why?* Why with her? Do you love her?"

"No," he admitted, frowning. "Not at all—it is hard for me really to love, Inès. You know that. But certainly it is—well—more than brotherly love at the moment. I think Stella will do quite well in Paris now that the occupation is over, there will be a lot of work for her. And you are doing fine here now, you have good clients—plenty of them—you will become more successful, make more money. You don't really need me anymore."

"I do," she sobbed. "I need you—there's never been anyone for me like you; there never will be."

"You'll find someone," he said coolly. "A girl like you—you'll find a new man."

"You bastard, you two-timing *macrou.* I loved you. How could you do this to me with that . . . *creature?*" She was becoming hysterical now. The thought of losing Yves was insupportable. It couldn't happen, he was her life.

The sound of running water ceased abruptly. Inès knew that Stella was probably listening at the bathroom door. Stella—her best friend. She was filled with pain and rage and grief. Suddenly memories of the Italian she had murdered came flooding back. She almost wished that she could find that same razor, slice it into Yves and Stella, kill them both, the ache in her heart was so palpable.

"Yves—oh, God, Yves," she cried despairingly. "You've broken my heart today, just as if you'd smashed it into the ground. You've destroyed me, Yves—completely destroyed me." Fresh tears filled her eyes but he stopped her.

"Listen to me, Inès . . . I always thought you should make something of yourself. But I'm not the man to be with for that. You'll be better off without me, *chérie,* I know you will. You're young, beautiful—too beautiful to be a *poule de luxe* forever. You'll make a life. Find a good man—not a pimp, a *macrou.* Someone to really love you, because I know for damn sure I'm not the one for you."

Inès stared at him. "You are," she sobbed. "You are, Yves, you're all I've got, all I've ever had. All I want."

"Stop it, Inès—stop it, please, *chérie.* It's over, can't you see that? Where's your pride? It's over between us; you must understand that now."

"I'm going for a walk," Inès said in desperation, running her fingers wildly through her hair. "When I come back, I hope you and that—that—red-haired *whore*"—she spat the word, even though her voice was almost cracking with the effort of holding back her tears—"will be gone."

"*Chérie,* I'm sorry . . ."

"Good-bye, Yves," Inès said in a tiny, broken voice. "And good luck in Paris—*au revoir.*"

She strode from the room, her head held high, clutching desperately to what remained of her pride, her throat aching with unshed tears. She was not yet nineteen years old and she was completely alone in the world once again.

After Yves and Stella left for Paris, Inès wept bitterly for days, pounding her pillow in frustrated anguish, crying Yves' name throughout the long wakeful nights. But she was young and resilient, and after a period of both intense rage and grief-stricken mourning, she slowly began to entertain her clients again. It was, after all, her only livelihood, and to live in war-time London was expensive. She frequented nightclubs, jazz clubs, bars and restaurants, hoping to meet a man for whom she could feel something—anything. She wanted to find love—she desperately wanted to stop her life of whoring before it was too late.

She had been a prostitute since the age of fourteen, and though it had meant little to her then, lately she had begun to feel more and more contempt for men's lust; disgust as their sweat dripped onto her; loathing as she mechanically pleasured them with her mouth. She was so erotically expert in what she did that all her clients were completely enthralled by her. But she hated it, and she started to hate them too.

She wanted a real boyfriend, someone with whom she could build a proper life, marry. She wanted to raise a family who would receive all the love and attention from her that she had never had from her mother. She wanted to become a normal woman.

As the weeks and months passed, as Inès searched for the elusive commodity called love, she realized that to find the type of man she sought she must become worthy of him.

She began an extensive course of self-improvement of both her mind and body. Every morning she exercised vigorously, the window open to all the sights and smells of Shepherd Market. Then she meditated, as she had learned to do from an ancient book written by an Indian seer. She tried to cleanse her thoughts of her clients, their depravity and kinkiness, to fill her mind with purity. She started going to church, praying for her soul and the souls of the men who used her. She found an inner peace in the teachings of Christ and in the Desiderata. She was convinced that she would one day shed the decaying skin of prostitution and become a member of the human race again. She knew she had to.

She spent almost all her afternoons at libraries and museums, letting great works of art fill her with wonder. She read voraciously—philosophy, religion and art history; she went to the theater, to concerts and to the opera. She studied the newspapers, becoming so well informed about current affairs and world events that she started debating with some of her clients. Much to their amazement and delight, they soon found that the mind of this beautiful whore was almost as fascinating as her face, her body and her incredible sexual skills.

Sometimes, so involved would both become in a discussion of Buddhism or poetry or the work of some new artist that a client would forget the original intention of his visit, and sipping dry sherry, they would argue fiercely and debate long into the night.

Inès was pleased with her progress. The frightened whore-child, ignorant of everything but men's desires, was gone forever. Instead, a woman of intelligence, beauty and knowledge was emerging, a woman of whom a man could be truly proud.

11

*I*t was finally over. Six long and bloody years of hell ended on a warm
May night, and all London seemed to be in Trafalgar Square celebrating the
German surrender.

No one was in a more joyous mood than Phoebe and Julian, for it was
a double celebration. They had finally been married in Caxton Hall Registry
Office the previous weekend. Julian had been reluctant, but Phoebe was
pregnant. Ever the gentleman, Julian "did the right thing."

Now, along with thousands of other revelers, they danced, laughed,
cried with joy around the fountains in the square. The sky was illuminated
by a dazzling fireworks display, and everyone was singing "Rule Britannia,"
"God Save the King" and other patriotic songs in drunken, tuneless delight.
Groups of French sailors with their pompommed berets tipped over their
eyes drunkenly chanted the "Marseillaise" as they tried in vain to stay on
their feet.

In the grand houses of England the armistice was being welcomed with
lavish parties. Rare vintage wines and spirits were uncorked. Exotic tinned
fruits, hams, cheeses, quail eggs, pheasant, sides of beef and delicacies not
tasted since the outbreak of war adorned the groaning tables. Even the
most stingy of the aristocracy had on this occasion given in to the black
marketeers and were sparing no expense for this glorious celebration.

The ordinary citizens, the common people—the backbone of Great Britain—had taken to the streets to celebrate together. Thousands of them had gone to stand outside Buckingham Palace and cheer the King and Queen as they waved from the balcony. The crowds stretched down the Mall to Trafalgar Square, where servicemen in uniform frolicked in the shallow, cold water of the fountains alongside boys and girls, middle-aged mums and dads with their floral skirts or flannel trousers hitched uninhibitedly over their knees.

A few brave souls tore off their clothes in a frenzy of exhibitionism, posturing before the cheering crowds. Some of the younger people were so carried away with excitement that they openly made love on the backs of Landseer's colossal lions, guardians of Nelson's Column. Dozens of church bells rang out as the crowd formed circles, dancing the knees up, the conga, the rhumba, even the Highland fling.

Bottles of champagne and beer were tipped to laughing lips as groups of giggling young girls ran around hugging and kissing anyone who took their fancy, sometimes even those who didn't. Every car had its headlights on and its horns blaring, and every municipal and government building was brilliantly lit. It was the bacchanal to end them all, the party of the century. But in all the crowd's jollity there was a frenetic desperation, for many had lost loved ones or possessions and homes during the war.

"I love you, Mr. Brooks," Phoebe yelled above the din.

"I love you too, Mrs. Brooks." Julian laughingly kissed his wife's full lips, then was unceremoniously pulled away from her by a teenage soldier.

" 'Ere, give us a kiss too, lovely," said the boy with a cheeky smile, and Phoebe obliged him with a smacker.

"Strumpet." Julian looked at the vermilion lipstick smeared across Phoebe's laughing face.

"Scoundrel!" she giggled. "And, speaking of which, look at *that!*" They observed a naked young woman being powerfully serviced by a French soldier whose trousers were around his ankles, while another young soldier hung on to his arm and vomited into the fountain.

"Charming! What a delightful sight. I think I've had just about enough of this party, old girl. Let's go home and celebrate being married in a rather more traditional way." Julian slid his hand over her full bosom.

"Naughty boy—people looking." Phoebe slapped his hand away coyly.

"Who cares?" laughed Julian. "The war's over, darling—it's finally over."

"Okay, let's go home to make love, celebrate our new baby, celebrate *life,* my gorgeous husband. That's the only proper way to end a war."

"There's a bloke 'ere to see yer—says 'e's from a film studio or somefink."
The stage doorkeeper poked a grizzled head around the door of Julian's
minuscule dressing room, where the young comedian was taking a catnap
between shows. It was tough work performing seven times a day and night.
All right for Phoebe and the showgirls. They just had to wander across the
stage, tits up, feathers erect, perform a little bit of a song and dance, and
look sexy and pretty.

Julian had to think up amusing, hilarious and original monologues night
after night, day after day—and after eighteen months it was becoming more
and more difficult.

Before he could say anything the door was pushed open by a man in his
late forties wearing a double-breasted black cashmere overcoat, a black
homburg and gray suede gloves. He walked into the room and removed his
hat. His nose was full and fleshy, and his lips were those of a gourmet—a
man who appreciated only the finest in food, wine and, no doubt, women.
His eyes were masked by thick-rimmed, dark-lensed black spectacles, and
his skin was deeply tanned. He exuded an aura of supreme self-confidence,
that of a man used to giving orders which would be instantly obeyed, of
making decisions that would always be right, and of always having the very
best of everything which life had to offer.

"Good evening, Mr. Brooks. My name is Didier Armande."

Julian stood up immediately, impressed and excited. Didier Armande—
the Didier Armande. Probably the most important and influential film producer in Britain. Julian knew it was he who had produced the unforgettable
Romeo and Juliet, the extraordinary *Woman of Baghdad* and the revolu-
tionary epic *The Life and Times of Louis XIV.* It was he who had discovered
not only the legendary Elaine Roche, the gorgeous Maxine Von Pallach and
the dashing Jasper Swanson, but had helped his own sister—the sultry and
mysterious Ramona Armande—to reach the heights of international and
Hollywood stardom, in his avant-garde production of *Mata Hari.* What on
earth was Didier Armande doing here in this tatty dressing room? And what
could he possibly want with Julian Brooks?

"May I sit down?" The older man's faint accent gave the impression of
culture and education.

"Of course, of course." Hastily Julian brushed a pile of his discarded
clothes from a small chair.

Mr. Armande sat down, his silver-topped ebony cane resting lightly between his knees. Taking a leather case from the pocket of his overcoat, he
proffered what was surely the first Havana cigar Julian had seen since
before the war.

Havana cigars! Where the hell had he managed to find such a luxury? It
was hard enough in austere Britain to find a packet of Woodbines, let alone

a cigar. Julian accepted one, and Didier coolly lit both cigars with a heavy-looking gold lighter, into which the initials D.A. had been set in small diamonds.

"I know you don't have much time," he said, glancing at his slim platinum wristwatch, whose shape and design were of faultless taste, "but I have watched you perform for the last few days and I wanted to express to you my most sincere congratulations."

"Congratulations? Whatever for?" Julian was mystified. All that he'd done recently was to trot out some old gags, fumbling in his memory for a bit of business or some material that he could remember from other comedians' acts—anything with which to raise a laugh from that sea of servicemen who sat enthralled each night by the tawdry glamour of the Windmill.

"You are indeed a comedian *par excellence.*" The man inhaled deeply on his cigar, filling the tiny room with a haze of delicious blue smoke. "You made me laugh even when I'd heard the same joke before."

"Thank you." Julian was pulling himself together, feeling more secure with the compliments. "That's most kind of you to say so. I was always told that the hardest thing for any comic to do is to make the same audience laugh twice at identical material."

"Exactly, my dear fellow. It is an art, a true art. However, I realize from watching you carefully that you possess much more than just a talent to amuse, as dear Noël is so fond of saying. You were an actor, were you not?"

"Yes, I was. Still am, really. Now that the war is over, I hope to go back into acting, but so many of the reps are still closed."

"Perhaps you won't have to go back to repertory." Didier Armande inspected the glowing tip of his cigar carefully. "Have you ever thought of making films?"

"Films! Well, no, actually I haven't, I've always done theater."

"I'll get straight to the point." Didier leaned forward, his hands resting casually on his cane, on which Julian could see an eagle, its wings spread, emblazoned with some kind of writing.

"My company, Goya Films, will shortly be making a film about Charles the Second, and the fascinating relationship that he was reputed to have with one of his illegitimate daughters."

Julian leaned forward, almost tipping his chair into Armande's.

"You bear a most striking resemblance to some of the portraits of Charles the Second," Armande said. "Similar coloring, even bone structure. It is uncanny, actually, quite amazing."

"Oh," said Julian feeling at a loss as Sammy, the call boy, poked a cheery carrot head around the door.

"Five minutes, matey," he chirped.

Didier Armande handed Julian a white card engraved with his name, that of Goya Pictures, an address and a telephone number. "If you would be interested in screen-testing for the role of King Charles, please have your agent call my office within the next two days. You may want some time to think it over."

"Oh—no. No, I don't need any time, I'll do it—I mean, I'll test. I'd love to test, absolutely love to!"

"*Très bien,* Mr. Brooks, good news indeed. I shall have my people call your agent."

"Great, great, that's wonderful. Oh, God, I'm sorry, but I don't have an agent." Julian felt embarrassed.

"You have no agent?" Didier raised black brows eloquently—an actor without an agent? How odd. Even if agents didn't seem to do much, they were a necessity when things got rough.

"Well, no—you know how it is at the Windmill—nonstop work, nose to the grindstone all the time, never even have time to write a letter. Actually I was really waiting until the war ended to get an agent, and I just don't seem to have got around to it yet."

"Very well. That is of course no problem. If you will be so kind as to give me your telephone number at home, my people will contact you in order to make the necessary arrangements."

Didier Armande rose, pulling tight suede gloves over his muscular hands, which were the only thing about him that seemed less than elegant.

"*Au revoir,* Mr. Brooks, until we meet again at Pinewood Studios, I hope." He extended his hand to Julian, who clasped it firmly.

"May I inquire what the film is to be called, sir?"

"It's called *The Merry Monarch.* The script was written by the Academy Award-winning writer Irving Frankovitch, and it will be directed by Francis Lawford, who I'm sure you must know. We fully expect the actor who plays the King to be nominated for the Oscar next year. It's a hell of a role, Mr. Brooks, a hell of a role, and one for which you were born."

Julian Brooks and his career were both thriving. He looked wonderful as Charles II. His own hair was covered by a shoulder-length wig of lustrous tumbling black ringlets, and a delicate moustache enhanced his gorgeous face. He swashbuckled his way through the film: fighting, romancing, dueling, perfectly cast as the suave, vain, highly sexed and romantic King. The story was based less on historical accuracy than on the fertile imagination of the American writer Irving Frankovitch, but it was exactly the kind of romantic epic for which postwar film fans yearned, and Julian was the kind of romantic hero female fans lusted after.

Goya Pictures' publicity department moved in on Julian, typewriters and cameras clicking. When not wearing his seventeenth-century costume, Julian was dressed by the wardrobe department in a variety of well-cut threads so that Didier's number one stills photographer, Curly, could snap to his heart's content.

Bronzed by the wizardry of the makeup department, Julian posed for hours, self-conscious in the freezing stills studio, wearing bathing trunks or rolled-up blue jeans, tennis shorts or sometimes only his Restoration doublet and hose from *The Merry Monarch* and a bare chest. And the chest had better be bare. Modesty, also known as the Production Code Administration, or the Hays Office, regarded a hairy chest as a major cause of moral corruption. Therefore, on the morning of every stills session, Julian's pectorals would be painstakingly shaved by the makeup man and covered with deep bronze makeup which was then topped off with a thin sheen of oil. This made his chest glisten like polished mahogany, and many a maidenly heart beat faster when she saw her favorite in all his masculine glory smiling out from the magazines. Beefcake was big business, and Julian epitomized it totally.

Before *The Merry Monarch* was even released, publications all over the world were clamoring for more and more photographs of Looks Brooks. The fewer clothes he wore, the more his fans seemed to like it. It did not matter that as yet none of these fans had even seen him on the silver screen—he was a world-famous star before his first film had been released. He bared almost his all whether he liked it or not: on a beach, tossing a medicine ball, swinging an ax with convincing dexterity, pulling a rope, flying a plane, riding a horse, always dressed in appropriate gear. Once the crafty Curly even had him wrestling with a giant rubber alligator. Julian found this endless posing and shaving of his chest tedious, to say the least, but Phoebe, ever the pragmatist, and a teeny bit envious of all the attention he was receiving, encouraged him to do anything and everything which the studio asked.

"You want to be a star—well, this is how it's done," she told him bluntly.

After having miscarried their baby, Phoebe had made Julian's career ever more her concern. Not satisfied with the simple domestic life of their new flat in Cadogan Square, she appeared constantly on the set, watching over him jealously from the sidelines as he played love scenes with a succession of glamorous actresses. She inwardly seethed when he embraced them, her innate common sense beginning to founder in a sea of envy. Phoebe was not as pretty as she had been. Lines of discontent had started to form on her face, and her voluptuous body was becoming soft and flabby.

Superficially she reveled in her husband's success, but she began to have serious acting ambitions herself. These had lain dormant until Julian started riding the crest of success, and now she too wanted to bask in the spotlight of fame. Several times she subtly suggested to Didier Armande that she would be right to perform opposite Julian or even play a second lead, but Didier diplomatically laughed off her aspirations, pretending that he didn't really understand.

"One star in the family is enough, my dear," he would say, patting her plump, powdered cheek. "Our boy needs to be taken care of, Phoebe, and you do that so beautifully it would be a great pity to do anything to prevent the golden goose from laying his lovely valuable eggs."

Phoebe bit her lip and kept quiet, but the more famous her husband became, the more the long green fingers of jealousy gripped her heart.

Julian's career thrived. When he wasn't acting he gave interviews. He confided his life story to *Picturegoer* and *Picture Show, Illustrated, Photoplay* and *Look* magazines. He laughed and joked with the cameramen and crew as he posed beside boats, planes and cars with the all-important macho stare. He chatted long distance to the twin witches of Hollywood, Hedda and Louella. He was becoming the most popular actor in England, but he still considered movies as just a means to an end. His ultimate ambition was to do classical stage roles, with aspirations to the crown of Olivier himself.

"There's no doubt about it, not doubt at all—the man's got star quality," Didier muttered to his assistant, delighted with his personal choice of a leading man after seeing the first rushes of *The Merry Monarch*. Didier stared at the last frame of Julian's beautifully lit, handsome face gazing into the camera with tears in his velvet eyes, the black poodle curls and rakish feathered hat accentuating both his innate masculinity and a brooding sensitivity.

"Run them again, Johnnie," Didier commanded, slipping back in the gray plush chair, eyes half closed to bask again in Julian's aura. "Run them again."

"Star quality," he murmured softly to himself. "If you've got it, you don't need anything else—except perhaps a little bit of luck."

12

*N*ikolas Stanopolis stared at the thick blue envelope in astonishment. It carried a U.S. airmail stamp, and in the top left-hand corner was printed importantly:

MCCP Studios
7700 Melrose Avenue
Los Angeles, California

On the back of the envelope was a name that made Nikolas' heart leap with excitement, SPYROS MAKOPOLIS, PRESIDENT. With trembling hands he handed the letter to his wife, Elektra. It was addressed to her, but she smilingly handed it back to him.

"No, no, Nikolai, *you* open it."

He ripped open the letter, reading it with mounting elation:

MY DEAR NIECE ELEKTRA,

I was happy to receive news of Hydra, but so sorry to hear about your dear departed mother. My heart is very heavy at her passing, but I shall think of the good days when we played together as children in our sunlit paradise of a village.

My congratulations on your marriage to Nikolas Stanopolis. He sounds like a fine young man, and his interest in the business of filmmaking is most interesting.

If you are able to make your way one day to Los Angeles, I would be happy to see Nikolas as you have suggested, and perhaps give him an opportunity to work at this studio if he seems suitable.

Please remember me to Dmitri Andros at the old bar in the port—I am happy to know the old man survived the war and remains in good health.

I am enclosing a little gift which may help you if you decide to come to America.

Be happy, my dear young niece,

Cordially,
Your Uncle Spyros

"Oh, my God—Elektra, this is fantastic, wonderful news—America! He wants us to come to Los Angeles! Hollywood! Elektra, do you know what this means?"

"Yes, yes, Nikolai my love, I do." Elektra's face shone with joy as she looked up lovingly at her husband. "And look, Nikolai—look at this." Triumphantly she waved the check at him. "He's sent us money. My uncle is a truly wonderful gentleman."

"Money?" Nikolas grabbed it. "How much? "He looked at the unfamiliar writing on the check.

"*Five hundred dollars!*" Elektra gasped. "*Five hundred dollars.* That is a *fortune,* Nikolai. Now we can go to America, my darling, we can both go to Hollywood, and you can make great films."

But the passage to America was not as easy to negotiate as Nikolas and Elektra had hoped. A few days later, having changed the five-hundred-dollar check into drachma, Nikolas took the weekly ferry from Hydra to Athens to make preparations for their trip. His first disappointment was finding out that it was extremely difficult for a Greek national to visit America, and it involved a considerable amount of red tape. Then, in the offices of the new Olympic Airlines, he discovered that two airline fares to Los Angeles cost more than twice the amount that Mr. Makopolis had sent, and with a heavy heart Nikolas returned to Hydra to break the news to his wife.

"Never mind, Nikolai. You must go first to America, make Uncle Spyros give you a job, then in a few months I can follow you there."

"But I need you with me," said Nikolas sulkily, "I won't go without you, Elektra."

"No, Nikolai. No. You must go," the girl said firmly, pouring out two glasses of wine. "It will be too difficult for us if we both go now. You will be worried about me—about where we shall live—about too many things. First you must go and make money, then I will follow. Now eat your supper before it gets cold."

Nikolas marveled at his young wife's understanding, as she raised her wineglass in a shy toast. "To America, Nikolai, and to us."

Nikolas Stanopolis arrived at Los Angeles airport on a cold November night in 1945. Shivering in his thin cotton jacket, he stood outside the busy terminal, wondering what he should do. Why was it so cold? He had been told that California weather was warm, sunny, like the weather of the Greek islands. Well, they'd been wrong, those fools who had told him this. It was freezing; a light rain was falling, and a foggy, choking, dark mist wafted in from the Pacific.

Everyone seemed to be busy rushing somewhere, as if they had a purpose, knew exactly what they were doing, where they were going. Nikolas waited forlornly outside the terminal where the giant four-engine plane had brought him from New York. He felt lost and homesick as he thought of his beautiful Elektra, of his beloved Hydra, thankfully now slowly recovering from the war and the atrocities committed by Umberto Scrofo.

Scrofo—whenever he thought of that odious Italian, he felt blinding rage. One day he would find him and make him suffer as his mother, father, brothers, sisters and so many others on Hydra had. The desire for revenge consumed him almost as much as his desire to succeed in the film business. He had no clue as to where the Italian was living now: whether in fact he was still alive, but that did nothing to assuage his two burning ambitions.

Nikolas' English was limited, picked up mostly from an old man on Hydra who had once worked in London and from the movies, but he spoke enough to communicate his predicament to a porter. The man wore a red cap and a blue shirt and he had the black, shiny hair and olive skin of a fellow Greek; but he was Spanish, having himself only recently arrived from Barcelona. He took pity on Nikolas, escorting him two blocks to the sign DOWNTOWN BUS and chatting to him in a mixture of Spanish and English.

Nikolas stood shivering behind two round, gossiping women, not unlike the women of Hydra. When the bus arrived he gave the conductor five dollars, but became confused when asked for his destination. "Downtown," he said in heavily accented English. "Downtown L.A., please, sir."

The man shrugged, giving him a handful of change. "Downtown's a big place, kid," he said. "Whereabouts downtown?"

Nikolas had been given the name of a hotel by one of the Greek officials in New York. So he said proudly, "I'm going to Roosevelt Hotel, Hollywood Boulevard, in Hollywood, sir."

He was on his way.

The following morning Nikolas Stanopolis presented himself in a state of high excitement at the imposing entrance of MCCP Studios.

There was a flurry of activity around the high wrought-iron gates, but the uniformed guard told him bluntly, "Get lost, buddy, you're too early—no one's in the administration offices yet."

Nikolas pleadingly brandished his letter with the offer of employment written by Spyros but the gum-chewing guard barely raised his eyes from his copy of *Variety*. He barked something unintelligible in a harsh voice, but the body language was clear. Nikolas would not be able to get in, nor could he hang around the gates.

"I said, get lost, buddy," snarled the cop. "Git outta sight. *Now*."

In desperation, Nikolas crossed the road to sit on a bench plastered with advertising signs. Here at least he had a front-row view of the studio, and could see a good deal of what went on behind the iron gates. For several hours he sat completely fascinated, watching all manner of people come and go.

The costumes of the extras particularly enthralled him. Cowboys and Indians, peasants and soldiers, cops and robbers all milled about, fraternizing with one another. At eleven o'clock a group of beautiful showgirls, their long California legs encased in flesh-colored fishnet tights, trooped out from a huge building marked Stage Three.

Nikolas sat up, his eyes widening. These were women such as he had never seen before. The women of Greece wore modest, all-enveloping clothes—even Elektra covered herself from neck to calf. The thought of her body started to excite him as he looked longingly at the showgirls.

These women were crimson-lipped, their hair was marceled yellow, flame red or jet black. Hips swaying provocatively, they sashayed around the courtyard, laughing, smoking cigarettes, drinking Coca-Colas straight from the bottle. He saw the studio employees, men in work shirts and denim trousers, eyeing the girls lecherously as they passed, some of them making, he was sure, suggestive or lewd remarks at which the girls just laughed. Nikolas was shocked. Although he had seen women like this in movies, he was amazed that they could prance about half naked in public so brazenly, placidly ignoring the men who flirted with them.

One particular girl caught his eye. She was lissome, with luxuriant black hair tumbling halfway down her back, where it was caught up with scarlet feathers. Although slightly shorter than the other girls, she possessed the most magnificent breasts he'd ever seen, which were more than half exposed in their gold lamé bra.

Nikolas felt dry-mouthed with desire. How he missed Elektra. It had been more than a week since he'd last seen her, she who gave her body to him joyously yet modestly every night, every morning, and sometimes even in the afternoon. This buxom girl in red feathers reminded him slightly of Elektra, and shaking his head he walked down the boulevard, trying to rid himself of carnal thoughts, concentrating again on the problem of how to pass through the hallowed studio gates.

Spotting a telephone booth, he scanned his dog-eared letter to read the number, but unfamiliar with even a Greek telephone, it took him ten minutes and as many nickels and dimes before the number rang and a cheerful-sounding voice chirped, "MCCP Studios, good morning."

"Spyros Makopolis, please," said Nikolas, his Greek accent making his words practically incomprehensible to the telephone operator.

"Who?" she squawked.

"Spyros Makopolis." He enunciated each syllable carefully, as beads of sweat trickled down his forehead. The noon sun was at full blast and the kiosk felt like a furnace.

"Hold on a minute," the voice snapped.

"Mr. Makopolis' office." Another female voice, this one mellow and cool, was on the line. Gratefully Nikolas spoke in Greek, hoping that the voice would understand him. Several times he repeated his name, and the halting English words "My wife's uncle. I am nephew of him."

Finally the woman seemed to understand, but after her crisp "Just a moment, I'll see if Mr. Makopolis is available" the line went silent again.

For several more minutes Nikolas stood sweating in the cramped booth as occasionally voices came on the line instructing him to insert "Five cents, please." He was praying for Mr. Makopolis to answer before he gave up the last of his coins.

Suddenly the cool female voice was on the line again. Nikolas couldn't understand her, but he hoped salvation was at hand as she said, "I'm putting you through to Mr. Makopolis now, sir."

Then a deep friendly Greek voice came on the line: "Nikolas, Nikolas my dear boy, where are you?" Spyros spoke in Greek, his voice warm and welcoming. When Nikolas told him he was only across the street the old man said happily, "Come, I must see you now, Nikolas—I will leave a pass for you—come to see me right now." With enormous relief Nikolas knew then that everything was going to be all right.

. . .

However, things did not go as smoothly as Nikolas had expected. Instead of immediately giving him a job on a film set, as he'd hoped, Spyros Makopolis was blunt with him.

"There is no way that you could work on a film now, Nikolas."

"Why not, Uncle? You said you could give me a job."

"Well for one thing, you speak hardly any English, which, of course, will eventually be remedied," said Spyros. "For another, our unions are tighter than a rat's ass and newcomers to technical jobs are unwelcome, to say the least." Nikolas looked confused. "Listen, son—listen to me," said the old man. "The war has just ended. Young servicemen are pouring back to the States from Okinawa, Bataan and Anzio. A lot of these soldiers, sailors and marines worked at the studios before the war; now they find their jobs going to younger men, or sometimes to even older ones, who don't want to give them up." Spyros sighed. "And they're all having tricky times. All the studio heads are trying to repatriate and reinstate the men who fought for us. There's hardly any room for new blood, Nick."

Nick looked crestfallen and Spyros patted him comfortingly on the shoulder.

"Another major problem all the studios are facing is that they aren't sure what the public now wants to see at the movies."

Nick's face was puzzled. "Movies—they just love any movies, Uncle."

"No, my boy. Postwar audiences are tougher, much more discriminating than they were. The harsh realities of daily life are difficult. Appetites have become cloyed by the bland diet of musicals, comedies and lightweight films; audiences are demanding more robust fare. It's a problem, Nick—a big fat problem, my friend."

The old man was right. Escapist movies had been churned out during the war by every studio to boost the morale not only of the armed forces, but also of those who by reason of sex, physical disability or age had stayed at home to keep things running. "Serious" pictures were in vogue now. Some were blatant copies of Roberto Rossellini's *Open City,* a harshly neorealistic film about Rome during the war. Films about GIs returning to civilian life were extremely popular. *The Clock* with Robert Walker and Judy Garland, *Hail the Conquering Hero* with Eddie Bracken, and *I'll Be Seeing You* with Joseph Cotton and Ginger Rogers had all done well at the box office.

"Now MCCP is making its own neorealistic pictures, of course," said Spyros proudly. "We're on that bandwagon. And we're also making Westerns, gangster movies and musicals. We hope to entice whole new audiences into the cinemas, Nick; after all the studio is humming with activity. We've got eighteen pictures shooting, twenty-two in post-production, and at least eighty in the development stage."

"That's wonderful, Uncle," said Nick, relieved. "Then you must have a job for me?"

The old man sighed and fidgeted with some scripts on his cluttered desk.

"I'm gonna do my best, m'boy," he boomed. "But you're gonna start at the bottom, son—just like I did."

To Nikolas' disappointment the only position which Spyros Makopolis could find for his nephew-in-law was one of the lowliest jobs on the lot—in the mail room. But at least it was a job, a well-paid job, and Nick was going to take the opportunities he was given and run with them. He was ambitious, not only for himself and Elektra, but also for his secret plan. The foul cloud of hatred that hovered in his subconscious had to be expunged and there was only one way to do it.

13

*T*he end of the war meant little to Inès. It would hardly change her life at all.

Every evening, and many afternoons, she received one of her gentlemen callers. She now had an elite clientele, consisting of several of the most illustrious men in Great Britain. Unconcerned that by being a prostitute she was breaking the law, she was dedicated to self-improvement and to money. The money was her key to escaping from this life, and she saved every penny she could in her goal to live normally one day. She loved to hear the rustle of the crisp five-pound notes which men gave her. She squirreled them away in a copy of Stendhal's *Love,* thinking the title ironically apt. She had painstakingly cut out a square center section of the book, into the hollow of which she fitted her takings. *Love,* she thought with a wry smile, was only to be found in her bookcase, along with *Who's Who, Burke's Peerage, The Diaries of Samuel Pepys* and dozens of richly illustrated books on art, British history, the great houses and collections of England, and biographies of influential men and women.

Every Friday at lunchtime, elegantly dressed in one of the outfits she herself had made, she would take her thick wad of notes to Coutts Bank in the Strand, ceremoniously handing it over to the clerk, who would credit it to her ever-growing bank account. It had been Yves who had opened an account for her at the prestigious bank whose customers numbered not only members of the Royal Family but some of Inès' own clients. How Yves had managed this was still a mystery to her, since a client's breeding was often as important to Coutts as his wealth.

It gave her enormous pleasure, when shopping in the exclusive Burlington Arcade or in Bond Street shops, to pay for her purchases with a Coutts check. Certainly none of the salespeople would ever have imagined that this poised young beauty was a common prostitute. She looked, dressed and behaved like a lady. Although only nineteen, Inès possessed the manners and sophistication of a woman far older; she now prided herself on a quiet elegance which spoke of breeding and old money. It was one of the attributes which most intrigued her clients when they took her to dine at the 400, the Caprice or the Coq d'Or. In her perfectly cut chic clothes she seemed to belong in these places far more than many of the English matrons in their frumpish prewar dresses. As she snuggled into the womblike comfort of these establishments jealous glances were often thrown her way. Inès had the Frenchwoman's innate understanding of clothes, and was always beautifully and stylishly dressed in outfits mostly created by herself. During the day she lived the life of a woman of leisure. Sometimes she strolled up Shaftesbury Avenue on her way to the Queens Theatre or the Globe to see the latest play by Terence Rattigan, Noël Coward or Emlyn Williams, passing the Windmill Theatre, where she would glance at the front-of-house photographs of the seminude showgirls and the leering comics.

Now she never thought of herself as a whore, but as a courtesan, and had improved herself to suit her new role. She had decided to keep her once-blond hair dark. It framed her pale, high-cheekboned face with its slanting blue cat's eyes and sculpted chin. She had grown taller in London, her body svelte and toned, her legs those of a thoroughbred, her breasts magnificent. Underneath all her elegance, her mound of golden pubic hair was trimmed to a heart shape, which further fascinated her devoted clients.

Courtesan. She liked that word. A courtesan was a woman who shared the fantasies of a man's secret life, who knew everything about his occupation and all that it entailed. She knew about his wife, what that particular woman liked in bed, and what she didn't; she knew which schools his children attended, and even what they wanted to be when they grew up. She knew what wines he preferred, how dry he liked his martinis, how strong his whiskey and soda. She knew his favorite foods and sometimes, for a special client, she would prepare them for him perfectly. She knew which books he read, which plays he'd seen, in which sports he participated, what politics he favored, but most important of all, she knew what excited him in bed.

Inès was quick to discover what a man liked sexually. Most of the time it wasn't anything that he couldn't get from his wife, except that from what she'd discovered, most English wives were not keen on oral sex. Thanks to Yves this was one of Inès' specialties. Most women wanted to please their husbands but often didn't have the time, energy or knowledge.

A sexually inept female is a turnoff to most men, and Inès became accustomed to hearing many clients complain that their wives just "lay there like stone and never responded." She could bring a man to orgasm within minutes. When men kissed her breasts, or her mound of Venus, running their fingers and tongues into her most intimate places, arousing her, they made her body shake with lust, for Inès had become an accomplished actress. She made sure her clients thought that they were exciting her, and that excited them more than anything else. They kept returning to her, often referring their friends to her. But Inès was careful about whom she entertained. She had never forgotten the perversions of the Italian General, and in her cozy, well-decorated flat she interviewed prospective clients carefully, questioning them as strictly as a duchess employing a chambermaid.

Politicians, members of Parliament, aristocrats, industrialists, men of finance, power and position, these were the men she entertained. Credentials were essential. Most of them became entranced with her, more than one proposing matrimony, but although Inès was ready for that, she knew she had to fall in love. Visions of true love haunted her. She still thought about Yves, dreamed about him, his laughter, his magic, his crinkly eyes and his soft hair. And she also dreamed too often of the Italian whom she had killed that April morning, awakening with a scream on her lips, vividly reliving the horror. She never allowed a man to spend the night with her during the week, and only for her most special clients would she consent to spend a weekend away. In her search for love she found all men lacking, and the more she saw of their weaknesses and foibles the less she felt she would ever meet the right one for her.

Armistice night she spent alone, in front of her sewing machine, working on a velvet Maggy Rouff suit which she was copying from *Vogue*. Inès felt more truly alone than she ever had before. All her clients were with their families and friends, and she had no one with whom to share this momentous night. Not a man, not a woman friend, not even a cat. From her windows she could hear the boisterous sound of revelers outside singing, laughing, hooting with joy.

On the wireless the excitement in the voice of the normally severe BBC commentator was contagious. The BBC was broadcasting from every European capital, so that their listeners could hear how the rest of the free world was celebrating victory.

She sat quietly working, listening to a French-accented voice describing the frenzy of the Parisian crowds. When the announcer started to describe with poetic reverence the beauty of Notre Dame Cathedral completely lit up, glowing like an exquisite gothic fairy-tale castle, and surrounded by French patriots singing the "Marseillaise" at the top of their lungs, tears ran down her face for the very first time since Yves had left.

"Paris," she whispered, as her fingers deftly cut cotton and threaded her needle. "Paris. I wonder if I will ever see you again. I wonder if there's anything left for me there anymore."

14

*U*mberto Scrofo returned to his native village in Calabria a very rich man. With his spoils of war he was able to purchase the land to build an enormous house on the highest part of the mountainous region. The terrain was harsh, rocky, difficult to farm, but since the whole region was so desperately poor and even more so as a result of the war, Umberto found no shortage of peasant labor to cultivate his unproductive land.

Because of his now enormous assets and possessions, he was able to wield great power in Calabria. Not, however, as great as the power of the Cosa Nostra; they still ruled the lives and destinies of those around them with total and unquestionable authority. But Scrofo had more than enough power to guarantee him the serenity he longed for.

Inside his new fortress he had built a screening room where he reveled in his passion for the latest Hollywood movies. Most nights he sat alone in the velvet-tented room watching carefully, admiring the beauty of the young blond actresses he desired: young virginal types like Bonita Granville, June Haver, Mary Beth Hughes were his great favorites. Girls who gave the illusion of being fresh from puberty. Often, as he watched them, his Lilliputian penis would stiffen and he would pleasure himself.

Since his "accident" with the French whore in Paris, he had rarely indulged in sex. He had found the olive-skinned, black-haired women of Hydra unappealing, preferring his own secret fantasies to coupling with them.

In addition to the Hollywood films, he possessed a large collection of blue movies imported from Scandinavia. The cool Nordic beauties who frolicked naked in sauna baths and pastoral streams could always arouse him.

As he rested his overstuffed body on an overstuffed couch one afternoon, he looked up from the Christie's catalogue he was flicking through and saw, tending his flowerbeds, a young blonde of exquisite beauty. She looked up, caught his eye, then blushed and looked away. Scrofo found her beauty and innocence exciting. It was the first time in years that he had felt such a strong desire for a woman, and it stimulated him into action.

On making inquiries he discovered that she was the niece of his gardener. Her parents had been killed in a road accident and she had been adopted by the gardener and his wife. Her name was Silvana, and she was seventeen years old.

Umberto insisted that the girl be given a job inside the house as parlormaid. It would be her job to dust and clean some of the treasured objets d'art that glittered on the tables and in the display cabinets of his villa.

Every day Silvana performed her tasks happily, humming quietly, a smile playing around her gently curved, soft pink lips, blushing whenever she caught Umberto's intense stare.

Soon he became obsessed by the girl, his thoughts full of her breasts, her innocent gray eyes, the way her body undulated underneath the plain blue calico house dress. He ordered another uniform to be made for her by one of the village women—the costume of a French maid, just as he had seen in so many movies. Silvana was embarrassed to be seen in it, but Signor Scrofo insisted, and, after all, he was her respected employer.

One afternoon Silvana shyly entered Umberto's drawing room with a timid knock on the door. She was wearing sheer black hose, a short frilly black skirt, a white organdy apron and, perched on her abundant yellow curls, a little mobcap such as might be worn by an eighteenth-century maiden in a picture by Boucher. As she knelt to dust the legs of a console table, Umberto could see her lacy panties, and he caught a tantalizing glimpse of succulent white thighs above black stockings.

He strode to the double doors, quietly closing and locking them. Silvana was busy cleaning around the gilded crevices, and cried out in fright when Umberto crept up behind her, grabbing her breasts through the flimsy silk of her blouse.

"No, please, no, Signor," she whimpered, her frightened eyes exciting him so much that he thought his tiny cock would burst through his trousers.

"Yes, yes, my dear, yes, *now,*" he rasped, his harsh wheezing voice thick as he ripped open her blouse, exposing her mouth watering, rose-tipped breasts. "I must have you *now,* Silvana—I must. Be a good girl now—I won't hurt you."

Her terrified screams continued to inflame him as he wrestled her down onto the flowered Aubusson carpet. The velvet curtains were drawn against the afternoon sun, and the thick stone walls were as good as soundproof.

Umberto's gross body pinioned her to the floor and no one heard Silvana's cries as he raped and sodomized her throughout the afternoon. Blood ran down her face and back as he beat her, and after a while she mercifully lost consciousness. She reminded him of that French tart in Paris, and this drove him to hurt her more.

"Whore," he said viciously, slapping the girl's unconscious face. "Cheap whore, you deserve this."

At last he was finished; Silvana lay slumped in front of the fireplace, her uniform in tatters, her face bruised and puffed from weeping and his beatings, her body covered in blood. Umberto looked at her coldly as he zipped up his trousers. Her eyes opened, looking at him pleadingly. She was disgusting to him now. No longer desirable—a discarded toy.

"*Signor*—help me, please," she said, crawling across the carpet, her words muffled by her swollen lips.

"Get out," Umberto said curtly, mopping his hairless sweating head with a silk handkerchief and rearranging his clothes.

"*Out*—now." He turned away from her, pouring himself a brandy with a gratified smile. "I've finished with you, little slut."

So—he gloated to himself. He could still perform, and very well too. This was the first time in over two years that he had done something like this with a woman. Ever since that creature in Paris had robbed him of most of his sexual desire with her vicious attempt on his life. But that little whore hadn't succeeded. He was still a man, a stallion, a stud, in spite of the tiny penis which had caused so much mirth in the girls he had attempted to make love to when he was young.

And he was still young, was he not? He preened in the mirror, his eyes not seeing the bloated features, the thick lips, the short, scarred neck. All he saw was a facsimile of Benito Mussolini—a soldier, a patriot, a man of power, irresistible to women. Alas now dead, hanged by his own people in disgrace. But Umberto was too pleased with himself to dwell on Mussolini's untimely death. He felt his sexual vigor to be in full and potent flower again. He was ready to take other women now. Many others. He didn't give a thought to Silvana; she meant less than nothing now that he had had her. But perhaps she had a pretty friend, a sister, or a cousin? He would find out.

The following night as Umberto lay asleep in the canopied Empire bed which was reputed to have once belonged to Napoleon, the locked bedroom doors burst open, and four men, hats pulled low over their eyes, surrounded him. They said nothing as they pulled him roughly out of bed, nothing as he called out hoarsely for his servants. Where were they, why didn't they answer him? Where were all his bodyguards? His entourage of lackeys? But no one answered his screams for mercy, and the house was dark and silent as a tomb as the men bustled him roughly down the marble staircase, out across his manicured lawns, ghostly green in the moonlight, down to the rough pebbled beach.

Whimpering with terror, the scar on his neck throbbing, the soles of his feet bleeding from the jagged rocks, Umberto was experiencing a fear unknown to him before.

His hands and feet were tied tightly together with rope and he was tossed roughly into a small fishing boat resting on the shoreline. The four men climbed into another boat and began towing Umberto's tiny craft out to sea, into the notoriously dangerous currents which swept down the coast. They grinned in the reflected moonlight, but their eyes were dead.

"What are you doing to me?" Umberto choked, feeling his throat constrict. "Where are you taking me?"

"We're sending you to die, scum," the leader snarled. "Die, pig, alone and scared. If you live to come back to this place ever again, we'll find you and we'll kill you in a way that will make you wish you had never entered this world—you have our word on that."

One of the men then unhooked the tow rope and the swift current started to carry Umberto farther and farther out to sea. "Why? Why are you doing this?" he bleated. "What have I done?"

"This is for Silvana," the tallest man shouted harshly. "We are her blood brothers. If you return to Calabria we will cut off your balls, stuff them in your mouth, and then kill you—and you'll be begging us to do that by the time we're finished. Antonio Rostranni has given us his blessing to do so, and he wants to watch." The men laughed coarse, loutish laughter, and Umberto froze. Rostranni, the most feared name in the whole of southern Italy. The Padrino himself; the Mafia chief whose word became unquestioned law. If the girl Silvana was indeed related to someone in the Cosa

Nostra, he could consider himself extremely lucky that they hadn't slit his throat while he slept.

The boat was swept farther out to sea, and the four men sat motionless, staring after it. Umberto then noticed the oars, an earthenware jug of water and some dry biscuits, provisions for an existence of a few days, if that, and only if he could find a way to remove the ropes which tied his wrists together so tightly that his arms were starting to go dead.

"Where am I to go?" he whispered. "I can't survive in this boat. How can I save myself? Where do you want me to go?"

"Go to hell," the leader jeered as the two boats drifted farther and farther apart. "You belong with the perverts there, with the other scum, go to hell, pig."

There was much rejoicing in the small Calabrian village when the hated Umberto Scrofo suddenly disappeared. Although foul play was suspected, not a single one of Umberto's numerous servants had either seen or heard anything the night that he had mysterously disappeared. In spite of extensive police investigations, no trace of him could be found. Several months later the remains of a small fishing boat were found washed up on the northern shore of an Italian beach. It was smashed to pieces and contained only a few tattered scraps of what the police identified as Scrofo's clothes. With that evidence, Umberto Scrofo was then declared officially dead.

His palatial mansion was sold, and his magnificent possessions were divided between the remaining members of his family in Calabria. The cousins, aunts and uncles who had mocked and despised him as a child found themselves the heirs to the glorious pictures and booty which he had scavenged from Paris and Hydra.

A funeral of sorts was held, which the family attended, but no one could have been said to mourn him. Very soon he was completely forgotten by everyone in the world except for Inès Juillard and Nikolas Stanopolis. Neither of them could ever forget him.

Part Two

1

*E*lektra *knew that life wasn't going to be easy for her in America.*
Nikolas had sent for her about three months after he'd arrived, and now
she was almost beside herself with excitement as she caught a glimpse of
his tall wiry body leaning against a pillar inside the arrivals hall at L.A.
airport.

"Nikolai, oh, my darling Nikolai—I can't believe it's really you—" she
said ecstatically as she threw herself into her husband's open arms, which
were not as warmly welcoming as she'd expected them to be.

"What's the matter, Nikolai?" she asked tentatively as he pulled away
from her embrace with apparent embarrassment.

"Elektra, I'd like you to meet Errol," he said in Greek, gesturing towards
an enormous black man wearing a burgundy uniform, trimmed with an
excessive amount of gold braid.

"Welcome to L.A., Missus Nicky," beamed the man as he stood to attention. "Sure are glad to have you here—our Mr. Nick he's bin pinin' away,
he never stops talkin' about you."

"This is Errol—Uncle Spyros' chauffeur. Uncle Spyros has lent us his
personal car today. He wanted you to have a special welcome to this
wonderful country."

Elektra nodded in silence, wishing that Nikolas had come to meet her
alone. The chauffeur seemed pleasantly friendly, but Elektra was shy, and
she had wanted to be reunited with her husband in private.

A cheerful porter carried her only shabby piece of luggage through the jostling crowds as they all walked out to the sidewalk, where Elektra's mouth opened wide with amazement. Waiting at the curb was the longest black car she had ever seen. There were no vehicles of any kind on Hydra, and she had hardly seen any cars before except on occasional trips to Athens. She looked fearfully at the busy street where cars, buses and taxis sped by at terrifying speeds, and laughing pedestrians seemed to defy death as they dashed between them.

"Come on, Elektra." She thought that Nick's voice seemed to have a more authoritative edge to it than before. "Hurry up, stop gawking, we must get to the house before dark. Aunt Olympia has prepared a Greek feast to welcome you."

Clumsily Elektra climbed into the cavernous backseat of the Cadillac, conscious that her skirt had bunched itself up well above her knees. Blushing furiously, she pulled it down and huddled in a corner, looking anxiously out the rear window to see if the porter had brought her suitcase.

Nick jumped in effortlessly, and gave her a brief hug. He held her hand, talking to her excitedly in their own language for a few minutes, but then he became involved in a long conversation with Errol in English. The men were laughing loudly as Errol seemed to be telling some kind of amusing story. Elektra leaned her head back onto the lush leather upholstery, closing weary eyes. She hadn't slept for days. It had been a long and exhausting trip to California, but she was here at last on the other side of the world. She hoped it wouldn't take long to become as settled and Americanized as the loving husband who had left her only three months ago.

Olympia Makopolis was a warm, motherly, comforting woman so like the women of Hydra that Elektra felt immediately at home with her. In spite of her husband's enormous wealth and position in Hollywood, Mrs. Makopolis still insisted on cooking and preparing everything herself, and her vast dining table was laden with familiar dishes from their homeland. Great plates of taramasalata, dishes of baby shrimp, squid and pompano, *tzadziki*, vine leaves stuffed with meat and rice, succulent baby lamb with eggplant, crisp lettuce tossed with diced pieces of goat cheese, *bourekia* wrapped in pastry, and freshly baked bread, mixed with the powerful aroma of freshly chopped garlic in the *skordalia* sauce—a sauce so overpoweringly pungent that it was considered bad manners to eat it before a social event unless everyone was having it. Jugs of cooled white wine had just been put on the table when Olympia heard the crunch of the limousine on the graveled driveway.

"Welcome, my dear Elektra, I'm *so* happy to see my cousin's daughter at last," said Olympia, embracing Elektra warmly and feeling an immediate rush of affection for the shy girl.

"Come, come—we eat right away—you must be starving." She looked approvingly at Elektra's full-bosomed and rounded figure, in such contrast to the greyhound-sleek body of her very pretty niece Vicky Zolotos, who was Americanized to within an inch of her life.

"Vicky, this is Elektra, my wife," said Nikolas proudly.

"I'm thrilled to meet you, honey, Nicky has talked about you *so* much," gushed Vicky, her long shiny blond pageboy, tightly belted green gabardine suit, and tiny matching hat tipped over one ravishing turquoise eye making her appear to Elektra like a fashion plate straight from the pages of *Vogue*.

Elektra cringed. She couldn't understand a single word the girl said, even though Nicky, who seemed to possess such newfound confidence, quickly translated.

"Vicky also works in the mail room at the studio," he said rapidly. "Her father is one of Uncle Spyros' board members—she's just out of university—her mother is Greek and she's a cousin of Uncle Spyros. She's been helping me learn English, and we're both slaves of the studio system, aren't we, Vicky?" He flashed a confident grin at the beautiful girl who made Elektra feel hopelessly drab, dowdy and old-fashioned. Elektra's long serge skirt, sensible brogues and heavy lisle stockings were hardly a match for this American beauty's slim nylon-clad legs, sculpted bosom and perfectly made-up face. Although she thought that they must be about the same age, Elektra felt hideous and inadequate beside her.

Olympia had lived in California for nearly thirty years, but she was still a simple Greek woman at heart. Seeing Elektra, so small, frightened and awed by the sumptuousness of these alien surroundings, reminded her of herself three decades ago, and Olympia made up her mind to help this girl to make the difficult adjustment to the American way of life.

Later that night, as Nikolas gently undressed his wife, whispering passionate endearments to her in the language she understood, Elektra felt herself beginning to relax at last. The tension in her knotted muscles began to ebb away as her husband's sensual fingers slowly caressed her. Gently his hands encircled her breasts and his fingers as gentle as butterfly wings touched her nipples, causing gasps of joy to spring from her throat. Nikolai, her husband, the only man she had ever been with—the only man she could ever love—was still hers. He loved her. Now she knew that she had nothing to fear in America.

Nikolas Stanopolis, with a natural aptitude for languages, had learned English surprisingly fast. Now not only could he read and write with few mistakes, but he had become a master of American slang, almost a necessity in the movie business.

But for Elektra, adjusting to American life was a struggle. Everything confused her—the language, the hectic pace of Los Angeles, the motorcars, and the airplanes which shattered the afternoon peace of her siestas. The gadgets in her kitchen might as well have come from another planet, and the fast, streamlined supermarkets all made her feel a hopeless wreck. She felt stupid, dumb, completely alien to this modern world.

In spite of Olympia's patient coaching, and in spite of the beautiful, bright and breezy Vicky coming to dinner several times a week to help her with her English, Elektra couldn't manage to grasp more than a few words. Desperately she studied phrase books and dictionaries, read magazines and newspapers, but her brain, already befuddled with trying to cope with electric cookers, washing machines and refrigerators, and trying to cook with tinned and frozen ingredients foreign to her, simply couldn't cope. Nikolas, Vicky and Olympia insisted that she listen to the news programs, plays and variety shows on the radio, but the foreign language was still a foreign language to her. She tried gallantly to make herself understood at the enormous Food Giant supermarket on Canon Drive where Olympia had insisted she shop. Numbly, pushing her shopping cart around the endless aisles stacked high with colorful products, none of which she'd ever heard of, she was jostled by confident wholesome women in crisp shirtwaist dresses, their faces made up, their hair coiffed into soft curls or covered by a becoming hat. Elektra couldn't even begin to think of shopping for new clothes, even though Nick asked her when she was going to get rid of her dowdy dresses.

"Why don't you buy some new clothes, honey?" he asked her one night, grimacing as he saw the overcooked meatballs and eggplant croquettes which she'd done her best to prepare on the incomprehensible modern cooker. "We can afford it; I'm making good money now."

They were sitting at a shiny yellow Bakelite kitchen table in one of many little bungalows Spyros reserved for his nearest and dearest. There was a tight enclave of Makopolis relations living on the land which bordered his estate. Vicky Zolotos lived in one with a female cousin, Olympia's three sisters lived in another, and Spyros' uncle and aunt lived next door to them. Unfortunately for Elektra, all of these Greek immigrants seemed to have had no difficulty at all in learning English. They chattered away effortlessly, switching back and forth between English and Greek with the practiced ease of people who had totally adjusted to both cultures.

Nikolas was glued to Jack Benny on the radio, laughing at his jokes until tears ran down his face while Elektra silently ladled the hardened, lumpy meatballs onto his plate.

"You used to cook these so well in Hydra," he said during the commerical break. "What happened?"

"I'm sorry," mumbled Elektra, close to tears. "I just can't get this cooker to work."

Nikolas took another bite, and made a face. "You've got to adjust to the modern world, Elektra, this is 1946, the war's over now, the men are all back, everyone is competing in America for jobs—position—everything. You've go to compete too, Elektra—you must—you've got to try."

"I can't." She slumped down at the table with her head in her hands, starting to weep. "I just *can't* learn English—I can't cook with this stove—I don't fit in here, Nikolas. I don't belong in America. I want to go home—back to Hydra. That's where I really belong."

Nikolas stroked her hair sympathetically. He loved her very much, but he couldn't help but compare her simple rounded peasant looks to the glamorous women he came into contact with daily at the studio. Vicky was always flirting with him, joking in that sassy cute way so many American girls seemed to have. He liked it. He liked Vicky too, and why shouldn't he? After all, she was his distant cousin, albeit a couple of dozen or so times removed.

"Try, Elektra—please try—for my sake," he said, tuning back into another wisecrack from Jack Benny and Rochester.

"I'll *try,* Niko," sobbed Elektra despairingly, "I will, but I don't think I'll ever succeed. I don't have the ear."

"You must be patient, and try harder," said Nick firmly. "You *must,* Elektra—for us—for our family. Our future is here, Elektra—in America, in Hollywood—with these people. I'm going to become a director one day—Spyros has promised, I'm going to be a great director. This is our life here now, Elektra, and we're never going back to live in Greece. Never!"

Elektra nodded, trying to control her welling tears. "I know," she said sadly, thinking of the mountains, the sea, the beauty of her island. She felt a great lump in her throat and her heart was heavy as she realized that they might well never see Hydra again. "I will try," she whispered. "I'll really try, Nikolai."

And she did. She studied for hours each day. Olympia became a mother hen to her, and Vicky, if not quite like an older sister, at least helped her with her wardrobe.

"You've gotta get out of those dowdy duds, kiddo," she insisted. "You look like a total frump—it's time for you to get hip." She dragged Elektra off to Saks to sharpen her image in spite of Elektra's protestations that they simply couldn't afford to buy such expensive new clothes. But Vicky took no notice at all and they returned from their shopping trip laden with boxes and bags full of pretty cotton shirtwaist dresses, slim Capri pants, frilly blouses and shorts, most of which Elektra vowed that she'd be too embarrassed to wear.

Vicky laughingly contradicted her. "Honey, when the weather gets hot here you're gonna *live* in those shorts, and you'll wonder how you could ever have put on those old fuddy-duddy long black skirts."

After a very long time Elektra finally managed to learn to speak English, albeit falteringly, but she never felt completely comfortable with it. She still read, with pangs of homesickness, the Greek newspapers and magazines which were sent regularly to Olympia Makopolis. She never really found any American friends, preferring the company of Olympia and her three sisters to the wives and girlfriends of Nikolas' co-workers. But she both worshiped and respected her husband, and to her he was king.

As for the luscious Vicky, she still terrified Elektra with her stylish clothes, glossy pageboy and fast talk. Elektra suspected that she would never feel at ease with her. She still felt left out when Nikolas and Vicky chattered together for hours about the film business, sharing industry gossip and jokes together in the American slang with which they both seemed so comfortable.

Elektra's happiness flowered completely the year after her arrival in Los Angeles only when the first of her beautiful babies was born. Then she was in her element, taking care of little Alexis totally, eschewing the nannies and nurses which Vicky and Olympia recommended. To Vicky's shocked amazement, Elektra breast-fed the baby until he was more than a year old and she was already pregnant with her second.

I will never become Americanized, particularly now with my baby boy and girl to look after, thought Elektra, looking at her bonny plump reflection in her dressing table mirror. She didn't have time for sessions at the hairdresser or for afternoons browsing at Saks or Magnin. She was perfectly happy in their little bungalow with her lively children and her beloved husband, who alas, wasn't there as much as she would have liked. He was becoming more and more involved with his work at the studio, and although he was a good husband and a loving father to the babies, Elektra knew that work was fast becoming the most important thing in his life.

Elektra woke up gasping and choking, unable to breathe. It was pitch dark in the bedroom and strong hands were clamped around her neck trying to squeeze the life from her. The figure was on top of her, the wiry fingers so tight around her throat that had she not awakened she knew it would have been only a matter of seconds before she was asphyxiated by this maniac. She tried to scream for help but no sounds would come. Where was Nikolas? Where was he? And how had this intruder got into their bedroom?

Elektra fought for her life, hearing nothing but the harsh breathing of her assailant. She knew she had to attack his eyes before she lost consciousness but his body was strong and pinned her to the bed. She struck out blindly with the remains of her strength where she thought his eyes were and to her horror heard the man exclaim as her fingernails raked his flesh:

"You bastard. You fucking scumbag—this is it, pig. I've got you now and I'm going to kill you."

In panic Elektra heard her husband's voice screaming this litany of hatred at her. Nikolas trying to kill her. Oh, dear God, thought Elektra as unconsciousness threatened to engulf her. God, no. How could he do this? Her gentle, kind Nikolas. Was he mad? Weakly she tried to cry out, but realized that she was completely powerless. She was going to die. She was going to die at the hands of her husband—the man she loved. She could feel the last thread of consciousness breaking . . .

"Mama—Papa—what are you doing?"

The bedroom light suddenly illuminated little Alexis standing at the door in his pajamas, his eyes wide with fear as he saw his father straddling his mother, hands gripping her throat.

"No, Papa, no," the boy screamed, running to the bed and tugging at his father.

As if from some great distance Nikolas heard his son's voice and opened his eyes which had been tightly closed in rage. When he saw what he had been doing to his wife he stopped with a scream of terror.

"My God, Elektra, oh, Jesus, what have I done?"

The baby girl now toddled into the bedroom holding her teddy bear and crying, wakened by the noise.

Elektra moaned and drew deep, gasping breaths into her aching lungs.

"God, Elektra! Oh, God, are you all right?" cried Nikolas. He was weeping now with the horror of what he had done. The two children were crying and his beloved wife was groaning in agony.

"I—I'm all right, Nikolas," Elektra managed to say as she tried to sit up.

He pressed a glass of water to her white lips.

"God, I almost killed you." Nikolas looked like a man possessed. His hair was disheveled and his whole body was shaking.

"Go back to bed, children, Mama is all right," Elektra managed to croak. "Everything's going to be all right now."

"It was a nightmare," cried Nikolas after he had tucked the children safely back in bed and sought the sanctuary of Elektra's arms. "I thought you were Scrofo," he wept. "It was a nightmare, Elektra, I didn't mean it. You know that, don't you?"

"Of course," she soothed. "Of course I do, Nikolas."

"I thought about Mama's death," he said softly. "Then I saw him and I tried to kill him, but it was *you!* Oh, God, Elektra, can you ever forgive me, can you?"

"Of course I can—of course," she soothed again.

"The dream was so vivid," he murmured, his body still shaking, and sweating. "Where do you think he is now?"

"You mean Scrofo?" she said gently, holding him safely.

"Yeah, Gourouni—the bastard. Commander Umberto Scrofo."

Nick's eyes began to gleam with rage again in the dim light from the bedside lamp.

Elektra was surprised that he was still so obsessed with Scrofo. They had been in America for nearly four years. Surely his anger must be waning by now?

"Don't think about him, Nikolai," she murmured. "That's all over now—it's all in the past."

"Mother of God, Elektra—here we are in America, in this nice house with my good job—the American Dream." His face was contorted with fury. "And that fucking piece of scum is probably still alive somewhere." He pounded the pillow with all the force of his frustrated anger. "The murdering bastard is still alive, do you realize that? Do you?"

Elektra tried to calm him down again but he was like a wild man.

"Sshh, you'll wake the babies again," she admonished. "Stop thinking about Scrofo, Nikolai—you must stop—you'll make yourself ill."

"Elektra." He turned to face her, his eyes wide and full of passion. "I said it that day on Hydra, but I *know* it now—one day I'm going to find that bastard—and I'm going to kill him with my bare hands."

"Sshh—no, Nikolai, no." She tried to hold him but he leaped out of bed and stood before her—a naked avenging angel.

"I swear it—I swear it on the lives of our children—on the memory of my mother—I'm going to find Umberto Scrofo and I'm going to kill him if it's the last thing on earth I do."

Ever the nepotist, Spyros Makopolis had taken Nikolas and Elektra to his bosom. He often invited them to join his family at their table, which was always groaning with Greek delicacies. At work he pushed Nikolas for promotion after promotion. From the mail room he went on to become a gofer in the publicity department; from there he became assistant to the assistant editor in the cutting rooms. He stayed there for nearly four years until he understood everything there was to know about editing, splicing, dubbing and the entire technical process of filmmaking. Finally he graduated to the floor itself. Third assistant director, second assistant director, first assistant director, location manager, production manager, and finally, joy of joys, Spyros called him into his office one day to announce the promotion he ached for more than any other: director.

Spyros sat behind a desk covered with scripts, puffing on his ever-present Havana.

"Take a look at *that,* kid," he beamed, throwing a bound blue script at him. "Something special, something real cute and zany."

Eagerly Nick caught it, but his face dropped as he saw the title. *"Bobby Soxers in Space?"* Nick looked astonished. "What's this, Uncle—do you want me to give you a budget breakdown on it?"

"No! No!" the old man boomed out. "No, my boy, I want you to *direct* it."

"Direct *Bobby Soxers in Space?* My God! You've gotta be kidding, Uncle." Nick didn't know whether to laugh or cry. For years he had been yearning to direct a feature film—any feature—but *Bobby Soxers in Space?* Even he had his pride. The title was a complete joke, and the content probably much worse.

"My boy, I won't lie to you," Spyros said with a sigh. "Not to put too fine a point on it, our studio is in deep and rising shit."

"How can it be? According to the trades, our last five movies grossed millions. Is that a lie?"

Spyros nodded sadly. "Alas, my boy—the publicity department did a sterling job in telling the world that our last five films did well. I must admit, however, it's not true. In fact it's a fucking lie."

He paused, dabbing his florid face with an enormous silk handkerchief, choosing his next words with care. "Understand, my boy, that after the war, MCCP could do no wrong—no wrong at all.

"Spyros Makopolis could do no wrong, either," he continued. "As the major stockholder, president and chief executive in charge of production, I was the golden boy to all the bankers and brokers."

Nick listened, aware that his uncle was under intense strain. This was obvious from the puffy liverish bags under his eyes and in the way he leaned heavily on the vast desk to relight his cigar.

"What happened, Uncle?"

"Television happened," Spyros spat out bitterly. "Tee bloody Vee is *destroying* the film business, Nick, *ruining* it. Do you realize that after the war, *ninety* million people a *week* went to the cinema? You know how many go now?" he asked accusingly. "Three years ago, in 1950, only *sixty million* people a week. Down to only sixty million. It's terrible, Nick, just terrible, and it's getting worse all the time."

"But it's not just our studio——it's all of them, surely?" asked Nick.

"Yeah, yeah—Zanuck, Warner, Cohn—we're all in the same kind of shit. Our jobs are hanging by a thread, Nick. If this decline in movie-going continues, by the end of this decade movie studios as we now know them will be practically extinct."

"But I don't understand. Surely this space movie is just another piece of shit," Nick said. "Who the hell is going to see something like that?"

"It's something *different!*" cried Spyros excitedly, getting up from behind the desk to throw a beefy arm around his nephew's shoulders. "Something new, something zany, crazy—a novelty for the kids that adults will love, too. They'll love it, Niko, I know it. Now look, I know it's low budget, but if you can bring this picture in for one hundred fifty thousand, kid, I can guarantee it will gross at least ten times that. We'll bring it out for Easter vacation—the college students will love it. You'll be a hero, my boy, a hero." He patted Nick benevolently and smiled broadly at him. "Especially to me."

"But, Uncle, why do you want *me* to direct it when I've never directed before? I mean, I'm honored, sure, but what about Weston or Ratoff, surely they'd be better?"

"I have to be honest with you, Niko—none of them will touch it with my left testicle," Spyros admitted. "Only a newcomer can do this movie, Niko. Someone fresh, young, with new ideas. Someone who understands the youth market. It's a break for you, kid, a big break."

No one would touch it? This was bad, very bad. Nick had expected to start by directing low-budget films, yes, but hopefully more of the quality of *The Window* or *Laura.* With *Bobby Soxers in Space,* he could quickly become the laughingstock of the business; then he'd never be able to get a decent movie to direct. Hollywood was a tough, snobbish town where you were only as good as your last film. If that film was a turkey, or, even worse, a lemon, no one was likely to take another chance on using you again.

"Do I have to do it, Uncle?"

"Yes, yes, you can *make* something of this, boy—I know you can," growled the old man. "This is your big break, Nick. I could give it to one of the young contract directors but I'm giving it to *you*. It's not a bad script, it's cute. You can shoot it in Death Valley with a non-union crew and some of our contract players—it'll only take four weeks. If you do well, there'll be other scripts—I promise you, Niko. For the sake of the old country, for your mama, for all of us Greeks who must stick together—you direct this picture and there'll be plenty more, I promise you. Plenty. You've got the talent, boy. Just do this for me, and for the studio."

That night, with a heavy heart, Nicky began to read the ridiculous script. Hidden beneath the tired old clichés, the heavy-handed humor and the wornout gags, there were grains of originality—a modern twist which might well be hilarious. If he could get a decent rewrite from one of the contract hacks who wasn't a lush, use some of his own ideas—and he was never short of those—and get a couple of halfway decent actors, maybe *Bobby Soxers in Space* could turn out to be the sow's ear which became the silk purse.

2

*F*or *seven consecutive years Julian Brooks had been one of Britain's*
top box-office stars, each film propelling him to even greater cinematic
glory. The fans simply could not get enough of him. His films were
nearly all in the romantic adventure genre, and men and women alike
doted on them.

His first film, *The Merry Monarch,* had been the precursor of his swashbuckling roles, and he'd continued to play a succession of brave adventur-
ers and heroes on locations as far away as the Sahara Desert, the Amazon
and the South China Sea. Didier Armande had signed him to a viselike
contract, and in spite of the fact that almost every major studio in Hollywood wanted him loaned to them, Didier simply would not let Julian
Brooks go. He was unquestionably England's number one male star, he was
Didier's discovery, and the shrewd producer was going to get his pound of
flesh each and every year from the watertight seven-year contract. Not only
that, but Phoebe wasn't at all keen on going to Hollywood.

"Better a big fish in a small pond than vice versa," she snapped whenever the subject came up. "Here you're a star, there you'll just be one of the
players on C. Aubrey Smith's cricket team."

Julian was in his element for the first two years of his contract. Mr.
Christian—Beau Geste—Chopin—Sir Walter Raleigh—he played many of
the great romantic leading men, and he also starred opposite some of the

world's most desirable actresses. For even if Didier was not keen to lend them his most important star, American studios were more than happy to allow their beautiful contract actresses to cross the Atlantic to star opposite Julian Brooks. Soon there were few leading actresses whom Julian had not played opposite, and not only played opposite on screen, but off screen too.

He seemed irresistible to practically all women. For Julian, making love to each new leading lady was as easy as tying his Charvet tie. The actresses were all more than willing, and he was more than eager to please, as long as there was always complete discretion. That was the only provision in Julian's liaisons. He insisted that no breath of scandal should leak out to the gossip columns or magazines. He always made it quite clear before an affair began that he was happily married, and not prepared either to hurt his wife or damage his marriage. Many was the Hollywood siren who, having sampled the delights of Looks Brooks' lovemaking techniques, was loath to let him go when their director had called the final "cut."

"Not since Gary Cooper," one actress told her friend who was off to London to play Roxanne to his Cyrano, "not since Coop has *any* guy made me come so many times and *so* deliciously." She shivered with pleasure at the memory.

"That good, huh?"

"Yeah—better than Sinatra—much better than Flynn."

"What does the wife think about all these shenanigans?" inquired the friend—Candida Willow, one of MCCP's most promising young stars.

The redhead tossed her titian pageboy. "Oh, she doesn't care. He doesn't flaunt it—he lets you know it's just a fling—but oh, boy, what a fling! Honey, you're in for *some* treat, I'm telling you."

"You mean his wife doesn't *know?* She doesn't even suspect?" asked Candida, big blue eyes wide with disbelief.

"Sure she knows. But she's so busy huntin' at Harrods 'n' Hartnells 'n' hobnobbing with the gentry, that she turns the other cheek—know what I mean?" The redhead winked and Candida giggled.

"Well, I'm certainly looking forward to getting to know this Mr. Brooks," said Candida. "But I won't sleep with him, because I *don't* have affairs with married men—besides, you know I'm in love with Gerry."

"Just wait till Looks turns on the charm," laughed the redhead. "You won't be able to resist those navy blue eyes, honey. Take it from me."

"Well, maybe *he'll* fall in love with *me*," smiled Candida, confident in her twenty-two-year-old glory. "Then the shoe will be on the other foot."

"Forget it, honey—everyone's tried—Ava—Lana—Liz—they all got nowhere with our Mr. Brooks. Wham, bam and thank you so *terribly terribly* much, ma'am—that was absolutely delightful—I'll see you on the next picture."

"We'll see," laughed Candida. "I'll send you a postcard from Jolly Olde England and let you know what happens—you know I love nothing better than a challenge."

While Julian pursued his career and his leading ladies, money continued to roll in, and Phoebe became no slouch at spending it. Aware of Julian's little flings, she was equally aware that he would never leave her, and she proceeded to spend, spend, spend with zest.

As Julian's fame grew, so did their accommodations. By 1953 they had moved seven times, and now lived in a beautiful Queen Anne house in Connaught Square just behind Hyde Park. But Phoebe was already preparing to upgrade again, and had her eye on a large country mansion only a few miles away from Sir Laurence and Lady Olivier. The Brookses now numbered among their intimate friends the Oliviers, Ralph Richardson, John Gielgud, Noël Coward, and practically every other major film and theatrical name in England, not to mention many choice members of the aristocracy and a couple of minor royals.

In spite of Julian's looks, sex appeal and fame he was so funny and self-deprecating, so down to earth and nice, that all the men liked and admired him, while their wives simply adored him. Some of them lusted after him fiercely, often making it quite apparent, but Julian would never have an affair with the wife of a friend. Only actresses and single women not in his set were his province. Consequently he continued to enjoy the reputation of the man's man that he'd always had, while remaining supremely attractive to all women.

When two years of his seven-year contract with Didier had expired, he agreed to sign for two more, but only if he were allowed to appear in a West End play every eighteen months. This gave Phoebe the chance she had been waiting for and she cajoled and persuaded her husband to finally cast her opposite him in some of the classics in which he performed.

She was hardly a staggering actress, her only previous experience on the stage having been in skits at the Windmill, but she tried hard and she still looked quite attractive. Buxom, creamy-skinned, and with abundant red curls and a sparkling personality, she appeared reasonably successfully with him in *The Taming of the Shrew*, *Present Laughter* and *The Importance of Being Earnest*.

They had just finished a successful three-month limited run at the Aldwych. Julian was now preparing to go to Normandy to play the lead in a film of *Cyrano de Bergerac,* but this was going to be the first time that he had not played a romantic part. He was keenly anticipating the challenge of playing a character part, a character who, for once, does not get the girl.

He had decided to take his black Bentley across the English Channel to the Normandy location. He enjoyed long drives and was expecting Phoebe to fly over to join him the following weekend. They were dining together at the Caprice. It was a quiet Monday night and the softly lit peach walls of the elegant restaurant reflected the orange highlights in Phoebe's dyed hair as she nibbled and sucked noisily on a fat asparagus stalk.

"Darling, I've decided not to go with you to Normandy," she said, her lips glistening with melted butter, a trickle of which was running down her chin. Julian leaned across and wiped it off with his damask napkin.

"Why not?" he asked, popping a piece of pâté de foie gras into his mouth while Phoebe repaired her lipstick.

"Darling, how can I *possibly* go to Normandy in the middle of the season?" She bared capped teeth in what she assumed to be an ingenuous girlish beam, but which at thirty-three was beginning to look a little frayed around the edges.

"I mean, next week is the Derby, two days later the Cavendish wedding, then the Oliviers are having that big birthday party for Michael, and I promised that I'd help Vivien with the decorations." She paused for a sip of wine as Julian looked across at her with raised eyebrows.

"Do I detect a mild dose of social-climbing fever here, my dear? Nothing before has ever kept you from visiting me on location. How on earth will I manage without you?" he asked, his irony totally missing its target.

"Oh, darling—I *know.* Do understand, my pet—please." She patted his hand with the absentminded gesture a nursemaid might make to her charge, and prepared to tackle the beef Wellington with sautéed potatoes which a waiter placed before her. "It's just that it's a terribly bad time now, what with redecorating the house, all these parties, and then the charity. The actors' charity, you remember, darling, you're on the committee. Surely you're going to fly back for that, aren't you, pet?"

"Phoebe, how *can* I?" he asked exasperatedly. "I know it's for a very good cause and so forth and I know we're both on the board but I'm in practically every damn shot of *Cyrano.* I can't *possibly* get away in the middle of the week, even for a charity."

"Exactly," crowed Phoebe triumphantly. "So I'll have to be there to represent you—the Rahvis girls are making me the most divine gown—completely covered in beaded topaz flowers, darling—you'll love it, it matches the topaz necklace and bracelet you gave me for the opening night of *Shrew*."

"Mmmm." Julian was not listening. He picked at his roast chicken, his mind absorbed in his forthcoming characterization. He really didn't care whether Phoebe was with him or not on location. She was just a habit, always around like some annoying lucky mascot. He'd even become used to her complaints, which were becoming more frequent since she'd struck up an apparently close friendship with Vivien Leigh. Although Phoebe considered Vivien to be her best friend, Julian knew that she was little more than another one of the actress's sycophants. Phoebe was neither intellectually stimulating nor amusing enough to be an intimate friend of the scintillating actress.

"So you won't be coming to Normandy at all then?" asked Julian, not really caring what his wife's answer would be.

"Well, I'll *try* and pop over for a few days, darling," trilled Phoebe. "But don't forget there's Ascot—we're expected every day in someone or other's box or in the Royal Enclosure. The Denhams are having that big lunch for the Aga Khan, then Lord Cheltenham and the Countess of Rathbone have taken a huge tent for Ladies' Day, and of course, Binkie's special outing—Noël and Gertie are *definitely* coming to that—I couldn't *possibly* not be there, darling."

"To represent me, I suppose?" said Julian with even more sarcasm.

"Of course, darling," she answered, yet again missing the barb as her mind whirled with the dozens of new outfits that were even now in the process of being created for her by Norman Hartnell, Rahvis and Jacques Fath.

"What I *will* do, darling, is when I have to go to Paris for my fittings, I'll pop up to Normandy and see you for a few days—how would that be, pet?"

"That would be just dandy, dear," said Julian, signaling to the waiter and at the same time noticing that Phoebe had spilled gravy down her creamy lace cleavage. She was becoming quite sluttish recently, and many a couture gown had been spoiled by her greed and lack of dexterity at the dining table.

"Well, good. Than that's that, dear. You'll be fine without me, you'll have all your cronies with you, won't you?"

"Yes, of course," he said, thinking fondly of his makeup man, his dresser and his stunt double who always accompanied him on every picture.

"Then I don't really have to worry too much about you, do I, darling?" smiled Phoebe, dabbing with a damp napkin at her Hartnell lace collar. "You'll be quite all right then?"

"Don't give it another thought, my dear—I'll be perfectly all right." Julian smiled, signing the bill with a flourish. "I'll be perfectly fine."

Indeed, as it turned out, Julian was more than perfectly fine. As soon as his navy blue eyes connected with the sexy yet innocent blue eyes of blond Miss Candida Willow it was instant and spontaneous combustion.

Phoebe heard no rumor of the affair until three-quarters of the way through the filming. She had been so heavily involved in her social whirl that she had been able to think of nothing but society balls, garden parties and weekends with the Oliviers. She did not bother to stop off in Normandy when in Paris for her fittings, as Paris suddenly had a little flurry of *petite saison* before the *haut monde* rushed off in opposite directions to Deauville and the Riviera. So Phoebe's Parisian friends stole the time that she had earmarked for her husband. Not that said husband minded one whit. He was quite content living with his entourage in a charming farmhouse far from the bright lights of Paris, London and the Riviera. He was adoring playing Cyrano, the tragicomic figure with the enormous nose who loves the gorgeous Roxanne in vain. And the gorgeous Roxanne herself, Miss Candida Willow, was so hopelessly in love with him and, in addition, such a sweetly adorable girl, that Julian's cup was, if not exactly running over, most definitely full to the brim.

It was one of those idyllic summer film locations, shot in the wilds of the French countryside in which everything went completely according to plan from start to finish. The director was a poppet, the actor who played Christian was talented and affable, and Miss Willow was even more enchanting than her name, everything which a man could want in a temporary paramour.

The crew, many of whom had worked with Julian before, were, as always, well aware of what was going on, but such was their loyalty to Julian that no breath of scandal concerning the two lovebirds was allowed to leak into general circulation.

Phoebe breezed in and breezed out of the location one brief weekend between attending the Oaks at Epsom and the Henley Regatta. Julian dutifully performed his marital obligations with eyes closed, although for the past several years Phoebe had been a less than enthusiastic partner, but Julian persisted because he was still hoping that they would have a child. They had now been married for eight years, and except for being pregnant when they were married, Phoebe hadn't conceived since. Now at thirty-three her biological clock was rattling on very fast indeed, but Julian's sincere longing for a child far outstripped her own. Although she pretended to want a baby, and indeed did nothing to prevent its possible conception, she lost no sleep about her failure to conceive, having plenty to occupy her in other ways.

They were in his trailer and Phoebe was preparing to leave for the airport. "Well, darling, I'll see you in London in a few weeks then," she trilled, adjusting her new Dior cream straw hat which overflowed with silk strawberries and violet ribbons. Julian thought that it clashed rather alarmingly with her red hair, whose color had become more pronounced with each passing year, but things of that nature never seemed to bother Phoebe. She loved vivid colors and strongly believed that they suited her vibrant personality.

"Yes, dear, enjoy Cowes, won't you—give my love to Larry and Viv and the gang," he said, abstractedly examining his huge rubber nose in the mirror of his portable trailer. It was terribly hot today, and the rubber prosthesis applied so painstakingly this morning by Tim, the makeup man, was in grave danger of peeling off around the edges. Damn—he had a close-up to do after lunch and that would mean that Tim would have to come back again with his bottles of glue and his orange sticks and fiddle about for hours to attach it again properly. It was most important that this nose look perfectly authentic. The new film system—CinemaScope—showed up every tiny pore, each and every crow's foot. Every minute detail of a face was magnified a thousand or so times. Nothing would appear more ridiculous than for Cyrano's enormous snout to look like little more than something a circus clown might wear. It was desperately humid in the cramped little trailer, and with his heavy plum velvet tunic and breeches, yards of lace ruffles and two-pound wig, sweat was streaming down Julian's forehead, threatening to wash the nose away completely.

"Timmy," he shouted, "get in here right away and save this fucking nose. I think the bloody thing's about to slide off my damn face."

"Well, I'm off then, pet," said Phoebe, typically oblivious to his problems. "The limousine has to get me to the airport by three—I suppose if we leave now, I'll have plenty of time to catch the plane?"

"Yes, yes, yes," snapped Julian—why wouldn't the bloody woman leave and let him get on with his bloody job, for Christ's sake? This nose was killing him—it was made of solid rubber, smelled absolutely foul and seemed to weigh a ton. Now the tip was beginning to droop, making it look even more ridiculous.

"Bye, dear—bon voyage." He blew her a vague kiss, as he yelled again, "Tim, Tim—where the bloody hell are you?"

"Right here, guv—sorry, just finishing me dinner." The makeup man rushed in, almost colliding with Phoebe, who was floating out in her white silk frock like a ship in full sail. With a final wave to her husband she left, and Julian sighed with relief. Closing his eyes, he allowed Tim to probe about under his false nose with orange sticks covered with cottonwool and acetone.

"Hell, Tim, this elephant's trunk is bloody uncomfortable, you know. In this damn heat I feel about to explode."

"Well, you know what me dear old mum always said, old sport." Tim grinned, deftly picking tiny bits of rubber out of the gaping cavern of Julian's rubber nostrils.

"I can't say that I do, Tim," groaned Julian, squinting at his grotesque reflection in the mirror. "What did the dear old thing say?"

"You've got to suffer to be beautiful, duckie."

That night in his cozy rented farmhouse, Julian slouched comfortably on the sofa, his arm around the delicate white shoulders of Candida Willow. Candida was gently nibbling at his ear while he leaned his head back and they listened to extracts of *La Bohème* on the old-fashioned radio gramophone.

He was exhausted from the long day's shooting, and also from a whole weekend with Phoebe, which had not been without its usual share of squabbling. Now he was looking forward to some languid stress-relieving lovemaking with his delectable co-star, and then a long restful sleep.

"Julian, let's get married," the delectable star suddenly whispered, between licks, into his ear.

"What—what did you say, darling?" Julian sat suddenly bolt upright, all hopes of a relaxing evening dashed.

"I said I want to marry you, Julian—I love you—I've never loved anyone like this before. You love me too—don't you, darling? Let's do it—please, please."

Pleading eyes turned to meet his, eyes which looked so radiant and gorgeous on the huge CinemaScope screen, but which now welled with huge CinemaScope tears.

Julian was dumbstruck. Surely she must know the way this game was played? He was married. This was just a location romance—he'd told her that when they'd begun their affair. Why on earth was she carrying on like this? Lovey-dovey, getting all emotional—talking marriage babble? Oh, hell. Women—women—women—damn the whole bloody lot of them, he thought, Henry Higgins was right. His mind desperately searched for a way to get himself out of this situation with his dignity and her pride intact.

"Darling heart, you *know* that's impossible," he said sincerely, making the effort to appear serious and lovingly understanding, in spite of his growing exhaustion.

"Why—why? You don't love Phoebe. You couldn't. I saw her today. She looks like an old tart," spat Candida tearfully. "I saw her with you all weekend—it almost *killed* me." She burst into sobs, spattering her angora sweater with tears. "The thought of you together—in bed—oh, oh, oh, it was terrible."

"Were you spying on me, darling heart?" scolded Julian gently. "That's very naughty, you know. Very, *very* naughty."

"Yes—yes I was," wept the girl, her tears flowing unabated. "I couldn't *help* it. I looked through your bedroom window one night. I saw her in her nightdress—she's *fat*. How can you *possibly* prefer her to me?"

Julian maintained a dignified silence as his mind raced. Candida peeking into the bedroom windows like some Peeping Tom—what sort of a woman was she?

"She's not *right* for you, Julian. I can tell. I watched you. You're like chalk and cheese together. You must know she's not the woman for you—you can't possibly love her. She's so old, how can you?" Fresh tears erupted and he automatically handed her his handkerchief.

He didn't answer her. The heartrending strains of the last act of *La Bohème* were moving on to their inevitably tragic end, the finale in another sense of an almost perfect evening which Candida was now ruining. "Look, my darling girl," he said, gently wiping the tears from her cheeks, marveling as if for the first time at how fresh and beautiful she was, "I don't want to hurt you, dear, but I *cannot* and *will* not marry you—*ever*. Do you understand that? It simpliy isn't possible, dear."

"No," said the girl churlishly, picking up her glass of wine and tipping the contents down her throat. "I don't understand. You *told* me you loved me, Julian—you know you did—didn't you? Were you lying?"

It was Julian's turn to be churlish now, and he knocked back his brandy with frustration. Of course he'd told her he loved her; it was all part of the game, dammit—a game he'd been playing for years now. She must know the rules. You always told them that you loved them when you were making love to them; it simply wasn't gentlemanly behavior not to—but one never, ever spoke of love when out of bed. All his other mistresses had understood it perfectly well. Why didn't this little fool, for God's sake?

"The picture finishes next week." Candida sounded desperate now, tears still dripping from her eyes with a persistence which unnerved him. "I can't live without you, Julian—I can't go back to America, my darling—I need you and I want you. I want to be with you always—forever and ever." She threw herself onto his chest, her body shaking with sobs that were verging on hysteria. Julian heaved a long inward sigh, and held her shaking shoulders tightly.

Throughout the long and sleepless night Julian talked reassuringly to Candida. He explained patiently all the reasons why it was impossible for them to marry. He told her that she must be a big grown-up girl, and that she must accept that their relationship must end when filming stopped. By the time they attempted to sleep as he held her comfortingly in the big four-poster bed, Julian thought that he'd successfully calmed Candida down, and had at last made her see reason. He was wrong.

When Julian woke up to Tim's knock and his cheerful "Five thirty, Julian—time to open those baby blues, chum, coffee's on the way up" he found that the other side of the double bed was empty. He moved an exploratory foot over to the other side, finding it not only empty, but cold. Candida had obviously accepted what he'd said to her, and decided to make a dignified exit during the night. So much the better, he thought. He hated scenes and confrontations, and much as he had liked Candida and adored making love to her, he knew that she was just another one of his flings. She was a charming child, an adorable sex kitten, but if he were ever to leave Phoebe, a thought which had certainly crossed his mind from time to time, then the woman for whom he might consider sacrificing his marriage would have to have a great deal more character, intelligence and personality than some cute but limited California cupcake. He swung his feet to the cool wooden floor and padded into the bathroom.

Nothing could have prepared him for the appalling sight which met his eyes. Lying in the old-fashioned splay-legged bathtub, floating as peacefully as Ophelia in the rushes, was Candida Willow. One slim arm was hanging over the rim of the tub and the dark red slash in her wrist was making a rich crimson pool on the floor. Her eyes were closed and her head was submerged almost up to her nose.

"Christ Almighty—*Candida*—Oh, my God—*Candida!*" Julian leaped towards the girl, sweeping her up into his arms, aware that the bathwater was the color of rosé wine. "Tim—*Timmy!*" he called at the top of his lungs. *"Get in here, for God's sake!"*

Within seconds Tim, who was carrying a tray of coffee and croissants, rushed into the bathroom and dropped the lot as soon as he saw the ghastly tableau. "Jesus Christ, guv—why the fuck's she done this?" he asked as they hastily carried the girl to the bed. Julian applied mouth-to-mouth resuscitation while Tim swiftly and efficiently shredded pieces of Julian's discarded white shirt into strips to stem the flow of blood from her wrists. Candida had slashed both of them with a razor blade which lay bloodied on the bathroom floor.

"Is she alive?" breathed Julian hoarsely.

Tim nodded. He had been in the ARP during the war and had had more than his fair share of dealing with serious injuries during the Blitz.

"Just about," he said grimly. "But she lost a lot of blood—we've got to get her to a hospital and pronto—otherwise she'll snuff it, guv, 'n' then the shit'll really hit the fan."

"Oh, my God," whispered Julian. "Oh, God, the poor silly little girl."

"If I were you, guv, it's *me* that I'd feel sorry for," said Tim bleakly. "The girl'll probably recover, but if this gets around, you'll be in deep deep shit. You won't be winnin' any popularity contests after this little lot, I'll bet my bottom dollar on *that*."

Somehow the studio managed to keep it out of the newspapers. Candida was young and strong, and by pure luck Julian had discovered her just in time. She would only have had two days' more shooting before her role was completed, and Didier Armande's imaginative publicity machine concocted a story about a sudden appendicitis attack which had made it necessary for her to be flown back to America immediately. Candida stayed in the local Normandy hospital for a few days and then her mother and father arrived with a lanky young lawyer from Pasadena called Gerry, who turned out to be Candida's fiancé.

"We're engaged," he drawled, having managed to steal an hour away from his bedside vigil to watch some of the shooting.

"How long have you two been engaged?" Julian asked, as Tim raised an eyebrow at him.

"Oh, two years now. We've been going together since high school, but Candy—that's her real name, Candy Wilson—the studio thought Candida Willow suited her better—well, Candy wanted to wait to get married until she'd forged her career—made a success, you know?"

"I know," said Julian, scratching his great itching nose, which was starting to droop again in the heat.

"Well, that's all changed now," said Gerry brightly. "She's decided, for the best, I think, to give up all this acting stuff and come back and live in Pasadena with me. We're gonna get married next spring."

"Congratulations, mate," said Tim, busy once again with his orange sticks in the crevices of Julian's nose. "She's a nice little gal—we've enjoyed having her, 'aven't we, guv?" He winked at Julian cheekily, his face inches away.

"I hope you'll both be very happy," said Julian sincerely, trying to ignore Tim. "Candida is a lovely girl, very lovely indeed."

"I know," said the young man, "I'm a real lucky guy." And he looked over in surprise at Tim as the makeup man gave a snort of suppressed laughter.

Although the general public was never allowed to hear about Candida Willow's suicide attempt, before long the entire show-business community from Paramount to Pinewood knew the whole story. Julian's charm and sex appeal were magnified tenfold, and he became almost a living legend. Nothing creates so much excitement as a woman trying to kill herself for the love of a man, and Julian found himself in even more demand both as an actor and as a lover.

He had felt guilty and responsible for Candida's suicide attempt, and had tried to visit her in the hospital, but was told that only her close relations were allowed to see her. He sent her a letter and three dozen white roses, and tried to put the incident out of his mind.

Candida's recovery was swift. As soon as she was out of intensive care, and the doctors said she could travel, the studio rented a private plane and packed her and her entourage back to California.

Julian never did get the chance to talk to her, and his letters to her in California were always returned unopened. He decided to be a great deal more careful with his love affairs in the future. And he did try. But Looks Brooks found it hard to change. In a matter of weeks, he was continuing on his path of casual philandering once again, and Phoebe was continuing to squander even more of his money.

Although Julian never mentioned Candida's suicide attempt to Phoebe over the telephone from France, the West End jungle drums were not long in relaying the news to her. It was one of the two Hermiones who imparted this particularly succulent piece of gossip to her while the women were lunching together at the Savoy Grill. It was all Phoebe could do to hold down her *sole bonne femme,* while Hermione rattled on about the wretched girl's suicide attempt.

"In Julian's bathroom, if you please! And I gather that the whole thing has been kept under wraps by Didier's film company. My dear, can you imagine *what* would happen if the story ever got out?"

"I certainly can," said Phoebe grimly, pecking at a piece of melba toast in a vain attempt to diet. "The newspapers would destroy Julian."

"I know I shouldn't really be telling you all this, darling," purred Hermione, her evident relish for relating the sorry tale to the injured party seemed to increase her already healthy appetite for plump roasted grouse, mounds of mashed potatoes and Brussels sprouts, all of which were washed down with copious amounts of dry Chardonnay. "But although they say that the wife is always the *last* to find out, I think you *should* know, my dear. You deserve to hear the truth, don't you agree?"

"Absolutely," croaked Phoebe, almost choking on a fishbone. "Damn it, this thing is supposed to be filleted," she snarled. "Tell me everything, Hermione, everything you know."

"Well, we all *know* what Julian's always been like—don't we?" giggled Hermione coyly, intimating by a flicker of false lashes that she also might have been among the lucky ones to have partaken of Julian's charms.

Phoebe stared at her with exasperated sarcasm. "What *is* he like, Hermione, dear? Do tell me."

"You're such a clever girl, Phoebe, that I'm sure that he's never managed to pull the wool completely over your eyes—not *quite,* has he, my dear?"

"Never," snapped Phoebe, trying to pour some more Chardonnay into her glass but spilling it onto the linen tablecloth. She felt a deep flush of humiliation creeping over the collar of her fuchsia silk dress—now almost a perfect match for the color of her face. "I'm not stupid, Hermione—I've always known he played around, of course, all men do—especially actors."

"Of course you have, dear, we're women of the world, we've always known. Well, there's nothing you can do really, I suppose, except pretend that absolutely nothing has happened, put on a happy face as it were."

"I always do that," Phoebe said icily. "Turn the other cheek, all that sort of stuff—what the eye doesn't see..."

"The heart doesn't grieve over," finished Hermione with a patronizing chuckle. "Exactly, dear. My mother taught me that too. Funny isn't it? It gets you through life pretty well—especially with the way most men are."

"What do you mean 'most'?" said Phoebe viciously. "They're all alike, Hermione. You must know that better than anyone, surely?"

"Really? I don't quite see the point of that last remark, Phoebe." Hermione raised a questioning penciled brow. "What exactly do you mean, dear?"

"Well I suppose it's bad enough that everyone knows that Julian has been pathologically unfaithful to me for years," said Phoebe, lighting a cigarette, and allowing a cloud of smoke to drift across her luncheon companion's face. "But at least he's unfaithful to me with *women*."

"And just *what* are you implying?" asked Hermione, looking suddenly irritated and defensive as she shifted in her chair, fanning at the cigarette smoke with a lace-bordered handkerchief.

"*Really*, Hermione dear, is it honestly necessary for you to be quite so naive?" Phoebe laughed lightly, enjoying the look of growing discomfort on

Hermione's heavily powdered face, into which she blew another cloud of smoke.

"What I mean is that although *my* husband has been busy screwing lots of young girls, *yours,* my dear, has been equally busy with lots of young boys!"

"Absolute nonsense!" Crimson spots now appeared on each of Hermione's normally porcelain-white cheeks. "That's utterly ridiculous—it's a slanderous lie, Phoebe, and you know it."

"Oh, do come off it, Hermione. You can dish it out but you obviously can't take it. Your precious Basil is as queer as a seven-pound note—you know it, I know it, everyone in the bloody business knows it—even the press knows it, for God's sake, so don't pretend to me that *you* don't know. You just make yourself look even more of a laughingstock."

"Well, I don't believe it, and even if it were true—I don't care—it doesn't matter. Basil loves me—he simply adores me," stammered Hermione. "He worships the ground I walk on."

But Phoebe was too fast for her. Leaning forward she hissed with calculated vehemence into the other woman's face, "Listen, Hermione, Julian may cheat on me, but he's a man—a real *man*—and although he fucks other women he *always* comes back to me—*me,* do you hear? He makes love to *me,* and I'll have you know he does it bloody well—now, duckie, can you say the same for your Basil?"

Hermione glared back at her, speechless. Some of the other people in the restaurant had turned in their direction, watching with great interest the two well-known actresses in heated discussion.

"Well, I was only trying to help," said Hermione huffily, patting the frizzy curls beneath her flowered hat. "After all, that's what friends are for, isn't it? I was just trying to let you know, my dear, that you have many many friends who are fully behind you, while you're going through this perfectly horrible situation."

"Thank you, Hermione." Phoebe signaled for the bill. "But probably not *nearly* as many as dear Basil has had behind *him!*" With a flourish she signed, leaving an unnecessarily large tip and, brushing her friend's cheek with her own, said through clenched teeth, "Thanks for all your interesting advice, dear . . . I'll think about it, and I dare say I'll see you both at Binkie's on Sunday."

By the time Phoebe got back to Connaught Square she had worked herself into a complete fury. Ignoring her butler, who opened the front door, she raced up to the master bedroom and throwing her hat, gloves and handbag on the bed, stood in the middle of her Colefax and Fowler chintz extravaganza seething and shaking with rage. That smug bitch. The vicious back-biting cow. How dare she give advice on how to handle Julian and his affairs when everyone knew that *her* husband was camper than a row of tents, and more than likely hadn't made love to her in years. How could he want to anyway, when he had to look at a face like hers. She paced up and down the room, puffing furiously on one cigarette after another. There was no way she could stop Julian's philandering, she knew that. She had allowed him to get away with it almost since the first day they'd met at the Windmill. He knew that and she knew that he knew that she knew. She could hardly make him stop now—it was far too much of a habit for him. But obviously his affairs were heating up, becoming more than just meaningless flings. This little harlot—starlet—trying to kill herself for love of him meant that Julian must have made romantic promises to her, maybe even heartfelt protestations of true love. She gritted her teeth. God, if he'd started to do *that*, then her days as Mrs. Julian Brooks could really be numbered. Before she even knew anything about it he could make some girl pregnant—become all broody, and ditch her to become the daddy he'd always wanted to be. Maybe she should really try to have a baby. She pulled a face—the idea was utterly repugnant to her. Motherhood in any of its aspects definitely didn't appeal to her. But perhaps she should attempt that ultimate sacrifice. After all, she thought, Julian was getting to that vulnerable age for a man, when the right woman could steal him away from her if there wasn't a tiny little Brooks junior to cement their bond.

"Not while I'm still around and breathing," muttered Phoebe, and with a great burst of energy she disappeared into his dressing room.

A week later Julian returned to London to find Phoebe not at home to greet him as was her wont. Everything in the house seemed perfectly normal but when he went upstairs into his dressing room and opened the heavy mahogany doors of his wardrobe, he was greeted by a sight which, to a man who prided himself on his sartorial elegance, was one of ultimate horror. Three dozen or more Savile Row suits hung, perfectly separated by a precise three-inch space, dark to the left, lighter cloth to the right, but every last one of the jackets had been cleanly cut off at the elbow, and all the trouser legs had been chopped off at the knees. Julian let out a howl as he fumbled through the rest of his costly and extensive wardrobe, and found to his horror that his Turnbull & Asser shirts, his beloved Charvet ties, Huntsman cashmere and vicuña coats, and dinner jackets and tailcoats from Kilgour, French & Stanbury, had all been systematically and very deliberately slashed to ribbons. Everything was completely ruined, nothing was salvageable, not even any of his dozens of silk boxer shorts. Phoebe had taken a vicious petty revenge, and Julian, realizing the penalty had now been paid in full for his potentially fatal indiscretion with Candida Willow, knew that he should try to toe the marital line—at least for the moment.

In its autumn issue, *Life* magazine named Julian Brooks as The Most Handsome Man in the World. They featured him on a full-color cover in his costume from *The Devil Is a Man*. He was standing at the tiller of a ship, wearing blue jeans, and a black shirt open to the waist revealed the glistening muscles of his broad chest to their best effect. His head was thrown back, and he was laughing into the wind, which was blowing his unruly hair back off his famous noble forehead. The article and accompanying photographs inside the magazine painted an idyllic portrait of Julian and Phoebe as happily married lovers living in intimate connubial bliss in Connaught Square, and sharing the theatrical limelight in the West End. They showed photographs of the two of them seen enjoying a joke at Ascot in the company of Noël Coward and Sir Crispin Peake, and they even printed a picture of Phoebe in the kitchen of their house, wearing a simple dress and to many people's great amusement, a modest apron, as she stirred a steaming casserole at the stove. In the background Julian held one of their many Persian cats and smiled fondly at her. The text was syrupy. The female writer had evidently fallen heavily for Julian, and the article was a paean of praise to his charm, talent and physical beauty. Phoebe had dozens of copies of the magazine sent over from America, as it was hard to find in London, and sent them to all their friends. She even put one in an Asprey's silver frame on top of the grand piano.

Even though they were in the middle of rehearsals for *Hamlet* Phoebe still found time to give an interview to one of the more sympathetic journalists from the *Daily Express*. She was delighted when she read the text of the article which appeared a month before they were due to open, and which helped make the box-office grow. It was headlined "If he cheated on me—I'd kill him" and in it in no uncertain terms, Phoebe warned the women of the world to keep away from her man.

"I know very well that because Julian is regarded by many as the handsomest man in the world, women will always be chasing him," gushed Phoebe in the article. *"But I also know that he's completely faithful to me, and to me alone. Oh, yes, of course I've heard all those silly rumors about his flirtations with his co-stars when he's away on location, but Julian just can't help but be charming and helpful to everyone he works with. It doesn't*

really mean a thing. We've been married for over eight years and our marriage is as sound and loving today as it ever was. No woman could ever come between us, and if anyone did try to steal him from me—I'd kill her."

Several copies of the *Daily Express* were passed around the dingy hall in Camberwell where *Hamlet* was in rehearsal, and the cast couldn't help giggling when they read about Phoebe's bravura performance in the paper.

"My dear, she acts so much better for the tabloids than she does on the stage," exclaimed Sir Crispin Peake at the local pub during a lunchtime break.

"Frankly, if she carries on giving the newspapers these perfectly *wonderful* pieces of fictionalized nonsense, she'll be able to make far more money writing penny-dreadfuls than Julian makes as a film star."

3

ST. TROPEZ 1954

*O*ften *when the mistral whistled tirelessly through fragrant hills of cypress* and pine, Agathe Guinzberg would bring out her scrapbook. Unlike the more docile winds of the sirocco, on whose hot breezes the scent of Africa wafted, the mistral was a demon wind. The shrill clattering of the rigging continued ceaselessly on the many vessels moored in the tiny harbor of St. Tropez, and the larger boats heaved against each other with a sound like the groans of ravening beasts.

But Agathe could disregard it all as she slowly and deliberately turned the pages of her album to gaze at the face of the man she adored. If the mistral became fierce enough to whip the village women's long skirts above their knees, to whisk the kerchiefs from their heads, and force old men to chase through narrow lanes after their black berets, then the loudest church bell would toll three times. When Agathe heard the bell ring out from the old tower she felt relieved, as this was the signal that there would be no school today.

Then she would sigh with pleasure, snuggling back under her goosefeather quilt as she leafed through her scrapbook and imagined herself with the man who so enriched her life. Julian Brooks and Agathe were dancing together, in glorious Technicolor, their bodies melting into one, as the orchestra of the Paris Opera played Tchaikovsky's *Romeo and Juliet.*

Agathe had thrilled to Julian's romantic exploits and escapades in *The Merry Monarch* and the many other films which had made him the most glamorous leading man in England, and now she seemed to live only for those moments when she saw him on the screen.

There were dozens of photographs of him, cut from *Ciné Monde, Ciné Revue* or *Jours de France,* which she had pasted into her thick scrapbook. Although he was England's biggest star, the French still preferred their actors home-grown, so Gérard Philipe, Jean Gabin and Fernandel were the masculine faces most frequently featured in French magazines. But nevertheless Agathe still managed to find quite a few pictures of her idol. Here was Julian clipped from the cover of *Paris Match* wearing a blue turtleneck sweater, tweed jacket and—his trademark—a fedora tilted at that rakish angle she adored. He was leaning against an oak tree, an ironic smile on his face, this thick dark hair tumbling over his forehead as he gazed into the camera with the tantalizing expression which Agathe and millions of other female filmgoers worshiped. She knew it was ridiculous for a woman of thirty-one to have such a passion for a film star, but she didn't care. To her he epitomized all that was romantic, gallant, quixotic and mysterious—he was her life.

Reverently she turned to another page where Julian, suavely dressed in white tie and tails, with his hair slicked back, clasped the eighteen-inch waist of some ravishing actress. They gazed into each other's eyes, appearing deeply in love, while a remarkable authentic studio moon shone down brightly on their enraptured faces. Agathe sighed. She really didn't like looking at photographs of Julian with other women. She preferred to look at him alone, bounding out of the waves onto some beach, his chest bronzed, wet and glistening, wearing a pair of tight-fitting white shorts. That kind of picture always gave her a strangely thrilling feeling in her loins that she knew was wrong.

At thirty-one Agathe was still a virgin who had never been involved with a man romantically. Sometimes at night as she looked at Julian's photographs an overwhelming heat would make her tingle so much that she would touch herself guiltily as she had done in the cellar years before. But her sense of relief was always followed by such feelings of shame and self-disgust that she would feverishly turn the amber beads of her rosary, begging forgiveness from the Virgin Mother. Those beads and her prayers had been her comfort and salvation when she had been hidden beneath Gabrielle's house for eighteen months, and Jewish or not, she still treasured them.

The shutters outside her window banged loudly and monotonously against the ivy-clad, pink-painted granite of the little house. The terrible force of the wind was tearing the jasmine and mimosa, so carefully nurtured by Aunt Brigitte, from the lattice-covered wall. Even the Nazi occupation hadn't been able to make her aunt's mimosa perish, but now the pale blossoms were falling to the ground like confetti.

"Agathe!" Aunt Brigitte's cross voice interrupted Agathe's reverie, and with a sigh she slid the album under the safety of her mattress.

"Close those shutters, Agathe," her aunt shouted, her voice sounding feeble against the howling of the wind. "Now!"

Agathe opened her window to reach the shutters, and the wind caught her long white hair, whipping it around her face in a blinding swirl. She gripped the heavy shutters, pulling and locking them firmly with the rusty catch.

Her aunt peered into the bedroom with a suspicious expression on her lined face, then went off muttering under her breath. Aunt Brigitte was a faded woman of sixty-four, whose thinning hair and sad demeanor mirrored all the suffering and loss of the war years, including the death of a much-loved husband. Now all she had left was this strange niece whom she'd inherited when the war had finally ended, and with whom she had nothing in common. Aunt Brigitte had escaped Paris just in time and had fled to the south of France and relative safety.

When the repatriation of families decimated by the Nazis began, Agathe had been reunited with the last surviving member of her family. She had insisted that Agathe come to live with her, and secured a job for her at the local school, where she was able to use her ballet training to teach the young girls.

Aunt Brigitte always looked as if the troubles of the whole world rested on her thin shoulders, and Agathe often wondered if her grim-faced aunt had ever been carefree and happy even as a girl. She sometimes studied the yellowing black-and-white photographs on her aunt's dressing table, pictures of the extensive family which no longer existed. How many of them there once were, and how pitifully short their lives had been. Agathe particularly loved one picture of the father she had known for barely eighteen years. How handsome Papa was, with his tanned, intelligent face and his thick black curls. His arms were holding the beautiful young girl who had been her mother, whose eyes were laughing and filled with joy. They had obviously been madly in love. Agathe sighed. Would she ever fall madly in love? Or was she destined to spend the rest of her life as a childless spinster, a ballet teacher, whose only joy was collecting photographs of a man she would never meet?

Well, there would be no school today, the mistral had conveniently seen to that. The whole day now stretched ahead of her—hours of emptiness which somehow had to be filled.

She decided to take a walk into the village—maybe the new edition of *Ciné Monde* was out, perhaps even with a photograph of Julian which she hadn't yet seen.

In her favorite café on the quay, the locals sat about glumly sipping their glasses of Provençal wine or cognac, staring out at the churning gray sea with grim resignation. Each day of mistral was a day of work lost, so the fishermen's families would eat little tonight. In spite of the wind, the blazing sun glittered on the rolling mass like shattered diamonds, and the air was fresh and tangy.

In the distance she could see boats bobbing even more furiously in the waters of the normally protected port. The Mediterranean had whipped itself into a foaming frenzy, and now golden sand swirled like clouds of smoke through the narrow streets. It seeped through even the most tightly closed doors and windows, while the wind screeched incessantly.

Agathe yearned to leave St. Tropez, to go somewhere, anywhere, away from the stern prying eyes of her aunt.

She sipped her coffee, gloomily thinking that judges in the south of France tended to be lenient in their sentencing if a crime, even murder, was committed during the mistral. They blamed it on "mistral madness," because the unrelenting winds had often been known to drive people quite literally mad. Mad—maybe that was why she had no friends. Everyone in St. Tropez thought she was slightly mad; she herself thought it a miracle that she wasn't, in fact, insane. If only everyone knew what she had been through during the war, perhaps they would be more friendly towards her. She had no friends of her own age, nor indeed of any age; and men friends, as Aunt Brigitte said, were all a waste of time. "All that giggling and gossiping, going to cafés and dances. You have responsibilities, *chérie*—no time for such nonsense."

As she stared out to sea Agathe began to daydream. Visions of a soft meadow came to mind, where wildflowers grew in great tangles and a gurgling stream ran nearby; there she wandered hand in hand with a friend, a lover perhaps, sharing hopes and dreams and confidences. Not that Agathe liked men, they frightened her. Only with Julian did she feel she could come into her own. The unattainable Looks Brooks. Unattainable, like all her dreams.

4

"*D*ominique. *Dominique!* Regarde ici." *The girl, pigtails flying, raced* along the cobbled back street of St. Tropez, excitedly waving a piece of paper. "Dominique. Stop—*please,* you must see this," she called breathlessly to her friend, who stubbornly strode on ahead, a knapsack full of books resting easily on her sturdy shoulders.

"Not now, Genevieve," Dominique said impatiently. "You know I'm late for class and Madame will give me hell again. *Merde*, that's the second time this week M'sieur has kept me late for talking in his science lesson. I think he must hate me." She increased her pace as Genevieve, two months younger than the sixteen-year-old, and a few inches shorter, hurried to keep up with her.

"Look, Dominique. Look at this, please, you are *such* a stubborn idiot," the girl said firmly, thrusting her prized scrap of paper in front of Dominique's enormous green eyes. "They have been giving these away outside the school, at the patisserie and the butcher's shop and all over the village. Some Americans have come down from Paris and they are looking for someone—" she said secretively, her freckled face attempting a look of mystery—"someone like you."

"Oh, Genevieve, you're *so* naive." Dominique broke into a run as she heard the church clock strike three and realized she should already be in her leotard, ballet shoes and tights. Madame Agathe would even now be flouncing into the chilly practice room, dispensing sarcastic comments to the disgruntled group of twelve schoolgirls who all strived for the perfection which, alas, Madame Agathe had never achieved herself. But Agathe thought Dominique showed some promise, and she encouraged her constantly, helped her, grilled her, instructed her, perhaps seeing in her the young ballerina she herself might have been if it hadn't been for the war.

"If you won't look at it yourself, then I'll read it to you," squealed Genevieve, keeping up with her taller friend's strides with difficulty.

"Okay, okay, I'm listening," said Dominique, "but read it fast, Genevieve. Between Madame Agathe and M'sieur Millet, they'll finish me off. *Merde—les salopes.*"

"Listen." Genevieve blushed at Dominique's language, although she had heard it often enough before.

" 'Wanted to audition for American film: classical ballet and jazz-trained girls aged between fifteen and twenty. Must have some acting experience and be willing and able to travel to the United States to work. Bring dance clothes, sheet music of one classical and one modern dance piece. Ten A.M., Saturday, March fifth. Théâtre de Comédie, boulevard des Anglais, Nice.' "

"Tiens!" Dominique stopped dead in her tracks and, snatching the paper from her friend, stared at it in wonder. "Do you think this is some sort of joke, Genevieve? Maybe the boys from the parish school have printed this up to make us look like fools. We all turn up in our tutus full of great expectations, and that bunch of spotty creeps will be waiting there to giggle at us." Most of the young girls who lived in St. Tropez hated boys, or at least pretended they did. Refined young ladies had nothing in common with uncouth teenage louts, avoiding them as much as possible. Boys seemed interested only in *boules,* darts, football and wrestling with each other in the meadows of the surrounding Provençal countryside. Girls were a total mystery to them—just boring fragile creatures to be teased mercilessly.

"I don't really think it is a joke," Genevieve insisted. "Dominique, you simply *must* go!"

"Genevieve!" gasped Dominique. Her eyes were sparkling, her long hair, tied into a ponytail, glistened like black swansdown in the fading afternoon sun, her sensual gamine face radiated excitement. "This is *fantastic—amazing!* An *audition*—right here in the south of France."

"Well, not exactly right here," Genevieve pointed out pragmatically, peering again at the paper. "To get to Nice will take the best part of four hours on the bus. I suppose you could take the train, but Papa says it was only Hitler who managed to get the trains running on time, and that now they're even *more* hopeless than they were before the war."

"Never mind, never mind, never mind," cried Dominique, breaking into a run. "Even if I have to leave at *five* in the morning, I *must* go to this audition. Genevieve, *quelle chance!* I could meet Gene Kelly or Fred Astaire! I could even become a *Star.* Well, maybe," she said as her friend giggled. "Look, I must run now, I'm so late—but thank you, Genevieve. Thanks!"

In the cloakroom Dominique quickly changed. Hearing Agathe already instructing the dance class, she burst in flushed and rosy, her heart pounding with excitement at the prospect of her audition, and was scolded for her lateness. She tried to execute the complicated pirouettes and *jetés* that Madame Agathe was showing her pupils, but she couldn't keep her mind focused. It kept returning again and again to the audition. A Hollywood movie! Hollywood! America! Dominique had often fantasized about becoming a Hollywood star. No matter that she was French: so were Leslie Caron and Zizi Jeanmaire!

Sweat trickled down the neck of her tight cotton leotard, and her legs felt hot and sticky in their thick lisle tights.

"Pay attention, Dominique," Madame Agathe snapped, banging her slender silver-topped cane down hard on the parquet floor. She always carried this cane when she led the class; it gave the impression of authority which she needed to control the group of overexcitable adolescent girls.

Most of the girls made fun of Agathe behind her back—of her white face and hair, her gaunt body in its shapeless clothes, her eyes which possessed such a fierce flame of discipline that they seemed to burn right into anyone who made a mistake.

"Those who can, *do.* Those who can't, teach," Genevieve had once told Dominique—another of her father's observations. Dominique now stood, head bent, chastened because Madame Agathe was giving her a tongue-lashing for lack of spontaneity, in front of the whole class.

"I'm sorry, Madame," Dominique said, close to tears. Madame could be very cruel when she wanted to be, her criticisms always hitting the mark with brutal accuracy. "I'm very sorry."

"I want you to stay behind after class, Dominique," Madame said brusquely. "We will go over this *again*—the solo you were *supposed* to have practiced this weekend. Obviously your ballet homework has not been done, so you will have to do it *now.*"

"Yes, Madame," Dominique mumbled, exchanging a quick look with another girl, who shrugged sympathetically.

Sometimes Madame's tongue was so razor sharp that the girls joked that if she swallowed it she'd slit her own throat. There was no doubt that Madame could be quite a tartar. Her quiet, inhibited exterior concealed a savage temper and a fury with life which lurked just beneath the surface.

At last the class was over and the other girls filed out. Dominique stood alone and silent, while Agathe lectured her and then went on to demonstrate some of the steps. Suddenly Agathe showed an infinite patience; kindness radiated from her eyes, which were no longer burning points of suppressed rage, but warm and understanding.

Dominique felt a wave of pity mingled with affection for this woman whom the village children all rudely called "the mad old maid," and she decided to confide her plans for Saturday's audition. Excitedly she told Agathe how much she wanted to go.

"*Chérie,* this is very, very exciting," Agathe breathed, a faint pink flush coloring her pale cheeks. "Certainly it is a very important opportunity. You must be good. You must be more than good. Dominique, you must be the absolute best."

"Yes, Madame." The girl nodded, her eyes bright, her legs suddenly no longer tired. "Will you help me?" she blurted out. "I need to practice much more, I know I do. Oh, Madame—" she looked at Agathe, her young face flushed and joyful—"Oh, Madame, I want this—I want so much to go to Hollywood—can you imagine?"

"Yes, yes, I will help you," Agathe said simply. "I will rehearse you now and for the next three days before the audition, and you must practice at home too," she said sternly. "It will take much hard work, but you, more than all the others in class, have the talent, the potential to succeed."

"Thank you, Madame, oh, thank you," Dominique breathed, thrilled by her teacher's rare praise. "I will kill myself working, I promise you."

"And I will take you to the audition myself," Agathe said, looking fondly at her lovely young pupil. "We will work very hard now, *chérie,* and on Saturday morning you will be prepared, and . . ." She paused, her dark eyes twinkling now with an unaccustomed pleasure. "And you will be the best, Dominique. You will be given the part, you will go to Hollywood—and who knows, perhaps I will even go with you."

Dominique was so overexcited after her afternoon of intensive rehearsal and about the upcoming audition, that after an early supper with her parents and three young brothers, she took her bicycle and rode into the center of St. Tropez.

The sign "Gaston's Glacés" emblazoned in purple on a small yellow ice cream wagon looked so inviting that she propped her bicycle carelessly against a tree in the Place des Lices, and sauntered over to investigate.

"I'll have a *framboise,*" she said, fishing for change in the pocket of her shorts. "Double, please."

"It's on the house," Gaston said, not only giving her an extra scoop of ice cream, but also the benefit of perfect white teeth in a beautifully tanned face.

She smiled back. "Merci, *M'sieur.*"

He admired her gamine face, sparkling green eyes and long tanned legs. She had an aristocratic accent, but her attitude seemed modern and free— not like the snobbish young tourists from England and Scandinavia who usually bought from him.

Gaston instantly decided that she was a prize not to be missed and that there was no time to lose. He quickly locked the door of his wagon and matched her stride as she wandered into the tiny square.

"I'm Gaston Girandot," he volunteered. "I own the joint."

"So, I gathered—I'm Dominique du Frey," she said, licking at the melting pink ice cream.

"Daughter of the banker?"

"Yes," she said, watching him slyly out of the corners of her slanting eyes. *Tiens,* but he was very good-looking, better-looking than any of the boys at school.

"My parents have a patisserie on the Avenue Bazoche," he volunteered.

"I think our cook buys from them sometimes," said Dominique, looking up at him through thick black lashes with an expression which was both challenging and shyly sensual.

"Would you like a cup of coffee?" He felt gauche for the first time in his nineteen years. Because of his good looks, girls usually made advances to him, but it was different with this one. She was cool and, although very young, seemed quite sure of herself.

"Yes," smiled Dominique, "I'd love one."

In the outdoor café, drinking espresso and smoking Gauloises, they talked until nearly ten o'clock, when Dominique, noticing the time, jumped up. "Ooh, I must go, I have to practice my ballet again tonight. Madame wants me to practice three times a day. She says practice makes perfect."

She smiled her kitten smile at him. "Will I see you again?" he stammered.

"Of course," said Dominique, wise beyond her years. "You know we will, but probably after my audition. I must work like a dog now." She extended a slim hand, *"Au revoir,* Gaston Girandot."

He kissed her hand solemnly, gazing into her face as if he had just discovered a priceless treasure.

"Tomorrow—Tango Beach, eleven o'clock?"

She nodded shyly. "Maybe, Gaston—maybe, but I cannot promise." With a smile that took his breath away, she climbed onto her bike and pedaled off into the darkness, leaving him with stars in his eyes and a thumping heart.

That night, lying in her bed, Dominique thought about the beautiful boy and about the power she felt she had had over him during their brief meeting. Power. Power over men. It was an exhilarating sensation that she was experiencing for the first time. She didn't particularly like the local boys but this one was so good-looking, with his dazzling white smile, tanned face and tight black curls that she thought she might make him the exception.

The following day, after a hot morning of vigorous ballet practice with Madame Agathe, she decided to go down to Pampellone for a swim and some sunbathing. She pedaled fast over the two miles of hilly road outside central St. Tropez, arriving in good time at the beach and she wondered if Gaston would be there. There seemed to be only a few people on Tango Beach. The pale yellow sand was clean, and several sailboats and motorboats zoomed about on the sea, which was flat and invitingly deep blue. About a dozen empty wooden sunbeds covered by yellow-and-white-striped mattresses were lined up on the beach waiting hopefully for occupants. She paid the mahogany-skinned beach boy a few francs, and he settled her up near the sea, stuck a parasol in the sand, and brought her a small slatted wooden table on which he set a glass of Coca-Cola. She took off the short cotton sundress which she was wearing over her bikini and lay back on the mattress, letting the glorious rays fall on her body. Closing her eyes behind her sunglasses she was almost asleep when she felt a gentle touch on her shoulder.

"*Bonjour,*" said Gaston Girandot, squatting down on the sand beside her, his brown muscular body gleaming with Ambre Solaire, a shy grin on his face.

"*Bonjour,* Gaston," she smiled up at him through her glasses.

"What a perfect day," he said.

"Yes, it was so lovely after my practice I decided I needed a swim."

"So what are you waiting for?" said the boy. "Come on, Lazy Bones—get up, let's hit the water. I'll race you."

Laughing and protesting, Dominique allowed Gaston to pull her up, and they dashed into the warm inviting Mediterranean where they swam and frolicked until they were both starving. In the tiny thatched outdoor restaurant where bamboo tables with yellow checked cloths were laid for lunch, the sun filtered through the bamboo blinds which protected the diners from its fiercest rays, throwing striped shadows across Dominique's and Gaston's smiling faces. They ate salade niçoise, provençal chicken with fried potatoes, and *tarte tatin,* washed down with a robust Beaujolais Nou-

veau. They talked and giggled all through lunch, watched over benignly by
the portly proprietor who had known them both since they'd been children.

"Why have we never met before?" asked Dominique, feeling completely
satiated by the delicious lunch, and exhilarated by Gaston's company.

"I've been at college in Aix-en-Provence for the last three years," he said.
"Before that we probably saw each other here—at the beach." He bent his
head until it almost touched hers. "I didn't notice you then, nor you me—
but if you'd looked the way you do now I certainly would have."

Dominique blushed and lowered her eyes. She was experiencing such
new exciting feelings with this boy, that later when he brought his mattress
next to hers on the beach and they were lying half asleep, their bare
shoulders almost touching, Dominique knew that she would like to see
more of Gaston Girandot—much much more.

In her chaste, narrow bed Agathe was unable to sleep. She was too excited
by Dominique's news. She had herself read one of the notices which had
been distributed in the village and had experienced her own quiet thrill.
When Dominique had spoken to her after class, she had felt that the
forthcoming audition might be the key to an escape from her own dull life.

If the girl won the audition, if she were given the part in a Hollywood
film, *she,* Agathe, could go with her. Why not? Dominique's parents had
heavy responsibilities. Her father was a locally important banker. Her
mother was tied down by three young sons, and visibly pregnant again.
If... if... *if*...

Agathe was too agitated to sleep, the possibilities of the future too exciting. She turned on her light and took out her scrapbook to gaze lovingly
at the handsome face of Julian Brooks. Would she meet him if they went to
Hollywood? Maybe not; he was a British star, who worked in England. She
knew he had never been to America. But the joy, the freedom to leave her
bourgeois and claustrophobic life in St. Tropez, to go out into the real
world, to go to America! Everyone wanted to go to America. The golden
land of opportunity, where all men—and women—were equal. Agathe
would find friends there, a new life—she knew she would.

The past years had not been kind to Agathe. Nothing in her life of
freedom could ever minimize the damage of her time in that cellar, and
after that her years in L'Éléphant Rose. Watching the traitorous whores
fraternizing with the monsters who had destroyed her family, her life, her
future, had been purgatory. But worst of all was her deep sense of self-
loathing.

She felt that she was hideously ugly. Whenever she looked into a mirror and saw the gaunt white spectre reflected there, she remembered how she had been as a young girl. Almost as pretty as Dominique. Well made, a little plump, with dark sparkling eyes and blue-black glossy hair. Pretty and far more talented. She had never been vivacious, but her quiet charm had its own appeal.

It was gone now forever. All of it—her talent, her looks, her appeal. She had heard the whispered taunts of the village children: "Old maid." "Ugly witch." She saw her aunt's disapproval of her. Brigitte's pursed lips and lack of communication with Agathe revealed clearly enough what her aunt thought of her. But Agathe had no money. What else could she do? Where could she go? Only into her imagination, where she walked in fragrant meadows, hand in hand with laughing friends, or with Julian Brooks—only there was she always happy.

Unless Dominique du Frey could win that audition . . . and perhaps give her the key to a new life in America.

5

I nès had returned to visit Paris nearly two years after the end of the war,
and found sadly that she cared little anymore for the beloved city of her
birth. She thought her fellow countrymen brusque and cold, although she
had to admit they had reason to be. So many of them seemed bitter and
resentful about the long Nazi occupation, and now they faced a relentless
day-to-day struggle to rebuild their broken lives. All seemed involved only
with themselves and their families. Food, a national obsession, was still in
very short supply, although the grand hotels and better shops were well
stocked and open for business as usual.

After her years in London, Inès felt as if she didn't really belong in
Paris. She missed the English sense of humor, missed her pretty flat in
Mayfair. She revisited a few familiar haunts to look for old friends, but
her only real friends had been Yves, Gabrielle and the rest of her "family" from L'Éléphant Rose. When she went to the old familiar club in
Pigalle she found the building shuttered and locked with an *A Vendre*
sign on it.

She made inquiries of the neighbors and learned, to her horror, that
Gabrielle and many of the girls who had worked at the club had been
condemned as traitors and collaborators when Paris was liberated. They
had been publicly humiliated in a nearby square by having their heads
shaved, being stoned and abused by the local patriots, and then ostra-

cized completely. All of them seemed to have vanished without a trace, and Inès' efforts to track them down were fruitless.

Why hadn't the neighbors and Free French defended them and put the record straight? Told them of the sacrifices these women had made during the war? It was too unfair. They had all done so much for the Resistance from the headquarters at L'Éléphant Rose, and to be punished in such a brutal way was hideously unjust.

But Paris still held so many memories for Inès, both good and bad, that she found it difficult to tear herself away. Just wandering through Montmartre, Pigalle and the glorious narrow streets of the Rive Gauche brought a rush of nostalgia. She knew that there was nothing left for her here anymore, but she felt she couldn't leave just yet.

One day she sat at one of the rickety iron tables outside the Café Deux Magots, which was packed to capacity. Tourists, laughing students and a sprinkling of old men wearing the shabby black berets indigenous to France, and who could nurse a cup of coffee or a glass of red wine for hours, all sat watching the comings and goings at the Boulevard Saint-Germain. Inès sipped at a glass of cognac, remembering that day when she'd sat almost at this very same table and been propositioned by the odious Italian General Umberto Scrofo. What would have been her fate if she had not kept that fateful appointment which had ended in his death?

Would she have been condemned as a traitor and sent away in disgrace? Or would she have simply remained in Paris working as one of Yves' girls? Yves. At the thought of him her heart lurched in spite of herself. Did one ever get over the infatuations of youth? It had been nearly three years now since he'd left her, but whenever she thought of him it was still with a pang.

She stared out into the busy street, and her eyes suddenly focused on a thin man, a grubby beret perched sloppily on his untidy brown curls, a cigarette hanging from his lips, who was walking slowly down the Boulevard Saint-Germain. It couldn't be, it couldn't.

"Yves! *Mon Dieu,* Yves!" Inès jumped up, the people around looking at her irritably as she stumbled through the tables and chairs to the street and grabbed his arm. It was almost as if she'd willed him to appear.

"Yves—it's you—it's really you!" Inès' eyes shone, her face was flushed and glowing as the man swung around and turned to face her.

"My God—Inès!" Yves smiled slowly and she noticed that his teeth had become yellowed from too many Gauloises, and there were deep lines around his eyes.

"What the hell are you doing in Paris?"

"I came to see the sights," said Inès breathlessly, "visit old friends—

except that there don't seem to be any old friends around anymore. But now I've found you." She saw that his cheeks were gaunt and unshaven, and that the collar of his blue shirt was grubby. "D'you have time for a cup of coffee with me?" she asked eagerly. "I'd love to talk to you."

"Of course," he said. "I don't have anything else to do. I have all the time in the world, *chérie.*"

They weaved their way back to her table, and he ordered coffee and Armagnac for both of them.

"But you'll have to pay for it." He winked at her wryly. "I'm a little short today."

"Of course," Inès smiled brightly. "So tell me about yourself, Yves. What are you doing? Are you still with Stella?"

He shook his head, lighting another cigarette from the stub of the old one. His hands were shaking, his fingernails dark with dirt, and the index finger of his right hand was deep yellow with nicotine stains. Yves had always been extremely fastidious, and Inès was startled by his transformation.

"Stella—poof—she's gone."

"Oh." Inès didn't know whether to feel a frisson of triumph over an old rival. Certainly this Yves, this man in the shabby overcoat with a three-day growth of stubble, was by no means the handsome dandy she'd always remembered him to be. "Why did she go?" she asked.

"A better offer." He laughed bitterly. "A better *macrou.* Someone who gave her more thrills in bed."

In spite of herself Inès felt herself blushing. Yves had always been a superb lover if nothing else.

"That's ridiculous—you were wonderful in bed—why should she leave for that?"

"*Merci, chérie,* but *malheureusement* a little problem arose when our great country was liberated." There was no mistaking the bitterness in his voice now, and she saw sadness in his eyes as he threw back his brandy and signaled to the white-aproned waiter for another.

"Do you really want to know what happened to me, Inès?"

"Yes," she whispered, "I do—tell me—please, Yves."

"You won't like it," he said bluntly.

"I don't care—tell me—tell me everything."

"When Stella and I came back here from London in 1944 the war was not yet over, you remember—although Paris had been liberated by the Americans. We found a flat, near here actually, and Stella went back to work. She was a good worker but times were bad, food was short." He paused and Inès leaned forward to hear his voice, which had become quieter. "I got involved in the black market. I was doing it in London, you remember, and I still had some contacts here."

"Yes, I know." Inès took a sip of brandy, listening intently, watching Yves' dead eyes growing more impassioned as he continued his story.

"One night a truckload of champagne was coming into Paris from Epernay. I'd arranged with my contacts to buy it—ten million francs, almost all the money I had, but New Year's Eve was on the way and there was a growing demand for all the best champagnes and wines; everyone wanted to celebrate. Don't forget that even though people had suffered during the war, many of them made a great deal of money from it."

"Yes, I know that. Go on, Yves," she coaxed. He'd stopped, the pallor had returned to his face and his hands were now shaking badly. She pushed her Armagnac across the table to him, watching as he drained it immediately.

"I was supposed to meet Gino, you remember Gino? He was one of my most trusted boys, at eleven o'clock on the Quai d'Orsay. He was driving the truck, I had the money. I gave him the cash, then I drove the truck on to my warehouse. I distributed the cases to the clubs and restaurants through my boys—and then I went home—"

He stopped again and Inès saw it was becoming more difficult for him to continue.

"Then what happened?" she coaxed. He didn't answer, lighting another cigarette, his hands as frail and shaking as an old man's. Both their glasses were empty, and she motioned to the waiter to bring more brandy.

"I don't know why I'm telling you all this." He gripped her hand suddenly, his bloodshot eyes those of a frightened animal. "You won't like it, Inès."

"I don't care, Yves—please—please tell me—you must—maybe I can help you."

"Help me—ha!—that's rich—that's very funny indeed." The waiter brought the brandies and Yves downed his in one gulp. His hands stopped shaking and he continued. "Three nights later, while Stella and I were asleep, they came for me."

"Who—who came for you?" whispered Inès.

He shrugged. "Them—the boys—the mob—who knows? It was a set-up, and I was the patsy. They dragged me off in the middle of the night." His voice dropped to a whisper and tears began to roll down his face. "They took me to a warehouse—somewhere near Les Halles I think it was, I could smell the stink of the fish." He stopped, the muscles in his neck quivering.

"And then," Inès prompted quickly.

"The bastards accused me of watering down the fucking champagne. They accused me of fixing it to make a bigger profit. Do you know what,

Inès? It wasn't champagne at all in those bottles, it was some kind of cheap colored fizzy water. Someone—and to this day I don't know who—palmed three hundred cases of fake champagne off on me and they blamed me— the scum blamed *me,* Inès."

He was sobbing quietly, unashamedly now.

"So what did they do to you?" Inès almost didn't want to hear the answer.

"Guess?" He looked up at her with a cynical smile. "What's the worst thing you could possibly do to a pimp?"

"I—I don't know," said Inès, mesmerized by this pathetic wreck of a man whom she'd once loved so desperately.

"They castrated me, *chérie.*" He put his face very close to hers and grinned horribly. "They made me into a eunuch."

"Oh my God, Yves—no, it's not possible." Inès felt faint as Yves' calloused hands clutched hers tightly on the iron table.

"They cut off my balls and they told me that was the *lightest* penalty that they usually gave to someone who tried to doublecross them. Emasculate them, turn them into a *nothing.*"

Inès' head was swimming. This couldn't be—this couldn't have happened to Yves. Yves who had lived for making love, who had taught her everything she knew about it.

"*Mon pauvre* Yves, I don't know what to say—I'm so sorry, so terribly sorry." She was crying now, and took out her handkerchief to wipe her eyes, oblivious to the curious stares of people at other tables.

"Don't be sorry, *chérie.* I hadn't exactly been Prince Charming in my life, I probably deserved it."

"*No! No! No one* could deserve that," said Inès in horror. "It's barbaric— did you go to the police?"

"Police?" He laughed bitterly. "You must be joking, *chérie,* they knew what my game was. They despise black marketeers. I got as much sympathy from them as Adolf Hitler would have got if he'd been bleeding to death in a concentration camp. They took me to the hospital, of course, sewed me up. It's not serious, you know—being a eunuch. It doesn't endanger your life or anything, but it sure as hell fucks up your sex life." He laughed again, a hollow dead sound, and lit another Gauloise. "A dead cock. A neuter. It makes you a laughingstock, but people pity you, too."

"So what did you do? What do you do now? How do you live?" Inès stammered, her face flushed and hot.

"I have a few friends left," he said. "I do odd jobs, this and that, betting on the horses, fencing a few bits and pieces, nothing too expensive, of course. I'm okay. I'm fine." He smiled, trying to reassure her, and Inès could see that the Armagnac had done its work in making him more confident. He had obviously become completely dependent on alcohol. Now he sat up straight, his hands no longer trembling, his gaze direct. "Stella left, of course, like a poxy rat deserting a ship—I can't say I blamed her. She liked a good fuck, did Stella, and she couldn't get it from me. Well, *chérie*—that was more than two years ago—I suppose we all have to play the cards that fate deals us—that was a shitty hand for a *mic* to get but I've coped with it. I've tried. What about you, have the gods been good to you?"

"Oh—I'm—well, I'm fine actually," mumbled Inès, her mind still reeling from his revelations. "Pretty good, really."

"Got any good clients?" he asked. "Rich mugs?"

"Yes, oh, yes—very good—I mean—yes, they're all right." Inès felt stifled, even though it was cool outside the café.

"I bet none of them can do this," exclaimed Yves and he flicked his tongue into his mouth with the burning cigarette on it, closed his lips and stared at Inès with the wide-eyed comical look that had so entranced her when she was a little girl. As she watched in dismay, two long puffs of smoke came out of Yves' ears.

Inès felt she had to escape. She wanted to run—run like the wind. She wanted to go back to her hotel and weep bitter tears for her erstwhile lover, who smiled, pleased with himself as he stubbed out the damp cigarette and looked to her for approval. She smiled weakly and he grinned back.

"Good, *chérie,* that's good. You always were a clever little *poule de luxe,* Inès, one of the best, you deserve to do well."

Suddenly Inès wanted to leave Paris right now. She felt sick, dirty, sullied. She wanted to cry for this sad little man she had loved so much, for the friends she had lost. As if reading her thoughts Yves leaned towards her, brushing her cheek briefly with dry lips.

"*Au revoir, chérie,*" he said briskly, arranging the beret on his graying curls. "I have to go now. Thanks for the drink." He stood up, the sun shining on his lined face, and Inès could see clearly how much he'd changed, how the years had taken their toll. "Good luck, Inès."

"*Au revoir,* Yves," she whispered. "Good-bye."

He tipped his beret, and as he walked off down the Boulevard Saint-Germain, his shabby overcoat flapping around his thin body, Inès silently thanked God that her heart was no longer in Paris, that her life was in England now.

The next day Inès stood outside the Ritz Hotel in the Place Vendôme, staring up for one last time at the window of the room where she had killed

Umberto Scrofo. She was on her way to the airport back to London, and she knew now that Paris held nothing for her but sad, bad memories.

During the next few years in London Inès became more and more disenchanted with her life of prostitution, even though her clients were all rich and reasonably attractive. The frightened, ignorant teenager had matured into a sophisticated, chic woman of the world who suspected that true love existed only in novels and women's magazines. The pain of Yves' betrayal had never really healed and she had not found a man to inspire feelings of truly belonging to someone body and soul.

As the years passed and her savings grew, Inès gradually eliminated most of her clients, keeping only a few of her most powerful and influential customers. Apart from Viscount Benjie, for whom she had a special affection, a series of mentors had kept her—in particular three rich, middle-aged Englishmen. One was an aristocrat who had come out of what he called a "good war" with a chestful of medals to prove it; the other two were more bourgeois men of the City, securely married industrialists who between them appeared to own half the home counties.

They had given Inès money—though not an enormous amount, since "old" English money is never thrown around by those who possess it. But what they had given her that was infinitely more precious than cash, expensive trinkets, or the occasional visit to Deauville, Cannes or New York, was knowledge—an understanding of politics, of stocks, bonds, equities and market prices. They had imparted secret share tips to her, and insider advice on futures. An overheard phrase in a business telephone conversation at her flat, an artfully veiled question or two from her, and she would call her stockbroker to buy coffee beans, nickel, tin, gold or silver. Knowledge is power, and Inès learned fast. Her portfolio grew, as with a shrewd Frenchwoman's understanding of financial matters she made it her business to protect her future.

Inès became resigned to never finding her own man, to never falling in love. She supposed it was her fate never to settle down in security with a safe husband and two-point-three children. One day soon, however, she would have enough money to stop working and to retire. What would she do with herself then? It was a thought she did not like to dwell on. Her flat was filled with expensive, beautiful objects, and revealed no clue to her profession. But there was no one to admire her pretty things. No one to share her life when she would finally end her "career."

Inès had felt little emotion for any man since Yves—only a vague fondness for them, an almost niecelike attitude. To her, men were all the same:

mostly selfish, sexual animals. The more they used her for their pleasure, the less she felt for them. Week after week, month after month, year after year, as she plied her sexual trade, she yearned for a romantic love which, in her heart, she believed did not exist.

She had met many eligible men—young men, handsome men, clever and ambitious men, some with great futures. None of them had moved her one iota. She tried desperately to fall in love, to feel some small part of the passion, ecstasy and joy which she'd known with Yves, but she felt nothing. Sometimes she wondered cynically if it was Yves' magic tricks which had so entranced her and that at heart she was still eleven years old.

Then one afternoon she went to a matinée performance of *Pygmalion* at the Aldwych Theatre. There on the stage was a tall handsome actor with curved black eyebrows and a face like an archangel. His dark hair was severely brushed back, tortoiseshell spectacles were perched on his aristocratic nose, and a deerstalker hat sat on his head at a jaunty angle. From her seat in the stalls, surrounded by the rustle of chocolate wrappings and the excited murmur of the matinée matrons, she could sense his innate sensitivity spiced with roguish masculinity and humor.

His name was Julian Brooks, Looks Brooks, the Idol of the Odeons, as he was known in the tabloid press, and not since Yves had Inès seen a man who so captured her heart and her imagination. When he was on stage, Julian entranced her with his charisma and waspish sexy charm. Her eyes never left him for a second. She perceived in him a quality of warmth and wonderful fun that she knew was real, and not just the actor playing a part. Inès knew that she had to meet this man.

Inès did not miss a single matinée performance of *Pygmalion* for the remainder of its run, and she made it her business to find out every scrap of information she could about the man who had started to inhabit so many of her waking thoughts.

6

*A*s *Julian became a bigger and more glittering star, Phoebe had grad-*ually changed into that kind of dreadful snob which only a middle-class Englishwoman can be. She loved two things beyond all else: money and social position. Her main interest in Julian's career, other than landing herself a plum part, was the position in society and the wealth which it could bring them. She rarely spoke to any of the cast or crew with whom Julian worked, choosing only to speak to stars and important directors. The artistic side was of no interest to her; she couldn't have cared less whether her husband was starring as Othello or Charley's Aunt. She loved being Mrs. Julian Brooks, close friend of the Oliviers and the Redgraves. She loved the life of a star's wife: the society rounds of Royal Ascot, Wimbledon, the fourth of June at Eton, Cowes, Henley; charity balls and weekends at country houses with the aristocratic and the famous, as well as gleaming black limousines and accounts with all the best couturiers and shops. Fueled by Julian's success, her acting ambitions came into full flower when she had forced him to cast her in his plays. She would have made his life quite intolerable had he not given in to her. Appearing on stage with Julian gave her even more cachet with her friends, and naturally she always insisted on having above-the-title billing: not just a star's wife, but a star in her own right.

But at this moment she was absolutely furious with Julian. She had in fact been fuming ever since he'd categorically refused to allow her to play Eliza Doolittle in *Pygmalion.*

At thirty-five, she looked at least a dozen years too old to play the part of the waiflike cockney flowergirl, not to mention the indeterminate number of excess pounds which gave her the look of a well-padded matron.

"I'm perfect for the part, *perfect,* you always *said* I was," Phoebe yapped. Lipstick was smeared on her front teeth, and her heavy makeup did nothing more than bring the deepening lines of discontent on her face into sharper focus. The henna which she used so liberally to brighten her fading locks glowed garishly in the thin afternoon light which filtered into Julian's dressing room at Pinewood Studios. He was in the last stages of shooting *The Buccaneer,* another swashbuckler for Didier Armande, and in the middle of intense casting and preproduction sessions for a stage production of *Pygmalion.* Exhausted after two long months on such a physically demanding movie, he had been trying in vain to take a nap on the daybed in his dressing room when Phoebe burst in, dismissing his dresser with a typically waspish "Get out. I don't care if he *is* asleep—I'm his bloody wife!"

"Phoebe, for God's sake," Julian pleaded, looking up bleary-eyed at his once desirable wife, now an outraged, overweight virago who stood before him, hands on hips.

"How *could* you have cast that *slut* Louise James as Eliza?" she said, spitting venom. "She's *hideous.* She can't act and she's *far* too old!"

"She's twenty," Julian said simply. "She won a Tony award on Broadway last year, she's been acting since she was eleven, and, what's more, she happens to be very pretty."

"*Pretty?*" Phoebe screeched. "You call that baggage pretty? She's got a face like a . . . like a cheap china doll. *I'm* your wife. How about some loyalty to me, *me!*"

"Phoebe, please. Please do be reasonable." Julian was trying hard not to lose his composure, not to say his temper. He had an important emotional scene to play this afternoon, and Phoebe's rages were far from helpful. "You're just too old for Eliza, can't you see that, dear?"

"No, I bloody can't." She started to cry the crocodile tears which Julian had grown to know so well. "I'm the same age as Vivien. She plays young girls."

"Look in the damned *mirror,* for Christ's sake. It doesn't *lie,* you know. You're almost thirty-six. You *can't* play an eighteen-year-old, Phoebe, you just can't, and that's that."

"I *can,*" she wept. "Oh, Julian, *please please* let me. I'll lose some weight, I'll be so good . . . Look at my reviews for *Present Laughter*—they said I was enchantingly young and vibrant."

"That was several years ago, old thing." Julian knew he had to remain adamant; Phoebe was doing everything she could to manipulate him, and he couldn't allow the balance of power in their marriage to shift in her direction. God knows she tried all the time. It was always an uphill struggle, but he had to remain in control. He believed in the dominance of the male, and just as importantly, the strong professional standards he wanted maintained.

"Nearly five years ago, Phoebe," he went on, "and the role of Joanna was of a woman of the world. Eliza's almost a *child*. I'm sorry, but it's done now. I've cast Louise, and the announcements go out to the press tomorrow."

Phoebe stopped crying and looked at him warily. "I see," she sighed, wiping her smudged eyes with a mascara-stained handkerchief. "Just like that—humped and dumped. Thanks a bunch."

"Don't be so bloody ridiculous, Phoebe. You've got a damned good life. I try to give you *everything* you want. You've been in practically every one of my plays, but you're just not going to be in this one. So let's finish this stupid argument, and for God's sake let me get some sleep."

Phoebe thoughtfully fingered her huge Kashmiri sapphire-and-diamond ring from Garrard's, then adjusted her gold-and-pavé diamond choker from Van Cleef & Arpels and toyed with the buttons of her beige cashmere Jacques Fath couture suit. These were all too familiar signs to Julian that she was plotting something. He threw himself back on the couch with a sigh, his body craving rest. He'd been up since five that morning. Phoebe had insisted that they go to the opening of *Ring Around the Moon* the night before, and afterward to yet another of Binkie Beaumont's lavish parties. He had slept for only three hours and was shatteringly exhausted.

"I'm so tired, Phoebe," he said simply. "Would you mind leaving me now? I need a bit of a doze—got an important scene this afternoon."

"Oh, yes, I'll leave, all right," she said frostily, pulling on her beige suede gauntlet gloves trimmed with mink and shrugging her new sable jacket from Bergdorf Goodman of New York City over her hefty shoulders.

"I'm not exactly happy with you these days, Julian. I don't think I'm going to enjoy being around London while you're rehearsing with that talentless trollop."

Julian sighed again. What now? Which threatening ploy did she have in mind this time? Was this bitch never satisfied?

"Last night at the party Hermione was telling me that she wants to take a little trip," she went on. "I think I'll join her. I'm sure we'll have a lot of fun together; Hermione's so amusing."

"Wonderful, dear," Julian sighed, closing his eyes, praying that she would now leave. He heard the assistant director knocking at his leading lady's dressing room next door.

"Where will you and Hermione go?" he asked, more out of a sense of politeness than interest.

"Around the world," Phoebe snapped, striding to the door. "It's expensive, of course," she added with smug satisfaction. "About ten thousand pounds for the best hotels, restaurants and so on. But since I'll be bored being around here with you and that James girl, probably fucking like rabbits, I know you won't mind too much forking out. Oh, by the way—" she stopped at the opened door—"don't forget—you've promised me Ophelia. *That* I will never give up. *Never.*" She sailed out, slamming the door just as Julian's dresser appeared carrying his usual wake-up cup of espresso.

"Everything okay, guv?" he asked sympathetically, seeing the evident strain on Julian's face.

"Fine, Freddie, fine. Thanks, old boy. Tell Tim in makeup I'll be over in five minutes."

Ophelia my arse! he thought tossing down the bitter but reviving espresso, and pulling on his black leather boots. The way Phoebe looked now she'd be a more likely contender for Gertrude. Maybe even Gertrude's mother if there was such a part. He was in a black mood when he stomped into the makeup room, only to be greeted by a warm smile from his current leading lady.

That evening, after shooting had finally ended, Julian was a most welcome visitor in the dressing room of his gorgeous, pouting co-star, Rebecca Chamberlane. There he released all his anger and pent-up frustration, leaving them both so delightfully sated and fulfilled that their liaison continued right up until the movie was finished.

"*Jesus, what a bunch of dogs.*" *Bluey Regan leaned back in his seat in* the darkened auditorium of the old theater in Nice. He studied the lineup of forty-seven nervous teenage girls who huddled together on the stage in their skimpy black leotards, mended tights and shabby ballet shoes.

"Not a decent body among them," he muttered to Nicholas Stone, the talented young director who was leaning forward in the seat next to him, staring intently at the girls. He was whispering something rapidly to his secretary, who was writing as fast as her limited shorthand would allow her.

"They've got no *tits,* Nick," complained Bluey. "Not one of 'em has anything more than a thirty-two A-cup. *That's* going to look *real* great in an off-the-shoulder period gown, in glorious Technicolor, up there with Julian Brooks trying to act as if he wants to screw her brains out."

"Shut up, Bluey," Nick snapped. "Haven't you heard? We're doing the sixteenth, not the eighteenth century. She's supposed to be a princess and she'll be dressed in something loose. Just *forget* tits for a minute, if that's remotely possible for you. Just look for raw talent, photogenic faces, the innocent but sexy quality of these girls. If you don't want to watch, go for a walk, go get laid, go get lost! I'll weed 'em out myself."

"Yeah, well, remember, you're the Charlie who's gonna be directing her."

"Yeah, and I know what I'm doing," said Nick implacably. "If you stay, keep your mouth *shut,* Bluey. When I want your advice I'll ask for it, and tits are no big deal in this case."

"Okay, okay," Bluey said, slumping back in his seat. He looked again at the group of terrified girls, muttering one last disparaging remark loudly enough for Nick's French secretary to hear.

"Please do not forget, *Meestair* Regan, that we have only come out of a war—an occupation—less than nine years ago," the woman said frostily. "These young girls 'ad very leetle to *eat* when they were babies and that is why they are so small—the *contraire* of your well-fed *American* girls."

"Well, I guess a few good American steaks, fries and chocolate malts would fatten 'em up. Get 'em lookin' as good as Marilyn Monroe and Jane Russell quicker than you can say Metro fuckin' Goldwyn Mayer, right?" Bluey smiled lazily, offering the woman some chewing gum.

"Quite," said the Frenchwoman, refusing. "But I don't think any of these girls are quite that type of *mademoiselle.* They are all French—*typiquement française*—and you will find, very proud of it, *Monsieur!*" She turned away from him, unable to disguise her extreme dislike for Nick's leathery assistant.

A frail redhead in a burgundy leotard and tights which did nothing for her coloring stepped forward on stage, shyly handing her sheet music to the pianist. She performed the dance of the dying swan from *Swan Lake;* it was technically perfect but had no passion at all. Shaking his head, Nick Stone whispered to his secretary to dismiss her. She was the fifteenth applicant they had seen so far. This was going to be much harder than he'd anticipated.

An hour later, Bluey was snoring loudly when Nick nudged him excitedly. "Take a look at this one," he whispered. "Now *she* is much more the type I had in mind for Isabella. What do you think?"

Bluey sat up, watching with a critical eye as Dominique danced a fandango from *Carmen* with such style and barely suppressed sensuality that both men found themselves aroused and intrigued.

"Hot damn, she's *good,*" breathed Bluey. "Fucking good, eh, Nick? And getta load of those legs. Looks like the kid's got star quality if ever I saw it."

"Yeah, she sure does," Nick agreed, scribbling notes and tossing them into a folder. "She's sure one helluva dancer, helluva looker too. Maybe she's the one, Bluey."

"About time too," said Bluey. "At least this hasn't been a complete waste of time."

At the back of the auditorium, Agathe clasped her hands joyfully as she saw how well her pupil was performing. All of her extra rehearsals had paid off. If there was any justice in the world, Dominique must get the part, be off to Hollywood, away from this Provençal backwater. And with a little luck, Agathe would be going with her.

"Well, what d'you know." Bluey stared with mounting admiration at Dominique as she finished her second audition piece, a perfectly executed version of Eleanor Powell's tap dance from *Broadway Melody*.

She had thrown a short skirt around her black cotton leotard which accentuated her tiny waist and small, firm breasts. Her long hair was loosened and it seemed to float in the air like soft black tendrils around her flushed face.

All but five of the girls had been dismissed. They sat watching cross-legged in the wings, cardigans and shawls draped over their shoulders, grudgingly admitting to each other that Dominique was very good, far better than any of them. She was more than good. She had a magical presence, a powerful charisma, a sweet gamine quality which could change like quicksilver into smoldering sensuality.

Dominique had now finished, and stood flushed and shaking with nerves, in the center of the vast stage. She waited, trembling, as the two men approached her.

"Very nice—*very* nice indeed," Nick said. Since his recent success he had become partial to the suave Fred Astaire school of dressing. He wore cream gabardine slacks with an open-necked pink shirt and a navy blue polkadot cravat. Even with his black curly hair greased down, it still looked wild, accentuating his boyish good looks. At twenty-seven he now had two major movie hits under his belt in less than a year, and he was considered one of the hottest of Hollywood's new generation of directors.

Bobby Soxers in Space had been the teenage cult movie of 1953, grossing over twenty million dollars at the box office, and giving Nick his first taste of the critical acclaim which he'd longed for. His second movie, a screwball comedy, had done equally well with critics and audiences alike, although the original script had been fairly mediocre. But Nick had a magic touch with film. He understood and respected it, he revered it, he could see the whole film in his mind's eye before he even shot it. He was sizzling in Hollywood, MCCP's golden boy, Spyros Makopolis' favorite, and now for his third film they had given him the prize plum of the year to direct: *The Legend of Cortez*.

After shaking Dominique's hand, Nick handed her a stiff white card with his name engraved on it in bold black letters.

"Come and see me this afternoon at three o'clock at the Carlton Hotel in Cannes. Can you get there all right, honey?"

Dominique almost fainted. She barely managed a nod and a whispered "*Oui, Monsieur,* I can. May I bring my chaperone?" She nodded towards the dim figure of Agathe shrouded in gloom, far beyond the footlights.

"Of course." Nick smiled at her. She certainly was adorable. Sexy, fresh and sweet too. "Bring your mother and father, your grandmother and all your aunts and uncles too, if you want. We are going to talk business, young lady, and I think you're going to like what I have to say."

Dominique smoothed back her waist-length hair so that it framed the perfect oval of her face as she shyly looked up at Nick through her forest of lashes with green lynx eyes.

"*Merci,* M'sieur Stone," she whispered in a girlishly sexy voice, which both men immediately realized would be another major asset to her. But those eyes. Nick found himself entranced by them, and Bluey's experienced gaze roamed over her young body like a gourmet before a feast. Gorgeous—yes, she was gorgeous all right. A tasty young dish to set before a king—or in this case an explorer.

In the darkness of the auditorium Agathe smiled to herself. She sensed the reaction of the two men to her pupil but clenched her fists in spite of her pleasure in Dominique's performance. It was always the same with men. Show them a young, pretty girl and they turned to putty. Once a woman was no longer young, no longer pretty, no one would bother to give her a second glance. In spite of her good wishes for her young pupil, Agathe felt a twinge of jealousy. If it hadn't been for the war, that could have been her up there.

8

In the spring of 1954 an American film company came to Rome to shoot a frothy escapist movie featuring two famous stars of the thirties. Ramona Armande and Gregory Mendelson were playing a middle-aged couple who find both adventure and autumnal love in Rome, amid its romantic beauty and its broken stones.

The film company had been setting up lights and equipment in a small piazza for a scene between Ramona and Gregory. It was unusually hot, and the stifling room above the café, which had been provided for Ramona's relaxation, was becoming uncomfortably warm.

She decided to walk a little, to explore the endlessly fascinating side streets of Rome, where each shop seemed to hold even more eye-catching, exquisite treasures than the last. Ramona adored collecting, and the more bizarre the objects the better they could be shown to advantage in her exotic house in Acapulco. She looked the height of chic in a beautifully tailored cream linen belted suit from Balenciaga, and a large beige straw hat, laden with silk lilies of the valley, perched on her shining black hair. Dark sunglasses covered her famous amber eyes, but even with them the sun was so blindly strong in the piazza that she squinted against its brightness.

"Principessa, where are you going?" asked Tinto, the first assistant director, with a concerned expression on his permanently anxious face as he hurried after her.

"Don't worry, Tinto my dear." Ramona smiled in the charming manner with which she always managed to endear herself to the crew. "I'm just going for a little stroll down the shaded side of the Via Babuino. I shan't be gone for more than half an hour and by that time you should have finished lighting the set, *si?*"

"*Si, Principessa,*" smiled Tinto, admiring the slim straight-backed figure as she wandered off up the cobbled and sun-dappled street. She was still a beautiful woman, even though there was no question that she would ever see fifty again.

Ramona strolled slowly along the hot dusty street enjoying the faint breeze which gently ruffled her hair. Each little shop was a treasure trove of beautiful things, and she lingered in several of them, admiring an eighteenth-century painted lace fan with an ornate silver gilt handle, then a pair of 1920s emerald-and-diamond ear clips, and finally a beautifully sculpted bronze figure of a muscular youth throwing a discus. But it wasn't until she found herself outside the last shop in the street that she caught her breath. The ivory-and-ruby bracelet which lay on a black velvet cushion in the window was truly breathtaking. To her experienced eye it was of museum quality, with its sugarloaf cabochon rubies surrounded by brilliant-cut diamonds all set into a wide cuff of creamy ivory. Immediately intrigued, Ramona opened the door and stepped into the cool, darkened interior. An extremely ugly fat man who reminded her of a toad sat behind the glass counter examining a diamond bracelet through a loupe. He looked up at her, and as the bright sunlight from the street only illuminated her as a silhouette, he did not immediately recognize her.

"May I help you?" he inquired, his voice sounding harsh and uncultured. Ramona thought she detected the southern accent of a Neapolitan or a Sicilian, certainly not the refined tones of a Roman gentleman.

"Yes—the ivory bracelet in the window—I'd like to see it, please."

"*Prego*—sit down, *Signora.*" The man gestured towards a carved eighteenth-century bergère, which she noticed was of superb quality, like everything else in the shop.

Ramona looked around her admiringly at all the shelves and cabinets which were full of jewels, small enamel and gold boxes, carved figures and other objects d'art. Obviously he was a man of taste in spite of his grotesque and off-putting appearance and that curious rasping voice.

"There—it is ravishing, is it not?" He placed the cuff gently on a velvet pad, watching her carefully as Ramona reverently picked it up.

"Beautiful—it's absolutely stunning," she breathed, removing a glove and admiring the bracelet on her slim wrist. "Such quality. How much?"

"Ah ... for you, *Signora,* a very special price indeed," beamed the *antiquaire,* having recognized her when switching on the desk light. "Only ten million lire to you, *Signora.*"

"It's superb," breathed Ramona, "truly beautiful—ten million, you say?"

He nodded encouragingly. His tiny eyes were slits, his hands clasped across his imposing stomach. But Ramona noticed how the excellent quality and cut of his suit managed cleverly to disguise so much of his bulk, and that his watch and cufflinks were from Cartier.

"I have an idea," she said as she leaned forward, removing her sunglasses to give him the full benefit of the amber lynx eyes which had captivated so many audiences for more than three decades. Their magic obviously still worked, for she saw him swallow, and a faint pink tinge begin to suffuse his sallow complexion.

"This bracelet looks wonderful with this dress, don't you think?"

He nodded, quite captivated by the extraordinary glamour and mystery of the woman.

"We're in the middle of shooting a movie down in the Piazza Barbarini—" Ramona clasped his arm with her delicate scarlet-tipped fingers like an excited child. "Let me wear it in the next scene. The production manager will be there to see to the insurance and all of that sort of thing—and—" she positively glowed as she continued—"when we've finished filming this afternoon, *Oggi* is shooting a photo layout of me all around Rome. You know the sort of thing, throwing coins into the Fontana di Trevi, wandering around the Forum and the Piazza di Spagna. If I was wearing this bracelet, I should *insist* that the magazine give your shop a credit for it in the article—then perhaps the price might be a little less?" She smiled ingenuously, pleased with her little plan, and he couldn't help but smile back. She was certainly an enchanting woman. A woman of the world—no doubt at all about that—but with a childlike charm which he found quite irresistible.

He pretended to heave a great sigh and then shook his shiny bald head from side to side. "The Signora drives a hard bargain." He smiled. "But as it is you, Madame Armande, such a great, great star—" he gave a little bow in her direction and Ramona acknowledged it by inclining her head regally—"I can see no way in which I could refuse you—with one proviso, of course."

"Which is?" asked Ramona, unable to tear her eyes away from the glorious cuff and the diamonds which glittered brilliantly on it in the dim light.

"That I might be allowed to accompany the Signora on her trip around

Rome this afternoon, perhaps even to show her some sights that she has not yet seen—then perhaps—if she would permit—to have the honor of escorting her to dinner tonight at Taverna Livia?"

Ramona studied him. He would certainly be an unprepossessing escort—short, fat and ugly. But she found that he had a certain kind of charm, and obviously from the exquisite contents of his shop, he had an enormous knowledge of art and a great eye for beautiful things.

She was becoming bored by the fawning Italian gigolos who had found their way to her suite in the Grand Hotel. Bored too by the labored huffing and puffing of her co-star Gregory Mendelson during their occasional bouts of lovemaking. They had indulged in a torrid affair some years ago, when he had been a desirable stud and the idol of millions, but unfortunately time had been unforgiving, not only to his hair and waistline, but also to his sex drive. Although he'd made a valiant effort to satisfy Ramona in bed for old times' sake, their perfunctory couplings had become less than gratifying for them both.

"Very well." She inclined her head to him again. "I should be happy for you to accompany me—and delighted to accept your invitation to dinner." She glanced at her wristwatch. "Oh dear, now I must go—it's time for the filming to start, I mustn't be late. Won't you join me, *Signor?*"

Pulling a bunch of keys from his pocket and carefully locking the door of his little shop behind them, the jeweler followed Ramona out into the blistering Roman sunshine.

He picked her up at the Grand Hotel at nine o'clock. His car was an open black Lancia, and his portliness was again adroitly disguised in a midnight blue shantung suit from Caraceni. He was wearing a white silk shirt from the Burlington Arcade, and a fairly garish crimson tie. If it weren't for the ugliness of his face and body and the cloying cologne in which he seemed to have bathed, he would indeed have cut quite a *bella figura.* As it was, he complemented Ramona, who was elegance personified in a champagne lace cocktail dress which nipped her tiny waist into a handspan, and gave her a cleavage that Miss Marilyn Monroe would envy. Around her neck was a simple diamond necklace from Fulco, and on her wrist she wore the beautiful ivory-and-diamond bracelet. They made an arresting couple as they walked through the lobby of the hotel, and several people turned to stare in genuine admiration at Ramona's style and presence.

He couldn't help feeling pleased with himself. He had never gone out with a woman as ravishing and as famous as Ramona—in fact no beautiful or even pretty girls would even give him a second glance unless plenty of lire changed hands. But Ramona seemed not to care about his lack of height or looks. She seemed more interested in his knowledge of jewelry and pictures. As they drove in his open car through the streets towards the quieter outskirts of Rome, she covered her hair with a chiffon scarf and listened carefully to the replies he gave to her many questions.

Ramona was an excellent listener, a natural expert in finding out every detail about a person's past. With a subtle and well-chosen question or two, she tried hard to piece together her escort's life story. As they sat at a table outside the elegant restaurant in the balmy night air, sipping champagne from heavy Venetian glasses, Umberto Scrofo told Ramona Armande everything that he thought she should know about his past life.

Umberto had been an extremely lucky man. When the Mafia thugs had left him to fend for himself in the tiny rowboat off the coast of Calabria, it had been a moonlit night and the sea flat and calm. Without the aid of a compass, and with more luck than skill, he had managed to drift around the cape of Calabria, the southernmost part of the Italian mainland, and through the Straits of Messina. There he had been found floating by a fisherman out in his boat who had rescued him and taken him, half dead, to his home in a tiny Sicilian village. When Umberto had recovered he contacted an old army friend, not a member of the Cosa Nostra, who had, with the help of a few gold coins, taken him to Rome.

Always prepared for an eventuality, Umberto had made it his habit to sleep with a money belt around his waist, in which he kept some ancient gold coins and a small fortune in loose diamonds, emeralds and rubies. The Mafia gang had luckily neglected to give him a full body search when they broke into his room, so he was a rich man when he arrived in Rome to begin yet another new life.

After a few months he opened an antique shop on the Via Babuino with many of the precious things that he had stolen from the French and the Greeks, and had shipped to Italy for storage during the war. Because so many of his pieces were from lesser-known museums and the great houses of France, he soon owned one of the most beautifully stocked antique shops in Rome.

He shrewdly released only a few selected items from his looted plunder onto the market each year, being extremely careful not to attract the attentions of Interpol, who were still on the lookout for the thousands of works of art that had been stolen during the war.

The gold rings and bracelets of all the unfortunates who had been tortured and sent to their deaths during his regime had provided an excellent income for him. He still had many of the silver and gold icons, enamel vases, alabaster figures and candlesticks pilfered from the Greeks, and from France he still had what he referred to as "my pictures." Among these were masterpieces by Manet, Van Gogh, Renoir, Cézanne, and three large and highly important cubist canvases by Picasso. These were all kept secured in an underground vault in his new house close to the Piazza di Spagna, waiting for the rainy day when he might need to sell them.

Umberto was a rich man, but a bored one. The pleasures of the flesh no longer titillated him much unless they were of a truly bizarre nature, and it was becoming tedious sitting in his shop day after day. He certainly didn't need the money. What he really needed was something to stimulate him, but apart from sex, he could not think of anything.

But when he stepped into the Piazza Barbarini that sunny day and saw the huge arclights glittering down from the iron girders, saw the hustle and bustle of the film company, the glamour and enthusiasm which everyone seemed to have, he realized at once that at last he had found the answer to his long days of ennui.

It was during the making of *One Sunday in Rome* that Umberto and Ramona became firm friends. Umberto, who had always been intrigued by Hollywood, began to be even more interested by the fascinating business of filmmaking, and he became a regular fixture on the set. He met the producer, Henry Hornblower, an over-the-hill grizzled Hollywood legend, almost ready to be put out to pasture, but still full of gutsy anecdotes and stories about the days before talkies were invented. He met the director, a brash young whiz kid well on his way up the ladder, ambitious as hell and absolutely sure both of himself and of his talent; and he met the money men, the mysterious financiers who had managed to raise the money for the movie like conjurors. He expertly picked all their respective brains, convinced that he too could find the money to both finance and produce a film in Italy. And why not? It was now an open city for filmmaking, the very hub of the movie industry in Europe.

All roads truly led to Rome in the early 1950s. The Via Veneto was a constant hive of activity, as busy as the terrace of the Carlton during the Cannes Film Festival. Every table at Doney's and the other cafés was packed with producers, financiers, writers and entrepreneurs, as well as a heavy sprinkling of Italian and American movie stars. The Via Veneto was the place to be seen, to be noticed, to clinch a deal.

It was hard to tell the difference between the aspiring starlets who table-hopped from group to group with calculated charm and the prostitutes who plied their timeless trade up and down the Veneto. Both groups were equally attractive in their tight low-cut dresses, bouffant hair and made-up faces.

Everyone seemed to have a movie which they wanted to make or were about to shoot, and everyone had a deal or a contract ready to be signed. Rome was Little Hollywood on the Tiber, and movie people from around the world were flocking in hordes to the Eternal City.

When Umberto confided his plans to Ramona one evening as they were sitting at the Café Doney, sipping *crème de menthe frappé* through long pink straws, she turned to him in surprise and exclaimed, "Why Umberto, I never knew you were interested in this crazy business. When did all this happen?"

"Well, a long time ago, I suppose," he laughed, eyeing a sloe-eyed blonde slowly cruising the street looking for some action. "During the war we used to see many American movies—some with you in them, my dear." He kissed her hand gallantly, his downcast eyes in fact following the progress of the young blonde's swaying buttocks up the pavement. "Those were always my particular favorites."

"How sweet of you, my dear Umberto, how very very kind you are."

"Not at all, my dear. But you are so much more beautiful in life than you ever were on the screen."

She laughed girlishly. "Now, Umberto, don't go too far, my dear, after all I am nearly forty, you know." She lied with a smile, as he smiled back, playing along with the joke.

"Forty or not, you are lovelier than *any* of these girls walking here tonight."

Another tall slender blonde, wearing a figure-hugging red sheath dress which was cut completely down to the vee of her bottom, tossed her hair and winked at Scrofo as she swayed past their table. He feigned indifference, but remembered her well from the week before. She'd been very hot indeed. He still had her number somewhere. Tonight he would call her—later. Much as he liked and admired Ramona he did not find her sexually attractive at all, and he was only too aware that the feeling was mutual. So much the better. Business and lust never made good bedfellows.

Ramona was well aware of his eyes on the red-sheathed blonde, but pretended not to notice. Removing a black Sobranie from her platinum Boucheron cigarette case, she carefully placed it between her vermilion lips and waited for him to light it, which he did immediately with a heavy gold lighter.

"Umberto, I have a little proposition for you," she said, leaning forward confidentially, allowing him to peek down her white chiffon décolletage—if he felt so inclined.

"What is it, *cara?*" He smiled at her, aware that at the surrounding tables everyone was whispering about her. He was pleased when a couple of paparazzi snapped photographs of them deep in discussion, and he posed casually, without looking at the cameras. There had already been several photographs of the two of them together in the Italian magazines, and she had also been snapped in his shop for the *Oggi* layout. The gorgeous bracelet on her wrist had created so much publicity for his business that he now had to have an assistant working in the shop.

"What is your proposition, *cara?*" he asked after the paparazzi had moved off in search of fresh prey.

"I have a wonderful script that was written for me last year. It's an art film of a kind, but it also has so much scope for action and spectacle," she said excitedly. Umberto's face was impassive as he sipped at the sticky *crème de menthe*. "My brother Didier in London has some backers who could put up more than half the money, and we're looking for the rest, and also for someone to produce the film. That someone could be you, Umberto," she said, her voice rising so that an American posse of journalists at the next table stared at them curiously. "Would you be interested?"

"I could be—in fact I could be very interested indeed, my dear." Umberto tapped his cigar into the ashtray, his heart beating fast with unexpected excitement. But he did not want Ramona to know how truly he wanted to grasp this key that she was offering him.

"Tell me something of the story—what's it all about?"

"It's called *La Città Perduta—The Lost City,*" she told him excitedly, "and it's wonderful, Umberto, just wonderful—it'll probably win every award at all the festivals next year—it's tough—gritty—and very modern."

"And I'm sure there's a great part in it for you," he smiled, his mind racing.

"Naturally." She smiled archly, puffing on her cigarette. "I would play a grandmother. A young one, of course, darling," she giggled, "poor, destitute, hungry, who has a teenage daughter with an illegitimate baby all living together in Rome. It's the story of her courageous struggle to build a life for them all after the war."

"It sounds promising," he said, chewing on his cigar.

"It certainly does. I'm not a complete fool, Umberto—I know that there are younger, prettier, more bankable actresses than me out there today. They're the ones who are getting the pick of the roles, girls like Grace Kelly, Ava Gardner, Marilyn Monroe. I'm no longer among the top boxoffice stars anymore, I'd be the first to admit it, but I still do love to work."

He patted her beautifully manicured hand, adorned as it was with the staggering forty-carat diamond which he knew was a present from her husband, the mysterious Prince Kasinov, and told her, "You're *Numera*

Una with me, *carissima,* and if this movie is half as good as you say it is—I would like very much to become involved with it."

Ramona beamed at him. "Wonderful, Umberto, wonderful. I have a copy of the script back at the hotel—I'll give it to you to read tonight."

"One thing," he asked, "how much money did your brother say that you're looking for from the other side?"

"Oh, peanuts, darling, only peanuts," trilled Ramona. "I will work for virtually nothing, of course, just a percentage of the profits. We will cast an unknown girl for the daughter, and this new young director on *Sunday in Rome* is very talented; I'm sure we could get him for a song. So the above-the-line is minimal. I would say about four hundred thousand dollars—"

"Excuse my ignorance, *Principessa,* but what does 'above-the-line' mean?"

Ramona laughed lightly and said, "That is the salaries for the stars and the director, Umberto. I suppose we would need about one million dollars total financing, certainly not much more." She looked at him, batting sooty eyelashes. "A million dollars isn't really too high a price to pay to get into the movie business, is it, Umberto, darling?"

"Not if it means working with you, *carissima,*" said Umberto, a sudden burst of adrenaline making his heart pound. The movies! At last. Umberto Scrofo, a film producer—no longer an obscure antique dealer, but someone truly to be reckoned with again. A wheeler-dealer. A force. A *bella figura.* "What about the film's promotion and distribution—all of those kinds of things?" he asked. "I know absolutely nothing about all that, you know."

"Oh, Didier will take care of that—I'm sure. He's the expert of the family. He wants to do everything to help me, and I know he'll want to help you too." She smiled dazzlingly, raising her glass to him, her face looking amazingly young and joyous in the light of the Via Veneto streetlamps. "To *La Città Perduta,*" she breathed, "and to a long, happy and profitable association with you, Umberto."

And Umberto Scrofo clinked glasses with the beautiful star and smiled triumphantly.

9

Even though Dominique had many things to do before she left for America she found her mind whirling with thoughts of Gaston Girandot. After she had told the thrilling news that she was going to Hollywood to star in a film to Maman, Papa, Genevieve and all her relations and friends, she felt she must tell him too.

It was a humid evening when she pedaled her bicycle once again to the Place des Lices and saw with a lurch of pleasure the little van with its gaily painted slogan, GASTON'S GLACES.

Leaning out of the hatch onto the ledge where he was serving a couple of lanky teenage boys was Gaston Girandot, more handsome than ever, and Dominique was thrilled to see him.

"*Bon soir,* Gaston." She smiled innocently as she slid five francs across the shallow wooden counter. "I would like a double *framboise,* please."

"Dominique, *quelle surprise!*" His white smile and tanned face made him look more than ever like James Dean, screen idol of all the girls and boys in France. "I haven't seen you for ages—I expected by now you would be flying off to Hollywood, giving Leslie Caron a run for her money." He winked at her and slid the coin back. "This is on the house."

"*Merci,*" smiled Dominique, licking her ice cream with a pert pink tongue as her eyes searched the boy's face for signs that he was still interested in her. They were certainly still all there, and his eyes burned into hers so steadily that she felt a hot blush start under the bodice of her blouse and spread to her cheeks.

She turned away and started to walk across the little square to where the old men were smoking Gitanes and playing *boules* outside the Café des Lices.

"Where are you going?" He was beside her, slowing his stride to match hers. "Would you like to go for a ride on my new motorcycle?"

"Oh, Maman would *murder* me if she knew I went on a motorcycle ," squealed Dominique, the forbidden thought of it nevertheless filling her with excited anticipation.

Gaston sensed it. "Come—come with me," he said in a suddenly proprietorial manner, and taking her arm, steered her out of the square and down one of the narrow cobbled streets. "There," he said, proudly gesturing to a shining green machine parked boldly next to the gendarmerie. "Isn't she a beauty?"

"Beautiful," breathed Dominique, hearing her mother's voice instructing her that she must *never* accept rides with any men. Especially on scooters. "Absolutely *ravissant.*"

"We can go for a little ride now, come—" he said, quickly jumping astride the black leather seat and patting the space behind him invitingly.

"Oh, no— I *can't.*" Dominique was of two minds now. He looked even more like James Dean as he sat astride the machine, smoke from the cigarette in his mouth making his eyes half close in a sexy way that she found extremely tempting, his blue jeans tight across his muscled thighs.

"Come on," he said insistently, "don't be scared, it won't bite you— neither will I."

"Oh, all right," said Dominique tentatively, sliding onto the pillion. "But only for a little while, Gaston. I *must* be home by ten-thirty, promise?"

"Right," said the boy as the motor sprang to life, and she clutched him around his waist with both hands as he guided the motorcycle carefully down the stony streets. "We'll go to Tango Beach," he said, "it's not too far."

The beach was dark and deserted and only a sliver of pale moon illuminated the black sand.

"Goodness, it's so dark," Dominique shivered. Instead of feeling nervous she was experiencing thrilling new sensations in the pit of her stomach. The ten-minute ride with her arms and head nuzzled into Gaston's cotton shirt had excited her, her mouth was dry with anticipation of an unknown which she felt sure she was going to like.

He turned off the engine and they sat for several minutes listening to the almost-silence. Dominique was sure that he could hear the thumping of her heart mixed with the faint lapping of the waves. A soft breeze ruffled her hair, and all was very still.

Without words Gaston took her hand and they walked across the sand to the water's edge. Simultaneously they flopped onto the sand, still slightly warm from the afternoon sun, and for a long moment sat staring up into the star-littered sky.

"It's beautiful, St. Tropez, isn't it?" breathed Dominique, conscious of Gaston's muscular arm resting lightly on her shoulder.

"Beautiful," he said softly, "but not nearly as beautiful as you, *chérie.*" His head turned to her and she saw the pupils of his eyes were so dilated they almost hid his irises. "*Mais tu es belle, Dominique,*" he whispered. "*Trop belle—trop, trop belle.*"

His lips were on her hair now, searching for the softness of her neck.

"No, Gaston, no." Dominique heard her faint yet unresisting voice as his soft lips gently bit her neck. "No."

"Yes," he said insistently. "Yes, Dominique, yes, yes." He bent her body back slowly onto the warm sand, and she could feel the cool water of the sea lapping at her feet as his mouth traced a pattern of exquisite pleasure around her lips. His tongue was delicate, probing, sensitive. It seemed to know where she wanted it to go. Her mouth opened to his kisses and she felt the heat of desire starting to burn through the thin cotton of her skirt. She shivered as waves surged over her feet, and she felt his hands move to the buttons of her blouse.

"No—Gaston, not here," Dominique said, almost starting to giggle with nerves. "We're right in the middle of the beach, what if someone comes along?"

"No one is going to come here at night, little goose," he said. "But I suppose you're right. Let's go up to the restaurant—we'll be safe there—come." He helped her to her feet and they ran towards the dark outline of the beach bar.

It was pitch dark in the interior and smelled of cooked garlic and herbs, a warm, comforting smell. Gaston held Dominique's hand tightly as they fumbled their way through the stacked tables and chairs to the back of the bar. Piled against the wall were dozens of the striped mattresses that were used for sunbathing during the day.

"Here," said Gaston as he helped her clamber up onto the top one. "Up here, Dominique—it's nice here."

"I feel like the princess and the pea in that fairy tale," giggled Dominique, feeling incredibly grown up, nervous and excited all at the same time. "Lying on top of so many mattresses—ooh, Gaston, I hope we don't fall off."

"I won't let you," mumbled the boy, his hands busy with the tiny buttons of her blouse. "Don't worry, Dominique, my darling, I will protect you. I promise."

With the scent of Ambre Solaire filling her nostrils and the gentle sound of the sea in the background Dominique abandoned herself to the fervent kisses and caresses of the young ice-cream vendor with a sigh of pleasure.

From then on they met several times each week, and Gaston taught Dominique many new delights. Their silent private world at the back of the beach hut was a haven of pleasure where Dominique amazed Gaston by her sexual ardor and enthusiasm. She had no prudery or false modesty. Her only fear was that she might become pregnant, but he protected her from that. She was a willing, wanton partner, and as he often told her, "made for love."

When the crisp telegram finally arrived from MCCP studios informing Dominique that it was time for her to leave for Hollywood to prepare for the filming of *The Legend of Cortez* the young lovers wept copiously.

"I won't forget you, I promise," cried Dominique, clinging to Gaston in the comforting darkness of their love nest. "I'll write every day—every single day."

"I will, too, my darling," said the boy, desperately trying not to weep. "I will not stop loving you, Dominique, and I will be waiting for you when you come back from America."

A few days later Gaston Girandot stood on the upper level of the white concrete terminal at Nice Airport, watching Dominique and Agathe board the huge Air France four-engine airliner which was taking them to New York. Dominique was dressed formally in a new black-and-white checked suit with black shiny buttons on the jacket and a tight black belt. The skirt was full and mid-calf length, and she wore a small felt hat on the back of her flowing hair which was tied with black grosgrain ribbon. Around her neck was a white Peter Pan collar trimmed with a small black bow, and in her white-gloved hands she carried a black patent boxy handbag which matched her high-heeled shoes. She looked grown-up and sophisticated as she posed prettily at the bottom of the airplane's steps for a lone photographer from *Nice Matin*.

In the background Agathe, the chaperone, smiled proudly at her young charge. At last they were off. After months of waiting they were being summoned to the magic land of Hollywood. In little more than twenty-four hours they would be there, and maybe some of Agathe's dreams would finally come true.

10

*T*he applause was deafening. Even by Julian's standards, it was an unusually enthusiastic and tumultuous first-night ovation, and he reveled in it. Handsome and romantic in black cotton tights and a loose white linen shirt, he held hands with the woman beside him, smiling at her with well-concealed fury, bowing yet again to the thunderous applause. The bloody bitch had been upstaging him all evening. Each time he had turned to her during their scenes on stage, Phoebe had managed to remain two or three steps behind him, thus enabling the audience to see all of her, but only three quarters of him. He was the star, after all—Julian Brooks *was* Hamlet. Ophelia was just a supporting role, and the redheaded witch was trying to muscle in on his territory to beef up her part.

But what was even more galling was that he knew that the Oliviers and Johnny Gielgud were in front, watching what Phoebe was doing. No doubt they were having a good laugh at his expense. "Ophelia upstaging Hamlet— what *is* the theater coming to?" they would be saying. "Julian must be going *mad*, darling."

True, he had promised his wife some seven years ago that if he ever played Hamlet, she would be his Ophelia, but she'd been more than two stone lighter in those days. He had finally given in wearily after her vastly expensive trip of revenge with Hermione. To play Ophelia she had lost fifteen pounds, and with a three-foot-long, curly auburn wig and brilliantly cantilevered costumes, she wasn't altogether terrible. Certainly not Vivien Leigh, but not Sophie Tucker either. Julian had naively thought that by letting Phoebe share some of his glory, it might help their marriage. But on the contrary, it only served to show her up as the mediocre actress she undoubtedly was, and make him look a complete fool for having cast her. To top it all, their marriage was now practically in name only.

He was reminded of the story about the flamboyant actor-manager Sir Donald Wolfit who, on a tour of the English provinces, stepped towards the footlights after his curtain call, announcing to the audience in stentorian tones, "Thank you, dear people, for your most kind reception tonight given to our play. Next week we shall be presenting here at the Alhambra Theatre, Shakespeare's *Othello*. I myself shall be playing the stately Moor, and my lady wife shall give her Desdemona."

A voice from the gallery called out, "Your wife's an old ratbag."

There was a very long pause. "Nevertheless," continued Sir Donald, "she shall *still* be playing Desdemona."

That was him and Phoebe, thought Julian, knotting his dressing-gown cord savagely. He was the star and she the ratbag, and an upstaging ratbag to boot.

Even though they took eleven curtain calls, he was still seething in the dressing room, as he roughly wiped makeup from his face.

"Now look here, Phoebe, I've had just about enough of your continual upstaging. Dammit, how many times have I told you that in my 'Get thee to a nunnery' speech, you *must* stay downstage. Are you *deaf* or something?"

"Oh, I *know* you did, dear," fluttered Phoebe, as helpless as a leopard in a jungle. She sneered at him in the fly-specked mirror, rubbing a touch of the powder and paint from her cheeks and removing a smidgin of eye shadow with the corner of a Turkish towel. After all, there was no point in wasting perfectly good cold cream to take this lot off, when she would only have to put it all back on again for the party. Besides, she was too lazy. Excited by the first-night fever, she ignored Julian's exasperated tirade as she primped and fussed with her carroty curls in preparation for the tidal wave of backstage visitors. Even now, she could hear them coming down the drafty stone corridors of the Haymarket Theatre. They'll put a stop to Julian's nagging, she thought.

Vivien and Larry, Johnny and Ralphie, Noël and Sir Crispin, and the two Hermiones all burst into the dressing room together in a rush of excited praise. "Darling, you were *divine—*simply *marvelous,*" gushed one of the Hermiones to Julian, who stood in the middle of the cramped dressing room in his navy blue-and-crimson Charvet dressing gown, modestly accepting the sincere compliments of his peers, along with a glass of champagne from his dresser.

"Best Hamlet I've seen in *years,* old boy," said Larry, patting him on the shoulder. "Really bloody good." Then he bent down, whispering conspiratorially, "Better than Alec's last year—much better."

"Not really, Larry." Julian smiled broadly, luxuriating in the praise from the supreme actor's actor. "But thank you very much."

"Dear boy, you were good; very, very good indeed," said Noël, a twinkle in his Chinese eyes, an ivory cigarette holder clenched between his teeth. "I've never seen you better—you must do more of the Bard, dear boy, although I hear Hollywood's crooked little bejeweled finger has been beckoning you—right, dear boy?"

How did he know that? Julian wasn't really surprised. Noël knew everything that went on—not only in the West End, but on Broadway and even in Hollywood. He was a walking cornucopia of fascinating theatrical gossip.

Another call from Julian's Hollywood agent had, in fact, come only yesterday. His agent was insistent that Julian make a film in America. He had missed the boat twice before and it was high time he didn't miss this one. Selznick had wanted him to play Rochester opposite Joan Fontaine in *Jane Eyre* but Didier had dithered for so long that the part had gone to Orson Welles. Three years ago they had wanted him again, this time to play opposite Joan's sister, Olivia de Havilland, in *My Cousin Rachel,* but he had been in the middle of a Restoration epic with Margaret Lockwood, so the role had gone to Richard Burton. Now Hollywood was beckoning again— with a juicy contract and Didier's blessing, lots of lovely dollars and a peach of a part: the title role in *The Legend of Cortez.* It was a difficult decision and Julian felt torn. Although *Hamlet* was only playing for a limited run, Phoebe was pregnant for the second time. He was delighted, but she wasn't happy about it at all—not that she was ever happy about much unless it involved spending money or hobnobbing with high society. It was almost an immaculate conception, as Julian had hardly gone near her at all since *Pygmalion,* but for Phoebe it was a trump card. Rumblings of incipient miscarriages and morning sickness kept him in line. She was hardly two months into her pregnancy, but she was more difficult, tetchy and discontented than ever.

"*Hollywood!* Over my dead body," she had barked at him that morning as she lay in bed in a maribou bedjacket, which always made her sneeze, while she cooed and caressed one of their five cats. "We can't leave the cats, and I *hate* Americans and their perfectly dreadful food—hamburgers and chili dogs—ugh, it makes me retch to think of it."

"Phoebe, what bloody difference does it make?" Julian roared, standing before her in his striped pajama bottoms, his face covered with shaving cream. "What the blazes—we'll import a bloody cook from England. We'll have fucking bangers and mash, boiled beef and carrots—whatever you want, Phoebe, but for Christ's sake, don't make me give up this big chance, *my* big chance, just because you don't like bloody Yankee food." Phoebe started to splutter, but he shut her up.

"If we go to Hollywood, I'll do this three-picture deal for Spyros and then we'll come back to London, I promise you. Then we'll buy that fucking house in Sussex, if that's what you want."

"The one near the Oliviers?" Phoebe asked eagerly.

"The one near the Oliviers," said Julian resignedly.

"I'll think about it," Phoebe pouted, pulling the green-and-pink chintz-covered eiderdown up to her chins. "I'll let you know after the opening tomorrow. I must rest now. Doctor's orders. Please leave me alone." She closed her eyes dismissively as Julian Brooks, matinée idol and leading male star of the British screen, stood helplessly in yet another fury of frustration.

Now, surrounded as he was by the *crème de la crème* of the theatrical profession, Julian tried once again to control his anger towards his tiresome wife. Tonight he was a great success; that was all that mattered at the moment.

"Darling heart, *go* to California, you simply *must*," said Vivien, her beautiful cat's eyes alight in her perfect face. "But *do* come to Notley Abbey next weekend before you go."

"I could think of nothing I'd rather do more," Julian said with a smile. That should placate Phoebe. She wouldn't have too much morning sickness down there, he was sure of that. Not with Larry and Viv and Johnny G., and Noël and Binkie Beaumont for company. She'd do her best to be the life and soul of the party, and she certainly always could be if she felt like it.

"Hollywood can be *the* most ghastly bore, of course, but the *money,* darling—you can't, you simply *can't* turn it down," said Sir Crispin Peake, ever the pragmatist. "Take it and run, my dear. I've just bought an enormous house near Windsor and the most ravishing little Renoir you've ever seen, and both with my last paycheck. You must come down and stay, if you ever manage to tear yourself away from Notley Abbey!" He winked as he was sucked into the crush of well-wishers.

"The British invasion, darling, that's what they call it," croaked Hermione One. "Hollywood simply adores the Brits, dear—they all play cricket

at dear Aubrey's every Sunday in white flannels, and eat cucumber sandwiches at every opportunity."

"It's nothing to be ashamed of—we've *all* done it," said Vivien, looking
over at her husband. "Even Larry, and he fought against it like a *dervish,*
darling—didn't want to go at all, did you, pet?"

"No—but once we went we had a glorious time. The weather is divine,
the work conditions excellent, and the natives are really quite amusing—
aren't they, darling?" said Sir Laurence, smiling fondly at his wife. "And the
women are terribly pretty."

"So are the men." She smiled back at him slyly.

"Go, dear boy, go, you simply simply must," said Noël. "Let's face it,
England is just a backwater these days, and who can ignore all that lovely
green lolly?"

"Certainly not Phoebe," answered Hermione impishly as Phoebe glared
at her, and Sir Crispin stifled a snigger. "She loves a buck, don't you, dearie?
Cannot say no to ye olde filthy lucre, never could, even when she was a
Windmill cutie."

"Well, now I think it's time for us all to go to the Ivy," announced Noël,
sensing a sudden chill in the atmosphere. "Let the revels begin, my children, it's fiesta time. Let us eat, drink and become very, very merry indeed,
and toast dear Julian's grand success."

The first-night party in the Edwardian back dining room of the Ivy bubbled
with the aristocracy of film and theater. Conversation was brittle and brilliant. The expensive smell of cigar smoke wafted through the air, mingling
with the dozens of scents worn by the glittering women, and Julian modestly accepted congratulations and praise from friend and foe alike.

Everyone was exquisitely dressed. In the theatrical world of the 1950s,
actresses were not afraid to look the part of the glamorous stars that many
of them were. The rainbow colors of their taffeta, satin and velvet gowns
were perfectly complemented by all the elegant men in their black dinner
jackets and crisp white shirts.

Television was not taken at all seriously by anyone in the profession.
Even actors who appeared in films were looked upon with a certain disdain
by their more respected thespian brothers and sisters, which was part of
the reason why Julian had decided to play *Hamlet.* He wanted the respect
of his peers, which he knew he would never earn by toiling in his romantic
potboilers for the screen. But he equally wanted, and Phoebe needed, the
large sums of money which he made from his screen career.

Phoebe's outgoing personality was spilling over, as were her enormous breasts, which bounced like two pale sponge cakes, half in and half out of her Norman Hartnell ice-blue dress. She circulated tirelessly, passing on snippets of theatrical gossip and naughty jokes with gusto. She was totally without diplomacy as she told vicious and hurtful stories about everyone. Many disliked her for it, but Julian was so popular that they put up with Phoebe's bitchiness and backbiting for his sake.

As the clock struck midnight the star of the evening suddenly found himself alone at the bar, with only a glass of Dom Perignon for company. He lit a cigar with his gold lighter—a present from Phoebe when he had played Othello at the Old Vic, opposite her far too curvaceous Desdemona. Slowly he became aware of a subtle scent and a pair of magnetic eyes staring at him.

He turned to meet the cool gaze of a tall young woman who was leaning elegantly against the bar, staring at him with barely disguised interest. She was beautiful in a sultry way, but there was an aura about her which spoke of much more than beauty. There was danger in her eyes, a look that signaled trouble for any man who got too close. She looked to be in her mid-twenties, with shoulder-length dark brown hair, and a thick fringe which seemed deliberately to draw attention to electric-blue eyes. They were boldly outlined in kohl and drawn in that doe-eyed slant which Audrey Hepburn had made so fashionable. Her lips, curved, full and sensual, were painted a deep, glossy scarlet; she now parted them, placed a cigarette between them and waited with a faint, expectant smile. All the while her eyes never left his.

Like all good actors, Julian always picked up his cue. In an instant he was at her side, gold lighter at the ready.

"*Merci.*" Her voice was low, husky, evocative of endless evenings in smoky clubs and long nights of love. He was instantly captivated. "You were excellent tonight," she smiled. "The best Hamlet I've ever seen. Better than Guinness. Maybe even better than Olivier."

"Thank you, *Mademoiselle,* you are really too kind. But I'm afraid you have the advantage of knowing who I am, while I don't know you."

"Inès," she replied softly. "Inès Juillard."

"A beautiful name for a beautiful woman." Julian couldn't help the cliché. He felt himself blush and noticed the girl's faint smile, but there was warmth there, and a sexual interest he could feel. Usually when he felt mutual attraction this strongly he went after it immediately. Having had many affairs during his marriage, he fully intended to have as many more as he wanted. No matter that Phoebe was finally pregnant, that was not going to stop him, particularly with this gorgeous creature who was oozing sexuality and fascination.

Suddenly he wanted Inès Juillard very much. He wanted to touch and caress her long, slim curves, wanted to feel those elegant hands with their short, unpainted nails rake his back, wanted to strip that severely chic clinging black dress from her body, feel her breasts against his chest. All those thoughts passed rapidly through his mind in the time it took for him to inhale his cigar, and for her to brush the ash from her cigarette.

Inès, of course, read them all instantly. She had been around men long enough to understand them completely, and since she had been intrigued by and attracted to Julian ever since she had seen him in *Pygmalion,* she was thankful that he obviously found her desirable. But she needed to be clever here. Very clever indeed. He was devastatingly good-looking, charming, famous, fascinating—and married. Looks Brooks—the most handsome man in the world. Every woman must be after him—some, so they said, had tried to kill themselves for love of him. She must make herself extra special, more than special to him.

"When can I see you?" Julian whispered urgently, as he saw out of the corner of his eye a particularly vicious gossip columnist who was bearing down on him. "I want to see you soon, Inès—as soon as possible. Please."

"Grosvenor 1734," she whispered, wafting away like some beautiful black wraith in a fragrant cloud of scent. "Call me during the day, any time. *J'attends,* Julian, *j'attends.*"

Julian could hardly wait. He had to see Inès Juillard. He rang her the next morning, she gave him her address in Shepherd Market, and he was out of the Connaught Square house and into a black cab before Phoebe had even opened an eye from her hangover slumbers. He knew that she'd have a fit when she saw her notices; he definitely didn't want to be around when she read them. The critics had not been kind to her, and although they praised Julian's Hamlet, they castigated him as producer for casting his wife in such an unsuitable role.

He was perfectly turned out in a camel cashmere belted overcoat, his caramel-colored fedora worn at its usual angle, so it was not surprising that the cabbie recognized him.

" 'Ello, Mr. Brooks." He smiled genially. "Good reviews, guv. Didja see 'em? Even James Agate liked it." London cabdrivers loved celebrities, often letting them travel for nothing in exchange for an autograph.

Julian smiled his thanks dismissively. He didn't want to talk to the cabbie. He only wanted to think about Inès. For the first time in years his interest in someone else overshadowed his interest in his reviews. His anticipation was electric. He felt like a small boy on Christmas Eve. He had not been able to put her out of his mind since last night. The cabbie took the hint, allowing Julian to be alone with his thoughts until they arrived at Shepherd Market.

Inès opened the door wearing a black polo neck sweater and a full black-and-white checked skirt cinched with a wide patent-leather belt around her tiny waist. She was ravishing, yet with a sweet vulnerability that he found incredibly refreshing. Her skin was devoid of any makeup, but her face glowed serenely, her complexion fresh and clear.

Julian noticed that on the walls of her flat hung exquisitely framed neoclassical drawings by Delacroix, Ingres and David. He thought he also recognized some early drawings by Boucher and Fragonard. The furniture was good, some of it very good, and there were spring flowers everywhere in blue and white pots. This was obviously a woman of considerable taste and style as well as great beauty.

Inès was playing him as gently and carefully as a fisherman landing a prize salmon on a slender trout rod. Finally he was in her flat. Julian Looks Brooks. The Idol of the Odeons in person sitting on her sofa, sipping espresso from one of her Sèvres cups, his eyes looking at her with steady desire.

She gave him no clue to her profession, gave him none of herself, either—not that day, nor the next, nor even the following week. For more than a month she refused to even let him kiss her. It wasn't until he'd convinced her that he was mad with love for her that she finally allowed him to possess her. And, of course, she made him think it had all been his idea.

He had suggested that after his Saturday performance they drive to his tiny cottage in the country. Phoebe had bought it in an uncharacteristic flash of country-life fever but had visited it only once, preferring the streets of St. James's and Piccadilly to the muddy lanes of Gloucestershire. He had talked Inès into it, and she finally reluctantly agreed.

Once there Inès concocted a gourmet feast on the old-fashioned cooker, produced a bottle of distinctive claret, and cuddled up to Julian after dinner in front of the roaring log fire with innocent seductiveness.

She knew the time was ripe for him to seduce her, and she resisted him girlishly until finally she succumbed to his ardent kisses. But once they were ensconced in the downy soft featherbed, Inès took the initiative, amazing Julian by her athletic ardor.

They made love all night long, and it exceeded his every expectation. It was an experience beyond his wildest fantasies.

Although Julian had had dozens of affairs, they had been mostly with English or American women, usually actresses, none of whom could exactly have been called passion flowers. They had moaned, groaned, writhed and performed with all the appropriate wiggles, thrusts and the "Oh, my *God,* darling, it's so good," but he had always felt that there was something important missing in his lovemaking with all of them. They gave their bodies enthusiastically enough, but he knew that their hearts were seldom truly in it.

With Inès it was totally different. The white heat of her passion seemed almost to scorch him, and he never wanted to stop. He knew it was real, he could feel that hers was not a performance, that it was just for him. Her skin drove him wild. It was the color of crushed pearls, and smelled like jasmine. When she wrapped her amazingly long slim legs around him, whispering eroticisms in that husky French voice of hers, he would become like a man possessed. He'd never been with a woman like her before. Few had specialized in the sexual arts and crafts which Inès had been perfecting since her teens. She was a walking mantrap, desire and lust incarnate. A wonderful wanton with such incredible sexual skills that even the sophisticated and worldly Julian was dazzled by them. That long weekend in the cottage as he tried to doze after yet another blissful session of lovemaking, she would take his sleeping cock in her mouth as gently and delicately as a snake would swallow a small mouse. She was insatiable and tireless, her tongue an instrument of pure pleasure, a lethal weapon, as were her mouth and lips, which she used to take him to the highest stratosphere of pleasure, from where he never wanted to return.

More than anything, Julian felt that her passion truly matched his. Her lust and physical need for his body were as strong as his for hers. After their affair started it was nothing for them to spend the entire morning together, and then the whole afternoon in her soft bed, until it was time for him to go to the theater. They made love at least three times a day, and at nearly thirty-seven, Julian became possessed with the sexual energy of a seventeen-year-old. He sometimes had odd pangs of fear that expending so much of his precious essence might somehow interfere with his performance on the stage, but in fact it seemed to do just the opposite. His Hamlet soared to new heights each night, and audiences cheered and applauded him until the rafters of the Haymarket Theatre seemed to shake. He often told her that, like Cleopatra, she never made his appetites for her cloy, but instead made hungry where most she satisfied.

Of course Phoebe soon suspected that another affair had begun. She had miscarried their baby again and, although secretly relieved, was making an enormous show of her misery. When Julian made a halfhearted attempt to make love to her one night, simply because he thought he should, Phoebe rejected him huffily.

"Don't point that tired old thing *near* me," she hissed. "You must wait at *least* three months. The doctor says I mustn't have sex until then, so just go and jerk off in the bathroom, like a good boy, or whatever else you've been doing." She bit viciously into another chocolate biscuit.

His wife's attitude suited Julian perfectly. He was totally consumed by thoughts of Inès, his angel, his gorgeous French beauty, his *grand passion*. He was her slave, completely besotted, and not only sexually. He had never felt such pure joy in a relationship with a woman, and soon he began to realize that he could no longer imagine his life without her.

Inès had still given Julian no hint of her true profession. At twenty-nine she knew that her years of successful and financially rewarding whoring were rapidly coming to an end. Julian was handsome, rich, successful, and a wonderful lover. She knew that he was the man for her, but she also knew that he lived by the usual convenient double standard, like so many Englishmen. He had been a philanderer and womanizer most of his adult life, which she was able to accept. However, she soon found out that her own past life needed to be practically perfect to please his curiously exacting moral values—he would never be able to accept the fact that she had been a whore. That was the one thing she would never be able to tell him. However much in love he was, she was sure that should he find out, their relationship would be destroyed.

Inès was in a difficult position. The chances of Julian's discovering the truth about her past were fairly slim, since most of her clients would be terrified of exposure themselves. She had stopped seeing all of them as soon as the romance with Julian began, telling them she was going away for a long time. She had concocted a thin web of lies about her life which Julian unquestioningly believed, and she prayed that he would never discover the truth.

She had told him that her parents had been killed in a car crash in Paris when she was very young. She had been brought up by a maiden aunt in Yorkshire who had died when Inès was twenty, leaving her this flat, some pretty and valuable bits and pieces, and enough money to live well on. He had believed her. In spite of his own promiscuity, Julian was extremely old-fashioned. He couldn't even think of Inès with another man. She had admitted to having had three boyfriends, but had refused to go into details about any relationships, saying that he mustn't be jealous of past loves.

Having completely sexually and emotionally enslaved him, and tangled him up in her beauty's web, prying him away from his wife was her next problem. And it was a major problem. Phoebe would not let Julian go without a fight. Even though she was no longer in love with him and the marriage was little more than a sham, she loved her life as Mrs. Julian Brooks and all that went with it. Phoebe was a tough, single-minded woman, both shrewd and clever. But perhaps not quite as shrewd and clever as her rival.

Inès had hinted at marriage but Julian had not been enthusiastic—why should he be? Phoebe always turned a blind eye to his affairs, realizing that they would all eventually come to an end and he would return to the marital fold.

And she was right, of course. Inès knew that there was a certain time between a man and a woman when the desire for each other was so strong that marriage was inevitable. If it didn't happen at that time, then it never would.

Julian seemed to be completely hooked now, and Inès knew the time was propitious to give him her ultimatum.

"Marriage, Julian darling," she said calmly as they sat by candlelight at her lace-draped dining table eating *coq au vin* from Spode plates. "We must get married."

"Darling girl—my angel, it's impossible, I've told you," Julian demurred. "Phoebe will never let me go, we both know that. Angel, can't we just stay the way we are? I'm so happy like this, Inès."

"No, Julian," said Inès firmly, aware that she was treading the trickiest of ground, but shrewdly knowing she had to do it. "In that case I can't continue seeing you."

"Of course you can, my angel," said Julian confidently. "We love each other too much, Inès, how could we bear to be apart from each other?"

At that moment Inès knew this was going to be much tougher than she had expected. She worshiped Julian, wanted desperately to marry him, to be with him forever. There was only one way to get him now—she had to play a brilliant game, and for high stakes. Julian was a rare prize.

The following day Inès withdrew from Julian's life completely. She packed a small suitcase and disappeared for a week without telling him. Then she sent a brief note to the theater telling him she was in the country and only giving him her telephone number.

Instantly he was on the telephone, begging to see her.

"No, Julian, no. I cannot see you again," Inès said firmly, her heart pounding with longing for him. "I love you too much to go on like this without marriage. We must forget each other, *chéri.*"

"No!" roared Julian, beside himself at the thought of losing her. "You can't do this, Inès, you simply can't. I've been going mad without you. What's your address? I'll come and see you, angel. Now, I simply must."

"No," said Inès softly. "No, Julian. It's marriage or it's over between us. We have been together now for seven months. If we don't marry I must get on with my life. If it has to be without you—so be it."

She hung up, leaving Julian staring blankly at the telephone. He knew she was right, of course, his marriage with Phoebe was a farce. Divorce. He would divorce Phoebe and marry Inès. That was the inevitable way it must be. Why not. He loved her. She was everything he desired and admired in a woman.

It had been a tough ultimatum for Inès. Please God, let it work, she prayed. Please God. She wanted to be with Julian forever. She had to be.

When Julian finally confessed his passionate affair to Phoebe, and his desire for a divorce so that he could marry Inès, Phoebe went berserk. Ranting and raving, she threw all her valuable painstakingly collected Chelsea and Bow porcelain at her husband in a furious barrage that lasted for hours. She threatened Julian with the most dire consequences if he left her.

"I'll create a scandal that will *ruin* you. That Candida *bitch* trying to commit suicide will be *nothing* compared to this," she screamed, her face ugly and puffy, her bloodshot eyes swollen with tears. "You'll *never* be Sir Julian Brooks now. Not with a divorce behind you."

"My dear girl," Julian said, trying to remain calm as he brushed bits of broken china off his sleeve, "I don't give a damn what you do. And I don't give a damn about becoming a knight. I'm an actor and that's all I bloody well care about."

"You're not an *actor*," Phoebe spat out contemptuously. "You're just a joke. When you first came on the screen as Charles the Second with that dead poodle on your head, everyone screamed with laughter. Everyone says you can't bloody act to save your bloody life."

"Thank you, Phoebe," Julian said quietly, "for those few kind words. Your undying loyalty is most touching."

"That French *whore*—I suppose *she's* loyal."

"Yes," he sighed. "She is."

"Does she know you're a pansy?"

Julian paled. Since his passing attachment to Wilson at school, he'd gone out of his way never to do, say or appear as anything other than the most masculine of men. But he had once in the early days of their marriage confessed to Phoebe his fondness for the boy. Like the elephant, she never forgot.

"And what's that supposed to mean?" he asked coldly.

"Nothing." She shrugged, realizing her barb had found its mark. "Nothing at all, Julian."

Phoebe had never suspected it herself, but maybe this man with whom she'd lived for nearly eleven years did have some homosexual tendencies. She always thought that Julian flirted with Sir Crispin Peake when they laughed and teased each other. Unfortunately, she had no proof. Pity—that would have been the perfect stick with which to beat him. He couldn't have put up with the stigma of being thought of as queer.

Julian's seemingly genuine love for this other woman enraged Phoebe. Whatever was wrong with their marriage, it was no worse than that of many other theatrical couples. Phoebe had always assumed that, like other couples they knew, she and Julian would last forever, conveniently if not romantically. Now he'd turned her whole world upside down all for the sake of love. *Love!* What a joke, she thought viciously. There was no such thing, it was all as Noël said, a very bad joke.

Julian tried to pacify Phoebe with offers of huge sums of money. He offered her the house, the furniture, the paintings, all of the possessions which they had carefully collected during their years together. He would give her everything in exchange for his freedom to marry Inès. But Phoebe refused.

It was Inès who at last found the answer. She had been thinking and analyzing the problem long and hard. She came to the conclusion that Phoebe would give Julian his freedom in exchange for a cut of his future earnings—for life. She suggested he offer Phoebe ten percent. After mulling it over for twenty-four hours, Julian confronted his wife with the more than generous proposition.

"Twenty percent," Phoebe fired back. "Forever and ever."

"Fifteen," sighed Julian wearily.

"Oh, all right, you mean son of a bitch," sniffed Phoebe. "Fifteen it is, then—for life dear, don't forget. Till death us do part, *lovey*."

"Done," said Julian, feeling as if some intolerable weight had been lifted from his shoulders. He was free at last. Free of Phoebe. Free to be with his perfect Inès for ever. Free to fly to Hollywood.

11

*U*mberto Scrofo *strutted onto the soundstage at Cinecittà Studios, his* cigar jutting from fleshy lips, his step self-assured. He was overseeing the final days of shooting of his film *La Città Perduta.* The word was out on the streets of Rome, on the Via Veneto, on the beaches of Ostia and Fregene where the film people gathered, even in the cutting rooms of the rival Scalera Studios, that Umberto Scrofo, this newcomer to their ranks, had a hit on his hands—and it was all his own work. Well, not quite all his own—after all, the script had been written by Irving Frankovitch, and Didier Armande had helped raise most of the money, but it was Umberto's name on the film, and everyone knew it.

He smiled with smug satisfaction as he stood watching carefully from outside the enchanted circle of arc lights, inside which his actors were performing. He had a proprietorial feeling towards his actors. It was as if they belonged exclusively to him. Not that they did; they had all, in fact, cost a fortune. Even Ramona had eventually demanded a salary, albeit minor. It hadn't been easy. Whoever told him that to break into the Italian film business was a breeze was a fool. He'd had to fight hard to get this script off the ground. Ponti, De Sica, Fellini and Visconti seemed to have rented all the studio space and hired every decent technician and piece of film equipment in Italy. He'd fought the American film companies as well. They had come to Italy in droves after the war, with falling stars of the 1930s and 1940s, plowing millions of dollars into crap, pure crap, and getting a guaranteed release, just because some faded Hollywood has-been's name was above the title and it was an American picture. Umberto had watched the Italian film industry thrive since the war, and with it the fortunes of the filmmakers, and he wanted to thrive, too. Oh, how he longed to succeed, how he yearned for Hollywood to beckon to him, and one day soon it would, of that he was certain.

12

*D*ominique *loved Hollywood and Hollywood loved Dominique. Each* morning on her way to the studios, she gazed with childlike excitement through the windows of her chauffeur-driven limousine, wondering what joys this day would bring. She adored California. She thought that hot dogs, hamburgers, drive-in movies, Hula-Hoops, the Santa Monica beaches and the California sun, which always seemed to be shining, were the best things ever. She especially adored the camaraderie with the other actors and dancers at the rehearsal studio. She laughed at their quick repartee even though she didn't quite understand it, as she studied hard, learning English, and the sensual dance she would perform in *The Legend of Cortez.* She loved the exciting bustle of MCCP's commissary, watching the comings and goings of the stars, but best of all she liked television, especially *The Jackie Gleason Show, Cavalcade of Stars* and *The Milton Berle Show.* There had been no television in St. Tropez, no hot dogs, no film studio commissary, no excitement at all—except for Gaston. Now she never wanted to go back there ever; California life was nothing less than terrific. She belonged here.

Gaston had written her several impassioned letters and she had sent both him and her family pages and pages of exciting news, but as each day passed, St. Tropez, her family and Gaston Girandot seemed farther and farther away. Soon she had almost forgotten what he looked like.

Only the memory of those nights on Tango Beach brought his image back to her. She imagined them lying together on the striped beach mattresses with the smell of Ambre Solaire in her nostrils, remembered how thrilling it had been. But it was all work work work now, no time for romance—which was just fine with Dominique. The studio wanted to make her into a new star and she was more than willing to help.

The only tiny fly in her ointment was her chaperone. With her eerie, bleached-looking skin, silver hair, those burning black, sad eyes in her haunted face, Agathe made most people uncomfortable. There was so much suffering in her face, such sorrow in her eyes, no joy in her life. Her clothes were old-fashioned, dark, dowdy—and far too heavy for California. Her manner was quiet and almost lethargic. What Dominique and others didn't realize was how thrilled Agathe was to be in Los Angeles; she was simply incapable of showing it.

Dominique, on the other hand, was bursting with vitality. In Levi's and plaid shirt, with her long hair in a ponytail, she had become hooked on the American way of life, its fashions and customs. She was almost beside herself with anticipation on this steamy November afternoon as they headed towards the studio for her first costume fitting.

"Oh, Agathe, I'm *so* excited I can hardly breathe! My first fitting—what do you think it'll be like?"

Agathe made no reply as the car pulled into the studio lot. She was, as always, mesmerized by the extras walking about. Today they were dressed in *fin-de-siècle* winter costumes, incongruous in the heat and humidity.

They drove down several winding streets, each of which had a completely different character, towards the wardrobe department. Here was a New York nineteenth-century tenement which connected to an exact facsimile of a part of London's Eaton Square, complete with perfect replicas of Regency houses, plane trees and laburnum shrubs. Here a cobblestoned French medieval village, the narrow houses with strings of washing hanging between them looking so authentic that both women suddenly felt a pang of homesickness for St. Tropez. This led to the wardrobe department, which was simply an unpretentious clapboard building with brown paint peeling from its drab exterior.

While Dominique was being fitted, Agathe explored the department, awed by the multitude of costumes housed there on endless racks, ranging from Roman togas to thousand-dollar beaded evening gowns. After the fitting Agathe suggested an uplifting visit to the Los Angeles Museum of Art, but Dominique had other plans. One of the dancers had told her about a new nightclub on Sunset Boulevard where all the young actors and dancers hung out. It was the ultimate in cool, she'd been reliably informed, and she was dying to go there to jive the night away.

"I'm exhausted." She smiled at Agathe, feigning a yawn. "I want to sleep for fifteen hours. Drop me at the hotel, then you take the car on to the museum. But I must sleep. Agathe, *ça va?*"

"All right," muttered Agathe, thinking how sophisticated Dominique had become after only a few weeks in Hollywood. The typically French school-girl seemed to have blossomed overnight into a genuine American teen-ager, complete with a mouthful of chewing gum, and all the right slang. Why was the girl so at ease while Agathe herself felt like a fish out of water?

"Now don't you worry, Agathe," Dominique said as the car pulled up outside the Château Marmont. "I'm going straight to sleep with a glass of hot milk, and I'll see you in the morning bright and early." Blowing a kiss to Agathe, she ran lightly up the steps of the hotel, giggling to herself. Poor old Agathe, it wasn't too difficult to pull the wool over *her* eyes.

Agathe stared unseeingly ahead of her as the driver edged into the heavy Sunset Boulevard traffic. She felt a terrible envy of her charge boiling up inside her, an envy which spread like some fast-acting drug through her veins, and she hated herself for it. Maybe it was because Dominique was so young—almost the same age as Agathe had been when she was banished to that cellar; or maybe it was because Dominique had her whole life before her, a joyful, exciting life filled with promise. At thirty-one Agathe felt that her own life was as good as over except for one thing: the prospect of meeting the star of *The Legend of Cortez,* Julian Brooks. When she had heard that he was to play the lead, Agathe had almost swooned. The prospect of finally seeing her idol in the flesh was so overwhelming that she had to lie down to stop the terrible dizziness. Now she waited each day, hungry with anticipation until the moment when she would finally meet the one man in the world that she knew was her destiny.

Dominique dressed carefully in the height of hip teenage fashion: a black sleeveless sweater, pencil-tight blue jeans, a wide black belt cinching her waist into an impossibly small eighteen inches, and red ballet pumps. She outlined her eyes with a heavy black pencil and carefully arranged her bed with pillows and towels to appear as if she were sleeping in it if Agathe came snooping around. She crept down the back stairs of the hotel to walk the eight blocks to the Rock 'n' Roll Club.

Although it was only nine o'clock, the small, smoky dive was already crammed with people, all young, all out for a good time.

As she waited for her friends to arrive, Dominique stood at the bar sipping Coke, and surveying the dancers bopping and jiving beneath the flashing colored lights. A good-looking black boy whose muscles bulged out of his short-sleeved yellow shirt, and glistened under the prisms of light, swaggered up to her.

"Wanna dance?" he asked in a bored, cool voice, extending a calloused brown hand without even looking at her. Dominique was thrilled. She had never danced with a black boy before; indeed, until only recently she hardly ever danced anywhere but at dancing school. This kind of dancing—close, grinding, primitive—was all new to her.

"Sure, love to," she drawled, trying to sound cool and bored herself.

"How old are you, girl?" the boy asked as he threw her out on the floor to the rhythm, catching her expertly and twirling her back to him.

"Sixteen," Dominique answered, feeling excited. This boy smelled different from other boys. There was an aroma of musk and sweat about him. He smelled of the West Indies—as she imagined them to be.

"What's your name?" she asked.

"Cab. Yours?"

"Dominique."

"Hi there, Dominique, I guess you're French, huh? And sixteen, huh?" He winked at her as he pulled her back to him. Then as the music changed he started to hold her close and she suddenly felt something large and hard against her thigh. "That's old enough then, ain't it?" he breathed, his lips close to her ear.

"For what?" Dominique asked, almost stumbling to the unaccustomed new slow beat.

"For a smoke, hon. Ya done it, ain't ya?"

"Oh, sure," drawled Dominique. "I've done it loads of times."

Dominique sensed danger, but was stimulated by it. The lights were flashing. The Dirty Dozen was playing a hot beat with pounding expertise, and the crowd seethed with sensuality and youth. The black boy—well, brown really—was deliciously different. Agathe would *kill* her if she knew, and so would her mother. She would be dead meat but it was deliciously thrilling.

"How old are you?" she yelled above the din.

"Twenty," he said, flashing snow-white teeth. "An' I've seen it all, hon. I want to show some of it to you, too—c'mon." The band finished, and as the teenage audience whistled and clapped enthusiastically, Cab grabbed Dominique's hand and led her through the surging throng out through the kitchen to the back door.

In a narrow alley, Dominique leaned breathlessly against a brick wall, watching Cab remove a few things from his pocket. Tobacco, cigarette papers, matches. It was so dark that she couldn't really see what he was doing but when he lit up, inhaling deeply, she could smell a sweetish, pungent odor which make her think of an exotic jungle.

"Take a drag on this, kid—an' let the good times roll!"

He drew deeply again on the cigarette, and Dominique watched, fascinated by his glittering dark eyes with their thick black eyelashes, and by his fleshy pale mauve lips.

She was tingling with anticipation and her high was already halfway there before she even took her first pull of marijuana.

"*Ooh la la.*" She coughed as acrid smoke hit her lungs. "What *is* this?"

"Jamaica Joy, babe," Cab said, taking the joint from her fingers and passing her a flask which he'd taken from his back pocket. "It's the best— it's crazy, man—real cool stuff. Now take a swig of this an' you'll feel better than you ever felt in ya whole life, girl."

Dominique tipped the flask to her lips, almost gagging at the harsh taste.

"Wow, what's that?" she gasped.

"Gin, of course, kid. Good old mother's ruin." He looked at her with amusement. "It won't hurt ya. You wanna feel real good, doncha, kid? Cool, crazy and real real good?"

"Mmm. You bet." Dominique nodded. Suddenly she certainly was feeling good. She was feeling excellent. She was experiencing a great rush of love for the whole beautiful world, for California, and especially for this exotic dusky animal who stood before her puffing on his magic weed and looking at her with glittering black eyes full of some secret amusement.

He passed her the reefer again and she drew it down deeply into her lungs, feeling the drug explode in her head like a Catherine wheel. It burned her throat with its bitter aftertaste, but it felt wonderful, delicious. Her head was as light as a puffball; it seemed to be stuffed with feathers, balloons, and those little globes of gossamer lightness which grow in summer meadows, carried by breezes to other pastures. It was as if her head were one of those puffballs, and if Cab's face came a millimeter nearer to her, his lips would blow it away, breaking her cottonwool skull into a million specks of dust. But she wasn't in a meadow. She was in the dank back alley of a club on Sunset Boulevard in Hollywood, surrounded by the putrid stench of dustbins and the raucous sounds of rock 'n' roll.

As if from a great distance, she saw Cab's enormous lips approaching her. Closer and closer they came, unattached to anything, like some figment of Alice's imagination in her Wonderland. He had no face, just those great mauve lips, coming towards her closer, closer—so close that her eyes

crossed, trying to keep them in focus. The lips were moving, saying something, but she couldn't hear what it was.

They looked terribly funny, those enormous lips, suspended in space, in
time, moving rapidly, yet with no sound coming from them.

Then suddenly, the lips were on hers, but they were not alone. A wet
snakelike tongue darted from between them, entering her mouth like a
reptile slithering into its lair. The slimy, slippery serpent filled her mouth
with its mushy wetness as the enormous lips tried to suck her mouth into
its cavern.

"No, no, *stop*—I can't breathe!" Dominique spluttered, the tongue still
probing her mouth and the great lips continuing to scour her face like a
wet mop over a kitchen floor.

"*Don't!*" She pushed him away hard, looking at him with distaste.

"What were you *doing?*" she gasped. "That was horrible!" Despite her
new and unaccustomed sense of power over men, Dominique was not
experienced in repelling unwanted suitors. When Gaston had kissed her it
was delicate, tender, his tongue exploring her mouth with gentle ardor.
This boy was rough, pushy, crude. She hated what he was doing.

The lips opened, revealing teeth as big as tombstones. "That's good, kid,
that's really, really good." The lips covered the teeth now, and the big black
head bent closer to hers as two huge hands grabbed her shoulders.

"You're messin' around with things ya don't know nothin' about, little
girl." Her head lolled from side to side as he shook her shoulders roughly.
"I give ya a joint and whadda I get? Eh? Horrible—ya say—*I'm* horrible.
That's great, isn't it, eh? I don't give 'em for nothin', ya know. Whadda I get
then, what's *my* reward for givin' ya a good time? C'mon, tell me—what?"
He started shaking her so hard that tears came to her eyes.

He tugged her head back by her hair, clapping a sweating palm over her
mouth. "Now you better keep away from me in the future, girl," he hissed
in her ear. "I know your kind of motherfucker. Pretend you've got the
jungle fever, then ya chicken out." He slammed her against the brick wall
until she hardly had any breath left in her body. "I'll have the word out on
you, so don't be hangin' 'round here no more if ya know what's good for
ya." With a final vicious shove at her, he strutted splayfooted back to the
club, muttering "Cock-teaser" under his breath. Loud blasts from the rock
band escorted him down the alley.

A few minutes later, Dominique limped her way down Sunset Boulevard
towards the hotel. The whole experience had been far from pleasant, but
she had felt stimulated by the danger and the knowledge that the menacing
boy desired her. He had been crude and offensive, but the delicious sensation she had felt when she smoked the reefer still lingered. She knew that

Cab's warning or not, she would go back to the club again. But next time she'd go with friends.

When she reached Agathe's door she heard the sounds of the television on. She crept silently into her own room to ruminate on this latest episode in her California adventure. "The perils of Dominique," she chuckled as she locked her door and took out her diary. "What a gas."

Agathe stared intently at the television screen. Wearing a highwayman's mask, a loden-green frock coat adorned with silver buttons and a black velvet tricorn hat pulled low over his forehead, astride a rearing black stallion with the muzzle of his flintlock pistol pointed at the beautiful, terrified face of Margaret Lockwood, was Julian Brooks. Agathe was riveted. She was watching one of a series of romantic swashbuckling films which Julian had made in England after the war, but it still held up. Agathe thought it was marvelous. How handsome he was, how dashing. She could barely breathe as Julian leaped down from his stallion, flung open the door of the carriage and pressed his lips to those of the frightened heroine.

"*Quelle merveille,*" breathed Agathe, her excitement mounting as their kisses intensified, and Miss Lockwood was swept with a passion which Agathe shared. How wonderful to have the lips of that man who looked like a Greek deity pressed against hers. She could almost feel the electricity between them, as her hand went to her mouth and her own lips opened to the barren dryness of her thumb. "Julian," she moaned softly, closing her eyes to everything but his television voice. "Oh, Julian, *Je t'aime. Que je t'aime, mon amour.*"

13

In a huge mansion hidden high in the canyons of the Hollywood hills, the legendary Ramona Armande was preparing for another evening out. A battalion of maids, hairdressers and *visagistes* hovered in reverential silence around the ivory-and-silver Ruhlmann dressing table at which the great star now sat, fastening diamond-and-emerald pendant earrings to her plump earlobes.

The pale, raven-haired woman had been a legend and a star for so long now that much of her early life was shrouded in mystery. Such was her exquisitely romantic past, which she'd read about in countless fan magazine interviews for some thirty years, that Ramona now believed each romantic word. The fact that she and Didier and their parents, Rachel and Eli Levinsky, had fled Hungary during the First World War, was not to be found in any of her biographies. The Levinsky family had been fortunate to find some relations in the East End of London, and Eli had continued as a fishmonger while she and Didier had been sent to the local school to learn English and the British way of life. Names were changed and both children's lives went on to great success.

Though small in stature, Ramona had a strong character. Woe betide the hapless menial who might misunderstand his mistress's commands at any time, but especially during her elaborate three-hour *grande levée*. Misunderstanding an order from the Princess would cause the unfortunate wretch to receive a withering look from her fabled amber eyes, fringed in lashes long and thick as spider legs, and a few well-chosen phrases from her were more than enough to terrify even the most insensitive.

In her vast bedchamber, lamps were kept dimmed to their lowest wattage to flatter her white, fine skin which was always covered with a special foundation created especially for her by Mr. Max Factor himself. It helped to camouflage the tiny wrinkles which, in spite of all the creams and potions which she applied every night, were multiplying over her precious face. What did it matter that her milky skin wasn't as perfect as it had been in the days of silent movies? She was still a star, and one who had every intention of remaining in the firmament, and she expected to be treated like one. Ramona was a true child of Hollywood, who knew the tricky ropes as well as Mr. Zanuck, Mr. Warner and Mr. Cohn. Tonight she was going to beat them at their own game.

"Bring me my diamonds, Maria," she commanded in the distinctive voice which had been her salvation when talkies had arrived. When many of her compatriots were being laughed off the screen because of their unsuitable voices, Ramona's dulcet tones had, thanks largely to her English education, appealed to the public, and her career had continued to flourish.

She thought about some of her contemporaries who had failed, as she studied her reflection in the three-way mirror. Poor old Jack Gilbert. Audiences had shrieked with laughter when they heard his voice. The great lover who had bedded so many stars of the silent screen and broken so many famous hearts, abandoning their beautiful owners to sob for him into their lace pillowcases, thought only of Greta Garbo, his one great passion. Garbo, Ramona thought, gritting her teeth—she'd certainly managed to pass the talkies test with flying colors. If it were possible, the public's love affair with her had grown even stronger when they all heard her first husky utterance: "Gimme a viskey, ginger ale on the side, and don't be stingy, baby." Audiences all over America had screamed with excitement, and Garbo had become the greatest star of all time.

Ramona frowned as she thought of her former arch-rival. Annoyingly, she was still continually in the American public's eye, as she slithered from yet another transcontinental train or transatlantic liner sheathed in a long coat, floppy felt hat, and always wearing those stupid sunglasses, stage-whispering, "I vant to be alone."

Ramona knew very well that this catchphrase was just another publicity ploy. She knew that Garbo really secretly loved the interest which her self-conscious mystery provoked. Garbo thrived on it. The more she "vanted to be alone," the less, of course, she was allowed to be. It was irritating and infuriating to Ramona, but Garbo was still continually in the newspapers and magazines, despite not having made a single appearance on celluloid for more than ten years.

Plucking a Lalique scent bottle from the massed ranks of expensive objects cluttering her dressing table, Ramona sprayed herself with a cloud of Shalimar, while her maid attached a diamond-and-tortoiseshell comb to her sleek black chignon. Ramona clasped the magnificent emerald, natural pearl and European-cut diamond necklace around her well preserved throat and surveyed herself critically. "Perfect," she breathed to herself, "perfect." She was ready at last, as ravishing as she could possibly make herself.

Tonight was another Hollywood party, this time to welcome the distinguished English actor Julian Brooks into the enchanted circle of Beverly Hills. He would be with Inès Juillard, the woman for whom he had left his wife, the woman all Hollywood was eager to meet. Their romance had been conducted discreetly because of his impending divorce, and few, if any, photographs had as yet appeared of the loving couple. The party was to be at the house of Spyros Makopolis, president of MCCP and one of the most important men in town. Ramona was determined to look more beautiful than ever before, fresh from her recent success in her new Italian movie. Tonight she would show the elite of Beverly Hills that Ramona Armande was still a star of the greatest magnitude—still someone very much to be reckoned with.

In the Aubusson-carpeted drawing room of her mansion, Ramona's escort for the evening and the producer of her new but as yet unreleased film, Umberto Scrofo, sat admiring her collection of Impressionists and sipping champagne while he waited patiently for her to finish dressing. This was his first trip to Hollywood and he was in a fever of anticipation about tonight's A-list party.

He couldn't wait to belong and to take charge once more.

"Spyros' house is lit up like a bloody Christmas tree!" Julian Brooks observed. It was true. Every window blazed with light, and the white Palladian-style villa, set in manicured lawns among tall cypress trees, had been strung with thousands of colored fairy lights, reflecting something which few Californians ever saw.

"Snow! *Mon Dieu!*" Inès exclaimed, leaning closer to the limousine window. "For goodness' sake look, Julian—it's snow! How could we have snow here? It's been over seventy degrees today."

Julian looked down at the thick sparkling expanse of virgin snow which carpeted either side of the long, winding driveway, and smiled at Inès, who was staring at a gargantuan jade-green Christmas tree, some thirty feet high, which was completely covered with sparkling baubles of every imaginable color.

The door to their limousine was flung open by a parking valet who was dressed, much to his own embarrassment, as one of Santa's elves. Most of these boys were out-of-work actors, so they managed to conceal their embarrassment fairly convincingly as they politely helped the glamorous guests from their cars with "Good evening, ma'am, sir, and a very merry Christmas to you."

Inès stifled a giggle at the sight of Spyros' impeccable English butler, Sanderson, now dressed in the unlikely costume of Santa Claus. His solemn face hardly matched the jolly seasonal red outfit and white beard. He had in fact refused point-blank to wear the costume, even threatening to resign, but Mr. Makopolis had finally persuaded him to don it in the way that he persuaded everyone to do anything: with money.

"This could never happen in England or France, could it, darling?" Julian whispered, squeezing Inès' hand as they exchanged amused glances. Inès was amazed. Ten years of associating with aristocrats and people of culture and breeding in London had given her a definite knowledge of what is done and what is not done. So far, what she had seen of the overdecorated Makopolis mansion had been frightful. A butler dressed as Père Noël? *Quelle horreur!*

"But, *chéri*." Inès was still puzzled. "Today I was sunbathing by the pool. How can it snow here at night?"

"Fake, my darling, fake," Julian laughed. "I'm quite sure that old Spyros had the prop department whip up this little concoction."

"But how?" A sophisticated woman of the world as far as most things were concerned, Inès found the ways of Lotus Land a total mystery. "You cannot make snow, Julian. How can you?"

"Crystals and cottonwood," he explained. "Must have cost the studio prop department a bloody fortune. Good old Spyros, he's an amazing old coot."

"But why would he want to do that when it is so pretty here without it?"

"One-upmanship, my darling," Julian said. "Next year everyone in Hollywood will have their driveways and lawns covered with *fausse neige*—and dear old Mr. and Mrs. Makopolis will be crowing to themselves because they were the first on the block to think of it."

Julian took a slim flute of champagne from a footman, this one ludicrously dressed as Rudolph the Red-Nosed Reindeer, and winked at Inès. Already half the female guests were eyeing him covertly and looking enviously at her. Muted chatter without beginning or end flowed throughout the room as Spyros and Olympia Makopolis bore down on Julian and Inès with overflowing bonhomie. Taking them in tow, they introduced them to the rest of the famous guests, all of whom were dying to meet "the new Olivier," as Julian had recently been dubbed by the MCCP publicity department, much to his embarrassment.

.   .   .

Ramona Armande stood to one side, talking to her brother and Umberto Scrofo. Didier was carefully eyeing his protégé while Umberto stared at the beautiful woman Julian was escorting. Ravishing, she was absolutely gorgeous. He couldn't see much of her face but her creamy décolletage was quite mouthwatering. Umberto appreciated rare beauty, and this woman was A-first class. He hoped he'd get a chance to meet her later on. She was obviously cultured; they could talk about paintings.

Didier thought Julian had done well—extremely well—since the time of their first meeting in his dingy dressing room. Didier always recognized those who possessed star quality, and those who did not. Julian Brooks had it in spades, and it had been polished and honed throughout the years until it radiated from him almost palpably.

In the years that Julian had been under contract to Didier's company, he had achieved precisely what had been planned for him. He had become unquestionably the biggest star in England. And this in spite of his bitch of a wife who, Didier thought, had always been an impediment to Julian. Phoebe and her social climbing, her pathetic attempts to become some kind of aristocrat, and all those damn cats of hers had not helped Julian's career. Happily, thanks to Inès, Phoebe was ancient history. All that the loving couple were waiting for now was the decree nisi. Once that obstacle had been cleared, they would be free to marry.

Inès observed the chattering throng in Spyros' vast drawing room, admiring so many faces which she'd seen in the movies since childhood. All the women were impossibly glamorous, groomed like prize fillies in the parade ring before a race. Their toffee-tanned, sleek bodies, even some of the plumper producers' wives, were corseted, girdled and brassiered to within an inch of their lives, and there seemed to be no such thing as a gray head of hair.

A sea of décolletage bobbed around. Breasts of all shapes, sizes and shades, many pushed up with underwiring and Merry Widow corsets, spilled seductively over the colorful satin, chiffon, lamé and lace gowns of Hollywood's most illustrious women. And their jewels! Inès had seen jewels like this only in the Tower of London or on the Queen of England.

But if Inès was fascinated by the women of Hollywood, the entire Hollywood community was more than curious to meet the woman for whom it was said Julian had given up everything but his talent. Despite the attempts of Julian and Didier to keep the terms of his divorce settlement quiet, the news had soon become common knowledge in the business. There were few secrets in the tight-knit community—none in fact—and everyone at the party knew every detail about Julian's divorce.

The women grudgingly agreed that Inès was very beautiful. The slim column of champagne silk worn with a simple string of pearls, the long, dark brown hair, unteased, unsprayed, uncurled, and the fine porcelain complexion with barely even a hint of cosmetic enhancement were in sharp contrast to the flashy looks of so many of them. Dark red lips and smoky kohl-shadowed eyes were her only makeup.

"She's so French," breathed one buxom starlet to another as they teased, sprayed and painted in the green marble splendor of the Makopolis powder room.

"Yeah, she just oozes class, don't she?" said starlet number two, painting an already pouting lower lip into a cyclamen moue.

"I bet she's from a *real* top-drawer family," breathed the first girl, inserting a hand deep into her cleavage to push up her breasts until her chin could almost have rested on them.

"Yeah—aristocratic all right. She sure didn't have to work to make out like we've had to."

"Yup," said the first, spraying a generous amount of Evening in Paris into her ample cleavage. "She's a real lucky dame. I bet it all came real easy to that one. Just as easy as pie."

"Ah, there's Julian," Shirley Frankovitch said as soon as she saw the English star. "Damn, he's great-looking, isn't he, Irving? No wonder they call him the handsomest guy in the world."

Her husband, a lugubrious man of nearly sixty, nodded. Early in his career he had written several fictional masterpieces and been hailed by the literate as the natural successor to Hemingway. Upon his meeting Shirley Horowitz, however, ten years his junior and ambition her middle name, his brilliant literary style had gradually been eroded by her demands and influence.

Ignoring the plays and novels of genius which were fermenting inside him and which his publishers begged him to write, he had become her mentor. He was in fact so besotted by her that it was *her* writing career which had become his obsession, while his own had taken a backseat.

In 1946 Shirley had had her first book published—a novel which had owed a great deal to Irving's literary talent and a certain amount to her own fertile sexual imagination. *Valentina,* the tale of a gorgeous courtesan in eighteenth-century France, had become an overnight best-seller all over the world. Soon Hollywood had beckoned, wanting Shirley to write the script for the movie. Shirley craved a Hollywood career, and who was Irving to argue?

They had taken the train to the West Coast from New York and installed themselves in the Garden of Allah. For six months they had partied with Hollywood's finest, between bouts of serious writing. The fruits of their labors—Shirley's *Valentina,* a dreadful yet successful movie, and Irving's infinitely better *Silence of the Damned*—both became box-office smashes.

Irving then went on to have enormous Broadway and London successes with his two plays about distinguished political-historical figures, while Shirley then wrote *Valentina and the King* and two more smash-hit sequels to her carnal heroine's adventures.

With Shirley's bawdy portraits of seventeenth- and eighteenth-century heroines, and Irving's critically acclaimed scripts, the Frankovitches soon earned a reputation for really knowing their onions when it came to historical melodrama. Who better than they to write the screenplay for *The Legend of Cortez,* which was being heralded as the greatest historical epic since *The Ten Commandments?*

Shirley licked her lips in anticipation of meeting the star of their movie. Julian was catnip to women, a fact she appreciated only too well. After all, she had been quite a swinger herself for a while, although her own un-spectacular looks had now turned to bloated flesh. But Shirley appreciated male beauty, aware, always, of the unlikelihood of her fantasies ever turning into reality. After all, a girl could dream, and it was Shirley's dreams which translated so convincingly onto the printed page.

There were so many people at the party that it was impossible for Julian and Inès to meet them all.

Every important star, director, producer and studio head had been invited, along with a spicy seasoning of contract starlets of both sexes. By nine o'clock there was such a heated crush in the three enormous reception rooms that Olympia Makopolis insisted that dinner be served at once.

Fifty tables covered with lamé cloths and each laid for ten people had been set up inside a giant red-and-white striped tent in the sprawling back garden. The walls of the tent were draped in evergreens, ivy and red poinsettias, and hundreds of tiny lights twinkled down from the ceiling, interspersed with more than ten thousand red roses suspended in silver mesh baskets. A vast eighteenth-century rock-crystal chandelier, some five feet in diameter, blazed down on the guests from the center, casting prisms of light on their expectant faces.

Spyros was known to give wonderful parties, but this one was set to top them all, it seemed.

A groaning buffet table, covered with scarlet satin and decorated with holly and silver lamé ribbons, held huge Baccarat crystal bowls of beluga caviar, silver salvers of lobster, baby crayfish, *foie gras* with the finest black truffles, smoked salmon flown in from Scotland, quail eggs and a profusion of exotic salads. At the opposite end of the tent a twenty-piece band in red dinner jackets played Gershwin and Cole Porter, and over a hundred waiters and waitresses, all dressed as fairies or elves, took the guests' orders from individual menus, written in exquisite calligraphy, which rested in front of each place card. Money was no object at the Makopolis house; after all, the studio was paying, and they were in the black this year.

Inès was seated between Spyros and the scintillating Cary Grant. Across the table Julian had Olympia Makopolis on his left—not much fun in the witty repartee stakes—but to his relief vivacious Rosalind Russell had been placed on his right and she kept Julian amused with a stream of fascinating and hilarious anecdotes.

In the center of each table an enormous cornucopia overflowing with Christmas goodies—tiny wheelbarrows filled with miniature Santa Clauses, jack-in-the-boxes, Raggedy Ann dolls, gift boxes, fairies, pixies and candy canes—spilled over in elegant yet ordered disarray onto the silver lamé tableclothes. In front of each guest was a present, a hallmarked silver Tiffany frame, wrapped in sky-blue paper and tied with silver ribbons and sprigs of holly. In the frame was a photograph of the smiling and paternal-looking Spyros Makopolis, Mrs. Makopolis, and their five children, all looking stiffly self-conscious.

"Hollywood, darling," mouthed Julian with a wink across the table to Inès as she opened her package. "Take it as it comes."

Inès sipped her heavily scented wine and smiled inwardly. So this was what it was really like. This was the Hollywood that the fans revered and the movie magazines gushed about; the magic place which intrigued everyone who went to the cinema. She would have to learn to like it, in spite of the incredible excesses of vulgarity she'd seen tonight, but she knew she could like anything as long as Julian was by her side. As long as she could be Mrs. Julian Brooks. How long—oh, Lord, how long would it be before his final decree was granted in London?

Across the sea of faces and noise, seated at a table of less important guests, the other newcomer to Hollywood gazed around in impressed delight.

Umberto Scrofo fingered the scar beneath his tight collar uncomfortably. As usual, when he was excited or ill at ease, it itched and burned like the devil. He fought the strong desire to rip open his collar and scratch it fiercely. Tonight he must behave like a gentleman even though he felt out of place. He'd felt like a country bumpkin when introduced to Grace Kelly, Marilyn Monroe and so many other stars. He was so overawed that his conversation dried up and he knew he was making a *bruta figura*. He was angry with Ramona Armande, who seemed to have deliberately ignored him from the moment they arrived. She flitted from group to group, laughing her affected laugh, stopping often to huddle with her brother. The two were known to be inseparable when Didier was in town, inspiring the nickname the Magyar Mafia. He noticed angrily that Didier had been seated at the top table with Julian Brooks, while Ramona was at an adjacent table far away from Umberto. Insulting bitch.

One of these days, I *will* belong there, at the number one table, he thought, maneuvering a dollop of caviar into his mouth. When these Hollywood people see my finished masterpiece, I'll be courted and admired the way Julian Brooks is with that woman who isn't even his wife.

He had caught another glimpse of Inès' profile earlier as her dark hair swung around her shoulders and she smiled at Julian. There was definitely something familiar about her—something which struck a strangely responsive chord in him. He'd wanted to get a closer look but she and Julian were surrounded by Gary Cooper, Errol Flynn and Clark Gable, all laughing, sharing secrets that men who looked as they did always seemed to share, so he couldn't get near them.

Umberto exchanged a few remarks across the table with Irving Frankovitch, who had written his superb script for *La Città Perduta,* then tried to listen to the boring babble of the woman next to him, a fat, overdressed monstrosity in a purple tent covered with flowered sequins. She had obviously tried hard, but failed miserably to pull herself together for tonight. Face powder in an unsuitable shade of orange caked the pores of her sweaty face, and her gray hair was frizzed and sprayed into an unfashionable style. But his jeweler's eye noticed that she was wearing a magnificent parure of diamonds and sapphires, obviously of extremely high quality, so she must be someone. Everyone here seemed to be someone.

He was becoming bored by her chatter, as he disliked ugly women, and it was only when Irving Frankovitch spoke to her that he realized she was Frankovitch's wife. While Irving was in Rome writing, Shirley had stayed in New York, so Umberto had never met her. Ah, this was much better. Shirley Frankovitch was a force to be reckoned with. A brilliant writer, an important woman in this town. He decided to cultivate her. She could help him with his plans of glory.

Shirley had been drinking steadily. Four or more glasses of Krug before dinner, and three glasses of Stolichnaya with her beluga had been downed faster than a sailor on shore leave. She had signaled to her waiter, good-looking even though he was dressed as an elf, to keep her wineglass topped up. By the time Spyros was making his introductory toasts, she was feeling no pain. Irving had tried to stop her drinking but she reprimanded him sharply. She felt good—she liked the way she felt when she'd really blasted a few.

Shirley hadn't been a heavy drinker when she was a teenager, but as she grew older and Mr. Right hadn't crossed her path, drinking had somehow become second nature to her. She had less than fond memories, in the days when she'd been a struggling writer in New York, of getting drunk night after night—always in the company of men, none of whom could ever have been remotely considered the answer to a maiden's prayer. Shirley had been so shy, insecure and intimidated by almost everything and everyone that she tried to lose herself in the romantic worlds which she created in her writing. But in sober reality, constant rejection was more the order of the day. Rejection from the publishers, rejection from the men. Only a diet of pink ladies, dry martinis and champagne cocktails could instill in her the illusion that she really mattered. Through her haze of alcohol she was able to amuse some of her male drinking partners enough to end up in bed with one of them occasionally. But the following morning she would always wake with a throbbing hangover. Sometimes she would find herself slumped across crumpled linen sheets in a shiny penthouse in uptown Manhattan, but more often than not her puffy eyes opened to a peeling fly-specked ceiling in some dingy midtown bedroom. There the object of last night's lust, typically some bleary-eyed blue-jawed brute, would avoid looking at her, which made her feel even cheaper.

It would have been stretching it to have called Shirley attractive, but she was eager to please, longed to be loved, and had good legs and big breasts. When the lights burned low and the hour was late, many men would lose their former powers of discrimination through drink, and slake their lust with Shirley. She always knew that she was never the first, second or even the third choice of her passing parade of paramours, but she never let her bitterness show. Instead she made every effort to become the life and soul of whatever party, club or bar she happened to find herself in. As she knocked back cocktail after cocktail, the skirts of her evening dresses hitched steadily higher as the evening progressed, revealing a tantalizing glimpse of garter belt and white thighs to entice the boys.

Occasionally, one of the boys would prove to be more than just a one-night stand, his attentions lingering towards her for a week or two, even for a month, but these liaisons always seemed to wane rapidly, and the shapely legs, the thirty-eight-inch bust and the increasingly bawdy repartee were never enough to sustain any permanent interest.

By the time Shirley Horowitz met Irving Frankovitch, she was pushing thirty-five and filled with an inner discontent and anger with a life which she felt had dealt her a rotten hand. Irving, however, the unassuming, unattractive, but brilliant writer from Hoboken, fell heavily and totally under her spell. He thought Shirley was the wittiest, funniest and sexiest woman in the world. The fact that his experience of women was severely limited, due largely to his shyness and unassuming looks, did not bother Shirley at all. Finally she had hooked herself a man.

Both sets of parents in Brooklyn and Hoboken breathed a communal sigh of relief when their respective only children were finally married in a burst of post-austerity glory. At the strictly Jewish wedding where the guests tucked into mountains of smoked salmon and sturgeon, potato *latkes,* wedding cake and expensively imported French red wine and champagne, Shirley became very drunk indeed. When Irving had finished his wedding speech, she rose, her veiled headdress of orange blossoms askew on her mouse-colored hair, and drawled triumphantly to the assembled throng.

"I know that all of you probably think that Irving doesn't look like much, but at least he's all mine, so hands off, girls, I've staked my claim."

Some of her girlfriends giggled, but a disapproving murmur echoed from the older members of the Frankovitch clan, and Shirley's mother raised a warning eyebrow at her daughter. But the bride, taking another few sips of champagne, would not to be halted. Swaying from side to side, her massive breasts pushed up so high by her underwire bra that they seemed on the point of an escape attempt, she hiccuped loudly several times, then said, "Yeah, I know he's got a body like a shrunken little runt, but he's a real tiger between the sheets, girls—real hot stuff." The younger members of both families screamed with laughter, as the parents, uncles, older cousins and aunts sat rigid with disapproval, and Irving's normally sallow face flushed deeply as he lowered his head in embarrassment. Clutching her new husband's hand, fueled by the laughter and the sea of upturned smiling faces around her, Shirley couldn't stop herself. Grabbing Irving's glass of wine she downed it in one gulp and screeched.

"You may all think he's got a face like a big rabbit too what with those big ears and that funny twitchy pink nose of his, but let me tell you, girls—" her voice dropped to a conspiratorial stage whisper—"I'm delighted to tell you he sure as hell fucks like one!"

Shirley let out a screech of delight as she threw back another glass and almost everyone except Irving's parents screamed with laughter. The new bride could feel great waves of love washing over her, as the laughing faces looked up at her with admiration. She reveled in it. Taking no notice at all of Irving's pained discomfort, ignoring the furious stares of his parents, Shirley threw her enraptured audience a final outrageous tidbit:

"Confidentially, girls ..." She steadied herself with her hands on the table, whispering in such a way that the hundred guests had to lean forward to catch her every word. "Between you 'n' me—he's the greatest little sex machine I've ever known, and believe me I've known more than my fair share, much *much* more. He can go *all* night 'n' every morning and although his little *schlong* may not be up to very much in the size department, what he lacks in inches he sure makes up for in staying power, he can *shtup* the night away, girls, and the afternoons too."

Her audience was in the palm of her hand now and Shirley had never had such a good time. Heedless of the disapproving maiden aunts shepherding the juvenile members of the party out of the room, oblivious to the guffawing waiters, some of whom had rushed from other parts of the hotel to hear her, she turned to her flushed and shell-shocked bridegroom and planted an enormous open-mouthed kiss on his gaping lips. "This little *putz* is the greatest *shtupper* I've ever known, and I've known a helluva lot!"

The whole room burst into applause, except for Irving's horrified father who was fanning Irving's deeply shocked mother with his fringed *tallith*. They were unable to comprehend why their precious only son had married such a vulgar drunken slut. A small gaggle of wide-eyed nephews and nieces stood snickering at the door, not understanding what Aunt Shirley had said, but knowing from the reaction of their elders that, whatever it meant, it sure was hot stuff.

That night, in the privacy of the honeymoon suite, Irving gave vent to his anger and burst his bride's balloon of happiness.

"You behaved like a cheap tart, Shirley," he told her, a pulse beating in his neck, the only physical sign of his shame and rage. "Worse than a street-corner tramp. I know that isn't the *real* you, which is why I forgive you, but I beg you, *please,* honey, you must stop drinking—it doesn't suit you, Shirley, and it's so undignified."

"Why should I?" snapped Shirley, tossing her orange-blossom headdress to the floor and gratefully unfastening the tight ankle-strap sandals which had been pinching her feet for hours. Irving was a spoilsport. He was bringing her down from an all-time high. Why was he trying to ruin everything now when everyone had adored her this afternoon?

"It's degrading," he said mildly. "It makes you look foolish, Shirley."

"Foolish, shmoolish, what the fuck—who *gives* a damn—they *loved* me—all of those people—all our relatives, and friends—even Mom and Dad. They never gave a shit about me before but they were laughing their heads off—did you see 'em laugh, Irving? Didja?"

"Yes, I did, Shirley," said Irving patiently, noticing that Shirley was calming down, becoming herself again as the effects of the lethal alcohol wore off. "I did see them laugh, but they were laughing *at* you, honey, not *with* you. There's a difference—don't you see that, honey?"

"No, I don't. I had a great time, Irv, and you're bringing me down now."

Shirley flounced into the bathroom, her eyes bright with hot tears, and slammed the door. Then Irving heard her violently throwing up, and shrugged. He was a kind and patient man, who loved this woman, his new wife, recognizing many of her fears and insecurities. But the *Beaujolais Belligerence* she evinced when drunk would have to go. He would see to it that she stopped drinking. He felt sure he would be able to handle her now that they were married.

Irving glanced over at Shirley as Spyros started talking. No doubt about it—she'd had much more than a snootful. From the way she was glaring at everyone, she looked about to explode at any moment. He sighed, mentally fastening his seat belt for the bumpy ride which looked now to be inevitable.

After dinner Spyros introduced Julian, who rose with a modest bow to enthusiastic applause from the guests. How Hollywood loved a true thespian from the British theater. The *crème de la crème* of the cinema always felt inferior, somehow insignificant, beside an actor who regularly performed the classics on stage. With all their fame, looks and wealth, many of these stars were desperately insecure about their abilities and envied Julian his impeccable theatrical reputation.

Many also respected his brave stand against Phoebe. Few of them would have given up a perpetual slice of their earnings, a house and all its contents, just for the love of a woman. Consequently Inès was the object of enormous conjecture and gossip, most of which subsided as she passed her test with flying colors. Her beauty and style couldn't be faulted on any level. Those who talked to her found her charming, witty and cultured, not bitchy in the slightest.

Julian started to speak now, his melodic baritone entrancing the guests with a particularly amusing and self-deprecating joke at which the crowd roared its approval. Inès looked at him, admiring his poise and his velvet voice.

Shirley glanced around the room irritably. Every eye seemed riveted on Julian or on the woman across him. No one was looking in her direction.

Why not? *She* too was a Star. A star writer and a star novelist who had written the script that had enticed Julian to America. *She* had single-handedly kept MCCP afloat through the lean, tough times after the war when audiences didn't know what the hell they wanted to see. But they'd all gone to see the movies she'd written, hadn't they? Especially the *Valentina* series. If it weren't for writers, nothing would ever happen in this town. No one seemed to appreciate how important they were to the movie product. No one.

"He's a lucky guy to have a woman like that," Irving said admiringly.

"And what's so great about her?" Shirley slurred belligerently. "She looks like a cold fish to me."

Irving ignored her as Julian told another joke and the rapt faces laughed again.

God damn it. Suddenly Shirley realized furiously that she wasn't even at the top table. Shit, shit, shit. What a bummer. Okay, so she was seated with Zanuck and Orson Welles—neither of them exactly *schleppers* in the business—but she still took it as a personal insult. After all she'd done for Spyros, this was his appreciation. Voices inside her seemed to be having a furious argument as they battled for supremacy. Good little Shirley was telling off bad little Shirley, but bad little Shirley seemed to be winning. Shirley knew she was losing control. Her head felt stuffed with cottonwool, her mouth dry. She quickly slugged back another glass of champagne, looking around the room with a challenging expression.

Irving's eyes were glued to Julian. Or was it Julian's French mistress he was staring at? Shirley squinted, trying to figure out *who* held her husband's attention. Yes, she was right, bad Shirley thought triumphantly. He was staring at the stuck-up Frenchwoman who looked as if butter wouldn't melt in her cocksucking mouth. Irving should be looking at her—her, *her!!* He was *her* husband, for Christ's sake. If he loved *her,* he should be paying attention to her.

Angrily, Shirley stuck a Lucky Strike in her mouth, turning to Irving for a light. He ignored her. He's ignoring you, Shirley, said the bad voice. As if you were nothing, no one, a fucking stranger!

"Gimme a light, Irving," she snapped, so loudly that Julian paused momentarily in his speech to look over at her.

Irving gestured that he had no matches, ignoring her again as his attention returned to Julian. In a fury, Shirley scrabbled through the cornucopia in front of her for matches. Some of the guests began to notice the disturbance and to make shushing noises. There were no matches in Santa's goodie box, and no one was smoking at Shirley's table.

"Fuck, fuck,*fuck!* Where are the motherfucking matches?" she screamed.

Julian stopped speaking as every head turned towards her and collectively Hollywood tut-tutted its silent disapproval of the bleary-eyed writer. Empty glass in hand, unlit cigarette dangling from slack lips, she was obviously completely, unbecomingly smashed.

Julian resumed his speech as Shirley's cute-looking waiter-elf dashed forward and struck a match for her. Inhaling deeply, she watched the sycophantic faces as they turned again in unison to listen to the actor's speech. What bullshit, she thought. They're all full of shit, every single one of the motherfuckers.

No longer giving a damn what anyone thought, Shirley suddenly stood up and said in a sarcastic, belligerent voice, "Everything that you say is absolute bullshit, your lordship. Everything in this room is bullshit— everyone in Hollywood is just a piece of *crap!*" She belched loudly, weaving violently as Irving grabbed her and pulled her into her seat.

"What the *hell* are you doing?" he whispered furiously. "For God's sake, behave yourself, Shirley. You're way out of line and making a complete fool of yourself again."

Everyone was looking at her now, some even standing up to get a better view. The whole damned tent—five hundred pairs of curious eyes were staring at her in shock, yet with the secret pleasure that tomorrow they'd all have something really juicy to gossip about.

That's the way it ought to be, Shirley thought, pleased with herself as she greedily downed another glass of champagne. They *should* be talking about her. Then she hiccuped so violently that the glass of champagne she was drinking spilled all over the front of her sequined tent dress. When the pretty waiter rushed forward to try to help her, he tripped over a piece of loose grass-green carpet and landed head first in Shirley's ample cleavage to shrieks of shocked laughter from the guests. Then, to add to Irving's intense embarrassment, Shirley's humiliation and the rest of the guests' hilarity, the two of them plummeted in slow motion to the floor, the tiny waiter in his elf's costume almost disappearing into the massive folds of Shirley's caftan.

Hollywood, of course, hushed up the story and closed ranks, as Hollywood always attempted to hush up the scandals and peccadillos of its darlings to the outside world. Nothing at all appeared in the press. But telephone wires hummed the next day throughout the Hills of Holmby and Beverly as chattering tongues broadcast the delicious news of Shirley's scandalous behavior to friends and acquaintances who'd neither had the luck nor the clout to have been invited to what must have been the party of the season.

Exaggerations abounded. By the end of the week, the story had been completely blown out of proportion. Not only had Shirley Frankovitch been completely drunk, but she'd ripped off her dress, danced half naked on the table, then pulled the waiter under the table, where she'd tried to give him a blow job. Olympia had become hysterical and had to be given a sedative by Dr. Zolotos. And Spyros had threatened Shirley that he would never use her again on a movie and fired both her and Irving from *Cortez.* Tittle-tattle and scandal. How the town loved it—revelled in it. Gossip, power and the movie business, these were the three ingredients that made its world turn and its inhabitants thrive.

On the way home from the party Inès couldn't stop talking and laughing about the party and the excesses of vulgarity she'd seen.

"Don't worry, darling," Julian smiled. "It's not always quite as tawdry as that—actually, many people who live here do have the most wonderful taste. Some of the most knowledgeable private art collectors in America live here. Many of them are even actors, believe it or not."

"Who?" inquired Inès. "I would like to meet them, Julian. Some of the pictures I saw on Mr. Makopolis' walls were absolute fakes. Anyone could see that. The original of the Renoir above the fireplace in the library is in the Louvre! How can Mr. Makopolis be so gullible?"

"Good old Spyros. He knows everything about the movies but not much about the art world. Tell you what, darling. Next week we'll go and see Eddie G. Robinson or Vincent Price, they both know everything about pictures and have marvellous collections."

"Mmm, I'd love to." Inès rested her head on Julian's shoulder as he drove them through the darkened empty streets of Beverly Hills towards their hotel. "But all I want to do now, *mon amour,* is to go home and make love with you."

"You've got yourself a deal, *Mademoiselle,*" said Julian gravely. "And you are not allowed to go back on your word."

*E*ven though it was December it was a boiling hot day. Dominique was playing volleyball on the Santa Monica sands with a group of shrieking teenagers, mostly boys, leaving Agathe with little to do but lie in the sun—something which she hated—or to eat lunch, which she'd already done. She decided to go for a walk. She wandered down the asphalt pavement which bordered the beach, thinking, thinking, thinking, oblivious to the cars speeding past, to the high, bright sun, indeed to anything at all except the vision of Julian Brooks which now filled her thoughts constantly.

They had met at last. Well, not exactly met. She had been having lunch in the MCCP commissary with Dominique and Kittens, the costume designer, when he'd come over to introduce himself. Agathe felt a deep flush suffuse her entire body as he stood chatting charmingly at their table. The flush seemed to rise from her between her legs and engulf her until she felt that her face was a scarlet mirror in which he could read all her most secret thoughts.

She hardly dared to meet his eyes; she just listened to his melodious voice as he spoke and laughed with Dominique and Kittens. The easy camaraderie the three of them seemed to share goaded Agathe into a silent jealous frenzy. Julian stood so tall and easy, one hand casually resting on the back of Dominique's chair, while the girl giggled up at him, chattering nineteen to the dozen. Agathe had frozen. She had been unable to meet his eye even for a second or two, conscious of the sweat which trickled down her back, the flush on her face and the horrible, embarrassing tingling in her groin. He could sense it—of course he could sense it. That was why he was ignoring her, wasn't it? Julian tipped his hat to the women as he left, and Agathe felt herself relax. Dominique's face was flushed and happy as she bit into her hamburger.

"Golly, he sure is cute for an old man, don't you think, Agathe?"

Kittens nodded in agreement.

"I'm sure I don't know what you mean," said Agathe stiffly.

"He's terribly good-looking," sighed Dominique, then leaning towards her chaperone, she whispered, "I hear that practically every actress he's ever worked with has fallen for him!"

"Don't say things like that, it isn't right for young girls like you to have thoughts like that," snapped Agathe. "Eat your lunch."

Dominique grinned to herself. If Agathe only knew what thoughts she did have, the poor old thing would probably have a nervous breakdown.

Inès woke up to the Beverly Hills sunshine, which streamed into the hotel room through the cloudy muslin curtains. She was nauseous and her head felt fuzzy. Strange, as she usually was able to handle champagne. Julian had left early for the studio's Malibu ranch for the first of his stunt-riding lessons. It was essential to be an expert horseman, and the end of the eight-week instruction period would hopefully guarantee that Julian would be able to deal with a horse better than the grizzled handlers at the ranch.

The telephone rang, the shrill sound making her head throb. It was Julian calling from the ranch.

"Darling." His voice was warm. "How are you feeling?"

She lied and assured him she was feeling fine.

"Good, good. Darling, I've just bumped into Flynn down here at the ranch. He's asked us to dinner tonight at Romanoff's—will you be up to it, angel?"

"Of course, *chéri.* I liked him so much when we met last night. And I've always wanted to go to Romanoff's."

"Good. Okay, I've got to run, my love. God, my arse is so sore from the damn horse. They must have been supermen in those days to ride without saddles."

"I'll kiss it better when you come home," Inès murmured, laughing.

"Can't wait, darling. See you later—dinner's at eight. We'll meet Errol there."

After a lazy, relaxing day, Inès dressed carefully for dinner, in a black *peau de soie* cocktail dress with a full mid-calf skirt. Her only jewelry was Julian's simple diamond engagement ring, small diamond stud earrings and her lucky bracelet, but she looked ravishing and Julian couldn't stop telling her so.

Romanoff's was on Rodeo Drive. One of the most famous restaurants in the world, it was owned and run by Prince Michael Romanoff, a self-styled exiled Russian prince with impeccable manners and immense charm. Because there were no top tables at Romanoff's—hence no Siberia—he managed to have half of Hollywood dining there regularly without ever offending any of their fragile egos. Stars always sat where Prince Michael put them and never complained.

He now stepped suavely forward to greet Julian and Inès as they came through the thick glass doors into the foyer. Every table was in full view and most of the diners looked up as they entered. Though small in stature, Prince Michael was big on personality. Inès could feel the power behind his twinkling brown eyes as he charmingly kissed her hand, murmuring to Julian, "Looks, m'boy, you've done it again as usual—what a ravishing gel—French too—excellent. I'm very happy for you, m'boy—come, Errol's waiting."

He led the way down the carpeted stairway while everyone in the room stared at Inès and Julian. It was as if the restaurant had been designed for people-watchers. None of the booths was high-backed, so one group could easily chat to another at the tables on either side and behind, and could see everything else that was going on.

Julian nodded hellos to Cary Grant and Darryl Zanuck as they wended their way to the table where Errol Flynn sat beside a pretty girl who looked young enough to be his daughter.

Prince Michael took their drink order in his clipped English accent, then, clamping his cigarette holder firmly between his teeth, left them to greet the ravishing Grace Kelly, who was standing at the top of the stairs with a handsome escort.

The room buzzed and then went silent as every detail of Grace's hair, makeup and outfit was analyzed by the women, while every man marveled at her beauty. Inès thought she was breathtaking. She deserved her title of Hollywood's reigning princess. She was flawless, besides being a highly talented actress.

It was an exhilarating dinner, and Errol was in top form, although drinking heavily. His young companion spoke little, content to giggle shyly at his jokes, most of which she didn't really understand, and to eat everything put before her. Errol embroidered on the fracas created by

Shirley Frankovitch at Spyros' party the other night, and had everyone in stitches.

Several studio executives stopped by the table, ostensibly to pay their respects to Errol, but after a perfunctory greeting to him, they seemed far more interested in Julian. By the end of the evening his pocket contained half a dozen cards from some of the most influential men in town, with instructions to call them as soon as possible.

Flynn was not given even one card. Although only in his mid-forties he was almost finished in Hollywood. He had been a great star, but he was now considered box-office poison, having outraged moral Middle America with his amorous antics, his philandering with underage girls, his drunken brawls, and his "I don't give a damn" attitude. Studio publicists had been unable to hold down the lid on his scandalous behavior, and he'd become Hollywood's whipping boy—almost a pariah. But he was wonderfully charming, Inès thought, full of humor, and a truly great raconteur. He must have been glorious-looking once, she decided.

When Inès went to the powder room, the peach-mirrored haven was empty but for one girl whose enormous overly tanned cleavage swelled out of an unfashionably short tight white lace dress which cupped her too-plump derriere in a most unflattering way. Her big lips were painted with thick pink gloss, and her mane of platinum hair heavily teased. Inès realized that the girl had gone to enormous trouble to try to look as much as possible like Jayne Mansfield, one of the town's leading sex symbols. The starlet was a true Hollywood cupcake. She eyed Inès' simple black Balenciaga dress admiringly while she applied yet more hair spray to her platinum helmet.

"I saw you the other night at the Makopolis party," she confided in a friendly way, removing another cosmetic necessity from her pink plastic and rhinestone bag, bending over so far that Inès could see her nipples. "I just *love* the way you dress. It's so chic—so French!" she gushed.

Inès murmured a thank you. What a pitiful girl—professional, obviously; Inès could always recognize one of her own. And this one was on the brink of losing her looks. Poor thing, Inès hoped she'd been clever enough to put some money away. She wondered who'd had the bad taste to bring such an obvious tart to Romanoff's. She soon found out.

Outside the powder room a tall, thin man stood waiting. He turned to Inès, and with a shock which electrified every nerve in her body she recognized him immediately. She tried to move away, but it was too late, he had seen her, and he pounced.

"Inès! Hello. Well, goodness gracious me. What the blazes are *you* doing here, old girl?"

"Benjie." Inès' voice was a hoarse whisper. "What a surprise. Oh, dear, I'm terribly sorry, Benjie, but you must excuse me—I have to go back to my table—they all want to leave." She moved away, but Benjie grabbed her arm, and with growing horror she saw that they were now in the foyer of the restaurant, in full view of the whole room. What was Benjie doing here? He never left London except to go to the country or Monte Carlo. Beverly Hills was Non-U to his set.

"Oh, no you don't—I'm not letting you get away again. I've *missed* you, Nanny." He bent his head closer as she tried to edge away. She could smell the gin on his breath which had always made him desperate to play his kinky sex games.

"Benjie's missed Nanny, vewy vewy much." He was lapsing into baby talk now, much to Inès' discomfort. "Benjie's been bad, a vewy *naughty* boy— needs Nanny to spank him *hard,*" he whispered, looking pleadingly at her, his long, bony fingers still holding tightly onto her arm. She could hardly put up a struggle in front of Hollywood's elite. He would never dare behave like this in London at the 400, the Café de Paris or any of the haunts that he and his friends frequented. Benjie had always behaved with the most impeccable manners everywhere in London, the perfect English gentleman. Only when he'd been in bed or drinking heavily, which was obviously what he'd been doing tonight, did his aristocratic demeanor lapse.

The door to the powder room opened and the Barbie Doll minced over, patting her hair. Benjie loosened his grip on Inès' arm as he greeted his platinum-haired companion.

"Well, it's been very, very nice to see you again, Inès," he said with a sly smile, taking the blonde's arm in a proprietary way. Inès was even more amazed. In London he would never have allowed himself to associate publicly with such an obvious tart.

"We must get together, I'm here until Sunday at the Bel-Air—where are you staying?" he asked.

"Oh—er—with friends," Inès said. "They're waiting for me. I must go— good-bye, Benjie."

At that moment Prince Michael came over to escort the couple to their table, but before he walked away, Benjie, sotto voice and with a wink, said, "Do give my very best regards to *Nanny!*"

Inès felt her face flame, truly shaken by this unexpected encounter. Her past seemed to be catching up with her already. Benjie had recognized her instantly, of course. With her pale matte face, red lips, kohl-rimmed eyes and distinctive long, dark bob, she would always stand out in a crowd. Most women today wore their hair in a curly, short poodle style, or in a gamine cut. Inès had not changed her look for nearly ten years.

She walked unsteadily back to her table, and Julian watched her curiously. She seemed flustered, and Inès was a woman who was rarely flustered.

"Wasn't that old Benjie Spencer-Monckton you were talking to?" he asked. "I remember meeting him once or twice at White's in London."

"Yes, it was," she said, taking a long cooling sip of ice water as she saw, to her dismay, that Benjie and the starlet-tart were being seated in a booth almost opposite theirs.

"You've never mentioned him," Julian persisted. "How do you know him?"

"I don't," Inès lied. "I mean, not really. We met at a weekend house party in the country once. I'm surprised he even remembered me." She laughed, the sound ringing tinnily in her ears, her eyes scanning Julian's face for any sign that he might not believe her. But he'd obviously accepted what she'd said. This time.

The blonde looked over at Inès, smiling amiably through lipstick-smudged lips. No doubt she was questioning Benjie about Inès, just as Julian was questioning her about Benjie. Would Benjie tell her the truth? He wouldn't dare—surely? They had been too fond of each other. But if he did tell this hooker that Inès had also been a whore; if he told her of the perverse games that they had played together, the occasional *ménage à trois* they'd had with some of his friends; if these stories began to circulate in Hollywood and Julian heard of them, her life with him would be finished. Inès couldn't bear to think about it. She didn't know what Benjie was doing in Hollywood nor what he was now whispering to the giggling girl. All she felt at that moment was the imminent danger that she might lose everything.

Inès' premonition proved horribly accurate. Later that evening, after having said good night to Errol and his girlfriend, who had decided to join another table of friends, she and Julian were standing outside the restaurant, waiting for their car to arrive. Suddenly Inès went rigid with fear. This was too much, much too much. It simply couldn't be true, it just wasn't possible.

Escorting a sable-clad Ramona Armande from Romanoff's was a short, bald paunchy man. Even though she only glimpsed his profile, Inès recognized, to her unspeakable horror, the loathsome face which had haunted her dreams for so many years. That squat body, the thick neck, that bullet head—she could never forget him. Eleven years had gone by, along with most of his hair. He was much fatter now, deep lines had etched themselves into his forehead and between his nose and mouth. His fleshy lips were

thinner and pulled into a grimace which he no doubt thought was a charming social smile, as he leaned towards Ramona to whisper in her ear.

But he was dead. She'd killed him, hadn't she? She had washed his life
blood from her hands with the perfumed soap at the Ritz. Wiped it on the
soft white towels. But there was absolutely no doubt about it at all. It was
the face she knew from her most terrifying nightmares. It was undeniably
Umberto Scrofo. The man she thought she'd murdered in the Ritz. The man
who had worn the uniform, bristling with medals, of an Italian general. The
man who'd forced her to have brutal, sadistic sex, who'd degraded and
beaten her so violently that the thought of his repeating those vile acts had
made her kill him.

She had always believed that she'd killed him. But if he were dead, how
could he possibly be here, standing outside Romanoff's on Rodeo Drive in
Beverly Hills? Was she going mad? Was this another nightmare? Some
horrible, sickening hallucination? Or was this reality?

Inès felt about to faint. Her palms were soaking wet and her heart
pounded like a piston. Her sense of panic was so suffocating that she could
hardly breathe. Umberto Scrofo, here, alive, in the all—too—gross flesh.

She turned her back, facing Julian so that the man couldn't see her
features. Would he recognize her? She prayed he wouldn't. Surely she'd
altered physically a great deal since Paris in 1943—but had she changed
enough?

"I want to look like this." Inès handed the hairdresser a photograph of
Grace Kelly that she'd cut out of *Look* magazine, and watched him expectantly.

"But you look so great the way you are," the hairdresser said in amazement. "Why d'you wanna change, honey?"

"Please, just do it," said Inès simply. "I want to, that's all."

The hairdresser shrugged indifferently. He would never understand
dames as long as he lived. Here was an original beauty, distinctive, classy,
a real elegant European lady, who wanted to change herself into another
Kelly clone. Well, he thought, at least she didn't want to look like Marilyn
Monroe, the other great flavor of the fifties. So what, he'd do it, he was
getting paid to do hair, not to be a psychiatrist.

Inès buried herself in a book while he mixed his colors, and she didn't
watch as he cut and colored her long dark hair. Only when the hairdresser
had finished his work did she look at herself critically in the mirror. It was
uncanny—the transformation from a dark-haired, sultry, European-looking
sophisticate to a distinctly American-looking rose was extraordinary. She

was almost unrecognizable but, happy to see, still beautiful. Her hair was cut into a short bob which skimmed her earlobes, with a low parting and soft waves around her forehead. The new color was masterful. A pale ash gold, almost the color of champagne, not the bright yellow gold of her teenage years, but a subtle, classic color with delicate bronze highlights. The style and shade were different enough to separate her from her past and anyone who had known her then.

Inès spent the rest of the afternoon at the Elizabeth Arden salon, completing her transformation. She invested in a complete new range of cosmetics, powder blue eyeshadow, light lipstick, pale rouge, and a new wardrobe for the upcoming Acapulco location. Pastels, frothy chiffon and light cotton gowns in pink, powder blue, lemon yellow. She would no longer wear those favorite severe blacks and whites of past years. She would be transformed. A new life. A new image. A new Inès.

Inès Juillard the courtesan was now dead. She was going to be Mrs. Julian Brooks in only a few weeks. No one from her past would ever be able to recognize her now, nor could they ever hurt her again, of that she felt sure.

15

Umberto Scrofo sat glumly in his Hilton suite waiting for the telephone to ring. He had called every single studio head since he had been in California, trying to arrange a meeting or a screening for his film. Not one of them would even take his calls. He was always sloughed off to one of their assistants who, with smoothly insincere voices, gave Umberto a dozen excuses as to why their bosses were too busy to see him.

"So what if the picture stars Ramona Armande?" Spyros Makopolis had growled to his second-in-command. "Who cares? She's an old has-been. She's been around longer than Garbo, for Christ's sake—and no one's interested in some goddamn Italian art film, even if it is supposed to be better than Rossellini's."

"Mr. Makopolis will let you know," the silken-voiced secretary had informed Umberto. And so indeed would Mr. Zanuck, Mr. Warner, Mr. Cohn and Mr. Schary. All had given him the cold shoulder, the frozen mitt. He was feeling unspeakably frustrated.

Didier Armande, who had been responsible for most of the financing, had seen a rough cut of *La Città Perduta* and had thought it a minor masterpiece. But although he was a powerful film producer in England, Didier didn't have the same clout in Hollywood, and even he couldn't persuade the tycoon moguls to attend a screening.

Umberto scratched furiously at the thick keloid scar on his throat until it was almost raw. Even the underage prostitute whom a bellboy had procured for him the night before hadn't managed to alleviate his rage. He had pummeled into her pale quivering body until she had cried out with pain, and he had to slap her across her sniveling face until she was silent. But he had never tried to do again what he had done with that little blond whore at the Ritz all those years ago, or in Calabria with Silvana. The revenge that had been meted out to him had been too terrible. How he had survived either attempt to destroy him had been a miracle. Whenever his secret erotic senses told him what he wanted, where he was headed, he always managed to stop in time. Thoughts of parched and starving days adrift in a fishing boat filled him with dread, and the memory of the blond tart's terror-stricken face as she slashed his razor across his throat would haunt him forever. The authorities had never found her. Was she still alive? Probably, but if she was she would now be some broken-down old strumpet selling her poxy, raddled body in the back alleys of Montmartre for a few sous. It must be eleven years ago, but he had not forgotten. He would never forget, he thought, as he once again scratched at his constant reminder of her.

He looked out at the fine blue December sky, but couldn't see too much of it. All his attempts to get one of the best suites at the Beverly Hills Hotel, the Beverly Wilshire or the Bel-Air had failed miserably. Money didn't talk in Hollywood. Power and fame did. Umberto had a great deal of money, but no one here knew or seemed to care who he was. He had only managed to get this suite at the Hilton which had no view at all and was decorated in a revolting shade of orange, by heavily bribing the man at the front desk.

He decided to go for a walk down Wilshire Boulevard to take some air. He had loved walking in Rome recently. There he was somebody. People stopped him in the cafés, glad to see him. *"Ciao,* Umberto, *come sta?"* they asked, eager voices showing their respect and admiration. On the Via Veneto he was the new king of the movies, ever since the word had spread about *La Città Perduta.* Here he was treated like a piece of shit. He put on a green mohair cardigan, similar to one he had seen Dean Martin wearing at a golf tournament. Tying a poison-green paisley scarf around his throat to hide his scar, he put on large dark sunglasses and a pristine panama hat, so new that it shrieked vulgarity.

He sauntered down Wilshire Boulevard towards the Beverly Wilshire Hotel, smiling at the few pedestrians who ignored him. He passed the shining red-lacquer door of the Elizabeth Arden beauty salon and idly looked into the windows at the displays of delicate lingerie, casual sportswear and cosmetics.

When the red door opened and a waft of subtle perfume caught him, he turned to see a delicate profile, a waterfall of shining champagne hair and a tall, lithe body dressed in powder blue. The woman walked briskly, disappearing in the direction of I. Magnin. Puzzled, he stared after her. He knew that woman, he was sure of it. There was something terribly familiar about her. He had thought he'd recognized someone like her at the Makopolis party too—but that girl had been a brunette. This one was a classic blonde. But she struck a definite chord. Now where had he seen her before? He shrugged. It wasn't important. What was important, all he cared about now, was getting Zanuck, Makopolis or Jack Warner to see his movie. If they didn't he might as well get out of this ghastly place and go back to Rome.

Part Three

*T*he above-the-line cast and technicians began dribbling into Acapulco early in January. Set designers, architects, carpenters, painters, plasterers and prop men had already been there for four months creating the grand and elaborate sets needed for *The Legend of Cortez*. The film's plot, which didn't even pretend to be historically accurate, given that this was a Cine-maScope epic, was fairly thin. In 1518 Hernando Cortez and his fellow adventurer Francisco Pizarro were sent by King Charles V on a mission to find gold. Their expedition landed in Mexico with only six hundred men. At first Cortez was received by Montezuma—who was to be the last Aztec emperor—like a god, but Cortez repaid this honor by imprisoning him and-later-by conquering his entire empire.

When Cortez' men attempted to leave Montezuma's capital, then called Tenochtitlán, the Aztecs finally rose up against him. They unsuccessfully fought Cortez and his troops in a pitched battle, largely because so many of Montezuma's men deserted and went over to the side of the Spanish invaders.

The Aztec emperor died in prison, leaving Cortez to win the heart of his fiery, beautiful daughter, and they supposedly lived happily ever after.

But Spyros Makopolis needed a much stronger plot than that. Historical epics were in vogue, the bigger the better. Chariots, togas and ruins were fascinating audiences everywhere, as long as the historical facts were beefed up; and Irving and Shirley Frankovitch had been hired to try to glamorize the life of Señor Cortez. They had started diligently researching and writing early in 1953, spurred on by Makopolis' offer of an unprecedented hundred-thousand-dollar advance plus seven percent of the gross profits. The following year, the studio sent teams of scouts all over the world to find the most suitable yet cheapest locations for this four-million-dollar Technicolor CinemaScope extravaganza. MCCP had high hopes for a box-office bonanza and were sparing no expense to achieve it.

Location scouts had returned from months of all-expense-paid trips to dozens of exotic places to inform the studio, that with its thirty-eight lush beaches, dozens of gorgeous tropical bays and lagoons, clear, calm water and incomparable sunsets, Acapulco was the most perfect location for the movie.

After Irving and Shirley had written their first two drafts in New York and their third in Los Angeles, they arrived in Acapulco to give it the final polish. The couple now sat on the vine-covered balcony of their Villa Vera suite, sipping *piña coladas* in the humid dusk and waiting for the new arrivals.

"Here comes Julian with his fiancée." The perpetually inquisitive Shirley was able to get a good close-up view of the couple with the help of a strong pair of binoculars.

It was obvious, from the proud looks she gave him, and by the way in which she held his arm, that Inès Juillard, svelte in champagne linen, was utterly devoted to Julian Brooks. He looked a little overheated for such a handsome star, Shirley thought. Under his cream panama hat beads of sweat shone on his matinée-idol brow, and his usually crisp moustache appeared to be wilting.

Inès spotted the glint of the binoculars in the reflected sunlight, looked up and then smiled at Julian. She wondered who could be watching them. No, not them, *him,* Julian; he was the star, the one the world was interested in. She knew that the studio and the Frankovitches had gone to considerable lengths to make the part of the buccaneer-adventurer Cortez to fit Julian, who at thirty-eight was now at the height of his masculine beauty.

Although the split from Phoebe had taken its toll on him financially, in the time Inès had been living with Julian she believed that he had found true contentment. He really loved her. More than he had ever loved anyone before. But he was, after all, an actor, so if he ever did stray a little, she knew that she would have to turn a blind eye. Her years as a courtesan had taught her that so many men were just like little boys. Sex was a sport, a hunt and a challenge to them. Even when they loved their wives madly, the best of men thought little of sexual infidelity. Unfaithfulness had been accepted in Europe as a fact of life for centuries, and intelligent wives had always ignored it. Inès had played brilliant sexual games, intrigued Julian with her quick mind, her knowledge of art, politics, music and finance. She had also woven a bond of sexual magic that made him feel as he never had with any other woman before.

Now, with the new year Inès would soon start a whole new life as Mrs. Julian Brooks. She was now nearly thirty years old. Beautiful, intelligent and desirable. To make her situation completely perfect, she suspected that she might be pregnant. Julian had often spoken of his desire for a child, and although they were not yet married she felt confident that he would be thrilled if her Los Angeles doctor confirmed her suspicions.

Julian smiled at his bride-to-be. She was the perfect woman for him in every way.

It never ceased to amaze him that after a grinding fourteen-hour day at the studio or on location, fencing, riding or performing his own difficult stunts, she could make his homecoming an event. An ice-cold martini would be waiting, made just as she heard his car coming up the winding driveway of their house. Exquisitely but simply dressed in the latest fashions from Paris, coolly elegant, she always managed to reveal a glimpse of something which would be guaranteed to arouse him. Perhaps the curve of a perfect breast through some transparent chiffon, or a creamy shoulder emerging from the depths of velvet, or her gorgeous legs through a split satin skirt. She would rub the back of his neck to relieve his tension, her cool fingers caressing his tired muscles. From this massage, Inès could always gauge his mood. She could tell if he'd be receptive to lovemaking or not; he almost always was. They would bathe together in the cool marble bathroom, in the shower which had powerful yet soothing jets positioned in strategic places, where she would wash his tired body with scented Guerlain soap.

As she kneaded his cock gently and lovingly with the soap, the tips of her nipples would brush lightly against his chest and he would harden; then her tongue would make its way into his mouth, as the strong jets burst into power, and she would position his body where the water would touch him most pleasurably.

She never seemed to mind that her makeup and hair were ruined by these few blissful moments. The only thing which truly mattered to her was giving pleasure to her man. Sometimes she left him, still tumescent after the soaping and the kissing, to withdraw to her bedroom to anoint herself with various oils and moisturizers. Usually he would come and take her as she stood in her curtained dressing room, possessing her fiercely, with stallion speed. But often they would linger in the shower. Before it was over, and when he was almost bursting with pleasure, she would take him to one of the many places that she'd designed for love. She knew all the answers to a man's tired libido and used them cunningly. Afterward, she washed him gently, leaving him to doze on cool linen sheets while she prepared dinner, which she would take to him on a tray. While he ate she would watch him. If he wanted to talk, she chatted away. If he craved silence, she would be as quiet as a mouse; if he wanted to study his dialogue, she would read a book. She was the perfect woman who wanted to be the perfect wife: a tigress in the bedroom, a sophisticated lady everywhere else. The only thing about her which displeased him was the new color of her hair. He had adored her long thick dark brown hair, loved twining it around his hands like silken ropes. This new style, although soft and becoming, made Inès somehow lose the aura of strength and individuality. It made her look more ordinary.

Never mind, it was probably only temporary. Her Grace Kelly style would be nothing more than a passing phase, and before long she would once again return to being his ravishing brunette. But whatever color Inès' hair might be, it didn't ever seem to stop men staring at her admiringly wherever she went.

Many men coveted Inès, sensing her almost palpable sexuality. But she belonged to him. Whatever relationships she had had in the past, they were now meaningless. She had told him about her only three lovers, refusing to go into any detail at all in spite of his pressing insistence. She was a clever woman. Julian knew that the more she told him the more he would jealously want to hear about her past. For Looks Brooks, Inès had no past. Her life had only begun when he met her.

*U*mberto Scrofo sat in his drawing room in Rome, surrounded by some of his favorite furniture, pictures and sculptures; he was picking his teeth with a paper clip and reading an airmailed copy of *Weekly Variety.*

La Città Perduta—*The Lost City,* in English—was a massive success. He had been right to insist on a European publicity tour with Ramona and the rest of the cast. *La Città Perduta* had received a phenomenal boost, and despite the actors demanding perks like grand hotel suites and limousines, it had all paid off handsomely. The picture was a smash hit in Europe. It was his first taste of cinematic success, and he was immensely pleased with himself.

His young housekeeper entered the semi-dark room which was shuttered against the afternoon sun, her manner subservient.

"May I get you something, Signor Scrofo?"

"Yes," Umberto snapped in his croaking voice, wondering why she always sounded so fucking apologetic. "Iced coffee with plenty of sugar, and don't spill it on the tray like you did last time."

"Yes, *Signor,*" the girl bobbed and hurriedly disappeared. Signor Scrofo terrified her, but she wanted to keep this job. It paid well and her large family needed the money.

Umberto sighed. He was bored, and Umberto disliked being bored. It was about time for another visit to Signora Albertoni's apartment in the Via

Sistina. *She* never bored him. Not when she stood tall and Aryan in long black boots and black silk stockings, a lacy suspender belt cutting into the flesh of her strong thighs, her blond hair flying around her flushed face, as she let him whip her with any one of the assorted implements which she kept for her clients' pleasure.

Five minutes later the housekeeper fluttered in nervously. "It's the telephone for you; I think it's America." When she smiled her face looked almost pretty. America. He knew how she'd love to go to America. So would he. He yearned for it. Maybe he would, now that the picture was a success.

When he'd been in L.A., Umberto had signed with the William Morris Agency, unconcerned that they represented almost three hundred producers worldwide, but his ego was big enough to stand the competition because he knew he had produced a great picture. Everyone in Rome had said so, and Umberto was a man who had never lacked a highly developed sense of his own worth. Even though he was ugly, he thought himself irresistible, witty and cultured. It was everyone else's stupidity that they couldn't seem to see it.

He opened one of the shutters and glanced outside at the tourists milling about on the Spanish Steps, cursing to himself that they were ruining his beautiful neighborhood with their loud voices and their cameras.

Gia brought him the telephone and he heard the crackle of the long-distance line as Abe, his agent, came on the line.

"Hi, Umberto, how ya doing?"

"I'm doing fine, Abe, just fine. What's the latest news on the movie?"

"Picture's doing great business in Europe as you know, Hubie baby. I'm sure you've seen *Variety*. We've had some interest in you here too," he said.

"Really?" Umberto lit his cigar, his fat face beaming. "Any of the majors?"

"Well, not exactly the majors, but there's been some independent interest—Roger Corman, for instance."

"Roger Corman!" Umberto spluttered. "He makes horror films, for Christ's sake—I'm beyond that now. I told you, Abe, that after *La Città Perduta* I want to produce something in Hollywood—haven't you been trying?"

"We're trying, we're trying," said Abe in the Hollywood agent's usual semi-placatory tone which they used on actors and producers alike. It didn't really matter a fig to Abe whether Umberto Scrofo made a film in America or not. Producers grew on palm trees in Hollywood; they hardly needed to import them from Europe.

Umberto's film was a success in Europe, but it had caused little excitement in America. It couldn't even get distribution. Abe, overworked and underpaid, was not about to go out of his way to push Scrofo. He was just one of thousands of William Morris clients, and this was simply a bread-and-butter call.

"If you read the European grosses in *Variety,*" Umberto asked, "why don't you tell everyone about them, for fuck's sake?"

"Yeah, yeah, we told 'em it's a great picture, real great. We're tryin' to get it to Cannes for the festival, you know. I just want you to understand that we're working hard on a whole lot of things, Umberto," the agent said easily. "A whole bunch of things. Something could happen very soon, believe me. Just keep the faith, sweetheart, keep the faith."

"I am a good producer, Abe, maybe even a *great* producer," Umberto said coldly. "Not only *Oggi* but *Gente* and *Tempo* said I am the new De Laurentiis—and those putzes in Hollywood—Makopolis, Cohn, Zanuck— they wouldn't even go to *see* my movie."

"I know, I know, Umberto baby," said Abe soothingly. "Just be patient, something'll come up—something big—so hold on for a little longer, be patient, we'll get a picture for you soon. Listen, I gotta go now. We'll keep in touch. *Ciao* for now, baby."

"Ciao, Abe," said Umberto crossly as he banged down the receiver. He swallowed his iced cappuccino with a scowl. If this picture was so big in Europe, why wasn't America interested? It had become his obsession to make an American film, to be an important man in Hollywood. To be up for an Oscar, to go to parties at Jack Warner's, Ray Stark's and Charlie Feldman's. He had adored the Makopolis Christmas bash. It was a stinging blow to his ego that the excellent reviews for *La Città Perduta* hadn't led to anything in the States. But he wasn't going to sit around and feel sorry for himself. He had three European projects on the boards, and he was dedicating himself passionately to them.

"Fuck America," he said to himself, rubbing the itching scar on his neck. "Who needs them? I'll stay here." Better a big fish in a small pond ...

He gazed now at a beautifully lit Manet which hung on the pale gold damask-covered wall. This picture always gave him enormous pleasure, although the blond girl in it vaguely reminded him of that whore who'd tried to kill him at the Ritz. Maybe he'd find her one day. Then he would exact the revenge he'd dreamed of so often. Meanwhile, he had motion pictures to make.

3

"*I could live like this forever,*" *chuckled Bluey Regan.* "*Who needs the* movie business when you've got a boat?"

The Irish-American Bluey Regan had been an assistant director since the talkies began. As he would constantly remind people, there was nothing he didn't know about the picture business. Full of life, always cheerful, he was a director's dream, and Nick Stone valued him immensely as his right-hand man; what Nick didn't know, Bluey would.

Nick agreed with Bluey. It was perfect. Nothing was more exhilarating than the camaraderie between men on a boat.

It had been thirty-six hours since they'd left the Los Angeles marina on a cold, misty morning. The seas were a sulking, churning mass in which a hundred-foot ketch had great difficulty maneuvering just to get out of the port. The *Jezebel* with its crew of five had traveled some fifteen hundred miles in this bad weather. In spite of Nick's Greek boyhood as a fisherman and a love for the sea which matched Bluey's, he had succumbed to bouts of *mal de mer*. But this was all behind them now; the icy gray Californian Pacific had gradually turned blue as they sailed closer to the tropics. Both men were bronzed, fit and muscled as they stood at the helm taking turns to steer, caught up in an easy flow of jokes and conversation.

Bluey was forty-eight, with hair bleached yellow-white by the sun, and wrinkled skin sunburned to the color of caramel. His blue eyes danced with humor; he was never happier than when sailing on a trip like this. He was in a state of total relaxation tinged faintly with the anticipation of the work ahead.

Nick was less sanguine. Against his will, he'd been persuaded by Bluey to make the trip down to Acapulco by boat. Much as he adored the sea, his first instincts had been to fly down, as he had much to do and many decisions to make before shooting started.

But his first assistant had been adamant. "Heck, Niko, it takes almost as long to fly to the damned place as sail. First, you've gotta drive to Tijuana on that shit road that takes at *least* six or seven hours. Then you grab a broken-down, two-engine plane left over from *Wings*—Richard Arlen's probably still the pilot. When you finally get to Mexico City, ya gotta stay overnight, and there's so much crazy fuckin' night life there you'll end up with a hangover the next day that'll make your teeth fall out, which is when you'll have to take Aero Nervoso de Mexico, or whatever the fuck it's called, and boy, oh boy, will you be needing a handful of their sick bags then, kid."

Nick could feel himself smiling as Bluey went on.

"I'll tell you the truth, Nick, you won't get me on *any* plane that hasn't got a good ole American pilot in the cockpit with at least five years' service in the US of A Air Force." He smiled beguilingly. Nick was laughing now.

"Come with me on the *Jezebel,* kiddo—you'll have four days to relax, work on the script, you'll arrive in *great* shape, and I promise I won't keep you up drinking all night."

The crew, all Bluey's buddies, doubled as bodyguards, companions or valets when they weren't being stewards or cooks. Bluey's "boys" had been together for years, so the atmosphere was that of a close fraternity, in which practical jokes and laughter were the order of the day.

Nick was worried about his line producer, Zachary Domino, who hadn't been well recently. Zack was sixty-eight and tired. With more than fifty years' experience, starting as a runner on some early Chaplin films, graduating to camera assistant on Mary Pickford features, then assistant director in the twenties with Clara Bow in *Red Hair* for First National Pictures, he was an excellent, knowledgeable and tough producer. He understood every aspect of the movie business and Nick was looking forward to learning a great deal from him. In fact he needed him badly. This was Nick's first major blockbuster movie, and everyone, not only in the studio but in Hollywood, would be carefully watching the results of this one. If it was a flop, he would be back to directing *Bobby Soxers in Space,* and then only if he was lucky. If MCCP lost its bets on *Cortez* he would probably never work again.

So Nick was understandably edgy about *Cortez.* He knew many people at the studio didn't want him to direct it, considering him more of a boy-wonder cult director, in spite of the fact that the two pictures he'd directed had been box-office successes. There were so many other directors they preferred. George Cukor had been first choice, followed by David Lean and Fred Zinnemann. But dear old Uncle Spyros, waving his nepotism like a tattered flag, had insisted on using Nick, and since he was the ultimate arbitrator, the studio had had to capitulate—for the moment.

MCCP's administrators couldn't believe that Nick was capable of handling this huge assignment. He was only twenty-seven. This picture needed a man of immense experience, a director used to dealing with thousands of extras, handling fragile star temperaments, coping with the thousand decisions which needed to be made daily on a picture this size. They didn't believe that Nick could do it, and they were waiting to be proved right. But Sypros had great faith that Nick would do an excellent job on this film, particularly with Zachary Domino as line producer to help him. Good old Uncle Spyros—he'd come through at last.

Bluey threw an affectionate arm around his friend's shoulder as he expertly handled the tiller with the other.

"What's the matter, Niko?"

"I just hope Zack holds up," Nick replied quietly. "I read the doctor's insurance report, Bluey. He smokes sixty a day, drinks like a fish, and he's had a heart murmur for years. But he's still one helluva great producer and we need him with us on this."

"Don't worry, kid, Zack's a *fighter*—tougher than an army boot with rusty nails in it. He'll have whipped everyone in shape, kicked their fat asses, and got all the wheels in motion on location by the time we arrive. Stop worrying, Nick—everything's gonna be okay."

On the flights all the way from Los Angeles, Dominique had kept up a nonstop stream of excited chatter. Her girlish enthusiasm increased the closer they came to Acapulco. The trip had taken almost two days and Agathe felt that she would scream if Dominique didn't stop babbling. The girl had bought every single movie magazine at the airport, and had scanned them all intently for any photographs of the stars who might be in *Cortez* or vacationing in Acapulco while they were making the movie there.

Agathe's head was splitting with one of the migraine headaches which were becoming more prevalent lately, but despite her telling Dominique that she was feeling terrible and needed to be quiet, the girl didn't stop to draw breath.

The noise of the plane's engines exacerbated Agathe's headache and she had absolutely no interest in looking at the celebrity photographs which Dominique insisted on pointing out to her.

"Look—*voilà*—Julian Brooks. Ooh, wow, Agathe, he is *magnifique, n'est-ce pas?* A really cool guy."

Agathe snatched the magazine out of Dominique's lap. Magnificent was an understatement, she thought. He was a god; a giant among men, a true living Adonis. The pit of her stomach churned as she feasted her eyes on his glorious dark perfection. His arm was around some woman, probably his latest leading lady.

"The fiancée," Dominique said, jabbing the photograph with her finger. "He's now engaged. She's beautiful, too, don't you think?"

Fingers of ice curled around Agathe's heart. Fiancée? Julian was engaged? Agathe stared at the woman, who was in profile, her long dark hair almost obscuring her face, but from the way Julian was looking at her they were obviously mad about each other. Who was she?

Viciously Agathe threw the magazine back to Dominique. *"Tais-toi,* Dominique," she snapped. "I'm not interested in these movie stars. Rest now and stop all this chattering, you've got important days ahead of you."

She closed her eyes and tried to sleep, but a jealous disappointment gripped her whenever she thought of Julian and the new woman in his life. How could Julian be marrying someone else *now,* now that Agathe was so close to being with him at last? How could he be doing this to her?

*A*s soon as he arrived at Villa Vera, Nick called Elektra, who was thrilled to speak to him. He unpacked, showered, changed and within twenty minutes was sitting in one of the hotel suites, which had been turned into a production room. His entire production staff were assembled around a table—art directors, set designers, costumiers, assistant directors, stunt coordinators, editors, the writers—that baleful-looking New York couple, the Frankovitches—and most important of all, Zachary Domino, Nick's line producer. Zack's eyes were weary, his shoulders stooped, and he chain-smoked Camels with nicotine-stained fingers.

"How are you feeling, *amigo?*" Nick asked.

"Not so hot today," Zack's smile was halfhearted. "But don't worry, I think it's just a touch of Montezuma's famous revenge. He's probably mad at us for doing his life story."

The crew all chuckled, except for the costume designer, Kittens.

"Montezuma's revenge doesn't last for three weeks, Zack," she said anxiously, then aside to Nick, "He's been feeling bad for a while, Nicky. We've been worried."

Nick clenched his fists. Jesus, he'd only been in the place for an hour and already everyone was worried about the main cog in his wheel.

"I *told* him to take Pepto-Bismol and not to eat salads," said Shirley Frankovitch impatiently. "But he wouldn't listen, would he, Irving?"

"No, dear," said Irving. "He wouldn't." Irving spoke little, his mind spinning constantly with new and different ideas for characters and situations in *Cortez*. Half the time he paid no attention to Shirley at all. Her embarrassing drunken antics at Makopolis's party had caused him to become more aware than ever of what a vulgarian his wife was. He didn't like to think about it, so he chose to ignore her most of the time.

Irving glanced out of the window of the second-floor suite. The sky was the softest blue, tinged apricot by a sun which was beginning to sink behind one of the hills. Irving sipped his drink, imagining what the effect of coconut milk on the taste buds of his hero would have been when he first reached La Roqueta island. He looked at the palm trees, their branches which were vivid green swaying softly in the breeze. Abundant foliage grew in the hotel courtyard. Acapulco was a luscious, tropical paradise, and the variety and beauty of its plant life were a continual source of wonder to Irving. He wasn't really listening to Zack, who had been talking about some of the multitude of technical problems which they'd discovered in transporting their equipment on to La Roqueta.

Irving was brought back to reality when Zack announced that the studio wanted the scene in which Cortez first makes love to the beautiful princess to be much more erotic, albeit within the bounds of censorship. The MCCP top brass insisted on sex, lust, sensual romance. Barrages of telephone calls and cables were constantly arriving from Hollywood. They wanted more sex and they wanted perfection. Now it was up to Irving and Shirley to make the script the best goddamn script of the decade. As writers, they could only do so much—because once the script fell into the hands of the actors and directors, God only knew what damage could be done to "great" dialogue. The Frankovitches were old campaigners on the Hollywood trail. Irving had seen two of his scripts destroyed by studios and others badly butchered, so he and Shirley intended to be around all the time, even though a writer on a shooting set was as welcome as a nun in a whorehouse.

The heat in the production office became more oppressive as the sun sank lower. The room was stifling, and even the ceiling fan made little difference. The men were all shirtsleeved but sweat glistened on their faces; Shirley wore a muumuu, one of many which she had bought at the local market. Shirley adored a bargain, and clothes here cost a fraction of what they would in New York or Beverly Hills. The muumuu was the perfect solution for her figure as her weight had ballooned in the past months.

She glanced at Zachary Domino, wondering how on earth he was going to survive the eighteen weeks of tough location work around beaches, mosquito-ridden swamps, forests and rivers.

Zack lit another Camel in spite of doctor's orders. In Los Angeles he had visited his doctor for the usual studio checkup. Dr. Zolotos had assured him that he was in fairly good health for his age. "Just remember to take a salt pill every morning, never drink the water—in spite of what the Mexican government may say, it's poison! Stay away from raw fruit and vegetables, especially lettuce, don't exert yourself too much, and stop *smoking!*"

Easier said than done. When you were line-producing one of the major motion pictures of the decade—quite impossible. Zack was practically living on cigarettes and coffee. He sipped some salty-tasting mineral water. Everyone at the meeting was smoking, no one giving a thought to what they were doing to their lungs or heart. Zachary inhaled deeply, trying to contribute to the discussions.

Across the table, Shirley's cunning, laser-beam eyes glared at him. There was no love lost between them. He thought her a pushy shrew and a lush who constantly and irritatingly interfered during production meetings. Zack tried patiently to explain to the Frankovitches that their latest rewrites would be much too expensive to shoot.

"Money, money, money—that's all you ever fucking *think* about Zack," shrieked Shirley. "This is *art,* you fucking moron. *Art!* Who gives a *shit* about money."

"We don't *need* two hundred and fifty extras watching Cortez and Princess Isabella strolling along the seashore." Zack tried to remain calm. "It's supposed to be lyrical, romantic. We don't *need* a bunch of fucking voyeurs standing around them just staring." He raised his voice, his efforts to stay calm failing. "I'm taking them *out*—do you understand, *out. No* extras. And that's that—*finito."* He hated shouting matches, but knew he had to win this point, otherwise the Frankovitches would walk all over him.

Nick nodded his approval. "I agree totally. I'm sorry, Shirley. Zack's right, we don't need any atmosphere in that scene, so that's that."

Shirley was not about to give up her two hundred and fifty extras without a fight. *No one* messed with Shirley Frankovitch. She was a star writer. She looked over to Irving for support, but he just shrugged. Although Irving possessed infinitely more talent than she, he'd subjugated it much too often to her pleading banshee wails, sly feminine wiles, and insidious whining.

It meant a great deal to Shirley to win. She wanted *her* script to be the one that was shot. She wanted the studio to know that *they,* the fabulous team of Shirley and Irving Frankovitch, were the most brilliant writers on the Hollywood scene. But it was evident that at this lengthy production meeting they were not winning. Many of their most daring and innovative ideas were being shot down—by both Nick and Zack. The meeting, like the room, was becoming increasingly heated. Expletives were bandied about and the air hung heavy with the smell of hostility, sweat and cigarette smoke.

Irving raised a laconic eyebrow in Shirley's direction. They would thrash this out later, privately. He sighed, remembering fondly his rapport with Umberto Scrofo during the shooting of *La Città* in Rome a year ago. Irving had praised Umberto to Shirley highly—he had been sympathetic to everything that Frankovitch had wanted—and Umberto Scrofo had been more than eager to cultivate the most important screenwriter in Hollywood.

Even though Shirley had made a fool of herself at the Makopolis party, it hadn't stopped Scrofo from wining and dining the Frankovitches during his Los Angeles trip. Shirley found Scrofo amusing. She liked his acerbic wit and bitter comments, which perfectly matched her own cynical attitude to the world. She thought that his *La Città Perduta* was excellent and had invited Spyros Makopolis to a screening, but at the last moment the old Greek had canceled and she had been unable to get him to reschedule.

Scrofo agreed with Shirley that the script was absolutely the most important ingredient in filmmaking and that everything and everyone else was secondary. It didn't matter if the movie had the most shimmering stars or the most elaborate sets, if it wasn't on the page the public wasn't going to see it on the screen.

Nikolas Stone shifted uneasily in his chair. His instincts were turning out to be right. Shirley Frankovitch was a meddling bitch, and her husband was a pathetic, pitiable excuse for a man. He thought their script was good in parts, but too overwritten, too flowery, too excessive. He envisioned a simple tale of adventure and discovery, of the battle of wills between Cortez and King Montezuma. He wanted a simple sensual love story between Cortez and Princess Isabella. He wanted to show the untouched beauty of the Mexican country, the incomparable lagoons, the ravishing sunsets. He wanted to reveal real people with real emotions, ambitions, passions. The Frankovitches didn't seem to want this at all. Their script was one gargantuan battle after another, an endless array of wounded, bleeding men being dispatched by the point of the hero's sword; scenes of sticky passion so trite that they'd be out of place in a shopgirl's weekly. And now, the sight of Zachary, his most important support, obviously unwell, was not a promising omen.

Suddenly Zack called a halt. The production office had become so unbearably hot that tempers were frayed to boiling point.

"Let's sleep on everything, boys and girls," he said quietly. "We've still got a few days before shooting starts to sort out our problems. Tomorrow, ten A.M. sharp, we'll have a read-through with some of the cast. Until then, let's get some rest."

. . .

Inès was suffering a mixture of jet lag and morning sickness which seemed to continue well into the early evening of their arrival. She was sleeping so soundly that Julian decided to accept Nick's invitation to dinner on the terrace of a restaurant away from the Villa Vera. They wanted to escape from the prying eyes, the clacking tongues and the electric tensions which always fill the air before a movie begins. The cool veranda looked down to the curve of Acapulco Bay where the ink-black water seemed striped with thin slivers of luminous silver.

A faint breeze blew in from the sea as they dined on *ceviche*—raw fish marinated with onions, lemon and avocado, charcoal-grilled prawns, and a great deal of tequila and beer. They chain-smoked as Nick shared his problems with Julian, who listened attentively, becoming increasingly aware that Nick was facing some serious hurdles.

"If Zachary is totally on your side," he said, "then what's the difficulty? You're the director—he's the producer—you've both got the final say, after all. Tell the Frankovitches to get stuffed."

Nick stared at him with a worried frown. "I don't know," he said. "I just can't figure it out. I don't think Zach's up to par, and that bitch Shirley is out to have his balls for *huevos rancheros* on her breakfast tray. I want to make this film as realistic and as modern as possible. I want the audience to *identify* with Cortez. Oh I know he's a sixteenth-century man but I want him to be a man of the moment—a today kinda guy. I know that's what audiences are looking for now. They've had too much escapist crap, musicals, biblical epics. They've gotta believe this man is made of the same flesh and blood as them. I just hope the studio isn't going to try and sabotage it. I think the Frankovitches have got enormous pull with Spyros in spite of the bitch getting plastered at his party. Jesus, Julian, some of their new dialogue is unspeakable—a couple of the scenes are straight out of Grand Guignol!"

Julian smiled. "I don't believe they're as bad as you think, Nick. I got the rewrites earlier this evening, but I'll look them over again tonight. So what are you going to do about all of this?"

"Tonight, my friend, I'm going to get very drunk," Nick drained his tequila with a wicked smile. "Then tomorrow, like Scarlett O'Hara, I'm gonna think about it, and work my ass off to get it right. Maybe it's just my old Greek instincts working, pal, but I'm worried."

5

Dominique arrived at the Villa Vera the following afternoon. She looked around her luxurious hotel room and giggled, "What a dump," á là Bette Davis in *Beyond the Forest.* She pranced to the window and gasped. Thick pink-flowered bougainvillea curled around the stone terrace, the ocean glittered invitingly, and the brilliant cobalt sky, which shaded to a bluish gray as it met the curving hills surrounding Acapulco Bay, made the view breathtaking.

Her portable record player was in her luggage, along with her much treasured box of records. She flipped through them, finally choosing one of her favorites, Edith Piaf singing "La Vie en Rose," then lay back on the sofa feeling gloriously grown-up and romantic as she thought about Gaston's latest love letter and the naughty things he wrote.

Feeling a sudden surge of energy, she got up to look through her suitcases for something to wear to the pool. The studio had provided her with plenty of clothes for the many photographic layouts they expected of her. Dozens of coordinated summer costumes had been carefully packed in layers of tissue paper by the wardrobe department and she rifled through them, humming happily.

Putting on a tiny pink gingham bikini with a matching short skirt, she grabbed a straw hat and her script and skipped down the stone steps towards the inviting swimming pool. Thankfully, Agathe was sound asleep, as the tropics didn't agree with her, and she was exhausted after the long flights from Los Angeles and Mexico City. Dominique loved being on her own, particularly when she had new pages of her script to study. It was just after two o'clock, and most of the Villa Vera residents were at lunch. There was nobody at the pool except for a lackadaisical Mexican boy removing crumpled, damp towels from the deck chairs.

Placing her towel on a chaise longue, Dominique put on her sunglasses, perched her straw hat on top of her head and gazed contentedly around. Gorgeous, there was no question of that. The pool was edged with tiny blue-and-white square tiles and looked truly inviting. It was set into reddish-pink, rough-hewn stone, and surrounded by huge pots of flaming bougainvillea. Their color was dazzling—lilac, mauve, fuchsia, cyclamen, shocking pink—a riot of reds and purples. Beyond the pool lay a garden dominated by tall palm trees, whose thick leaves gave shelter to a wide lawn and tropical flowerbeds. Floating on the pool were dozens of white, red and yellow hibiscus blossoms. A tulip tree, its flaming red torchwood branches standing like bayonets, shaded most of the far end of the pool. Farther away were sharp spires of banana trees, hibiscus bushes, frangipani and an occasional banyan tree with its huge, ancient twisted roots, an ideal shelter for the birds that flew about happily in the jasmine-scented air.

In spite of the heat, Dominique could feel a refreshing breeze as she lay under her umbrella. A smiling waiter appeared, asking in Spanish if she wanted a drink, Latin eyes drank in her lissome body, and a flash of lust crossed his adolescent features. Dominique was getting very used to men responding to her sex appeal. She asked for a Coke and lay back comfortably, the *Cortez* script in front of her. The only sound was the splashing of water into a small stone pool around which enormous velvet-winged butterflies hovered and danced. The sound was soporific and soothing.

From down on the beach, came the music of mariachis and the gay chants of a Mexican band. She'd heard that Acapulco night life was exciting, although nothing compared to that of Hollywood. She knew that Lana Turner, Tyrone Power and Errol Flynn were all staunch aficionados of Acapulco, coming here regularly. Perhaps she might even meet them.

From his secluded terrace on the first floor Julian Brooks looked down at Dominique as she buried her glossy head in the script.

In the time he had been with Inès he'd been as dutiful and loving as any man could be, never tempted once by the many offers to which his striking looks and fame made him subject. Inès was attentive, beautiful, kind—what more could he want? What more, indeed, he thought—except now the sight of Dominique's ravishing face, waist-length black hair and honey-colored limbs was suddenly a powerful stimulant. Most intriguing of all was her undeniable resemblance to Inès. She seemed like a younger version, with the same appealing mixture of sensuality and innocence. Odd, perhaps, but this similarity made Dominique an object of great interest to Julian.

He pulled his panama hat down farther over his eyes, watching intently as she stood up and peeled off her tiny skirt, revealing a bottom so round and peachlike in her bikini that he caught his breath.

Stretching unselfconsciously, unaware of her admirer up on his terrace, she ran her fingers through her hair, removed her sunglasses and dipped her feet in the pool. The sun, filtering through the leaves of a palm tree, dappled her shoulders. Thinking about the bathtub scene she would have to film next week, and not wanting any white marks on her shoulders, she slipped off the straps of her bikini top. Then looking around to make sure no one was near she undid the hooks, tossing it to the edge of the pool, then slid slowly into the water until it barely covered her breasts.

Julian's mouth was suddenly dry. This was one of the most erotic little scenes he'd witnessed for a long time. He was, after all, only a man—a fact which the discomfort inside his immaculately cut linen trousers confirmed. He thought he'd seen few more glorious sights. This golden-skinned goddess, almost naked in a swimming pool, wet black hair flowing around her shoulders, was deliciously and enchantingly exciting. . . .

Out of the corner of her eye, Dominique had become aware that she was being observed. She lazily splashed water over her shoulders, enjoying the coolness on her sun kissed skin. She realized that it was Looks Brooks who was watching her beneath his panama hat, and as she started to sing "La Vie en Rose" in her best Edith Piaf voice a secret smile crossed her beautiful face.

6

*A*gathe *was unable to sleep. A full moon shone through the bamboo*
window slats, and the ceiling fan did little but churn the sluggish air. She
was roasting, her cotton nightgown soaked with sweat, her mouth like
cardboard. The carafe next to the bed was dry as a bone. She got up to
get some water from the bathroom tap, then remembered all the dire
warnings she'd been given about not drinking the water. Searching
through her valise, she found nothing to drink except a bottle of cough
syrup.

Slipping off her nightgown, she threw on some shorts, a short-sleeved
shirt and rope-soled espadrilles. Grabbing the room key and a handful of
pesos, she glanced at the seductive moon suspended over the black sand,
closed the door quietly and ran down to the lobby. It was empty except for
a fat concierge dozing over a copy of *Hola*. She asked him in French and
English where she might find something to drink, but he understood
nothing until she spoke the magic words Coca-Cola. His greasy face, slippery with sweat, perked up as he jabbered away in Spanish, pointing across
the road to the beach.

There was little traffic on the road. She heard the occasional *fut-fut* of a
motorcycle, and in the distance mariachis playing. From some nearby
houses came exciting-sounding Spanish love songs which made her senses
quicken. How she'd love to dance to that music. How she would whirl and

twirl—if only Julian could be with her too. She could show him how well she danced. He must have arrived in Acapulco by now.

The beach was deserted, the sand pockmarked with a thousand footprints. There were a few thatched-roof beach huts on the sand, around which abandoned chairs and tables were clustered. A few yards away, a larger hut boasted a flickering neon sign saying something incomprehensible in Spanish. She would surely find a drink there, she thought, as she made for the light.

Four tough-looking Mexican men sat at a cigarette-scorched table, playing cards. Behind them were several tired hookers, their black hair and exotic Spanish dresses only emphasizing their state of fragile weariness. At the bar stood half a dozen truculent-looking men, most of them drunk. Agathe blushed, wishing she'd worn a bra and panties underneath her skimpy clothes. The barman looked less ferocious than the others and she quietly asked for a coke.

Unsmiling, he passed her the bottle and a damp, chipped glass. She drank fast, eyes downcast, and asked for another, while hostile eyes stared at her.

She asked the barman if she could take the bottle with her, then, throwing some coins onto the zinc-topped bar, casually walked out, pretending not to hear remarks in Spanish from which she could make out the words *guapa* and *linda*. In spite of herself she felt flattered that the men had noticed her and admired her feminine charms. It had been a long time since anyone had.

Enveloped by the sultry night, her thirst satisfied and her adrenaline pumping, Agathe didn't feel like going back to the hotel yet. It was barely midnight. She would take a stroll along the beach.

In the distance she could see the lights of the town, and some brightly lit boats. She walked slowly along the shoreline, enjoying the sensation of the cool waves lapping at her feet, catching the scent of jasmine and the salty tang of the sea. She thought about the upcoming film with excitement. As Dominique's chaperone she knew that she was only a tiny cog in the wheel of *Cortez*, but still, she was important. Everyone was important, because she knew that filming was a group effort. But the most thrilling thing of all was that she would be near Julian Brooks. She wondered if she would see him soon, so that they could talk of mutual interests—of art, philosophy, religion. She knew that he must be a man of superior intellect to match his superior looks. She fingered the small crucifix which she always wore around her neck. The tiny amber beads on the fine silver chain were her talisman—her luck. Superstitiously she believed that if she didn't wear it, something unspeakable would happen to her.

Lost in reverie, Agathe did not hear the muffled footsteps approaching her. Coarse hands grabbed her from behind and another pair clamped themselves over her mouth. There were two men—or three?—she couldn't tell. Their arms seemed to be everywhere. As wiry as she was, there was no way she could overcome their combined strength, try as she might. She heard hoarse drunken voices mocking her and, with a surge of fury, brought the bottle in her hand up behind her with all her strength. She heard a satisfying crack as it connected with a nose, and with a yelp, one man was out of the fray, blood pumping from his nostrils. But two still held her. One of them yanked at her blouse viciously as the other tried to pull off her shorts, but they had loosened their grip on her mouth and she started screaming desperately for help.

In the moonlight she could see the sharp stubble on the men's chins, their bloodshot eyes; smell their unwashed bodies, the beer on their breath. There was no doubt what they were intending to do. They threw her on to the sand, tearing off her shorts and shirt. She tried to crawl away, as she heard them unzipping their trousers. She was a thirty-one-year-old virgin, this couldn't be happening to her. Not after everything she'd been through in her life.

"No, *mon Dieu, no,*" she sobbed as one of the men tried to force his sweating bulk on top of her naked body. With a dancer's dexterity she twisted away, scrabbling sideways over the sand like a demented crab. With trousers around their ankles, both men were at a momentary loss, which gave her the edge. Screaming for help, she ran as fast as she could across the slippery sand. Their heavy footsteps were coming closer, gaining on her. However fast she ran, they were stronger and quicker. She knew she couldn't outrun them, it was a losing battle. She heard them cursing harshly, yelling with drunken rage as they were in danger of losing their prey—she could almost feel their blood lust. Where was everyone? Oh, sweet Jesus—was there no one to help her?

Four hundred yards away pleasure boats bobbed gently in the bay. She saw their lights, heard faint music, the gentle laughter of women. Civilization, but still too far away. She must get to the boats before these animals caught her—she had to. She felt a hand grab her nude back, but slick with sweat, she twisted free. The thundering feet ran faster, she could smell the sour, garlicky stink of their last meal.

Julian was the first to hear the faint cries. He'd spent the evening with Nick and Bluey on the *Jezebel,* discussing the continuing problems: Zack's health, Shirley's subversive bitchery and various studio vendettas. Inès had decided to give Julian an evening out with the boys, but now he was eager to get back to her. Straining his eyes across the darkness he thought he saw a naked girl being chased by two men.

"Good God," he whistled, running down the gangplank, calling out for Nick and Bluey. "Damsel in distress, boys. Let's go."

As he got closer, Julian saw it was that weird Agathe woman, Dominique's chaperone. What the blazes was she doing on the beach at this hour?

With Nick and Bluey hot on his heels, Julian launched himself at the nearest ruffian. The trio made short work of Agathe's attackers with a few well-placed kicks and punches. It was over in a matter of seconds, and the Mexicans ran off shouting empty threats.

Agathe sank to the sand, trembling with fear and shame, trying in vain to cover her naked body. Tears streamed down her face, and she was covered with painful cuts and bruises.

"Here," Julian took off his shirt and handed it to her. "Put this on. We'll go back to the boat. We've got first aid stuff there."

She put it on quickly, thankful that it was long enough to cover her thighs. Nick went off to retrieve her clothes as Julian helped her down the beach. She looked at her watch—only five past twelve. Everything had happened so terrifyingly fast. What would those men have done to her if Julian had not saved her? She couldn't bear to think of it, or of what he must think of her. He must think her insane.

"You must be insane," he said with a gentle smile, putting his arm around her trembling back. "What on earth were you doing on the beach at night? Don't you know how dangerous it is?"

"I was thirsty," she said in a small voice, realizing how ridiculous it sounded. "I went to a bar."

"Well"—he smiled—"that doesn't exactly explain a helluva lot, but come on board. You need a stiff drink, my dear. "

Julian helped Agathe onto the deck of the *Jezebel*. She seemed so frail and vulnerable with that ice-white hair and skin; she obviously needed protection. Any woman stupid enough to wander alone at night on a Mexican beach could hardly be called mature. Old-fashioned feelings of responsibility stirred in him as he ushered her into the main cabin. She collapsed onto the sofa, trying to get her breath, and Julian strode over to the bar. He poured her a large drink which she sipped gratefully, the amber fluid warming her comfortingly. He smiled at her and she smiled shyly back. What would Dominique say if she heard about her midnight stroll? She'd surely think she was no longer either fit or responsible enough to be a chaperone. Now she was just a frightened waif, dirty and bruised.

"Why don't you take a shower?—Clean up, you'll feel a lot better," said Bluey. "C'mon, I'll show you where the head is."

"Thank you," said Agathe, blushing as Julian's eyes smiled sympathetically into hers again.

Invigorating needles of water tingled on her aching body, and she scrubbed away until she felt completely clean. Bluey's rough towels smelled strongly of camphor but they felt good; she was relieved to rid herself of the sand, the sweat and the touch of those filthy, grasping hands. She pulled on her shorts, managing just barely to secure them with the loose top button, and Julian's shirt. There was a brush on the dressing table, and she tried to tame her tangled hair. She looked at herself in the mirror. Better. Although still frightened, at least she was no longer a total wreck. She padded back into the salon where Bluey, Nick and Julian were sitting with large drinks at a table strewn with yachting magazines and books. Julian stood up.

"Come and sit down, Agathe," he said benevolently. "You look done in, poor dear. Drink up."

Agathe took another sip of her drink, grimacing at the strength of it.

"Bluey's special remedy." Bluey winked at her. "Good for what ails you, sweetheart—seasickness, tummy upsets, first-day nerves on the set, whatever it is, the Bluey Special will cure it."

"What is it?" she asked tentatively. Though she rarely drank anything alcoholic except for an occasional glass of wine, she was beginning to like the taste.

"Ah-ha, that's a secret," Julian said, smiling at her. She was such a strange, quiet girl, but she seemed sweet, and terribly innocent, with her soulful eyes and tragic face. Certainly not his type, though he realized from the way she was gazing at him that she could probably fall for him much too easily. Agathe seemed so demure—she even wore a little crucifix around her neck. But he could sense that there was something lurking beneath the surface, something odd about her—what was it? Oh, Lord, he could almost see the look of love growing in her eyes. It made him nervous. He'd never been in the business of encouraging lovesick women in their fantasies. That he saved for the screen.

"Drink up," he said looking at his watch. "It's nearly one o'clock. We've all got to get up early for the reading tomorrow. And we don't want anyone to find out about what happened tonight, do we?" He winked conspiratorially at Agathe who smiled nervously.

"Oh, no, they would think I was such a fool—everyone warned me about going out alone. Please promise you won't tell anyone."

"I promise, Agathe, so do the boys," Julian said, his voice so gentle it seemed to her almost like a caress. "It's our little secret, Agathe." And she felt herself flush with pure happiness.

Agathe was too excited to sleep. In her humid room she hugged a pillow to her aching body and, closing her eyes in a kind of ecstasy, relived the enchanted hour that she'd spent with Julian. It had almost been worth being attacked, she mused, to have had her idol's attentions so intently focused on her. Her pulse fluttered as she remembered how his firm brown hand had gently stroked her hair away from her forehead. His shirt. She still wore the blue cotton shirt which he'd so gallantly taken off and given to her. It smelled of him—of his Turkish cigarettes, the faint and far from unpleasant smell of his sweat mingled with a subtle trace of his after-shave.

She rubbed the loose shirt up and down her body, between her legs and across her breasts. She began to feel feverish as his face filled her imagination; in her mind, his eyes gazed into hers with tenderness and love. His bare chest streaked with rivulets of sweat was next to hers now ... his muscular arms encircled her shoulders, his lips kissing her hair. She felt herself rising to peaks of pleasure which she'd never known before. Rocking from side to side, eyes tightly closed, with Julian's shirt squeezed between her legs, her body stiffened into a series of shuddering and glorious spasms of release as she breathed his name over and over again in the darkness.

7

Zachary Domino had achieved something which Hollywood believed to be impossible. He had a secret mistress for more than five years.

He and Ramona Armande had enjoyed their on-again-off-again clandestine affair. It suited them both. He was single, and even though Ramona was married, her husband was absent so much that few people had ever seen him in the flesh. Hollywood had always been intrigued by Ramona in all of her thirty years on the scene, but no gossip had ever surfaced about her. No one really knew exactly how old she was, but she was certainly well into her fifties. Her face was almost unlined, however, her body lithe, and her sexual vigor that of someone half her age.

She and Zack were in her extraordinary villa on a hill high above Acapulco Bay, their privacy guaranteed by a highly efficient security system of guards and German shepherd dogs.

She had cooked dinner for him herself: chicken enchiladas, and his favorite—refried beans with tortillas, which she believed had aphrodisiacal qualities. She had given him a good claret to drink and a fat Havana cigar to smoke after dinner. Now they were discussing the film and especially her part in it. She was unhappy with her role and had accepted it only because parts for women her age were rather thin on the ground. Playing Dominique's mother deeply rankled with her.

"I've been a star," she complained. "One of the biggest stars in the history of movies. It's a *scandal* that all I play now is a supporting role." She spat the "supporting" from between her lips as if it were a piece of tobacco from the end of a cigarette. "I had a wonderful part in my Italian film— wonderful. I don't expect to play leads anymore, but I wish I had more to do in this one Zack, really I do."

Zachary gently stroked her arm, looking hopefully towards the bedroom. He didn't feel like getting into yet another discussion about Ramona's career. He wanted to change the subject as quickly as possible. He wanted to get laid, then go home to his own bed and study the script again. He wanted to get his rocks off and not listen to the woes and complaints of an actress. Staying overnight with Ramona was taboo, on the off-chance that her husband might appear unexpectedly. He had had a bitch of a day. Between the appalling Shirley Frankovitch's continuous whining over the script, Irving supporting her with threats of returning to New York, Sir Crispin, who was playing King Montezuma, having a tantrum over his wig, the studio screaming about everything under the sun, and the postponing of the first day's shooting until the script problems could be worked out, he'd had a bellyful.

"Hell, let 'em go," he'd insisted wearily to Nick earlier when both Frankovitches had flounced out of the room, slamming the door. "We've got a halfway decent shooting script, we'll bring in someone else from Hollywood to rewrite certain scenes if it's necessary. We don't need 'em. Fuck the Frankovitches. They're more trouble than they're worth." Nick had agreed with him; the two men were formidably strong allies, God knows they needed to be.

Now Zack sighed. He desperately needed to forget all his problems in the arms of his sultry mistress. As if anticipating his needs, she looked at him seductively and glided gracefully into her vast white bedroom. He quickly followed.

After they finished making love, Ramona rose immediately from her bed and padded across rose-colored rugs to her marble bathroom. There she deftly massaged Zachary's semen into the skin of her face and neck, an invaluable beauty tip which her friend Mae West had taught her years ago.

"Forget all those expensive face creams and fancy lotions, hon," Mae had drawled. "If guys are good for only one thing, it's that essence they produce. Don't forget, honey, they use *us,* we can use *them*—*I've* been doin' it for years—and my skin's gorgeous ain't it?"

Ramona smiled as she thought of raunchy Mae while Zack lay on the bed smoking his usual après-sex Camel, watching the tropical fish darting about in the aquarium which covered one entire wall of the bedroom. He idly wondered about the whereabouts of Ramona's husband, the White Russian

Prince Ivor Kasinov who was even more mysterious than his wife. Why was he always so often away on business? No one had any idea what business the Prince was involved in, but he seemed to be colossally rich in cash and other assets—one of which was this magnificent mansion and its precious contents. Scheherazade was a palace in the tropical jungle. Made of onyx, marble, glass and stone, all supported by marble Corinthian columns brought from Italian quarries at phenomenal expense, the villa was like a Visconti film set.

Ramona had been married to Prince Kasinov for more than a decade. After the war she had returned to Hollywood from making a movie in Vienna with the diminutive Prince in tow. Hollywood bowed and scraped to both of them, impressed with Ramona's pedigree prize, and she had queened it in Beverly Hills for several years until the Prince had decided to move to Mexico for unexplained reasons. She then became the most celebrated society hostess in Mexico, an invitation to one of her parties being most coveted. She was throwing a gala next week to launch *Cortez*. Dozens of Hollywood celebrities would be flying in, as well as the society and show-business press of the world.

Other than her intimates—of whom there were few—everyone who knew Ramona never called her anything but Princess. Unless she was working on a film, when she became democratic. In some small way this compensated for the decline in her movie career, as did her glittering parties and, of course, her lavish photo-layouts in all the best magazines. She was determined that this party would be the most dazzling to date, an event to remember.

Looking at the Cartier clock on the bedside table, Zack saw it was time for him to leave.

The key technical crew and main actors were congregated in one of the assembly rooms of the Villa Vera for the ten o'clock read-through. All were punctual, but Zack had not yet appeared, which was unusual, as he was always the first to arrive. The room was dominated by a huge oak table around which everyone could sit comfortably. A silver urn dispensed coffee, and there were ash trays and bottles of mineral water on the table. Nick glanced at his watch nervously; it was nearly a quarter past ten. He wanted to give a short motivating rah-rah speech to everyone, but he needed Zack's support. Where was he?

"I think I'll call him," Nick said to Bluey. "He's *never* late—he's probably overslept."

There was no answer from Zack's room and Nick looked over at Bluey with concern.

"I don't understand this at all," he muttered. "It's not like him."

"Hang up. Let's start the reading anyway," Shirley rasped. "We don't need to wait for him. C'mon, Irving and I have written a coupla new scenes—we want to read them to you."

"No, we can't do that, we must have him here, we need him. It's just not right," Nick replied.

He looked over at Shirley, whose shrewish face was puffy and shiny with perspiration. God, she was a malevolent bitch, and a drunkard into the bargain—a lethal combination.

Julian was chatting with Agathe, whose eager black eyes never once left his face; although she was blushing she still managed to retain a pinched, cold look, icy in spite of the heat.

Dominique sidled up to Julian, green eyes sparkling, perfectly shaped breasts seeming to point deliberately at his chest. "Did you sleep well, Julian?" she asked with a sly grin.

"Like a log." He smiled, aware more than ever of her resemblance to the young Inès. It was truly striking. They were the same height, had the same oval face, small nose, sensual lips—but this little girl was years younger. Jail bait. "Don't even *think* about it, Julian," said his conscience. "It could never be worth it in a hundred years."

"I'm so excited," Dominique sighed. "This is going to be a *thrilling* film, *n'est-ce pas?* And I'm so honored to be playing opposite you, Julian." She was giving him the sexual come-on. He had never been wrong about female vibrations before, and this one was only a teenager! But what a teenager. He remembered the sight of her luscious body in the swimming pool and his eyes flitted appreciatively over her breasts, barely covered by a flimsy pink blouse. "Yes, it certainly is going to be exciting," he said. He felt that disturbing stirring again, and moved away from her to the safety of the coffee urn.

"And, I'm looking forward to working with you, too, Dominique my dear," he said as he poured himself a cup of coffee while the girl smiled secretly and Agathe glared at her jealously.

"I'm going to Zack's room—find out what's going on." Nick banged down the phone. "I'll be right back," he said, and strode out.

The cast and crew started to gossip and chatter. Dominique monopolized Julian's attention again discussing the script, and completely cutting Agathe off from the possibility of any further conversation with him. She went to the window to stare sulkily at the view and to relive last night with Julian on the boat. Suddenly the telephone rang harshly. Bluey answered it.

"Oh, my God, Jesus Christ—no, I don't believe it." Bluey's face hardened and he leaned against the wall for support. The room became hushed. "I'll be right there. Have you called the doctor?"

"What on earth's the matter old boy?" Julian asked.

"It's Zachary, he's—er—not well, it seems." The normally unflappable assistant director was trying not to sound flustered. "I'm going up to see if I can help."

"What do you mean, 'not well'?" Julian insisted. "What's wrong with him?"

"I don't know, I'll go and see. Don't worry, I'll be right back," he added as he raced out.

The group began muttering. This sounded ominous. A film crew has a sixth sense about one of their own, and they realized something must have happened to Zachary. Something which could affect the movie.

His face the color of chalk, his eyes open, blank and staring, Zachary Domino was lying on the bed. He had obviously tried to get up because of the strange angle of his body, but he hadn't been able to make it.

"He's dead," said Nick numbly. "Oh, Christ."

"Jesus," Bluey gasped. "How the hell did it happen?"

"I don't know," sighed Nick. "I suppose it must have been his heart."

He felt for Zachary's pulse but there was nothing, even in the heat the body was cold. He'd obviously been dead for some time—maybe several hours.

Julian came in, immediately followed by the frantic hotel manager, who crossed himself, raising his eyes to heaven when he saw the corpse. Death was terrible for business in the hotel trade. He wondered if they might be able to hush it up. They wouldn't be able to rent this room for a while, that was for sure.

"Oh, God," Julian groaned when he saw Zack's body. "Poor old chap."

Nick nodded slowly, staring at Zachary, his eyes brimming with tears. He had seen his mother, father, baby brothers and sisters, almost all of his family, in death, and he had always tried not to weep, but somehow the sight of this stalwart old man, who had meant so much to him, who had helped him and guided him, touched Nick deeply. Tears ran down his cheeks as he heard Bluey's shocked voice saying, "Well, Jesus H. Christ! Who the hell is going to produce this fucking movie now?"

Shirley Frankovitch was immediately on the telephone to Spyros Makopolis, but he had already heard the news half an hour earlier and had called an emergency meeting of the MCCP board.

"We need a new line producer down here right away," she said in her gravelly voice. "I've just had a *great* idea, Spyros, it's simply *great.*"

"And what's that?" Spyros asked. He'd always had a soft spot for Shirley. Her films had made the studio pots of money. She was smart, despite being a woman, an ugly and occasionally drunken one at that, but he admired her talent, especially her undoubted ability to make the coffers of the box office rattle.

"Umberto Scrofo," Shirley said triumphantly. "He produced *La Città Perduta*, the film Irving wrote in Rome last year. He really is a *wonderful* producer, Spyros darling, very talented. Irving can't speak highly enough about him. You met him at your party, remember? He came with Ramona. He's intelligent, cultured; he has innovative, brilliant ideas. He's great with budgets, understands cast and crew, and I think you can get him cheap."

"Well, I was thinking of Gregory Ratoff," Spyros said after a slight pause. "But I'm told he's shooting in Egypt. We've already contacted the agents for Spears Farnsworth and Jack Hall, but they're both probably booked. We can't afford to waste any more time, Shirley. It's already costing us more than ten thousand dollars a day just to keep everyone in Acapulco. Our studio has no acceptable producers available at the moment."

Shirley shot back with a triumphant "Well, let's use Scrofo—take a chance on someone new for a change—someone who isn't part of your family." She realized she had probably gone too far with that but Spyros answered as if he hadn't really been listening.

"How do you know if this Scrofo guy is free?" he asked.

"I spoke to him last week in Rome," Shirley lied. "He's a good friend of ours, Spyros, he's available, and I *know* he's ready to do an important American movie. You did see *La Città*, didn't you, darling?" she asked, knowing he hadn't.

"Sure, it was great." It was his turn to lie, and, covering the receiver, he hissed at his assistant to find a print of *La Città Perduta* right away.

"And he brought it in for under a million," Shirley persisted. "With that amazing cast—Mendelson, even Ramona." A sarcastic tone crept into her voice. She was not enamored of Ramona Armande; indeed, she didn't like actors in general, considering them shallow, vain creatures whose only interest was getting as many close-ups of themselves as possible. Her only exception was Julian Brooks, whom she admired in spite of herself.

"Give this guy Scrofo a call," Spyros conceded. "If he's available, have him telephone me at my office immediately. We've got to get moving on this, Shirley, this delay is gonna cost us *thousands*—and the stockholders are gonna blow their stacks."

"Right away, Spyros my darling," crowed Shirley. "I'm on the blower to Italy now."

Shirley hung up, a victorious smile splitting her pumpkin face. This is it, she said to herself. Signor Scrofo, you better be good to us now. This is a gift I've given you—a fucking *gift*. And picking up the telephone, she instructed the operator to place a call to Rome immediately.

It was six o'clock in Rome. The vast apartment was chilly and Umberto Scrofo was freezing. His southern Calabrian blood never seemed to have adjusted to the cold Roman winters. He picked up the telephone receiver after only two rings.

"Pronto," he snapped. He'd been receiving a good many unpleasant calls recently, perhaps because of the excessive nudity in his movie which had caused some offense to the Catholic community. The shrill tones of Shirley Frankovitch crackled down the transatlantic line.

"Umberto, it's me, Shirley, Shirley Frankovitch. Do you remember me?"

"Of course," he said gallantly. "How could I forget you Shirley?"

"I have some *great* news for you, Umberto. Tell me, are you working on anything right now?"

"Well, there are a few things in the pipeline, Shirley my dear, many things actually," Umberto hedged, glancing at the small pile of dreadful scripts on his desk. "But I must confess, nothing definite—nothing I'm really excited about at this moment."

"How about coming to Acapulco and taking up the reins of our movie *Cortez?*" Shirley asked excitedly. There was a pause as Scrofo digested this. "Hello—Hello, Umberto, can you hear me?"

"Cortez? The Makopolis film with Julian Brooks? Of course I've heard about it, but I thought Zachary Domino was producing."

"He's dead," Shirley stated triumphantly. "He died this morning. Heart attack, they think. I've spoken to Spyros about you coming down here to produce it, Umberto, and he seems keen. Are you free? Can you do it?"

"Well, yes, yes, I am free actually, I certainly am." Umberto couldn't keep the eagerness out of his voice. "Er, how sad about Zachary, he was a fine producer." The realization of what this could mean to his career was hitting Scrofo like the rush of cocaine, and excitement made his voice even harsher than usual.

"Then call Spyros Makopolis right away. Here's the number—Crestview 77933. Get your ass on the first plane out of that Eternal fucking City," cackled Shirley, "and fly on down to Acapulco. We've got work to do, Umberto. Lots and lots of work."

"Ciao, Shirley—and thank you, *cara,"* shouted Umberto. "I shall be there *subito."* As he replaced the receiver his heart was beating so erratically that he thought it might stop altogether, and all his dreams would be ended before he even clambered on the first rung of his stairway to Hollywood

success. Quickly he dialed the international operator but was frustrated to find all circuits to the United States were busy.

He took his solid-gold pen, an "end of picture" gift from Ramona, and started to doodle on a pad. PRODUCED BY UMBERTO SCROFO. Somehow that didn't look right now. Not that there was anything wrong with Italian names. On movie credits they hadn't hurt Carlo Ponti or Federico Fellini, but there was something . . . well . . . unpleasant about *his* name. Scrofo—in English it sounded like "scruffy," or "scrofulous," a bad connotation. No, it wasn't right for an above-the-title important Hollywood producer; he needed something better.

He doodled some more, leaving out the S. CROFA, CROFF, CROFT. Croft—now that was a good surname. It sounded vaguely Scottish to him. Croft. It reminded him of a charming cottage in the Scottish Highlands that he'd visited once. Umberto, of course, he would change to Hubert. Hubert Croft. Excellent. One thing was missing, though. He thought of the producers who were his idols: David O. Selznick, Jack L. Warner. Darryl F. Zanuck. A middle initial—that's what he needed. He would take the *S* from Scrofo. Hubert S. Croft. Now that was a fine name for a fine Hollywood producer. He tried the international operator again and this time he got through to Spyros Makopolis.

He was on his way at last.

*A*s the day of her party dawned, Ramona woke up in her shimmering
white bedroom with an appalling headache, Zack's tragic death still fresh in
her mind. Her maid brought her breakfast in bed, along with a copy of the
Acapulcan News. It was crammed with gossipy details of tonight's lavish
celebration for *Cortez.* According to the society reporter, this would be the
most spectacular society event here of the whole year. Lana Turner and
Linda Christian were flying in from Hollywood, and so were Errol Flynn,
Ava Gardner and Gilbert Roland. Miguel Alemán, until recently the President of Mexico, had also promised to attend as had many prominent dig-
nitaries and politicians from America. The festivities would begin at sunset
because Acapulcan sunsets were of such particular and extraordinary
beauty, and probably not end till the equally spectacular dawn came up .

Ramona had hired two bands to play: one dance band from Mexico City,
and a strolling group of mariachi players called Los Paraguayos who would
play Mexican folk songs.

Ramona regularly made "the ten best hostesses in the world" list in the
glossy magazines, and for this occasion she determined to live up to her
reputation in spite of her sorrow over her secret lover's death. A small army
of servants had been up since dawn, scrubbing, scouring, polishing and
sweeping the vast areas of marble, glass and stone. The two swimming
pools were to be covered with a floating veil of flowers, hundreds of

imported white roses, costing thousands of dollars, and so much more unusual than jasmine or hibiscus, would float in her brilliantly lit pools tonight.

The fiesta was going to cost a minor fortune, but Ramona wouldn't be footing the bill. Although the Prince indulged her every financial whim, her childhood in Hungary had left her with a solid respect for the value of money. Didier, who had himself started at the bottom of the film ladder before finally becoming the most powerful producer in England, had taught her all she'd needed to know about finance. His advice was: "Never pay for anything yourself if you can get someone else to pay for it." Didier had scolded her when he'd discovered that she'd been buying her own stockings and gloves for a movie in which she'd only had a small role. "Always charge *everything* you can to the production—that should be your credo." Ramona had learned well from her brother, so when Zack had approached her to give the *Cortez* launch party, she'd agreed, provided, of course, that MCCP would be footing the bill.

Pragmatically unsentimental, Ramona wasn't going to allow Zachary's death to spoil her day. To her, there was no point in mourning too long after the departed had been sent off in a civilized manner. It had been three days since Zack's funeral. That was long enough; the show must go on.

She dressed quickly in a cream cotton caftan. Catching her sleek hair back with a tortoiseshell comb and leaving her skin bare of makeup, she began her long list of household checks.

Everything must be perfection tonight, not only to impress the glamorous guests, but because she was looking forward to again seeing her friend Umberto Scrofo, Zachary's replacement as producer. Irving Frankovitch had let slip last night that it was to be him, but that Umberto had insisted on changing his name. Not only had she enjoyed working with Umberto in Rome last year, but he'd also been an interesting and knowledgeable escort. She had played one of the starring roles then. Now she hoped that Umberto might be persuaded to build up her role in *Cortez,* something Zachary hadn't been prepared to do in spite of their relationship.

Scheherazade was a vast, multilevel mansion modeled after an Arabian mosque. From the top level, which was some ten stories high, an old white wooden cable car with creaky metal gear teeth and thin wire pulleys ran down the side of the house to Ramona's private beach. Although antiquated, the cable car always had regular safety checks, and all visitors to Scheherazade used it to take them down to the secluded beach.

This top level was a huge open terrace paved with diamond-shaped mosaic tiles. A fountain gushed in the center and palm trees and tropical plants grew in luscious profusion. There was an enormous white marble bar, and here and there, as if resting at some oasis, stood a dozen or more white stone camels.

On the second level were six guest bedroom suites, nestled together in an intimate group around their own swimming pool.

Down winding steps lined on each side by jungle foliage, through sparkling white arches so bright that they dazzled the eye, was the unbelievable vista of the main salon. From here there was a panoramic view of the Pacific revealed in all its glittering glory, for where the south wall should have been was only the peerless beauty of the sea. Around the salon snaked the main swimming pool, its very edge the horizon. Were it not for the marble figures at the edge of the pool, pool and sea would appear as one.

A large golden snail with *trompe l'oeil* butterflies painted on its shell guarded the entrance to the grotto, where revelers were often serenaded long into the night.

Set into the wall was a huge shell of shimmering pearl big enough for a small woman to sit in. Ramona had done that herself once for Zack, wearing just a pair of golden stockings and a smile. He'd been quite insatiable that night. Poor Zack.

At the bottom of more steps was her own private beach—the only private beach in Acapulco—and Ramona used it with pleasure and great pride.

It had taken Ramona and her Prince five years to construct Scheherazade—five arduous years during which the most brilliant architects and designers from Mexico, New York and Paris had created this fantasy masterpiece. Now the perfectionist Princess Ramona reigned supreme, secure that it was the grandest house in Mexico.

Nicholas Stone shaved with his customary speed. He hated wasting time on shaving and showering and other mundane things. His mind constantly whirled with every tiny detail of his movie which would finally begin shooting on Monday morning. The jet-set party tonight held no interest for him. Parties of any description were just not his scene. He was a simple man, and having to make small talk with the *beau monde* was not his idea of a good time. He had tried to telephone the new producer, Hubert S. Croft, the night before, but had been informed by the hotel operator that Mr. Croft was sleeping off his arduous trip from Rome and was not to be disturbed under any circumstances.

He had, however, spoken to Elektra and his children, and in spite of a bad connection he could hear the warmth in their voices which always brought him such happiness. He knew it was time now to pick up Bluey at his boat and, grabbing his keys, he glanced briefly into the mirror and made a face of resignation at the boring evening that stretched ahead of him.

In complete contrast to Nick, the newly christened Hubert S. Croft spent a great deal of time on his toilette. Unfortunately, his beautifully cut cream-colored suit from Caraceni of Milan did nothing to minimize his bulk, and his sallow complexion was not enhanced by a striped voile shirt with a tight white collar. He had hoped that the midnight blue silk tie would give him the look of respectability and authority that he craved. It was most important that he make the right impression tonight.

He knew how much was at stake. With a big Hollywood film to produce, he needed to earn the trust of the director, encourage the actors, ingratiate himself with the crew and show everyone that he knew exactly what he was doing. He'd succeeded in Rome; he would succeed in Hollywood at last, and he had excellent ammunition in that he believed in himself. He also had strong allies already in the Frankovitch team and Ramona Armande—a good set of cards in his hands. Very good indeed.

He flicked back what little remained of his hair and doused himself with the pungent French cologne which he'd worn for so many years. Inserting a pair of gold links set with enormous sapphires into his cuffs, he wondered if his favorite sapphire stickpin might not be a little too fancy for the tropics. He was already sweating profusely, even in the relative cool of the hotel room. He hoped it would be cooler at Ramona's party. He must make a *bella figura* tonight—he had to let the cast and crew know who was boss. And the first person he must convince of this would be the young hotshot director, Nicholas Stone.

Inès looked in the mirror and put the finishing touches to her makeup, liking what she saw. She was glowing. A one-shouldered sarong dress of pale green silk complemented her elegant figure. It was clasped at the shoulder with a jade-and-ivory brooch which Julian had given her just this morning, on receiving a letter from Dr. Langley in L.A., confirming her pregnancy. Tiny jade studs gleamed in her earlobes, and her hair was tied with a simple emerald-green ribbon. On her wrist she wore as usual the delicate amber-and-silver bracelet given to her by Yves. She never took it off; it was her lucky mascot. The only night she had not worn it was the night she had killed the Italian General with his own razor. She shuddered. Forget about that night, she told herself. Why was it so hard to forget?

Julian, casually immaculate as ever, tanned and handsome, looked her up and down approvingly.

"Darling, are you sure you're up to tonight?" he asked. "I'm worried about you. You know how we both feel about the baby, I don't want you to risk overdoing it."

"Don't worry, my love," she said, coming close to him, touching his cheek with her gentle fingers. "I feel fine—it's just a touch of morning sickness and Dr. Langley told me that almost every woman suffers from it, particularly with the first baby."

"I hope you don't get it with our next one," said Julian sincerely, cupping her face in his hands and gazing lovingly into her eyes. "And the ones after that. You know how much I love you—want you—want to be with you all my life, don't you, my angel?"

"I do, darling—I really do," Inès whispered, her heart full of love for him.

"This is going to be a tough film for me, darling—I just need to know that you'll be as understanding as ever—and that you'll always, always be here with me."

"You'd better believe it, Mister Brooks," Inès replied with a big smile. "Looks, honey, you ain't *never* gonna get rid of this particular woman."

"And I never want to—ever," he said, his expression so penetrating and sincere that Inès looked surprised.

"Julian—darling—what is it?" she asked. "You seem so worried suddenly—why? What's the matter?"

"I don't really know," said Julian, moving away and looking out the window at the dark blue velvet of the sea.

"Everything's so perfect, Inès. Almost too good to be true. Everything. You—the two of us together—the baby—I just couldn't bear anything to go wrong, ever."

"Nothing's going to go wrong, silly," said Inès lightly, thinking that it was so unlike Julian to voice this kind of thought. "Phoebe has agreed to your terms, we can be married as soon as the decree comes through—the baby's fine, and Dr. Langley says he sees no reason why I can't have *lots* more—so why are you so suddenly worried, darling?"

"I'm not—I'm not, forget it." He scooped her up in his arms and kissed the soft fragrance of her neck. "I'm just behaving like a stupid superstitious actor before the show starts. Come on, old girl, let's get off to this dreaded gala."

She kissed his cheek, feeling the rush of pleasure from the knowledge that she was going to have his child.

He smiled back at her tenderly. She was the woman he wanted to be with forever. He loved her so much—but how he wished that these new and alarming erotic images of Dominique would stop coming into his head whenever he made love to the woman who was not only carrying his child but who was soon to be his wife.

After Dominique had awakened from her afternoon siesta she stood under the shower, letting the tingling cold water revive her. She was looking forward tremendously to this evening. She loved parties, the new thrill of dressing up, painting her face, designing her hair in some daring new style. She loved to flirt—and now, she especially loved to flirt with Julian. Julian Brooks. So famous and charming—and the handsomest man in the world.

She knew she had his male libido in a spin. She smiled to herself as she sat at her dressing table fiddling with her lipstick. Although her face hardly needed any cosmetic assistance, playing with paints and brushes gave her more time to think. Looks Brooks liked her. She smiled like a cat while she applied Revlon's Fire and Ice to her full lips. He more than liked her—he desired her, too. She'd become aware of that when she'd spotted him watching her in the pool. On the few occasions that they had met since, it was increasingly obvious to her how he felt.

Dominique was beginning to understand how desirable she was, how much power her youthful beauty gave her. She loved it. So Looks Brooks wanted to play, did he? At sixteen she was hardly an expert in the game of love, but she was going to try and experiment. She'd enjoyed her affair with Gaston in St. Tropez very much. But she'd had to come to America for this film just as she was really beginning to enjoy his lovemaking. What would it be like to make love to Julian?

That Julian was both engaged and in the middle of a divorce didn't bother her at all. Love was all only a game, wasn't it? she thought as she clipped on a pair of big golden hoop earrings. After all, Inès was French too, and Frenchwomen understood about these things. So she wouldn't mind if Dominique flirted with her fiancé—it was all part of the game.

Dominique chose a short strapless dress from her wardrobe. The waist was tightly cinched and the hemline high, which drew attention to her splendid legs. Her hair was dry now, and she brushed it until it tumbled in luxuriant splendor down her bare back.

She knocked on the door of the room next to hers. "Ready, Agathe?" she called out in her breathy little girl's voice with its newly acquired American accent. "Let's hit the road, baby."

Tonight she was determined to have a wonderful time and perhaps to captivate Julian Brooks even more.

. . .

Irving and Shirley put the finishing touches on their respective toilettes. He felt comfortable in a pair of loose cotton trousers and an old shirt; he cared little or nothing about his appearance; his only concern was his work.

Shirley fussed miserably in front of the mirror. The new caftan she was wearing, in its bright shades of orange and yellow, did nothing to disguise her ballooning girth. She was allergic to the sun so her face was white, and her salt-and-pepper hair clung to her head in tight, old-fashioned curls, giving her an uncanny, but hardly becoming, resemblance to Harpo Marx. She had done her best with her makeup, as she wanted to look as good as possible when she met Umberto Scrofo again. Or Hubert S. Croft—she didn't care what he wanted to be called. He'd rung the day before, informing the Frankovitches that now that he was making an American film, he wanted an American name. Since only Irving, Shirley and Ramona knew him as Umberto Scrofo, he would appreciate . . . must insist, actually . . . that they never refer to him as anything but Hubert S. Croft. Hell, she'd call him Donald Duck if it would help their cause. Croft was sure to be the Frankovitches' ally, the man to reinstate those violent battle scenes and those lyrical pages of prose to the shooting script. Zachary Domino and Nicholas Stone had callously sabotaged it; now Scrofo would be their savior. He would be as strong and authoritative as he had been in Italy, even inspiring fear in some of the cast and crew. That was good. That was how a producer should be—respected. A hard task-master. He would make this truly a Frankovitch film, not one for which the critics would praise only the director and the actors, leaving the writers unappreciated, as usual. Shirley smiled grimly as she pinned an emerald brooch to her cafton. Oh, yes, she'd call him anything he wanted as long as he helped the cast and crew of *Cortez* to realize the true worth of the Frankovitch team and give them the respect and glory which they so richly deserved.

*R*amona was a vision of composed loveliness as she waited for her guests in the center of her marble entrance hall. Wearing a slim column of white silk crepe, her ebony hair caught up with a diamond comb from the estate of the Prince's family, enormous pear-shaped diamonds glittering on her ears, and several diamond bracelets on each wrist, she was coolly elegant, but exuding that charming effervescence which is the mark of every good hostess.

Agathe and Dominique were the first to arrive, Agathe in a long matronly floral dress in which she appeared uncomfortable. Her normally expressionless white face was awestruck. Not only was she a guest at one of the most talked-about houses in the world, but soon her idol would be here. He would smile at her. They would chat wittily. He would see how bright she was, how cultivated.

She accepted a glass of mineral water and was content just to sit on a divan watching the fabled sunset and waiting for Julian's arrival.

Dominique sashayed around, looking older tonight than her sixteen years. Tanned to a golden honey-color, she mixed gaily with the arriving guests, chatting and joking with genuine camaraderie and charm.

Agathe envied her. Where had she found that poise, that sophistication, that ease with people? Just a few months ago she was a French schoolgirl; now she was a woman of the world, an actress—glamorous and confident. She made Agathe feel even more like some insecure country bumpkin.

Soon the marble floors echoed to the chatter and laughter of the jet set, Hollywood stars, local celebrities and politicians. Bluey and Nick were both impressed by the sheer scale of the house.

"Jesus H. Christ," whistled Bluey. "I've seen some pads in my time, but this takes the cake, cherry, icing and all."

Nick nodded. In spite of having lived in America for ten years, he was still unaccustomed to the palatial, often vulgar residences of the high-living Hollywood stars, directors and producers, but this extraordinary villa was more lavish than any he'd ever seen there. His director's eye was enthralled by the beauty of the landscaping, the exotic pictures, sculptures and other objects, the depth and dimensions of all the rooms. He set off on his own to examine them more closely.

The usually jaded photographers from *Life, Look, Vogue* and the movie magazines—*Photoplay, Modern Scene* and *Motion Picture*—were so excited that they jostled and pushed each other to take pictures. There were stars galore to fill both their columns and their lenses. Lana Turner, with her new husband, Lex Barker, had arrived; she, with her silver-blond hair, was more tanned than the Mexican waiters, and he was as handsome as any film star had a right to be. Hedda Hopper and Louella Parsons had sent only their stringers, but influential, fast-talking Walter Winchell from New York and Harrison Carroll from the Los Angeles *Herald-Examiner* had arrived in person, and now mingled with the chattering crowd, whose voices competed with the music of the strolling mariachis.

As the sun dipped into the horizon, the guests gathered at the end of the huge terrace to view its fading glory. Even the waiters stopped work to admire it, for to the Mexicans it is the symbol of eternal life. There were appreciative gasps as the sun made a dramatically rapid exit to the west, casting a soft apricot glow over everyone and everything. It was such a magnificent sight that spontaneous applause broke out. The mariachis played more wildly and the margaritas began to stir everyone's blood with fiesta excitement.

No one noticed the entrance of Hubert S. Croft as he stood at the top of the tall marble staircase and watched the partygoers as they oohed and aahed at the sunset. He gave a sneering smile. They all seemed so childish.

Ramona was the first to see him; she hurried over to greet him effusively. "Hubert, my dear Hubert, I'm *so* happy to see you again. You look very well." She was careful to use the new name which he'd insisted on.

Hubert took her hand and with European gallantry bowed his head over her fabled forty-carat diamond. "Ramona my dear, you are more ravishing than ever—and what a superb house. Magnificent, my dear, magnificent."

Ramona beamed as Hubert accepted a margarita from a passing waiter; then she whisked him off to be introduced to her other guests.

Across the sea of laughing faces, Inès froze in horror. No. Not again. Not here in Acapulco. Was this a dream or a ghost? Why was he here? Her eyes were riveted to the short, paunchy man who strutted around shaking hands and smiling and who in turn was being greeted with friendly smiles by everyone. But of course he must be some friend of Ramona's; she had seen them both outside Romanoff's last month.

As the man came nearer to her she could see the unmistakable face and squat body which had haunted her dreams. His fleshy lips were at this moment pulled into an expression which he imagined to be a charming social smile, but which made him look like some grotesque gargoyle. But there was no doubt at all that this was the face from her past. Inès clung to Julian's arm; her heart hammering as Umberto Scrofo advanced towards her with an ominous tread and with that ghastly smile plastered on his hideous face.

There was nowhere to hide.

"Bon soir, Julian," Dominique said, licking pink glossy lips and smiling up at him seductively.

Julian beamed. "Dear girl," he said heartily, "you look very pretty to-night, very grown up—doesn't she, Inès?"

"Thank you, Julian," Dominique smiled, her attention focused totally on him. She completely ignored Inès even though she was arm in arm with her fiancé. "And you look very—what is the word?—dashing. Yes, that's it, you look very dashing tonight, Julian."

Julian laughed, again finding himself uncomfortably bewitched. Damn, damn. This child-woman was irresistible.

"Would you have a few minutes to discuss something with me, Julian?" Dominique went on, her eyes now downcast shyly. "There's a scene that I didn't quite understand and I would so appreciate your advice about it."

"Well, this *is* a party, my dear. Perhaps tomorrow—" demurred Julian.

"I don't think I could sleep tonight for worrying about this, Julian," Dominique implored, looking up at him, again beseechingly with her Circe-green eyes. "It is so important to me, this film. And I am only a beginner, you can teach me so much, Julian."

Julian shot a quick look at Inès, but she was staring out towards the main salon with a curious blank look on her face. Probably admiring the decorations, he thought.

"Excuse me, darling—I hope you don't mind. Dominique and I are just going over to the edge of the pool to discuss a scene."

She nodded, not speaking, and Julian let go of Inès' arm and allowed Dominique to lead him into the shadows at the base of a nearby palm tree.

By God, she was having an amazing effect on him. He was becoming aroused just by the soft touch of her fingers on his hand. What was wrong with him—was he mad?

"Now which scene is it, Dominique?" he asked sternly, annoyed with himself as he felt his cock starting to harden.

"This one," she said simply, opening her pouting mouth to his, running a tongue full of silent promises across his dry lips, and pressing her yielding body to his. Before he had a chance to respond, she pulled away, looking up at him with a kittenish smile. "I thought that perhaps *this* should be how we did the first kiss after my dance, the firelight scene—what do you think, Julian?" She looked at him in mock innocence while she gently dabbed at her lips with her handkerchief, then wiped his with it.

Julian was dumbstruck. He had always thought that he understood the workings of the female mind, at least as well as, if not better than, the next man. But Dominique was so much more unpredictable than any other woman he had known—even Inès. She was flaunting her sexuality tonight like bunting strung across a pleasure boat. She was a pubescent jade, a wanton child-woman—and God, he desired her.

As Julian stood there dumbstruck Dominique reapplied her lipstick, whispering conspiratorially, "Think about it, Julian, *chéri*. It should be a tender moment, don't you agree? I mean, really sexy but sweet, like Liz and Monty in *A Place in the Sun. N'est-ce pas?*"

Before the spellbound actor could reply, the teenaged minx disappeared into the shadows with a roguish smile, and an embarrassed and tumescent Julian stared after her, alarm bells ringing in his ears.

Inès prayed that Scrofo wouldn't remember her, or that her scarlet face would not betray her. She had tried to disappear into the crowd, but after Julian had finished his talk with Dominique he had found her in the marble bar and taken her over to meet the new producer, who was with Ramona.

"Inès, my dear, I should like you to meet Hubert Croft—Hubert, this is Mademoiselle Juillard, Julian's fiancée," said Ramona.

"How do you do, Mademoiselle," said Scrofo in a rasping harsh voice. *"Enchanté."*

"Hubert is our new producer," beamed Ramona. "And we are very lucky to have him."

Inès felt faint and put her trembling hand on Julian's arm for support.

Producer? Umberto Scrofo was Zachary's replacement? It simply wasn't possible.

"How do you do," Inès mumbled. She knew she had to say something. She felt her knees starting to buckle, and only Julian's steady arm prevented her from swooning. So she hadn't killed him after all.

In horrified fascination she stared at the rim of a pink puckered scar which was only slightly concealed under his flashy shirt. *She* had caused that scar. It was because of her that his voice was a grating whisper.

For eleven years she had believed that she had murdered this man, who was here shaking her hand with a ghastly smile on his brutish face. This was certainly no ghost who held her gaze and rasped, "You're a very lucky man indeed, Mr. Brooks."

Umberto drank in Inès' loveliness with no visible sign of recognition, although he'd held her gaze for perhaps a second longer than necessary. But that was something Inès was used to. Her beauty often caused men to react in strange ways. Croft shook hands with Julian, expressing his delight at being on the movie and his admiration for Julian's fine work in the past. Then his eyes began flitting back to Inès. Faintly she could smell the same sickly after-shave that he'd worn that night at the Ritz. She wanted to flee to the other side of the room, to escape his probing stare, but Julian held her hand tightly. Her heart thumped so hard she felt sure someone would notice. How in heaven's name had Umberto Scrofo ended up here? Why had he changed his name? How on earth could he possibly be producing Julian's movie? But most of all, why wasn't he dead?

As if reading her thoughts, Hubert turned to look at her again with a penetrating stare.

"You're a very beautiful woman, Mademoiselle Juillard." He had barely a trace of an Italian accent. "Very beautiful indeed."

"Thank you," she murmured, gulping at her margarita, the salt that encrusted the rim of the glass stinging her lips. She looked at Julian for help, but he was busy talking to Hedda Hopper's stringer, who was scribbling in a notebook.

"Have we not met somewhere before?" His beady black eyes roamed over the contours of her breasts. "You look familiar."

"I don't think so," Inès said quietly, trying to move away, "I'm sure I would have remembered." Hubert took a step closer and yet another wave of his familiar cologne hit her. She felt her stomach churn.

"I never forget a face. Never." His eyes searched hers as he suddenly sensed her fear. Who was this woman? He felt sure he knew her from somewhere. But where? What was the story of this beautiful creature? He must find out. He would make it his business to find out. Hubert always needed to know every detail about everyone with whom he worked— knowledge gave him power.

"Where are you from?" he probed.

Inès felt as if she were going mad. She had murdered him, hadn't she? She remembered all too vividly the look on his face, the blood covering the bathroom floor, the hue and cry in Paris when they'd searched for his murderer. Her flight to England to escape certain death. Surely, though, there was little chance that he would recognize her today. She looked so very different from the skinny teenage prostitute of wartime Paris. She was now an elegant, chic woman of the world, in her prime. But she *had* tried to kill him. No one could ever forget a face seen in those circumstances, could they? But her face wasn't the same—or was it? The style and blondness of her hair were different, her cheekbones were more pronounced, she was taller, sleeker. She was *not* recognizable, she told herself.

But she knew she could not lie to him about her nationality. Everyone knew where she was from.

"London," she murmured. "I'm from London."

"London?" he said in surprise. "But you cannot be, you are French, are you not?"

"Yes," said Inès quietly. "I am."

"She lived in London for twelve years," smiled Julian, turning away from the reporter, his actor's instincts sensing tension. "That's where we met, isn't it, darling?"

"Oh really," Umberto smiled, still staring at Inès. "Where were you born, Mademoiselle Juillard?"

"France," she whispered.

"France?" he said, raising an eyebrow. "France? France is a very big country. Which part of France, Mademoiselle Juillard?"

"I was born in Lyon," she lied.

His eyes narrowed. "Lyon, really?"

"Yes." Then, more boldly, "Lyon. Have you ever been there?" She could barely keep the loathing from her voice.

A smirk crossed his slug-white face. She was *avverso* towards him, was she? He was used to that. It certainly wouldn't be the first time someone had disliked him on sight. He couldn't place her, but it seemed that she was most anxious to hide something from him. "Lyon, hmm?" He looked carefully at her again. "I was never in Lyon, but I know that I'll remember where it was that we met; it's sure to come back to me. As I say, I never, ever forget a face, or where I saw it."

He smiled craftily and strolled out onto the terrace to rejoin his hostess.

Inès felt as if she'd been kicked in the stomach. Julian had been right in thinking that everything was almost too perfect. She had to get away. Julian was holding court in one corner of the vast room. She needed to be alone, to have time to digest Scrofo's presence here.

As soon as Scrofo left her, she ran down the stone steps which led to the beach, and stood on the toffee-colored sand, staring out to sea with unseeing eyes. She was now sure that Scrofo would inevitably remember her as the whore who had slashed his throat. She shuddered at the word: *whore.* How would it affect Julian's career if the world found out that his fiancée had been a Parisian prostitute and a failed murderess? A woman who had serviced the enemy during the war? She couldn't bear even to think about it, or what it would do to their relationship.

However much he professed to love her, Julian would dump her immediately—she knew that. Although she believed that he truly loved her, she knew that Julian Brooks simply couldn't handle the ramifications of marrying a woman with such a sordid, even criminal, past.

No, her life would be totally ruined if Julian were to discover any part of her past. Ruined. His divorce was supposed to be final in two months. They must marry soon, before her pregnancy became obvious; before he had time to learn the truth. If he did, it would be the end. He would leave her, she knew. Oh, he would be kind—he would give her money, which she did not need. She had invested wisely and could provide for herself. She would be left with nothing of his except his child. No one even knew that she was pregnant. If they found out, that would no doubt cause another scandal, but not nearly as ignominious as the one Umberto Scrofo could cause.

Inès sat down on a rock, her mind spinning. What could Scrofo possibly want from her? She was no threat to him. But if he recognized her he would want his revenge, naturally, and from the way he stared at her it was only a matter of time before he did. She cursed the fact that her first name had never been changed.

She placed her hand comfortingly on her still-flat stomach. Sweat trickled down the inside of her thin silk dress and she took off her shoes, putting them on one of the rocks which lay like beached sea monsters on the sand. Across the bay in the dusk she could see a speedboat weaving about, filled with laughing people. The sea was flat and oily, without the slight wind that usually came from the bay. A fisherman suddenly emerged from the water in the crepuscular light, a baby octopus inpaled on his rusty spear, its saclike pink body hanging down limply like the scrotum of an elderly man. Inès shuddered. She had seen too many of those. The thought of ever again having to make love to any man except Julian was anathema.

She paddled her feet listlessly in the tide in the hope of cooling down, but the water was too warm, only making her feel stickier. She bent down to splash some water on her flushed face. Her mind was crowded with thoughts of the embarrassment, the humiliation, the indignity if her past were to be discovered. Julian would never be able to forgive her. He was the traditional public school English gentleman just as much as he was an important star. He'd sacrificed his marriage and a great deal of money for Inès, but she knew he wouldn't be willing to sacrifice his future. Her female instincts warned her that she was in grave danger. She had to do something drastic about Umberto Scrofo before he tried to ruin her life all over again.

Agathe had been looking forward with mixed feelings to the party. She usually felt out of place and ill at ease at social gatherings, but as Dominique's chaperone she had had to go. At least there was the presence of Julian to look forward to.

She sensed his arrival at once, almost smelling him across the room, the same scent she cherished in the fabric of his blue shirt. She had kept it hidden away under her mattress, and slept with it entwined around her body every night.

He was even more handsome than the last time she'd seen him, more sexually arousing to her just from across the room than during her fevered nights when her thoughts were constantly of his body curled around hers, their two mouths one. He was wearing a white shantung suit of exquisite cut, and the palest of blue silk shirts open at the neck to reveal the dark curly hair of his chest. His hair tumbled over his bronzed brow as he laughed into the face of the woman by his side—laughing joyously, intimately, with a slim ash-blond woman in a green sarong, his hand casually resting on her one bare shoulder.

Agathe drew in her breath with a gasp. The hair was different. The style, the sophistication had not been there. But there was no one from those wartime days Agathe could *ever* forget. What was Julian doing with that tart Inès?

How could he be with that slut-child who'd slept with half the Gestapo in Paris? Surely *she* wasn't his fiancée?

They were being greeted by everyone like an emperor and his consort, but Inès was no empress, Agathe thought. She was a cheap whore and a traitor to her country. Why was Julian, who deserved only the pure and the good, engaged to this . . . this personification of evil? The bitch must have put a spell on him, for it was impossible for a man so wonderful, so kind, so magnificent in every way to want to take a whore as his wife.

Agathe remembered the magazine photograph which Dominique had shown her on their flight to Acapulco. The woman with Julian had been in profile and had been dark haired so it was no wonder that she hadn't recognized her, but there was no mistaking the traitor now, even though she was blond.

The past came flooding back to her. This was the tart who'd killed an Italian officer. They had hidden her in the same cellar next to L'Éléphant Rose where Agathe had been made to stay for so long. But Inès had spent only a few days there before becoming hysterical. She had no stamina; she was weak and evil. Of course they had all rallied around the girl. Her pimp Yves, old Gabrielle, all of them who hadn't raised a finger to help Agathe until she was almost *dead* had done everything for Inès the whore. False passports, changing her name, coloring her hair, sending her off to the safety of England, spoiling the little bitch. Agathe had never heard anything about her again after that. But now, here, engaged to the man Agathe worshiped, was Inès Dessault, smiling at the world as if she owned it.

Bluey and Nick watched the sunset from the second level of Scheherazade, and Nick enthused, "It's the most goddamn gorgeous thing I've ever seen in my whole life, far more beautiful than the sunsets in Hydra. I want to be able to have this sort of look in the last battle scenes, Bluey—it could symbolize the tragedy of Mexico—the dying sun, the sun that the Mexicans so revere—dead and dying soldiers lying in the sunset when the battle's over—" Nick rattled on excitedly about the pathos and symbolism of the sunset, but Bluey, having seen it far too many times to wax lyrical, only noticed his margarita was finished.

"C'mon, let's get a refill, kiddo," he said. "There'll be plenty more sunsets, believe me."

Nick looked back at the amber sky, ideas fermenting in his mind as he reluctantly returned to the party. He had to capture this on the screen—had to.

The mariachi music in the main salon was only slightly louder than the conversation and laughter, now that all the guests had become more relaxed with one another. Nick and Bluey strolled to the bar, and Ramona, like a sliver of moonlight, drifted over to them.

"Darlings, our new producer has arrived. I've been looking everywhere for you. You must come and meet him."

"Of course, I've been waiting for this," said Nick as Ramona led him through the jostling crowd. "It's about time."

In the middle of a small group, consisting of Irving and Shirley Frankovitch, Dominique and Agathe, stood a short, overweight man, his back turned, wearing an expensive-looking tailored suit.

"You haven't met Hubert, have you?" Ramona smiled.

The man turned around to face Nicholas, whose heart almost stopped beating as he stared into the stony black eyes of Umberto Scrofo, his nemesis: the man who had murdered his mother.

Nicholas stood transfixed while introductions were being made. As if by remote control, he shook the sweaty hand of Gourouni, the man who'd destroyed his entire family in Hydra more than a decade before. His mouth was so dry that to speak was out of the question. He knew that no sound would come out of his throat. He couldn't even hear what anyone was saying, so loud was the pounding in his ears. He could only see the toadlike face of the man he'd vowed to himself he would destroy one day. Granted, with the passing years, with the fading of excitable youth, his burning hatred and desperate desire for revenge had diminished. But now, face to face with Scrofo on this tropical night in Acapulco, it surfaced again with deadly vehemence. And it was all he could do to hold back from throwing himself at the fat swine and screaming out that he was a murdering bastard who deserved to die. But he held his tongue and said nothing.

He knew that he must appear to be behaving stupidly. Ramona was looking at him quizzically, and Scrofo was eyeing him with a strangely patronizing expression. Through the fog in his brain, Nicholas heard the Italian say, "I'm delighted to meet you, Nick, we will make a great picture here, I know it. I like most of the script and we've got a terrific cast, haven't we? We need to meet before the others tomorrow morning so I can give you a few of my ideas."

Nick knew a remark was expected of him, but he was unable to reply with even the simplest platitude. He nodded, muttering something unintelligible under his breath.

Hubert Croft scrutinized the young director coolly. His appearance had so often alienated him from people that over the years he'd found ways in which to camouflage the rejection, including doling out saccharine doses of charm and heavy-handed wit. But this Nick Stone, the *wunderkind* of the 1950s cinema, was behaving in a particularly strange manner. Was he drunk? Had tequila taken its inevitable toll so early in the evening? Hubert smiled saying; "When I saw your first picture, Nick, I knew you had talent— anyone who could make something witty and fresh out of *Bobby Soxers in Space* must be a genius."

"Mmm, thanks," mumbled Nick, his throat so dry it was painful to speak.

"And your next movie was a work of art too—brilliant. I'm proud to be working with you, Nick—really thrilled."

Nick's gut instinct was to take the fat Italian's neck between his hands and squeeze the life out of him. He felt that he was no longer in Acapulco, but back in war-torn Hydra, a sixteen-year-old boy whose brothers and sisters had died in starving misery, whose father had been bludgeoned to death in front of all the villagers by Scrofo's men, whose mother had died at Scrofo's very own hand, and whose friends and relations had been either starved or tortured to death.

Less than a minute had passed when Bluey pressed a fresh margarita into his hand. Nick drained the glass, his eyes never leaving the Italian. Bluey looked at him in mild surprise. Nick seemed in a trance, like a man lost in a dream. His face was drained of color and he appeared to have lost both his tongue and his composure. Bluey cracked a joke as he was introduced to Hubert, who flashed him a beaming smile, glad to have his attention diverted from the dumb Greek director.

Mumbling some excuse about feeling ill, Nick desperately wanted to escape. This meeting was so unbelievable that he simply couldn't cope with it. He had to be alone. He had to have time to think. He must telephone Elektra. He was just about to leave when there was a sudden fanfare from the mariachi band, and Ramona, grabbing him firmly by the arm, announced that dinner was served. Nick was trapped. The Princess's arm was like a handcuff as she led him down the winding onyx staircase to the main terrace.

The tables were set exquisitely. In the center of each of the round tables for ten, all covered with gold lamé tablecloths, a thick, gold-painted palm frond was embedded in a gold pyramid-shaped container which was in what looked like fine golden sand. Circled around the sand were a dozen tiny flickering lights which cast a flattering glow on the faces of the guests. On either side of the pyramid, two sleepy-eyed ceramic camels nestled against each other. The knives and forks were of solid gold, as were the saltshakers and the peppermills, which were also shaped like camels.

Ramona considered herself an expert at the tricky art of *placement*. The first three tables were the most important, and table number one was naturally presided over by Ramona herself. She had placed Hubert on her right and, to his dismay, Nick on her left. Next to him was Shirley Frankovitch, which made Nick's spirits sink even lower. He actively disliked this pseudo-intellectual, mean-spirited woman, who thought herself some kind of literary giant, but who owed most of her success to her husband.

"Good evening, Nicky," she said to him sarcastically as he sat down. "Gorgeous party, isn't it? Ramona's got so much class, doncha think?"

Nick nodded briefly to her, signaling to a waiter to fill his wine glass. He needed to get drunk tonight—very drunk indeed.

Next to Shirley sat Julian, who was also not overly fond of the blowsy writer, but as if to make up for this, Ramona had thoughtfully placed Dominique on his left. Between Dominique and Inès sat the American ambassador to Mexico, who drank much and talked little.

To her utter distress, Inès found herself sitting only four places away from Umberto Scrofo's penetrating stare. The only guests between her and the vile Italian were Teddy Stauffer, owner of the Villa Vera, self-styled "Mr. Acapulco" and leader of local society, and beautiful Gene Tierney, "Laura" herself.

The celebrities, press, cast and crew at the other tables all seemed to be having a much better time than those at Ramona's. A movie company works and plays hard, and tonight was supposed to be playtime, but as an experienced hostess, Ramona wondered why on earth there was such a chilly atmosphere at her table. She chatted away animatedly with Hubert, who responded with his usual heavy-handed wit, but Nicholas Stone, she thought, was being little more than downright rude. His morose eyes never left his plate, and he gulped the Château-Lafite 1929 as if it were lemonade.

"You are as ever looking glorious tonight, *Principessa*." Hubert smiled oilily, raising his hand-blown Venetian goblet in a toast to her. "More ravishing than ever."

"Why, thank you, Hubert dear." If Ramona could have managed a maidenly blush, she would have summoned one up, but her thespian gifts were not that munificent. "You are so kind."

"Tell me, my dear, who is the woman who is engaged to Julian? I think I know her from somewhere."

"Oh." Ramona seemed disappointed that the conversation had so quickly turned away from her. "Julian met her in London, Hubert. She's French, from quite a good family I understand—orphaned before the war and brought up by an aunt somewhere."

"Hmm." Hubert sipped his wine, regarding Inès covertly as she attempted conversation with the ambassador. "Attractive woman, I'm sure I've met her before."

Ramona gave no answer, and Hubert realized that he had committed the cardinal sin of discussing another woman's merits too glowingly in front of his hostess, who was now attempting conversation with a sullen-looking Nick Stone. Croft leaned across Ramona to join in the conversation.

"I think one of the things we must do, Nick, is to build up the role of the queen, don't you agree?"

Nick nodded, unable to speak, still convulsed with fury. The nerve of the slime. Script and character changes already, and he'd only been on the picture ten minutes.

"Oh, Hubert, do you really mean it?" Ramona glowed, her amber eyes shining like a teenager's. "I've got *so* many ideas about my character—do let me tell you some of them."

"I'd love to hear them, my dear," said Hubert. "Tell me everything you would like us to do, I'm sure we can work it out to everyone's satisfaction."

Across the table Inès picked at her food, trying not to watch as Umberto Scrofo stuffed his odious face, occasionally dropping bits of food down his tie. Every few minutes her eyes would catch his, which were observing her carefully, asking silent questions about her identity.

She was beautiful, Hubert thought, seemingly aristocratic and elegant—meeting her would surely have left an indelible impression on him. She looked about twenty-eight or thirty, which meant that if he'd known her in the past, it must have been about ten or twelve years ago when she was in her late teens. And since he had visited London briefly in 1946—maybe he had met her there? Ten years ago he'd been on Hydra. She certainly hadn't been there. Twelve years ago, however, he had been in Paris. Could he have met her there? No, it was impossible, she would have been too young. He barely listened as Ramona prattled on, giving him ideas and suggestions about how the script could be vastly improved by making Princess Isabella's mother a more interesting character. He hardly heard her; he was concentrating on unearthing the mystery of the enigmatic beauty who sat opposite him, so pale and quiet.

Lyon—Lyon—Lyon? He'd never been to Lyon in his life, but he knew this woman.

Julian was unaware of Inès' distress because Dominique had decided to play footsie with him. She had slipped off a shoe, and her bare foot caressed his ankle as she gazed into his eyes, finding his desire for her incredibly stimulating. Julian looked towards Inès, but she seemed so totally oblivious to everything going on around her that he decided he might as well play Dominique's little game with her. After all it meant nothing. She was just a young girl testing the new waters of flirtation. He could easily handle her.

10

By the time they had returned to their hotel, Inès was feeling dreadful.
Throughout the evening the continual gaze of Umberto Scrofo had haunted
her. After dinner, when the guests drifted down to the lower terrace to
dance, she had wanted desperately to leave, but Julian was dancing with
Dominique, deep in conversation, so she hadn't wanted to interrupt him.
Inès understood that actors filming together needed to spend time getting
to know each other. Since Dominique was so young and completely inex-
perienced in the world of movies, Inès was sure that, being the true professional, Julian would want to help her as much as possible.

She was just coming back from the powder room when a damp hand
clutched at her bare shoulder.

"Why do you always seem in such a hurry to get away from me, dear
lady?" Hubert said. "Let us dance together."

"I'm afraid I'm not feeling very well," she said, pulling away from his
grip. "I don't want to dance."

"Then let us sit this one out," he said, firmly taking her arm and leading
her to a carved ivory seat close to the dance floor. "I want to talk to you."
Scrofo appeared to possess that formidable inner strength which came
from being used to having his orders carried out without question.

"I remember you now," he said suddenly, with a basilisk stare.

She looked back at him, struggling to keep her eyes expressionless.
"How could you? We've never met."

"Oh, but we have, my dear Inès." His voice was rancid oil. "We most certainly have." He paused, waiting for her to react, relighting his cigar, surveying her through narrowed eyes. Inès didn't flinch, willing him not to remember.

"Of course you look quite different now. Almost twelve years makes a great difference to a pretty young girl." He smiled, waiting for her reaction. She found it hard to stop her glass from shaking and her stomach felt as if it had turned to stone.

"Well, if you won't remember, then I shall have to remind you," he said ominously. "I'm sure you recall a certain hotel room in Paris in 1943?"

Her expression was impassive. "I'm afraid I don't. What are you trying to imply? This conversation is getting us nowhere—excuse me."

She made a move to leave, but he was too quick for her and his hand shot out to grab her arm. She felt the unforgettable frisson of cruelty in his viselike fingers.

"I told you I never forget a face. I never forget a name, either. Foolish of you not to have changed it; Inès is an unusual name—so beautiful that you decided that you wouldn't change it when you gave up your occupation. *Whoring!*" His lips were close to her ear now as he spat out the word; she saw the undisguised hatred which had turned his sallow complexion florid.

"Mr. Croft, I don't know what you're talking about. Please, let me go. My fiancé is waiting for me."

But she was unable to extricate herself from his tight grip. As if in a dream, she saw the dancers whirling around the floor, the band playing, guests laughing. She heard the faint hum of the nighttime insects, smelled the soft scent of jasmine—but all she could think of was the torture of this man's vicious attack on her, and how she had repaid him for it.

"Ah, yes, I can see you remember now, don't you?" His teeth split his face like a Halloween pumpkin. "You don't need to answer, Inès. Your silence is enough; besides, as I told you, my memory never fails me. You were that little tart who came to service me at the Ritz Hotel, weren't you? And then you tried to kill me, didn't you?"

Inès felt she was in a nightmare from which she could never wake up. Less than twenty yards away, the man she loved so passionately was dancing with his leading lady. She wanted to be close to him, to hold him, to be Mrs. Julian Brooks, as soon as possible. She wanted to escape. That was all she wanted—but this reptilian creature held her rigidly in his grip. To get away from him she would have to create a scene.

"So, Miss Prim and Proper, Miss Fiancée of the Star, Miss *Murderess*." He blew a cloud of blinding cigar smoke into her face. "So here we are—together again." He obviously hadn't changed much in all these years. He was still a monster.

"What is it you want from me?" Inès whispered.

"Nothing, my dear, absolutely *nothing*—yet. I just want you to be aware that I know who you are, Inès ... whatever your name has become. I remember you very well. You were a young prostitute, obviously you'd been one for some time. You were good—very, very good." He licked his lips in recollection. "And then you tried to kill me, didn't you?" He bent his face so close to hers, that she could see the tiny broken veins on his nose and the stubble on his chins, smell that sickening cologne.

"You nearly succeeded, too—bitch!" His fingers held her upper arm so tightly she knew that by tomorrow their imprint would still be there. "I almost died because of you, you lousy whore. Look—" Quickly he loosened his tie, pulling open his shirt to reveal the thick scar at the base of his Adam's apple. Inès gasped. The wound was three or more inches long, pinkish-white, shiny and raised.

"I was in that fucking military hospital for week after week after fucking week." He pulled her nearer to him, his saliva almost hitting her face, and Inès thought the whole room must be watching them now. Then he smiled—a rictus grin. "I shall have my revenge for this," he hissed ominously as he straightened his tie. "I've waited a long time to find you, young lady, and you are going to curse the day you ever met me."

Inès shuddered. "I don't know what you're talking about, Mr. Croft," she said defiantly. "Whatever happened to you was a long time ago, and it had nothing to do with me."

He was even more loathsome than she'd remembered. With a wrench she managed to pull her arm away, just as the dance number was ending and Julian sauntered over, his arm casually around Dominique's waist.

"I'm so tired, darling," Inès whispered, moving into the safety of her fiancé's arms. "Can we go home now, please?"

"Of course, we'll go now, darling. Goodnight, Dominique." His eyes held Dominique's for a fraction longer than necessary. "Hubert, good to have met you, I expect we'll talk tomorrow." Arm in arm he and Inès strolled away to say goodnight to their hostess.

Umberto Scrofo's eyes stared after them. However much she might deny it, he was positive that it was she. He knew it was. The whore from Paris.

So he'd finally found her. The girl who'd tried to kill him—the skinny slut he'd dreamed of meeting again—of doing the most unspeakable things to, of punishing her. Well, her punishment must wait—but only for now. Priorities. The *Cortez* film had to be number one on his list—and Mademoiselle Inès Juillard was going to be of great help to him in that particular direction, whether she liked it or not.

Inès slept fitfully, visions of the sadistic Scrofo tormenting her subconscious. She tossed and turned, thrashing in the humid darkness, crying out in her sleep. Julian held her close, whispering comforting endearments, feeling waves of love for her. He tried to make love to her during the night, to calm her unspoken fears, but for the first time in their relationship, Inès refused him. Julian, slightly piqued, tried in vain not to let his thoughts turn to fantasies of Dominique.

"I'm sorry," Inès said shakily. "I'm really sorry, darling. I ... I ... don't feel well; I don't know what's wrong with me, Julian, but please understand, my darling."

"Of course, my darling," said Julian soothingly as he held her closely. "I understand."

He drifted back into an untroubled sleep but she lay awake throughout the night, staring up at the ceiling, thinking only of her enemy.

The following morning Inès found patches of blood on the sheets. Horrified, she called her gynecologist in Los Angeles, but it was Sunday; he was out playing golf. Inès crawled back to bed, suggesting to Julian that he go off for the day by himself.

"I'll be fine, darling," she assured him. "I just want to rest."

She didn't tell him about the hemorrhaging. She only hoped that if she rested, it would stop.

Again she didn't want to make love.

Julian was as edgy, restless and nervous as are most actors the day before a production starts. Inès' second rejection of him, this time giving him no reason other than saying that she felt unwell, made him even more restless. Julian was a highly sexed man, and he needed an outlet for the eve-of-picture tension which was building inside him.

He was quite nervous about this film. Even though he had made so many films in England, this was his first American production, and there was much at stake.

He looked down at Inès who lay white and drawn on the pillow, a faint sheen of sweat on her normally cool forehead. "Are you sure you're all right, Inès?"

"Oh, yes, fine, just fine, darling," she murmured weakly. "Just exhaustion from the party."

"Well, I think I'll water-ski after the production meeting," he said. "Are you sure you don't mind being alone, my love?"

"No, I'll be perfectly all right," she said, not wanting him to leave at all, yet needing her solitude to think. "Have a wonderful day, darling—don't fall off the slalom. I'll see you tonight."

She blew him a kiss as he left the room, but he didn't return it, and Inès slumped sadly back on to the crumpled pillow, thinking that Julian's strange premonition of last night was coming horribly true.

*A*lthough *it was barely eight o'clock, the secret breakfast meeting was in* full swing. Irving and Shirley Frankovitch and Hubert Croft sat on the shaded balcony of Hubert's suite, the glass table in front of them piled high with scripts, revisions, budgets, coffee cups, tropical fruit, breads, assorted jams and preserves.

Hubert ate continuously as he talked. When he wanted to make a point, he would jab his finger in the air and gesticulate wildly. Whenever he did this, his resemblance to Mussolini was quite remarkable, thought Shirley, picking at another piece of fruit, Hubert's appetite inspiring her own.

"The main problem, as I see it, is that Nicholas Stone appears to have drastically changed the original script as *you* have written it." He glanced at Shirley. "It was a brilliant script, Shirley, my dear—you did your usual stunning job, absolutely brilliant."

"Every new suggestion we had—every idea—everything clever and innovative—Nick has shot down in flames," Shirley said bitterly, pleased by Hubert's praise. "It was a great script, wasn't it, Irving?"

"Bluey is Nick's main ally," Irving chimed in. "Between the two of them and Zack Domino, who had the total support of the studio, we were completely outflanked."

"No longer." Hubert smiled. "No longer, my dear friends. I've read both scripts—the one you wrote, which Zachary Domino and Nick Stone tried to ruin, and the one of which Nick approves. There is no question in my mind as to the one which possesses the greatest merit."

"Ours!" snapped Shirley, slipping another sliver of papaya between sausage lips.

"Yes, indeed. To that end, we now need to get the studio, and the rest of the cast on our side."

"Of course," Shirley and Irving both agreed.

"Ramona Armande is no problem," Hubert said. "She can, and will, be an excellent ally, as well as being an excellent actress of course."

"But she hardly has a part," Shirley frowned.

"I think we can possibly improve her role," Hubert said smoothly, "without damaging your script at all." Shirley looked dubious, as Hubert continued.

"The little girl—Dominique—what has been her reaction to both scripts? I tried to speak to the young lady last evening, but she seemed to have other things on her mind."

"You bet," Shirley smirked. "Looks Brooks' cock is on that young cookie's mind, and it'll be in certain other places besides her mind soon enough, I should think."

Irving shot his wife a disapproving look. Sometimes her gutter language repelled him.

"Really? Very interesting." Hubert made some notes in his brown leather folder. "Tell me more."

Irving sighed. He didn't believe the Julian-Dominique gossip which was circulating already. Shirley had been babbling on about seeing the young actress draped all over him the night before. She rarely missed anything; and her observations gave her a kind of vicarious pleasure, as her sex life with Irving was negligible these days. He tried hard, but basically he wasn't interested anymore.

"His fiancée is a very beautiful woman—why should he want to stray?" Hubert fingered his scar, images of Inès' elegant limbs flashing across his mind.

"He's an actor." Shirley shrugged. "You know actors—all cock and no confidence, most of 'em." She again ignored Irving's disapproving look and pushed some more papaya into her mouth. "He's famous for putting it into anything that's playing opposite him. Several of his co-stars have even tried to kill themselves over 'the handsomest man in the world,' " she sneered.

"I see. How do you find *his* allegiances then?" Hubert was still scribbling his notes. "Whose side is he on?"

"Middle of the road," said Irving. "He likes some of our stuff and some of Nick's. He's difficult to sway because he goes for the scene that he feels will be of benefit to the film; he's not nearly as much of an egomaniac as Shirley likes to make out, he's a team player."

"Hmm." Hubert prodded his teeth with a toothpick while he studied a yellow bird perched at the edge of his table, which was pecking happily at the remains of the food, but his thoughts were evidently elsewhere.

"Nick is on the phone *constantly* to the old man in Hollywood. He's some kind of nephew, y'know, and being Greek, of course, they all stick together," Shirley said sarcastically.

"Naturally." Hubert was not surprised. He remembered the fierce family loyalty of the Greeks when he'd commanded Hydra.

"And Sir Crispin?" he asked, referring to the world-famous and much-loved English actor who was playing Emperor Montezuma. "What about him?"

"Oh, just the usual full of shit, faggoty Old Vic actor-knight, who thinks he knows everything," Shirley said waspishly. "Always sounds to me like he's got his mouth full of plums. So far, he's kept a low profile though. Too busy making goo-goo eyes at beach boys. I think he rather fancies our Mr. Brooks, too, so he'll probably agree with anything the great movie star wants."

"We have to get *all* the actors on our side, then there will be no contest with the scripts," said the Italian. "The studio will have to go along with the majority, otherwise we will have nothing but unrest and trouble on the set. That costs money, and you know how the studio hates wasting money."

"Right," said the Frankovitches in unison.

"But how are you going to do that?" Shirley asked. "There's a production meeting with Nick in two hours. He'll fight our script, he always does."

"Leave it to me," Hubert said, Inès' pale face flickering across his mind like some old black-and-white movie. "Leave it to me, my friends—I'll find a way to shoot *our* script, believe me, that I guarantee."

At the official production meeting Bluey fidgeted uncomfortably—he hated confrontations. The only scenes he enjoyed were the ones he viewed from behind the cameras. But Nick needed him. Nick looked odd today. His olive skin was a greenish white, and his normally smiling mouth was clamped tighter than a rattrap.

The oily Italian, whom Bluey had disliked on sight, sat flanked by the Frankovitch team on one side of the table. As a trio, they'd be hard to beat in an ugliness contest, he mused. A war of words was in progress which was becoming even more heated as the tropical sun came beating through the windows.

Hubert Croft held two scripts before him, one red, one blue.

"I will make no bones about it, Nick," he rasped in that gravelly wheeze Nick remembered so well. "This script—" he held the blue one high above his head in a boxer's gesture of victory—*"this one* is magic, pure cinematic *magic.* I read it last night and I cried tears of happiness that I was *privileged* enough to be involved in a project that uses the talents of these two wonderful people who wrote these brilliant words."

Irving and Shirley beamed and nodded like ventriloquists' dummies as Bluey gave an audible groan.

"It's really up to the studio which script we shoot, isn't it?" Nick kept his voice crisp and businesslike, belying his fermenting fury at this man's astonishing audacity. One Italian art film unreleased in America was all he had under his too-tight belt—Nick had checked that out last night—and he was now giving orders like the Mussolini clone he'd always felt himself to be. The hairs on the back of Nick's neck rose as he thought of Scrofo on Hydra, remembering the squat body stuffed into the ridiculous medallioned musical-comedy uniforms, prancing and puffing his way around the island, creating havoc and hatred wherever he went. But he mustn't think about that now—he couldn't. He must get his film made the way *he* wanted it.

If this movie failed, he would be blamed. Not the loathsome trio of the Frankovitches and Scrofo, not even the stars. No, it was *his* ass, Nick Stone's, that was on the line, and all his years of yearning, struggling to be a decent film director, would end up on the scrap heap. God, *why* had Spyros agreed to send this toad, this scowl on legs, to Acapulco? He had telephoned the old man last night and had been told to "shut up and do your job—that's what you're being paid for." So much for family loyalty. With a film as expensive as *Cortez,* someone would have to be the whipping boy if it failed, and he knew that it would be he alone up there on the sacrificial altar.

The script Nick wanted was gritty, historically accurate, with battle scenes which showed the true horror of war. His love scenes were sensually realistic, not the lovey-dovey treacle syrup of the Frankovitches. And his dialogue was pithy and modern, in contrast to theirs, which was stilted and flowery.

Tomorrow they would shoot the first scene of the movie, where Cortez and his men greet Emperor Montezuma on the shore. Nick wanted to shoot Cortez and a small boatload of sailors arriving to greet the emperor, who would only have a handful of warriors with him. The Frankovitch script had six hundred extras with Cortez, and several hundred men on shore with Montezuma. It certainly wasn't going to be easy, but that scene was going to be shot *his* way, or not at all. Let them fire him, he'd go back to the mail room if he had to.

As soon as the production meeting was over Nick hurried back to his room to try again to telephone Elektra. She was his rock, his sanity, and she was wise, not so much in the ways of the modern world, but in the simple ways which really counted. Wise about life, about people, about relationships. Her brand of wisdom was the wisdom of centuries, handed down from generation to generation by the power of the family, by which all Greeks still lived. All international telephone lines had been down yesterday and he had spent a frustrated night, needing to speak to her.

"Elektra." He was so delighted to hear her voice that he immediately started talking rapidly in the Greek she still preferred, even after nearly a decade in America.

"What can I do, Elektra? They're all ganging up on me, I know it—I can't stand it, darling—I'm about ready to walk off this picture even if Uncle Spyros sends me back to work in the mail room."

"No, Nikolai." Elektra's voice was quiet but insistent. "You cannot do that. You have worked too hard for this opportunity—you cannot let it go, Nikolai—and you mustn't."

"But you don't understand, Elektra," he said despairingly. "You don't know who's producing this film."

"Who?" she asked.

"Scrofo," he said grimly. "Umberto Scrofo."

"What?" cried Elektra. "No, Nikolai, don't be ridiculous. It's not possible—Scrofo's dead—you remember we heard that he'd died in Italy years ago?"

"Well, he isn't dead," said Nick bleakly. "I'm afraid the bastard's very much alive. He's here, and he's about to make my life a complete fucking misery. I want to *kill* him, Elektra—every time I look at his monstrous face I think about what he did to my mother and I feel this urge to crush the life out of him."

He started to sob into the telephone as Elektra tried to soothe him.

"No, Nikolai, *stop it,* you cannot allow Scrofo to win. First of all you *must* go ahead with the film—you must, you have to—for us, for Uncle Spyros, for the children." She paused as she heard her husband's voice down the long-distance wires, still quavering but more in control.

"I know, Elektra—I know I've got to do it—but how in the bloody *hell* can I possibly work hand in glove with that murdering, thieving piece of scum? How can I?"

"I know it's going to be difficult," she said softly. "I know it will be hard for you to forgive him for what he did to your mother."

"Forgive him—*forgive Gourouni!* That slimy motherfucker! Forget it!"

hissed Nick. "I'll never forgive him—how can I? I thought that maybe my hatred had died, Elektra—I thought now that I'm older I could never have the same kind of thoughts I did about that bastard when we were on Hydra. But I was wrong, completely wrong—my hatred was only dormant. It never died."

"How, Nikolai, what do you mean, you were wrong?" she asked fearfully.

"I want to kill him." His lips were very close to the receiver and she heard the intensity in his voice as he spat out the words. "I want to kill him, Elektra, and I'm going to kill him."

"No, Nikolai, don't talk like that." Elektra was afraid as she remembered how he'd tried to strangle her in her own bed. Sometimes her husband's Greek temper and hot blood got the better of him. "You mustn't do anything foolish, Nikolai," she pleaded. "Please don't."

Talking to his wife had made him feel suddenly better, more in control, stronger. "Don't worry—don't worry about it now, Elektra. I'm not going to do it at this moment. I'll make this damned movie, I'll eat crow—I'll even work side by side with that filthy scum—but when it's *over* with—I swear to you Elektra, Umberto Scrofo will be a dead man."

It was lunchtime and as Julian walked along the burning sands to Caleta Beach, where the local water-skiing instructors were chattering like magpies beneath cool thatched huts, he thanked God that the production meeting was finally over. Frankly, he didn't really care if Cortez had six men or six hundred with him when he arrived in Mexico. Characterization was the most important thing to him, and the Frankovitches, Croft and Nick had nothing to say about that.

He ordered a *cerveza,* a local beer, instructing Angelito, the boat boy, that he wanted to go skiing right away.

"Oh, *Señor.* I'm sorry," said Angelito. "The Señorita Dominique, she book me for this afternoon."

"Well, what about you, then? Are you free?" Julian asked another boy irritably.

"It's fine with me, *Señor,* fine," smiled Miguel, the proud possessor of a perfect set of gold-capped teeth which must have cost him a year's pay. "My boat ees good—we ski well together, *Señor.*"

Suddenly there was a ripple of excitement from all the beach boys as Dominique arrived. Seeing Julian, she gave a little squeal of joy and rushed over to kiss him, letting her firm breasts crush against his chest through her flimsy *pareo.*

"I'm *so* happy to see you, *chéri,*" she gushed. "Why don't we ski together?"

"Well, I—I've just booked Miguel." Julian actually heard himself stutter.

"Oh, don't be silly," cooed the peach, flashing Julian an irresistible smile that would no doubt bewitch her future film audiences as much as it bewitched him. "We can ski together, we're both alone." She grabbed him by the hand and led him down the hot golden sands.

"You can teach me how to para-ski—they say you're so good at it." She smiled mischievously. "Come on, let's go."

Inès' doctor called her back from L.A. after lunch, ordering complete bed rest.

"Complete, you understand? That means you do not *move.* You stay in bed. You get up to go to the bathroom, but that's *it. No* sex for a fortnight, no moving about at all for at least a week."

"Oh, no." Inès was dismayed. "But the film starts tomorrow, and Julian wants me to be on the set all the time, or at least nearby, and well—you know Julian is a very sexy man," she said, feeling rather embarrassed.

"Well, I'm afraid Julian has little choice," said the doctor brusquely. "He can have you, or he can have this baby, but certainly not both. I warn you, Inès, if you exert yourself in any way, you could lose this child. I told you it was going to be difficult for you to conceive, you're lucky that you did; if you want this baby, be a good girl, stay put."

He prescribed pills through a local doctor and Inès asked the concierge to pick them up for her; then she lay back, trying to relax. She felt feverish, her head was a furnace, her mouth parched, but the more she drank, the more thirsty she became. She tried to lie still, but her knees were trembling with fear as she felt warm blood trickling slowly from her—blood that might be her baby.

She couldn't lose this baby that Julian wanted so desperately. Conceived in love, it would be so adored, she couldn't lose it. She drifted into a light, feverish sleep from which the deafening jangle of the old-fashioned telephone next to the bed woke her.

She instantly recognized the chilling tones.

"Mademoiselle Juillard," inquired the gravelly voice.

"Yes?"

"I know you're alone because I saw your husband on the beach this morning, going water-skiing with our beautiful young star."

"So? What do you want, Mr. Croft, I'm resting." Inès' voice was frigid. She refused to let him intimidate her. She was strong, a survivor. Her experiences with men, Scrofo in Paris, Yves' cavalier departure from her life, her perverse English aristocrats, had made her vow that she'd never allow any man to abuse her again. She was a woman of the world, engaged to a famous man, beautiful, secure, happy and pregnant. So she'd tried to kill an enemy officer years ago. So what? What could Umberto Scrofo possibly do to her now that could affect her life? She knew full well what he could do. But would he dare?

If Umberto let it be known to the cast and crew that she'd been a whore, and that he had been one of her clients, they would realize, if they didn't already suspect, that he'd been one of Mussolini's bloodiest generals. Many of the film crew had fought on the beaches of Anzio, Dunkirk and the Pacific, in the deserts of North Africa, or over the skies of Great Britain. The war had ended scarcely ten years ago, but many people still treated Germans, Japanese and Italians with antipathy, particularly if they thought that they had been actively involved in it. No, Signor Scrofo would make a bad mistake with everyone if it was discovered that he had been a high-ranking officer in occupied Paris. She held a good hand of cards in her well-manicured fingers—she could bluff him out.

"Since you're alone," continued the hateful voice, "I must insist upon seeing you. It is for your own benefit, Mademoiselle Juillard."

Inès groaned. "Listen to me. I'm unwell. My doctor has told me I must rest, which is exactly what I'm trying to do. If you feel you have any business with me, please state it on the telephone."

"Mademoiselle Juillard, right now I'm downstairs in the lobby of your hotel." Umberto's voice held more than a hint of menace. "I will take up no more than five minutes of your precious time, but I must see you." The "precious" held an insulting innuendo. "There are several people standing around here, including some crew members of *Cortez*. I do not think, Mademoiselle Juillard, that you would want them to hear what I have to say to you, do you?"

"Very well," said Inès with a deep sigh. "Room seventeen, on the second floor." And she banged down the receiver.

Julian and Dominique lay back comfortably on their brightly colored towels as the tropical sun tanned their bodies. The boat was a relatively crude affair, but Angelito was an expert at maneuvering it. Acapulco Bay was peacefully calm, and the boatman made a smooth circuit before turning towards La Roqueta Island.

Julian found Dominique's proximity, as she snuggled next to him, unnervingly erotic. Her eyes had cast a spell on him again, and her curved, honey-colored body, in the tiniest bikini, was driving his cock mad. He usually made love to Inès at least once a day; being deprived yesterday and this morning had made him acutely aware that the damn thing had a mind of its own, especially when it was near Dominique. His erection was becoming so obvious that he edged away from her before he made a complete fool of himself.

"Angelito, I want to ski around the bay," he ordered. "Stop the boat, I'll jump off here." The tiny craft slowed down and Julian leaped over the side into the sparkling water, thankfully feeling his erection subsiding.

Angelito threw him a ski and the rope. Julian signaled to the boy, with a jerk the ancient boat sputtered and accelerated, and Julian rose from the water on his slalom like an arrow. Dominique cheered, admiring his marvelous physique. She thought that Looks Brooks possessed a body and a face which even a Greek god would envy. His week of rest and rigorous morning workouts had brought him back to perfect shape. His hair was now slicked down flat to his head by the wind and water as he gestured to Angelito to go faster.

There were only a few luxury pleasure boats in the port and around the bay, but many speedboats and tiny sailing boats. Angelito steered the boat past the "morning" beach, where laughing brown children played together in the waves while their weary fathers stared blankly out to sea. Mothers, aunts, sisters and grandmothers ceremoniously laid out the Sunday lunch on the beach for the one day the family all spent together. The children, many of them naked, since bathing suits were a luxury few Mexican families could afford, waved excitedly at the passing speedboats.

They zoomed past the "afternoon" beach, the more tourist-oriented area of Acapulco, where under straw hats overweight vacationers from cruise ships sampled the pleasures of this new resort. Sipping *piña coladas,* they oiled themselves as the tropical sun turned their bodies various shades of scarlet. On the shore, Julian could see the skeleton of the new Hilton Hotel, its iron girders an eyesore. If those hideous high-rise hotels start being built along this shore, it will only be a matter of time before this glorious place is ruined forever, he thought. Saltwater stung his face as he crisscrossed over the wake several times with professional panache, until he finally let go of the rope and waited for the boat to pick him up.

"Bravo," cried Dominique. "Oh, Julian, you're brilliant. Where did you learn to ski so brilliantly?"

She leaned over the bow of the boat, looking so sexy that it would have been hard for any male over the age of seven not to have been affected by her. Julian had noticed the bulge in Angelito's trunks when the boy helped Dominique into his boat, brushing his arm unnecessarily against her lightly tanned shoulder. She was an incredibly sensual girl, a little minx who was learning—too well—the art of driving men crazy.

Angelito looked questioningly towards an island of mustard-colored rock shaped like a fat man sleeping after a good lunch. Julian nodded, and the boat sped across the bobbing waves.

One o'clock was early for lunch at La Roqueta, and few people were there. The jovial *patron* offered them the most secluded table in the restaurant, his eyes goggling at the sight of Dominique in her virtually transparent *pareo*. Angelito's brief words in Spanish gave him the lowdown on Julian, the big movie star.

"Let's have the biggest, strongest, most Mexicanish drink in the house," Dominique said, a mischievous glint in her eyes.

"What a marvelous idea," Julian laughed, already half drunk with her charms. "Let's have two each."

Soon they were sipping, through straws, from coconut shells in which pineapples, bananas, three kinds of rum, tequila, brandy and fruit juice had been expertly blended.

"Mmm. Delicious." Dominique smiled. "Better than a chocolate malt any day."

The tropical air on his skin, the sense of well-being and exhilaration from water-skiing, and the sight of this delectable female all left Julian feeling incredibly virile and young. Not even the most exotic lovemaking with Inès had ignited him in this way; he felt like a slow-burning coal which had either to be doused completely or be allowed to burst into leaping tongues of fire. He didn't understand himself at all. He didn't want to.

He downed both of his drinks fast, then blurted out, "God, you're so beautiful. I know this sounds strange—and I know I shouldn't say this—but I want to kiss you, Dominique." All inhibitions seemed to have flown and he watched the slow smile spread across her exquisite face.

"It's what I want too, Julian," she whispered huskily. "So much."

Her total lack of pretense and archness was so unlike the ways of the women he usually met that Julian felt like a schoolboy again. That delicious innocence which hadn't yet learned to say *no* when desire was saying *yes* made her sensuality more erotic than if she were lying naked in bed beside him.

After several more strong drinks and a lunch of plump grilled shrimps, lobster and rice, Julian and Dominique set off to explore the tiny, almost deserted island. Only the restaurant, now half filled with tourists, was evidence of any habitation. Julian felt as if he were going to burst. The touch of Dominique's hand on his arm was sending electric shocks of desire through his whole being, as they strolled around the rocks and out of sight of the few tourists.

Dominique felt a shiver of excitement and anticipation as they rounded a corner where an ancient banana tree shaded a small beach.

Julian stopped, held Dominique's lovely face between his hands and let his mouth gently explore hers. Her lips were petal-soft, more yielding than any he had ever kissed before. They were innocent, naive, the lips of a little girl—then as her tongue came to claim his, they became wantonly erotic. It was the mouth of a woman who knew exactly what she wanted and knew how to get it, and knew instinctively where all the pleasure sources lay. His hands dropped to the ribbons of her bikini top. How he longed to hold these glorious breasts, to trace their contours, exploring with fingers and tongue, to watch her excitement increase. But Dominique was not quite ready to grant his wish yet.

Moving away from him, she took a bottle of suntan oil from her straw bag and, leaning against the trunk of the banana tree, started to rub it slowly into her shoulders and chest. Her head thrown back, her eyes closed, Julian watched, mesmerized, as her bikini top started inching down and her rosy nipples became visible. Her breathing accelerated as she started to massage them with the oil. They glistened in the sunlight, her nipples, like pink shells, now erect. Julian moved towards her, but she stopped him with a gesture, continuing her erotic caresses—the ones that Gaston had taught her last summer. Her top was off now; her fingers had worked their way down to her flat stomach, to the band of her bikini bottom. Julian was now dizzy with desire as the vision shimmered before him in the heat. Soon she was completely naked, abandoned, leaning against the tree, her skin glistening, and her eyes signaled that now it was time.

Dominique's fingers entwined in Julian's thick brown hair as his tongue and lips pleasured her breasts and his own fingers encircled her soft but muscled rear. She gave little whimpers of ecstasy as she stripped him of his shorts, aggressively pulling him down onto the hot sand, oblivious to discomfort. She took his cock into her mouth as Gaston had taught her, and he felt the eruption start to rise deep within him, an explosion which took every ounce of his concentration and willpower to control. Her catlike eyes smiled up at him as her lips anointed him and she slid warm, hard, bursting skin in and out of her hot mouth.

He had to take her now—he could wait no longer. He forgot Inès—forgot their love, their baby, their marriage. All he could think of was this enchantress. Gently he lifted her from him, moving until his body lay on top of hers for a magic second or two, then with a groan of pleasure he entered her. She was a more than willing partner, moistly receptive. Their sweat mingling, lips and tongues entwined, her eyes wide open, smiling, willing him on, he plunged into her, his face contorted in fierce ecstasy as he set the rhythm of their passion. She could feel an imminent and unfamiliar convulsion building inside her.

"I love you," she whispered, "I love you, Julian. I love you," truly meaning it as she cried out his name in joy.

As the sound of speedboats hummed in the distance and the waves lapped near their bucking bodies, the lovers orgasmed together with cries which seemed to echo around the whole bay.

And from far away, the lone passenger in a small motorboat focused his telescopic lens and clicked the shutter of his camera again and again.

With her silk kimono sticking uncomfortably to her moist skin, Inès lay on her bed in agony listening to what the detestable Scrofo had come to say. "Please, get to the point, Mr. Croft," she said weakly, lighting a cigarette. "I must rest, it's my doctor's orders."

"Then you shouldn't smoke." His tone was irritatingly patronizing. "Especially since you are pregnant."

"How do you know I'm pregnant? No one here knows. Besides, it's none of your business."

His voice was steely. "I know everything, I'm the producer of this film and I make it my business to know everything about everyone." But he smiled inwardly. It had been an educated guess, but it had hit its mark. "Don't forget that, ever—don't underestimate me either, Mademoiselle Juillard."

"Well, what's your business with me? I have nothing to do with your precious film, so what do you want?"

"You have *everything* to do with the film. You're the fiancée of the star. It seems that the great star doesn't much like the excellent script which Mr. and Mrs. Frankovitch, writers of the highest proficiency and artistic merit, have written. He and Bluey Regan were quite difficult with me this morning." His pig eyes drilled into hers. "And the Greek, Nicholas Stone, the so-called *wunderkind* director who has directed only two films, he also does not like the script."

"But what does all this have to do with me?" Inès cried "I hardly know Nick Stone or the Frankovitches."

Scrofo's body oozed over the edge of the chair in which he sat while staring at her contemptuously. She felt a terrible stab of fear. How could this man not inspire terror, with his evil smile, twisted mind and grotesque body in his vulgar and self-conscious clothes. He looked ridiculous in his powder-blue safari suit, his hairy arms bulging out of the short sleeves, and the military-style gold buttons which looked about to burst from their buttonholes as they strained across his gross belly. In spite of herself a look of revulsion came into her face as she noticed the silk scarf knotted loosely around his neck, and the hideous scar for which she had herself been responsible. But he'd made her do it, there was nothing else she could have done. She shuddered at the memory of the agony and humiliation Scrofo had caused her, and a cold fury came over her as she pictured herself as that young girl in Paris. How could she ever forget the pain? Dr. Langley's sinister words suddenly came back to her: "You're a healthy woman, Inès, and there's no reason why you shouldn't have a beautiful baby, but you've obviously had a very bad time with someone. You have some scar tissue, you must have been injured once."

"Could it affect the baby?" Inès had asked tearfully.

"Not if you're careful. But you've suffered quite a bit of damage to your womb and cervix—and I'm not saying it necessarily will, but it *might,* affect your pregnancy unless, as I say, you're very careful."

Now as Inès stared back at Scrofo with undisguised loathing in her eyes, she suddenly understood. Of course, this man was the very reason why she was lying here in her bed of pain, bleeding, unable to move, all because of those monstrous and perverted acts which he'd inflicted on her years ago.

Scrofo moved from the wicker chair to stand at the end of Inès' bed, his brown boots clattering on the marble floor, his slug-white face covered with a thin film of sweat. Inès could hear luncheon being served and happy Mexican music from the patio below. She looked out at the beautiful day, at the sun-flecked cottonwool clouds. How she wanted to be outside, anywhere but here, alone with this horror.

"So," he said, his voice now becoming venomous and threatening, "I'll spell it out for you, you murdering whore." Involuntarily he fingered his scar, his lips twisting in that familiar and repulsive way she could never forget.

"Nobody knows anything of your past here, do they? Not even your precious fiancé?" He looked at her menacingly. "Do they, Inès? Prostitute, whore, streetwalker—from what age? How old were you when I had you? Thirteen? Fourteen?"

Inès felt her brain fill with a kind of red mist. She was reliving the nightmare—she could almost feel the razor in her hand as she'd sliced it across his yielding throat. She felt her stomach contracting in intermittent spasms of pain. Warm blood had made her thighs slippery. She made an immense effort to calm herself.

"It's none of your business, Scrofo! Tell me what you want of me, for God's sake." She stubbed out her cigarette, lighting another immediately. The bed was now wet with blood, but she couldn't move. There was a buzzing in her head. This spectre from her past was going to ruin her future, her perfect future.

"I'm not going to say anything more to upset you now." He looked at her in mock pity. "You're white as a sheet, you don't look at all well. You should get some rest, so I'll get to the point and then leave you in peace. I want to tell you just one thing. As I have told you, I have discovered that nobody either in America or on this film—and most certainly not Julian Brooks—is aware of your sordid past. I'm going to need your help at certain strategic times during the filming. I know you discuss the script with your fiancé, I know he depends very much on your advice. When I tell you—" he leaned towards her menacingly—"I repeat, when I tell you that I want Julian to prefer scene A to scene B, I want you to coerce him, exert every particle of influence that you have on him to see that he accepts my choice. *Do you understand?* If you *don't* comply with my wishes, well, let's just say there'll be very serious consequences."

She nodded silently. She would have agreed to anything just to get this creature out of her sight.

"All right, I will. I promise," she whispered, holding back her tears.

"Good, then your secret, as they say, will be safe with me, Inès my dear." He waddled over to the door. "The first two scenes will be arriving this evening. Be sure you insist that Mr. Brooks prefers the first one." And with that he closed the door behind him.

With an animal sound, Inès staggered to the bathroom, seeing, to her horror, that her blood was streaking the marble tiles scarlet.

"Oh, no," she cried. "No, no. Oh, please, God, no!"

12

After the incident with Croft, Inès had spent the rest of the afternoon attempting to recover. When Julian returned from his afternoon with Dominique, she was able to greet him with a semblance of normality. Caught up in her own personal trauma, she failed to notice that Julian was somewhat distant, lacking his usual affectionate attentiveness.

But he was still extremely concerned about her condition, even though she assured him that Dr. Langley had said that, as long as she was careful, all would be well. Julian was secretly relieved that lovemaking was forbidden for at least two weeks.

It would give him time to think, and to savor the enchanted afternoon he'd spent with Dominique, who had visited him in his dreams last night. He awoke, covered with sweat, and to feelings of guilt and horror, mumbling her name. But Inès was sleeping soundly, a pill helping her to expunge the memory of Scrofo's threats.

Julian was worried and ashamed of his behavior with Dominique. He tried hard to analyze what spell she must have cast over him, but he couldn't. Their lovemaking that afternoon had been both wonderfully enhilarating and quite exceptional, but maybe it was because she was so young, just a schoolgirl really, and the added spice of being outdoors and the possibility of being discovered had made it all the more thrilling.

He sighed heavily, looking at his frowning face in the bathroom mirror. "You're a rat, Julian Brooks," he mouthed to himself. "A dirty rotten rat. What the fuck are you doing?" He gazed at himself for a minute or two but his reflection gave him no answers. Throwing cold water on his face, he walked back into the bedroom and settled down to study his dialogue for tomorrow's scenes.

In the morning, while they breakfasted on their terrace, Inès and Julian chatted desultorily. This was to be the first day of shooting, and he seemed preoccupied. There was a dull ache in the pit of Inès' stomach—whether from a possible miscarriage or the fear of Scrofo's threats, she didn't know. She only knew that for the first time since they'd met she was pleased that Julian was going out. The previous evening she'd done her utmost to persuade him that the scene in script A was so much better for him as an actor than the scene in script B. Appealing to his ego seemed to have succeeded and she thought she'd managed to convince him, even though he went off with both scripts in his haversack.

She was left alone with her thoughts, and with only the sounds of the seabirds for company.

Nick tried hard to overcome his first-day nerves as he stood in the bay, starting to block the first scene of the morning when Cortez, Pizarro and their men arrive on the shores of Mexico for the first time. Cortez was to be greeted by Emperor Montezuma and his warriors, while his beautiful daughter, Princess Isabella, stayed modestly in the background.

Dominique had been enveloped by the wardrobe department in thick folds of embroidered linen. She had little to do in this scene but play the virgin maiden, eyes appropriately downcast as she sees bold Cortez for the first time.

She tried to catch Julian's eye as she was sitting on her canvas chair under a large umbrella planted in the sand. It was only eight in the morning, but the heat was already overpowering, encased as she was in the yards of itchy fabric, with an enormous hank of false hair under her headdress, which weighed a ton. She cooled herself with a woven straw fan and sipped ice water as her makeup crew buzzed around her.

Suddenly an aide came running down the beach waving two telegrams—one for Nick and one for Croft. When Croft had read his, a triumphant look came into his face. He knew victory was his now.

Julian had called him late the night before, informing him that he preferred the first script. Croft had also had a short telephone conversation with Dominique, who'd been anxious to do whatever Julian wanted. Sir Crispin too had agreed.

Now there would be a more audience-pleasing spectacle, more pomp and circumstance, more crowd scenes, more bloody battle scenes. Croft

and the Frankovitches would make *Cortez* a much more important movie—
a worthy successor to *The Robe, Quo Vadis* and the other epic blockbusters
of the fifties. The actors would glitter and shine like thirty-carat diamonds
in a Van Cleef & Arpels setting.

Nick stared in silence at his own telegram, which was also from his
uncle. He'd lost.

Spyros Makopolis had made it abundantly clear. He and the vice-
presidents of MCCP, having carefully reviewed the relative merits of the
two scripts, had been unanimous in their verdict. The most bankable script
was definitely the Frankovitch one. That was the one they wanted Nick to
shoot, that was the one he was going to have to shoot.

They wanted pageantry, histrionics, lavish spectacle and violent battles.
The Mexican extras were paid so little that it wouldn't make much difference to the budget if the film company used sixty or six hundred of them.
They were even now being outfitted in the uniforms of sixteenth-century
sailors and warriors, while two hundred and fifty others, stripping to the
waist, were having wads of black hair attached to their scalps and skimpy
loincloths draped around their hips.

"You've won, you leprous bastard," Nick hissed, grabbing the Italian's
arm with furious strength as Scrofo's livid face stared back at him in triumph.

"You may have won this round, pigface, but don't you *dare* tell me where
I should put the extras or the actors or any piece of fucking furniture in any
scene. Don't you dare tell *me* how to direct my actors—they'll say the motherfucking lines *my* way, and if you put your fat face near any one of my crew,
I'll slam it into that rock until it's mincemeat."

Dominique pricked up her ears and watched with the rest of the cast and
crew in amazement as Nick and Hubert Croft battled it out at the water's
edge.

Next to her sat Sir Crispin Peake, his noble brow beaded with sweat
which trickled out from under his large black wig. He now put aside his
Times crossword to watch the argument between the two men. He never
liked to miss anything, and he and Julian exchanged knowing glances.

Sir Crispin adored Julian, and they'd been in several West End plays together. He had agreed to appear in this film only for a substantial salary.
Although his *King Lear* had been a great success with the London critics, the
public, alas, had not flocked in any great numbers to see it. He'd accepted
this job partly in order to save face but, as he was fond of remarking, also to
"keep Tony in gold taps." Tony was his handsome young live-in companion,
who was constantly redecorating their two enormous houses.

As befitted his position as one of Britain's theatrical knights, he'd been
given his own personal dresser, the ubiquitous Alf, who busied himself

bringing "His Nibs" all that was required for his rarefied English blood to better withstand the tropical climate. Even now in the ninety-degree heat, Sir Crispin was sipping a hot cup of Lapsang souchong tea from a delicate china cup, as he held a Friebourg Treyer cigarette between his elegant fingers. A Chinese paper fan was doing little to cool him, and his patrician features were flushed.

Scrofo's much more plebeian features were also flushed as he strode about on the sand, waving his arms and shouting at Nick in his throaty squawk, his voile shirt already wringing wet and his few remaining strands of hair stuck to his scarlet scalp. He was exhausted. Unable to sleep last night due to a combination of heat and excitement, he'd been up at dawn, awaiting confirmation from Spyros Makopolis that the studio would agree to shoot the Frankovitch script. And he had! Success was his.

Nick and Bluey now found themselves outflanked, outnumbered and outvoted.

Umberto started to speak, but Nick's fingers, which were still holding onto his arm, dug tighter.

"You don't remember me, Gourouni, do you? But I remember you—I remember you very fucking well no matter what you call yourself now. I'd never forget you, never. I'll do this fucking script the way you and those two scumbags and the fucking studio want me to. I'll have the thousand fucking extras and the goddamn battle scenes and the charge of the fucking Light Brigade." The whole beach was now riveted by the screaming fury of the normally soft-spoken young director. He towered over the squat Italian, and even though the crew couldn't quite hear any of the words, the body language was unmistakable.

"But just watch it, you pasta-loving prickhead," Nick spat out venomously. "Watch your fat ass. I'll play *everything* by the rules, but it's gonna be *my* film, the way I want it, with or without a crowd of extras standing around scratching their balls." With a snort of contempt he released Scrofo's arm and the Italian stumbled, almost falling over.

Taking his well-fingered Greek worry beads out of his pocket, Nick started turning them in his fingers rapidly while calling, "Okay, Bluey, let's go. I want first team and all the extras for a line-up—*now!*"

As the Pacific ebbed around Umberto's handmade shoes, he was torn between elation and blinding rage. Yes, he'd won. He was going to produce a film with all the brilliance which he'd put into *La Città Perduta,* but the angry young director had berated and humiliated him in front of the entire cast and crew, made him look idiotic—weak—foolish. And God, how he hated to look a fool, for people to laugh at him.

Stone's hatred, Scrofo thought, was out of all proportion to their short working relationship. They'd know each other only for a few days. Since Nick was Greek, Umberto wondered if perhaps he'd lived on Hydra during the time of his command. So what? The Greeks were all so stupid. All those peasants had gone to their deaths without protest or resistance, whether it was by starvation, torture or firing squad, like silent and obedient sheep. He had no respect for any of them. Reluctantly, however, Scrofo had to admit that even though he'd humiliated him, this Greek had balls.

"Well done," Ramone said admiringly. "Well done, Hubert my dear." The sun was glittering on her heavily embroidered costume as she gushed, "I'm *so* glad we're going to shoot the Frankovitch script, darling, I *much* prefer it."

Umberto knew she preferred it only because she had a few extra scenes to play, but he smiled his thanks, even though he was seething, and conscious of the entire crew looking at him out of the corners of their eyes—probably laughing at him, he thought.

"Now, Hubert, I have an idea." Ramona linked a braceleted arm through his while they strolled across the beach towards the setup. "That wretched hotel where you're staying has no air-conditioning and such terrible service, I'm sure you didn't sleep much last night. You didn't, did you?"

Umberto shook his head.

"I'm in that huge house all by my little self," she said coquettishly. "I have more guest rooms than I know what to do with. You'd be *far* more comfortable staying there with me. You can have the whole second level of rooms for your offices and secretary, and of course we're only five minutes from the Villa Vera. What d'you think, Hubert dear, would you like that?"

"I should like that very much indeed. Thank you, Ramona my dear," he said. "You're very thoughtful, as usual."

"Wonderful," Ramona beamed. "I've also asked the little French girl, Dominique, and her guardian, to stay." She leaned confidentially towards him. "It's not safe for young women to walk alone at night in Acapulco anymore. I heard that the chaperone was attacked and almost raped on the beach only a few nights ago."

"Really?" Umberto raised his eyebrows, looking towards the ghostly, waiflike figure of Agathe who was hovering near Dominique. Who could possibly want to rape *her?*

Since there were never any secrets on a location, the entire crew seemed to know the story of Agathe's narrow escape from the thugs in the bar. And some of the boys were already taking bets as to when Julian would pack Inès off to Europe so that Dominique could move in on him lock, stock and eyeliner. It seemed to be even money on that.

13

*S*ir *Crispin Peake stared down the beach at Dominique's tanned danc-*
er's body as she played around at the water's edge with several of the
younger male crew members. They had been shooting for over a week
now, and she was friendly with all of them.

"Surely that child must be jail bait?" he asked Ramona, who sat sipping
iced orange pekoe tea with him beneath the shade of an enormous striped
umbrella.

"Of course she is," smiled Ramona, who had become more than a little
maternal towards Dominique. "But I'm quite sure she's still an innocent,
Crispin; after all she is only sixteen and she comes from a good family in
France."

Sir Crispin slowly nodded his head, which was heavy with the plaited
hair of a dozen Chinese maidens.

"I wouldn't believe that for a second, my dear. And what's France got to
do with it?" he asked, watching the squealing and giggling Dominique
being chased into the waves by one of the better-looking stuntmen. "She
certainly has oomph, but she looks as if she likes to do a great deal more
than just frolic in the waves."

Ramona took off her sunglasses in order to get a clearer view of the
laughing nymph at the water's edge.

"Nonsense, Crispin, Agathe guards that girl like a tigress. She couldn't *possibly* be anything but a virgin. There's no doubt she's destined for stardom, wouldn't you say? With that face and that unbelievable shape— how could she not be?"

"I wouldn't know, my dear, she's not really my type," Sir Crispin replied with an ironic little smile. He looked quizzically into Ramona's painted face. She really was a creature of cosmetic myth.

"My dear, it was your star which surely shone the brightest when the Hollywood dream factory was at its zenith. Now, of course, the star system, as we both used to know it, is fast disintegrating," he said.

"It most certainly is," agreed Ramona. "And the studios are signing fewer and fewer contract players each year; the big stars are now all trying desperately to be independent."

"Out of the dozens that they do sign, how much longer after the initial burst of fame do you think their moment of celebrity will last?" Sir Crispin asked dryly.

Ramona made no reply as she thought about her own long and eventful career, remembering herself at Dominique's age.

"What, I wonder, does *her* future hold," the old knight speculated, almost to himself. "Is she a Cinderella girl who will return to St. Tropez in a few years to become just another *femme de ménage?* Or will she become an addict of all the hoopla and idolatry, and throw herself away on a succession of unworthy men?"

"She'll hardly do *that*, Crispin," laughed Ramona. "She's so ravishing that they'll be standing in line to escort her. She's not a girl to lose her head over a man."

"Humph," said Sir Crispin enigmatically as Julian joined them, hot and sweating from the scene he'd just been shooting.

"Jesus, it's a scorcher," he gasped, ripping off his velvet doublet and pulling open his shirt to the waist. "How you stand that bloody wig on your head all day, old boy, I'll never know. Why on earth don't you take it off?"

"My dear fellow," Sir Crispin answered drolly, "this hideous object is attached to my poor scant-haired scalp by at least a pound of the most foul-smelling glue. I can assure you that its removal every evening is absolute torture, dear boy, worse than anything which could have been thought up by Torquemada and his frightful Spanish Inquisition."

Ramona and Julian both laughed as Julian's dresser brought him a cold glass of beer, which he tipped to his lips, watching the object of his new passion, who was still cavorting in the waves.

Sir Crispin turned his beady eyes towards Julian, paying particular attention to the muscles of his golden chest, which quivered deliciously as he swallowed his beer. Sir Crispin was always attracted to a magnificent male body, and few he'd ever seen were as magnificent as Looks Brooks'. Julian always reminded him of a breathtaking Bernini sculpture of Apollo that he'd once seen in a museum in Rome.

"Dear boy, we were just talking about yon vestal virgin," he said waggishly. "I was saying to Ramona that I thought she was *no* stranger to the world of the championship blow job. What do you think, Julian?"

Julian almost choked on his beer, and to his horror felt himself blushing.

"Now, now, Crispin, we'll have none of that," he said with a splutter as his dresser sprang forward to mop his velvet breeches.

"Crispin, you're terrible," chuckled Ramona. "Dominique's just a baby. How can you say such things?"

"It seems to me that the younger they are, the more sex they always want," said Sir Crispin authoritatively.

"Well, I suppose you should know, old chap, shouldn't you?" Julian winked, grinning at Ramona.

Suddenly Dominique let out an ear-piercing shriek as one of the men she'd been fooling around with jumped on top of her in the water.

"Our baby is growing up fast," observed Sir Crispin, his eyes glittering with amusement from behind his sunglasses. "And, my dears, if *she's* a virgin then *I'm* Edith Evans."

"Now you come to mention it, you've actually developed an uncanny resemblance to Edith recently," Julian teased, trying his best to ignore Dominique, who was now completely soaked, her long hair flying in the wind, as she was chased repeatedly across the waves by two large and excitable members of the camera crew.

"Yes, I think it must be the wig," laughed Ramona.

"That mass of hair, old chap, is identical to the one Edith had to wear as Cleopatra," Julian said, tears of laughter coming into his eyes.

"But I have bigger breasts than she has," Sir Crispin said archly, reveling in his audience's laughter. "I remember going to see a matinée of Edith's Cleopatra," he reminisced. "My dear, the audience consisted of three old ladies and an Afghan hound, and the Afghan hound appeared to be having the most fun."

They laughed again as Dominique, like a giggling dervish, streaked towards them, hotly pursued by her group of admirers.

"Julian, oh, Julian, help me please!" she squealed in mock terror as she threw herself down into his lap.

"These men, they're teasing me so much," she said, nestling her wet body against his warm chest. "Please help me, Julian," she said plaintively, peeking up at him through her wet, sooty eyelashes which partially hid the secret message contained in her eyes. "Please!"

As Julian felt an embarrassing erection stirring, he quickly but playfully tumbled her off his knees and onto the sand.

"What do you think you're doing, young lady?" he scolded. "Nick told me the next scene is with you and all of us, and here you are messing about in the waves. You're a very naughty girl."

Dominique pouted prettily up at him.

"Most unprofessional, dear girl," said Sir Crispin, wagging an admonishing finger. "Never keep them waiting on the set, my dear—better you wait for them—as alas we've all been doing for *hours.*"

"Okay, okay," laughed Dominique, cheekily grabbing Julian's beer from him and taking a large sip. "I'm going—I'll be ready in less than ten minutes, I promise, you know how fast I can be."

"We'll take your word for it," murmured Sir Crispin, noticing with a frisson of pleasure that Julian was rearranging the crotch of his trousers. He congratulated himself for not having missed the stimulating sight of Julian's sudden and impressive erection. "Oh, well," said Sir Crispin blithely, "where there's youth, there's bound to be gaiety—isn't that true, Julian dear boy?"

"Absolutely," Julian agreed, finishing his beer and casually picking up his script to cover his lap.

"She's certainly a bright and spirited young maiden, our little *mademoiselle.*" Sir Crispin smiled. "I daresay she'll break many a heart before we're all much older."

The small house party usually dined quietly each evening on Ramona's second terrace. Shooting finished at sundown, and after Umberto had attended a series of production meetings in his offices, spoken to Hollywood half a dozen times, and screamed at everyone who'd crossed him that day, a calm, civilized dinner would be served.

Dominique adored living in Ramona's palatial mansion; it was as if she'd found herself in some great big beautiful doll's house. Agathe was quietly impressed by some of the pictures and sculptures, and she lived in constant nervous anticipation that Julian might be invited to dinner.

When Ramona first extended a dinner invitation to Nick, the young Greek asked her bluntly, "Will Croft be there?"

"Why, yes—of course he will," answered Ramona, somewhat flustered by Nick's burning brown eyes. "He's one of my houseguests."

"Then thank you very much for the invitation, Princess," he said, "but I don't intend to spend any more time in the company of that creature than is absolutely necessary."

"I see," said Ramona, raising penciled brows, not seeing at all. "In that case perhaps it would be better if I didn't invite you again."

She seemed so piqued that Nick, always trying to be the diplomat and also a genuine admirer of Ramona, said, "Please don't take it personally, Princess. You know, as well as the whole crew does, that there's no love lost between Croft and me. In fact we loathe each other. Please try to understand, will you?"

"Of course," said Ramona graciously. "But I hope that one day you may change your mind."

He smiled grimly. "If the toad is guaranteed not to be there, then I'd be delighted to dine with you, Princess."

"It's a date," smiled Ramona, mentally removing Nick from the guest list which she kept permanently in her head.

Sir Crispin Peake, whose eccentric English humor livened up the sometimes somber gatherings, was one of Ramona's favorite guests. Attractive young diplomats from the American embassy, visiting socialites, film stars and politicians would also often be asked. Ramona's table was famous, and invitations from her were in demand, but to Agathe's disappointment Julian never came to her dinner parties.

Inès had become virtually a prisoner in her hotel suite. Dr. Langley had insisted that she spend the next seven months in bed if she really wanted to have this baby.

"Just get up for the wedding day. And *no sex*. Not even necking," he told her continually.

Although Julian had been extremely understanding about her condition, Inès knew there was a limit to a man's sexual altruism. She was torn between her love for him, and wanting to show it, and her longing to have his child. Every night they were together, and he studied his script while she lay in bed trying not to feel sorry for herself, trying to make bright and interesting conversation. But it was difficult to make interesting conversation when she spent every day flat on her back staring at the ceiling. Although Inès tried hard, she had the ominous feeling that Julian was drifting away from her, his mind on other things. She knew that the movie was arduous and that there was a good deal of tension on the set. What Inès didn't know was that each lunch hour and practically every day after shooting, Looks Brooks and Dominique were making passionate love behind the locked doors and curtained windows of her trailer.

14

The studio was ecstatic about the first week's rushes. Nick was doing a masterful job of injecting an intimate, realistic style into the Frankovitches' overly melodramatic and flowery script. The result was a brilliant contrast with the sixteenth-century grandeur and pageantry. The studio believed it was going to create a new look in film, and they were eagerly planning other historical epics for Nick to direct.

Each day Agathe would sit on the set quietly watching, saying little. The crew hardly ever spoke to her. With her strangely forbidding looks and manner, and her stiff and correct English, it was almost like trying to communicate with a wax mannequin. She rehearsed Dominique in her lines and watched over her while she daydreamed constantly of Julian.

Since Agathe's experience on the beach she regarded all men, with the exception of Julian, with great suspicion, but she was totally blind to the smoldering affair that was going on between him and Dominique. To her, Dominique was nothing more than a schoolgirl. Granted, she was an actress now and in a major motion picture, but she was still a child, a girl who knew nothing of life. Agathe's mind was a kaleidoscope of images of Julian. She couldn't keep her eyes off him when she sat on the sidelines at the beaches, lagoons and mountains, watching the shooting. Through her dark glasses and with a hat tipped over her forehead she would observe his every gesture, his every movement.

The fact that he was friendly, even flirtatious, with Dominique was attributed by Agathe to the natural closeness that all film people seemed to develop with one another. How she envied them that. The easy jokes, the sarcastic familiarity which bordered on a kind of rudeness, seemed to bind them all closely together.

The only person who spent any time with her, other than Dominique, was Sir Crispin Peake. He often sat beside her underneath a striped umbrella, regaling her with long-ago anecdotes and tales of the British stage. Agathe thought him tedious, since she found it difficult to understand his theatrical humor, but she tried to sit near him because Julian adored him and would always come over to talk to him between setups. With his doublet off, his chest gleaming with a faint sheen of perspiration, he would laugh his head off at the old knight's stories and captivate Agathe still more. After those days when she sat with Sir Crispin and Julian, Agathe's nights would be gloriously erotic and she would pleasure herself frantically.

One day, when no one was near, she purloined another of Julian's shirts from his trailer. It was of white cambric, one that he'd worn in a dueling scene. The wardrobe woman had several doubles of it, and this one had been ripped. As it couldn't be used again, Agathe didn't consider that she was stealing. She was just borrowing something of Julian's which would bring him even closer to her. She could almost feel his body next to hers when she lay with it at night.

As for that prostitute fiancée of his, Inès, she never appeared, although rumors were rife around the unit that she was pregnant and confined to bed. Pregnant! Agathe didn't ask Julian if it was true; she hardly dared talk to him at all, because she always blushed so furiously that she felt sure he could read her thoughts. But she was filled with bitter rage that this magnificent man could have sown his seed in the body of that traitorous whore.

15

Dominique now believed that she was madly in love with Julian. Two weeks of abandoned lovemaking made her want him all the more. When they were together on the set it was as if an electric current flowed and crackled between their bodies. Her eyes glowed whenever she was near him, and their sexual combustion on the screen was so visible that rapturous telegrams were sent from Hollywood to Nick congratulating him on creating and capturing such magical chemistry on film. The screen almost melted the first time Julian and Dominique kissed. Gasps of amazement rippled through the screening rooms, as many of the normally hard-bitten executives sighed with vicarious pleasure.

"More love scenes! These two are hotter than even Gable and Leigh, Clift and Taylor. Write more," went the gist of the telegrams which were fired off to Nick and Hubert Croft.

"More love scenes!" cackled Shirley, crouching over her ancient typewriter, a cigarette dangling from between her lips. "What a pity we can't shoot the hot ones going on in that hussy's trailer every lunchtime. I'll give 'em more love scenes—we'll scorch the screen with 'em."

Irving didn't bother to answer. He ignored Shirley when she was being a bitch. She was so obviously vicariously enjoying the steamy affair which was being played out right under everyone's noses that he thought he would give her the job of writing the new romantic scenes between Julian and Dominique that the studio craved. He was sitting at the other end of their Villa Vera sitting room with a yellow legal pad on his lap as yet again he rewrote the ending of the film.

Nick had not given up. Even though MCCP was still insisting on shooting the original Frankovitch script, Nick was such a perfectionist that he was constantly harassing the Frankovitches into changing a line here—making a scene better there—polish, polish, polish. Irving admired and respected his persistence, and he'd grudgingly had to admit that Nick was almost always right. Croft and Shirley were usually unanimous in *their* criticism and denunciation of all Nick's ideas, and the battles between them still raged on, but now with Irving more often taking Nick's side of the argument.

Shirley rat-tat-tatted away on her typewriter, spinning out the erotic scene in which the young Princess Isabella has to perform a dance for Cortez before they make love. She wondered what she could possibly do to make it really hot—"to melt their zippers" as she put it—to make it sexier than anything that had ever before been seen on the screen. She thought of some of the recent films: *The Robe* had been far too pure in its content, as had been *The Ten Commandments,* and even *Miss Sadie Thompson* with Rita Hayworth. Everyone in Hollywood had made such a big song and dance about her, but the movie had turned out to be as tame as a pet parrot.

"*Gilda*—now that was a sexy film," Shirley said out loud.

"What, dear?" Irving asked.

"The dance Hayworth did in *Gilda*—you remember, 'Put the blame on Mame, boys'—erotic, wasn't it?"

"Very," he replied. "But a little out of period for us, dear. We're trying to stay in the sixteenth century—*Gilda* was 1947."

"Hmmm." Shirley tapped at her teeth with a pencil. "What about Ava in *Pandora and the Flying Dutchman?*" she yelled across the room to him. "She sure lit up the screen in that scene where she swims out to the Dutchman's schooner in the nude."

"That was a great scene," recalled Irving, "and it really was shot in the moonlight too—on actual locations in the Mediterranean, I believe."

"Yeah, yeah, yeah—I'm gonna use it," said Shirley, tapping excitedly on her machine. "It'll be great, just great, Princess Isabella's gonna swim out to Cortez' boat in the nude," she said gleefully. "She's gonna climb on board, in the nude." Now she was becoming even more gleeful. "And *then* she's gonna do her hot little dance for Señor Cortez in the—"

"Don't be ridiculous, Shirley, you *can't.*" Irving was shocked and irritated at his wife's stupidity. "The Hays Office will have all our asses. We can't have any nudity on the screen."

"Oh, yes we can." Shirley picked up the telephone from her desk and barked at the hotel operator, "Get me Hubert Croft."

"We can and we will, Irv," she went on. "The studio'll love it—we can shoot it two ways—with and without veils." She cackled and shrieked into the phone. "Hubert—Shirley. Now listen, I've just had this great idea—can you come over and see us right away? Right—okay. You're just gonna *love* this scene, Hubert—yeah, I'm quite sure."

Julian was in a stupor of erotic tension. He hardly knew what had hit him. He adored Inès, worshiped her. His divorce from Phoebe would be final in a month, and his marriage to Inès had been planned for the following week. This was what he still wanted in his heart. But he knew that he somehow had to get Dominique out of his system. To do this he had convinced himself that if he made love to her as much and as often as possible he would grow tired of her. But the more wildly they made love, the more he wanted her. He simply couldn't get enough of this teenage temptress who reminded him so much of a younger version of the woman he really loved.

For him, Inès' illness was a blessing in disguise, although he suffered pangs of desperate guilt which made him drink more than usual. But Dominique's glances full of promise, her creamy lusciousness, her sensual touch, caused him to think of nothing but his hunger for her. One morning during shooting she deliberately teased him by repeatedly moistening her lips with her little pink tongue. This caused him a painfully embarrassing erection which lasted until she allowed him to take her, in a blazing burst of passion, in her dressing room during the lunch hour. They'd both been in full costume, but he'd plunged into her in such a frenzy of abandonment that the thin plywood walls had begun to rock, and many of the crew grinned knowingly at each other.

"Location romance, my foot," said Tim. "I ain't *never* seen the guvnor like this before—he's gorn, 'ook, line 'n' sinker."

Dominique loved it. She had found her ultimate power in the discovery of sex. This famous and gorgeous star, engaged to another woman, was hers to twist around her finger as much and in as many ways as her heart desired, and there was absolutely nothing he could do about it.

"It's quite impossible, Dominique. I could never allow you to do this scene—it's disgraceful, disgusting. Scandalous." Two red dots burned on Agathe's pale cheeks as she confronted Dominique with the new blue pages of script which had been delivered that evening.

"Don't be such a square, Agathe." Dominique yawned. "What's such a big deal about it? Why should I mind about a bit of nudity, it's perfectly natural—bodies are nothing to be ashamed of."

"It's immoral," spluttered Agathe. "It's—it's—disgraceful—it's demeaning and cheap—swimming out stark naked to a man—" her voice rose almost an octave—"then climbing onto the boat and dancing naked in front of Julian Brooks." Her tone had become so hysterical and outraged that Dominique looked up at her in astonishment.

"What do you care, Agathe—as long as I don't? I can't see what's the big deal—aren't you overreacting?"

"I'm your chaperone, young woman, in case it's slipped your mind," huffed Agathe. "I am supposed to look after your welfare, your morals, and help you sustain the values instilled in you by your parents."

"Bull," said Dominique rudely. "My parents didn't instill any values in me."

"That's a lie and you're a wicked, wicked girl to say so," Agathe shrieked. "I know your father. He's one of the most respected bankers in St. Tropez—*mon Dieu,* what will he say when he sees you prancing about in the nude? *Quelle horreur.*" She crossed herself and rubbed the little crucifix she always wore.

"Stop being such an old fuddy-duddy, Agathe," said Dominique. "Look— just take a look at this girl—she's French too, and her parents are *petit-bourgeois* too, just like mine." She threw over a copy of *Cinémonde,* the French magazine that she'd been reading.

Agathe picked it up and gasped at the photograph. A beautiful young blonde lay on her stomach, her hair covering the curves of her breasts, but her bare buttocks were prominently exposed and she was staring into the camera with an alluring and provocative smile.

"*Mais c'est porno*—what is the world coming to?" gasped Agathe, shocked to her foundations.

Dominique shrugged. "That's Brigitte Bardot," she said as if that were enough. "She's a couple of years older than me, maybe eighteen or nineteen, but that's what they're doing in France now—that kind of movie. They're shooting it now with a young director called Roger Vadim. It's called *And God Created Woman.*"

"I don't care if it's called *And God Created Shit,*" hissed Agathe in an unusual burst of blasphemy. "I'm going to see our producer right now and tell him I will never *allow* you to shoot this disgusting scene! *Never,* do you hear?"

Dominique shrugged. Agathe certainly seemed to be under a great deal of nervous tension recently. She wondered why.

Hubert Croft was trying unsuccessfully to take a nap when Agathe burst into his room unannounced and with only a perfunctory knock at the door. He'd taken off his shirt and trousers and was dressed only in his voluminous underpants and an undershirt when his visitor appeared.

"How *dare* you send Dominique this filth," she yelled, brandishing the pages of the scene under his nose. "I cannot permit my charge to perform this degrading act. She's my responsibility and *I forbid it.*"

"And what does your so-called charge have to say about it?" asked Hubert sarcastically, shrugging his bulk into a terry robe, complete with Ramona's royal crest embroidered in red and gold on the breast pocket. "I'm sure she probably doesn't mind the idea in the least."

"That's not the point—she's a child and she knows no better," Agathe replied stiffly. "I'm the adult who's responsible for her and I *will NOT,* indeed *cannot,* allow her to reveal herself in such a debasing and disgusting fashion. It's abominable, I'm calling her parents tomorrow to tell them what's happening. She's underage, you people shouldn't even suggest that she do it."

"Sit down, *Mademoiselle,*" said Hubert calmly. He gestured to a turquoise suede armchair, and Agathe sank into its depths, quite out of breath and fanning herself with the offending pages.

Just the thought of Julian seeing Dominique totally naked filled her with such conflicting feelings that her whole body was tingling. Her Julian—her love—watching Dominique perform this wanton dance wearing nothing but a smile. It was bad enough when she'd had to watch them making love for the screen. She had sat on the sidelines, out of sight, dry-mouthed with lust while the two of them kissed and caressed each other with such a passionate frenzy that she'd felt the moisture welling up in the most secret and private part of her body. It had almost been unbearable watching Julian hold that immature child in his strong arms, seeing his lips devour hers, her breasts pressed to his muscular chest, his arms holding her tightly. It had been a bittersweet sensation, particularly as Nick had insisted on shooting the love scenes from several different angles. She had suffered, oh, how she had suffered the pangs of jealousy and desire. She'd been unable to control herself, and had crept away to Dominique's empty trailer to relieve herself in the only way she knew. Whispering Julian's name, biting her lips until they almost bled, rubbing herself furiously with his scarf—another purloined object—she came to one torrential orgasm after another.

"Now, Mademoiselle Guinzberg," said Hubert, lighting a cigar and closely observing her through his narrowed eyes, "this is all a lot of nonsense. You know that, don't you?"

"I certainly don't," she huffed peevishly. "Dominique is only sixteen—I'm her guardian and—"

"Shut up, Mademoiselle Guinzberg," snapped Hubert. "Sit down and stop behaving like a two-faced bitch."

"What—what did you call me?" His sudden orders stunned her into confusion and anger.

"I said you're behaving like a two-faced hypocrite," he continued. "Do you think I don't make it my business to know what's been going on?"

"I don't know what you're talking about," gasped Agathe.

"Don't pretend to be as stupid as you look," snapped Hubert. "Listen to me for a minute before you start telephoning the girl's parents or the police or the fucking coast guard." He sucked on his cigar and pinioned her to the chair with his look of contempt. She squirmed uncomfortably, aware of the power of his penetrating stare. God, he was ugly. The crew, who all seemed to dislike him, made jokes about him all the time, and had christened him "the Toad." He looked like a great bulbous toad now as he sat hunched in the dark green robe, his bald head glistening with sweat, and stubble like black sandpaper covering his several chins.

"Don't for one minute think that I don't know *everything* that's going on in this film unit," he said slowly. "I mean *everything.*"

"And what's that supposed to mean?" Agathe tried to sound resolute, but there was no question that Croft not only repelled her but also terrified her. She disliked any kind of confrontation, and she was starting to wish that she'd never come.

"I know what you think, Mademoiselle Agathe Guinzberg." He leaned forward, staring so intently into her eyes that she had to look away. "I know your every thought when you're on the set watching Julian Brooks work."

"What—what do you mean?"

"You love him, don't you, Agathe?" He leered. "You're passionately in love with him, and you lust after his body."

"No—no, I don't, it's a lie, a monstrous lie."

"Nonsense, woman. I've *seen* you—I miss nothing, you know." Hubert's cigar had gone out, and he relit it with an elaborate gold lighter. "I've *seen* the expression on your face when you sit under the umbrella with Sir Crispin and Julian—I *know* what's going through your mind, *and* your body."

"You don't—you couldn't," said Agathe fearfully.

"Don't be a cretin, woman." He smiled triumphantly, knowing that his next revelation would prove the killer for her. "I've seen your book—your precious scrapbook. Did you think you could hide anything from me?"

"No!" cried Agathe. "You couldn't have."

"Oh, but I could, and I have. A lovely book, Agathe, so beautifully as-sembled, and with such affection. I must congratulate you on such a comprehensive selection of photographs of our dear Mr. Brooks." He laughed unpleasantly. "It's certainly been well thumbed, your scrapbook."

"How did you find it?" whispered Agathe, shame for herself and hatred for the Toad both rising in her like lava.

"I searched your room, you fool." He smiled again. "I had a suspicion you might have something like that—I needed to find it. You didn't conceal it very well, Agathe. Under the mattress—ha!—very original. Any one of those stupid maids who work here could have found it, even though it was well wrapped up—in one of Julian's shirts, if I'm not mistaken." His eyes gleamed.

"No," she said softly. "No. No, that's my property—it's private—private. You're trespassing."

"Now, Mademoiselle Guinzberg, I'm going to forget totally that we ever had this little conversation, but only if you go away right now like a good woman and allow Dominique to get on with her work. If you choose to make a scene, call her parents, or do anything of that kind, I will personally see to it that everyone on this picture, including Julian Brooks himself, gets to know of your pathetic, pitiful obsession with him. Do I make myself clear?"

She nodded, her eyes burning with tears.

"And of course if Dominique's parents ever find out that the very person they trusted to look after their precious daughter is no more than a sick, sexually obsessed *pervert,* you will be undoubtedly thrown off this film in less than the time it takes to shout 'Action'—I do make myself clear, don't I?"

She nodded again, still unable to speak, and rose to leave.

"Not a word of our meeting here tonight will you breathe to anyone, Mademoiselle Guinzberg. And we shall all continue to be one big happy family. Do you understand?"

His eyes never left her as she walked slowly to the door, her shoulders slumped, her head bowed in defeat. Pathetic creature, he thought, feeling an unaccustomed emotion—pity. He would spare telling her about Dominique's roaring affair with Julian—the shock would probably kill her.

16

It was a clear moonlit night when Nick decided to shoot Dominique's nude swimming scene, followed by her seductive dance for Julian. The studio had become terribly excited when they had heard about it. It was breaking nearly all of the Hays Office censorship codes. Spyros Makopolis knew that in the new and dangerous territory they were entering, the studio was creating a precedent for future erotic scenes in movies. If the censor passed the scene in *Cortez*—without cuts—it would open the flood-gates for other productions to shoot bare-skinned actresses and the public would demand more and more titillating scenes.

After arduous discussions with the Hays Office, with Scrofo, the Frank-ovitches and with Dominique herself, Nick had finally figured out a way to shoot it which would make it not only erotic and sensual, but would not actually show any censorable parts of Dominique's body. Only in long shots or in silhouette would the outlines of her beautiful figure be seen. To be completely safe, the following night they were going to shoot the iden-tical scene all over again, this time with Dominique in a primitive bikini.

Agathe spoke little as Dominique prepared for her first swimming shot. She stood completely and unself-consciously naked in front of Agathe, who had to avert her eyes while the makeup girl applied waterproof makeup to the girl's nipples. Her breasts were firm and up-jutting, her nipples dark pink. The makeup girl was trying to mask their color with the sponge so that the camera would not be able to see them from the boat, some two hundred yards away in the lagoon.

Dominique rather enjoyed the sensation of the soft sponge on her breasts, but her mind was filled with thoughts of what she and Julian would do together to while away the time tonight between shots. They both had cabins on the boat, and she knew that as soon as they finalized the first take, and he had glimpsed her glistening nude body rising from the sea, climbing up the side of the boat, he would feel a desperate urge to take her. She shivered at the delicious expectation, already becoming aroused by the thought of their passion taking place so close to where the crew would all be working.

She admired her reflection in the full-length mirror. Her belly was flat and tight, and at the base of her pubic triangle of black hair the wardrobe woman had pasted a small piece of flesh-colored fabric, not as a concession to her own modesty—which didn't exist—but to protect the footage from the potential wrath of the censor.

There was a sharp knock at the door, and Bluey's voice boomed out, "How we doin', Dominique?"

"I'm ready," she said happily, tossing her hair over her shoulders and smiling again at her gorgeous reflection. Agathe stole another look at her charge. The girl was exquisitely formed, there was no doubt at all about that. She seemed to have matured in the few months since she'd left St. Tropez; now she was no longer a schoolgirl but a ripe young woman in full flower. Agathe felt a surge of jealousy engulf her again as she imagined how Julian would feel when he saw the naked girl for the first time. She shuddered. She didn't *want* to think about that.

The wardrobe woman tied a large multicolored sarong around Dominique, who then tripped down the beach to where a small tent had been erected on the sand.

Nick was there waiting to meet her. "All set, Dominique? You look terrific, darling—how do you feel?"

"Great, Nick, great—I'm so excited, ready for anything."

"You really don't mind the nudity, you're absolutely sure?"

"Of course not." She laughed. "We all look the same without our clothes—it means nothing to me, Nick, less than nothing. I do think it's better for the scene too, more—how-you-say—*érotique, n'est-ce pas?*"

"Erotic, right." He grinned, admiring this girl's frankness and her refreshing joie de vivre. They'd made the right choice with this one, no question—she was a born star, and her sexuality seemed to gain in power each day. "Okay, now I'm going to get on the boat. Wait in the tent until you hear me call 'Action.' Then you come out slowly—look around you—to see if the guard is watching. When you get to the edge of the water you drop your scarf, and wade out very, very slowly into the sea. All the time you look towards the boat with an expression of anticipation. You're longing to see Cortez. Let me see how you're going to do it."

She rehearsed for him in the tent, and when he was satisfied with everything he gave her a big kiss on the cheek.

"You're gonna be great, break a leg, kid, and if you get a cramp in one while you're swimming, just yell—we've got divers all around—you'll be quite safe."

"I know." She smiled. "I'm a strong swimmer, Nick. Don't forget I live in St. Tropez."

He smiled to himself as he sat back in the speedboat which took him out to the majestic sixteenth-century schooner, whose masts towered impressively. If his instincts were correct, this was going to be quite some scene.

The crew were busy setting up on deck, and as he went over to consult with his lighting cameraman, he was accosted by Croft.

"I need to talk to you, my friend," the Italian said in an unexpectedly amiable tone, putting his hand on Nick's arm.

Nick pulled his arm away as if it had been stung, saying, "Okay, let's go down into my cabin then."

In his claustrophobic cabin, Nick nodded towards a chair for Croft to sit in. Ignoring the Italian, he stood with his hands on his hips thinking through his script with a frown.

"It's about this nude scene we're going to shoot," Umberto began.

"What about it?" Nick's voice was sharp. "The studio has agreed to this scene in principle, so what's the problem, Hubie baby?" He couldn't keep the sarcasm out of his voice, nor could he bear to look at the abhorrent creature who sat puffing on his stinking cigar.

"I want to know exactly how you're going to shoot it, to protect Dominique's modesty," said Umberto. "She's young—she shouldn't be out there flashing her snatch at the crew without a stitch on. I want to know that you're all going to behave like gentlemen."

Nick raised his eyebrows. "Since when did you become the moralist?" he sneered. "Since when did *you* know anything about gentlemen and their behavior? I didn't realize you were so concerned about protecting Dominique—I assumed that you had other ideas about her."

"And what do you mean by *that?*" snarled the Italian.

"Oh, nothing, nothing," said Nick, innocently glancing at his script. "You've got a cock too, Hubie baby—haven't you?"

"Listen, asshole." Umberto rose, his huge bulk, enveloped in clouds of cigar smoke, seeming to fill the tiny cabin. "Let's not have any more cracks about *me*—I'm still the fucking producer on this fucking epic whether *you* like it or not, you Greek shithead. *Here.*" He threw a crumpled telegram on the desk. "Read that."

Nick picked up the scrap of paper and read: "Hays Office most concerned sᴛᴏᴘ Despite them having agreed to pass nude scene it is essential that any shots filmed, repeat, any at all, must have no salacious content vis-à-vis body position or exposure of the girl sᴛᴏᴘ They unaware Dominique is a minor sᴛᴏᴘ Be very careful sᴛᴏᴘ Picture so far is great but we need this scene so get it right sᴛᴏᴘ Regards Makopolis."

"I've already had a copy of this," said Nick, throwing it back to Umberto. "I've spent all today and yesterday on this boat with the operator, the lighting cameraman and with Dominique or her stand-in. We've carefully gone through every fucking frame. Any time there's the minutest possibility that we might see a flash of tit or any of her other bits, we've always got a piece of sail or some scenery to cover it—does that satisfy your prudery, Hubie baby?"

"What about the crew—will they be able to see any of her body?" Umberto asked persistently.

"Of *course* they'll be able to see her!" exploded Nick. "But they're fucking professionals, for Christ's sake, not a bunch of Peeping fucking Toms." Like you, he almost added, but he badly wanted to get rid of the Toad. The sight and sound of the man always put him into a blinding fury, and he had to get to work right away. There was a great deal to be done tonight.

"Well, I'll be watching the whole time to see that you do *exactly* what you're supposed to," said Umberto, his eyes glinting at Nick like chips of coal. "And no one had better take advantage of that girl."

Least of all you, asshole, Nick thought to himself, but all he said was, "Right, have you finished now, Hubert? Are you satisfied?"

"One thing you should know about me, Nick," sneered Umberto, his face close to Nick's, "I'm *never* satisfied." With that he stalked out, slamming the cabin door.

Nick shrugged and made a couple of notes in red pencil on his script. This was just another typical day with Hubert S. Croft. Every day he tried to make trouble, and every day he succeeded in infuriating someone in the crew or a member of the cast.

Nick looked out of the cabin's minute porthole which faced the deck and saw Hubert talking angrily to one of Dominique's wardrobe women who was looking back at him with patient irritation. Nick grinned. He'd seen that particular look on parctically every one of the crew members' faces. They all loathed Scrofo. He put the Italian out of his mind as best he could and, as he strode purposefully back onto the deck, concentrated his attention on the forthcoming scene.

"Ready, boys?" he called to his two camera crews, both set up for different angles on the deck.

"Okay—ready, Nick," they shouted back in unison.

"Right—let's *go!*"

The clapper boy snapped his wooden sticks in front of camera one, then again in front of camera two. The sound operator called, "Rolling." Nick then shouted the magic words through his loudhailer: "Aaand—*Action!*"

Also on deck, out of sight just behind the camera crews Umberto Scrofo stood, a pair of powerful binoculars pressed firmly to his porcine eye sockets. He didn't want to miss a single second of this spectacle. Naturally he'd thought Dominique a lovely little creature since the first moment that he'd laid eyes on her, but she had resolutely and continually ignored him. If he ever tried to talk to her, she would only reply in monosyllables and with barely disguised boredom.

As she paused at the shoreline Dominique looked steadily towards the anchored boat. Slowly and with an infinite yet natural sensuality, she unloosed her flimsy sarong and let it fall with a faint whisper to the sand. The full moon illuminated her flawless breasts and gave an ethereal beauty to her whole body. She looked like a dark and less modest version of Botticelli's Venus rising from the waves. She was a divinely created masterpiece, the personification of youthful and feminine perfection.

"Madonna mia," muttered Scrofo, the lump in his throat almost as uncomfortable as the one in his trousers, *"Che bellissima ragazza— bellissima."*

He was far from alone in his admiration for the naked beauty who was milking her moment at the water's edge to the very utmost. Slowly, sinuously, she walked into the cool black waters. Pausing momentarily as the ocean lapped around the tops of her thighs, she gazed again with a look of undisguised desire at the deck of the boat where Julian was waiting for her.

"My God, what a dame," whispered Bluey to Nick, who stood transfixed, just gazing at her. "That's the fuckin' body of a fuckin' angel if I ever saw one."

Nick didn't bother to answer. The tableau was so exquisite in its simple timeless beauty that he felt he wanted to drown himself in it. Dominique took another two or three steps, and, as the water covered her waist, she gave a tiny cry and dived under the surface, to reappear seconds later with her hair streaming out behind her like black seaweed. She swam impressively and strongly towards the boat. The close-up camera was filming her face and shoulders, but the operator was concentrating on trying not to reveal any glimpses of her breasts.

"Fantastic," he murmured under his breath to his assistant, who was constantly adjusting the focus as Dominique swam closer and closer to the boat. "Fan-fuckin'-tastic."

Julian was standing between the two cameras, so that as Dominique swam within thirty yards of the boat she could see him clearly. She gave him a smile of such devastating innocence, seductively tinged with voluptuous adult longing, that he could feel his mouth becoming dry, and his cock, in anxious anticipation of the delights in store for it later, began its irresistible rise.

Finally she arrived at the rope ladder which hung over the side of the boat, and grasping it tightly climbed on board. For an instant she stood absolutely still, posing, allowing the cameras to capture the electric sensuality that emanated from her. Then with a passionate sigh she murmured, "Oh, Hernando, my love," and threw herself into Julian's open and welcoming arms.

"Cut," shouted Nick. "Beautiful, Dominique—absolutely beautiful—we don't need to do another one; that was perfection, darling—just great. Relax for an hour while we get set up for your dance—dry yourself off, have a hot drink. We don't want you catching cold."

The wardrobe woman had already draped Dominique with towels and a terrycloth robe, and she wrapped herself in them, twisting a towel around her wet hair like a turban. Julian stood nearby while her posse of helpers fussed around her, and she felt she could almost see his hardness through the material of his breeches. She shooed away her entourage and stood very still as he approached her.

"Can I buy you a drink?" he whispered.

"You could," she breathed. "But I'd rather you make love to me."

In the privacy of his tiny cabin, neither could control their desperate impatience. Julian sat on the bunk fully clothed, and she stood shaking between his legs—more from lust than from the effects of the cold water—as he slowly unwound the towels from her damp body.

They could hear the crew up on deck preparing for the next shot, and the gentle slap of the waves against the hull. A dim yellow lamp glowed from the table in the cabin, and as the towels fell away from her breasts it bathed them in a warm, golden light. His mouth went to each one in turn, licking and gently biting them until she threw back her head and cried out for him to stop—then his hands caressed her hips as he unwound the towel from her waist, laying bare her buttocks and her sex. He stroked the soft firmness of her muscled rear as his lips dropped down to her silky mound and his tongue found the exact place for which it longed.

She moaned softly as it probed her gently and softly. He now knew well how to please her, and in only a matter of seconds she came, her hands tangled in his thick hair, as he continued to massage her nipples gently with the palms of his hands.

Then she was on him like a wild creature and his cock leaped out at her as she unbuttoned his trousers. It seemed to her harder and larger than it had ever been before. Lovingly she put as much of it in her mouth as she could, rhythmically sucking it until he almost burst. Then she put him inside her, and rode him, gently at first, but gaining momentum until together they became two bodies but one flesh.

Bluey went to knock on Julian's cabin about an hour later.

"Is Dominique in there by any chance?" he said with mock innocence.

"*J'arrive*—coming right out," called Dominique happily, blowing her lover a kiss, and leaving him lying back on his bunk completely sated.

Nick was ready to rehearse the dance scene, so Dominique put on a leotard to run over it until Nick was completely satisfied that it was perfect. Umberto stood beside the cameras, cigar jutting out from his mouth, saying nothing, but his very presence making everyone uncomfortable and distracted.

The cameras were positioned in such a way that the areas of Dominique's body which were censorable were always masked by parts of the boat's equipment and rigging. It was a highly complicated and difficult shot and it took almost all night to get it. They needed to do more than fifteen setups with the three cameras to make quite sure that no mistakes were made.

Dominique was in her element. She found the idea of dancing naked in front of forty men, including her lover, enormously exhilarating. Each time that Nick yelled "Cut—it's a print—next setup" she and Julian would slink away to one or other of their cabins. No one disturbed them. Even though everyone knew exactly what was going on, and although lewd jokes and comments were bandied about by the crew, nothing was ever said within earshot of the two principals.

"Maybe we should call her the Submarine," joked Bluey to the camera operator.

"And why's that?"

"Because she's always going down," laughed Bluey, nodding towards Julian's cabin.

Julian was lying on his bunk after the fifth setup. They'd been shooting Dominique's dance for over six hours now and he was exhausted. Not from the dancing, as all he had to do was watch, but because Dominique was so sexually demanding. Every time they came back down to the cabin, she would want to make love again. She was in such a high state of excitement that it was becoming infectious. All the crew could feel it radiating from her, and almost every one of the men had a pleasurable discomfort in his loins as they watched her, each with his own fantasy.

Her body glistening with water in the lamplight, she leaned against the cabin door, eyeing Julian, who was lying back on his bunk.

My God, they'd done it four times already tonight. Surely she couldn't— wouldn't—be able to do it again, he thought—not after all that swimming and dancing. But he was wrong. Her robe dropped to the floor once more, and he could almost see her pulsing to receive him.

"Dominique, don't you think we've had enough for one night?" he said weakly, but only too aware that in spite of his physical exhaustion his expectant cock was rising yet again.

"Certainly not," she crooned, leaning against the mahogany door, look- ing like some wanton maiden, her hair falling shiny and wet around her full breasts.

"I want you to want me again, Julian—I want you again, my love—I want you now." She was touching herself now, in a way which she knew would drive him half mad with desire. Massaging her nipples gently between her fingers, she then slipped one hand down to between her legs, two fingers beginning to slide in and out of her moist pink sex.

"Of course I want you," he said, his voice made hoarse with passion. "I want you too damn much—you're an enchantress, you know that—a little witch, and you're driving me mad."

"I want you, Julian," she moaned, still leaning against the door, her fingers now moving so rapidly, and her breathing so fast that he could see that she was about to come again.

He watched spellbound as she did, crying out his name.

"Je t'aime, Julian, je t'aime, mon homme." He saw her whole body quiver with her own ecstasy.

"Come over here," he said huskily. "My God, what have you done to me, Dominique—what have you done?"

"Nothing," she whispered, "nothing at all." Her eyes were wide with rapture as he immersed himself into her once again.

"I've just made you love me—*j'espère*—because I love you, Julian, I always will."

As Julian walked from his cabin to the upper deck where the crew were filming he saw a man silhouetted against a pile of rigging in the shadows.

He paused for a second, his actor's instincts sensing something unusual.

Thinking himself unseen, Hubert Croft was leaning against a furled sail, his eyes fixed on the distant, dancing figure of a naked Dominique. One of his hands was moving fast and furiously in the pocket of his baggy linen trousers, his eyes were half closed and his breathing harsh.

"What the devil do you think you're doing, Croft?" hissed Julian.

The Italian abruptly ceased what he was doing and stared at Julian.

"Well, well, well, if it isn't our Mr. Brooks come to check up on his Lolita," he sneered, seeming neither ashamed nor embarrassed to have been caught masturbating almost publicly. He removed his hand slowly from his trouser pocket, looking at Julian with a mocking smile.

"Jesus Christ, Croft, you're acting like a bloody pervert," said Julian in disgust. "If any of the crew saw what you were doing you'd be thrown off the set."

"Let you *not* be the one to cast stones, Julian old boy," said Croft, mimicking Julian's impeccable English in his grating voice. "If any of the men saw what *you* have been doing with that little slut—deliberately flaunting herself in front of them—you would not be thought of any longer as the second coming of Olivier, but rather a pathetic aging Lothario."

"I'm not going to bandy words with you, Croft," said Julian, feeling his face burn. He knew what the crew were all thinking about Dominique and himself. He couldn't blame them, either. "It's none of your damn business."

"Oh, but it *is* my business," smirked Scrofo. "And my dear chap, much as I, the producer of the film, admire your performance on the screen, your performance *off* it proves that you are nothing but a vain, shallow actor, attempting to retain your youth through having repeated sex with that innocent girl."

Oh, sure, thought Julian. Dominique was about as innocent as a basketful of adders. Where she had learned her siren skills he didn't dare think.

"I'm wanted on the set, Croft," he said tensely. "I'd prefer not to linger any longer in this conversation. Frankly it's making me ill."

"Not as ill as Mademoiselle Inès is going to feel when she reads yesterday's *Herald Examiner,*" said Scrofo.

"Oh? And what, pray, is so interesting about that?"

"Read it and weep," said Scrofo, "as will your fiancée, no doubt. As I told you before, Brooks, don't throw stones—you'll only get mud on your shoes."

He chortled harshly as he waddled back to the set, and Julian stood quite still. What could possibly be in the newspaper that might affect Inès? He groaned silently. He knew only too well what it could be: some gossip about him and Dominique. It wouldn't be the first time that he had been grist for the gossip-mongers' mills, but, by God, if it hurt Inès . . .

He walked quickly back to his cabin where his makeup man was busily sharpening eyebrow pencils.

"You haven't by any chance got a copy of yesterday's Los Angeles newspaper have you, old chap?" he asked Tim casually.

"Naw, guv, you know I only read the comics," said Tim cheerily, blotting Julian's sweating face with Kleenex. "But some of the boys get it, guv. I'll see what I can do."

"Thanks, Tim, I appreciate it," sighed Julian, wishing this night were over. Talking to Croft always left him with a sour taste in his mouth.

Tim went around to the crew asking for a copy of yesterday's paper, while Kittens was retailing to the wardrobe women, in excited indignation, the fact that she had seen Croft peeping voyeuristically at Dominique's nudity and playing with himself at the same time. Within an hour the entire unit knew what their producer had been doing, and their dislike of him reached new heights.

The following night the whole scene was shot again, this time with Dominique clothed in a series of veils. These worked perfectly well when she was in the water, but as soon as she was out of it, the see-through chiffon clung to her curves in the skimpy bikini underneath in such a suggestive way that Hubert again cornered Nick in his cabin after the very first shot. The crew were then treated to a screaming match between the two men that could have been heard far away in the highest guard tower of Ramona's villa. Eventually the two protagonists emerged, both grim-faced, to consult further with Agathe, Kittens and the wardrobe woman.

It appeared that Hubert thought Dominique's nipples were clearly visible through the flimsy, saturated material, the censor would be forced to use his sharpened scissors, and the scene would be a write-off.

Dominique was summoned away from Julian's cabin where the two were about to indulge in yet another amorous session. She stood sullen and pouting in her cabin, fuming that she'd had to leave her lover, as they fussed around her. Nick was furious, but he did see that Umberto had a point. During Dominique's dance the wet fabric rubbed itself against her breasts and excited her already prominent nipples until they became clearly visible from several yards away. It was impossible for the camera not to see them in all these shots unless they could somehow be camouflaged.

"I really don't see what all this *fuss* is about," sulked Dominique, longing to get back to Julian. "*All* women have breasts, I can't understand why you Americans are so prudish about showing them?"

Everyone ignored her as Kittens and the wardrobe woman conferred in hushed voices. Eventually the men were shooed out of the room while the women performed various experiments to try to conceal Dominique's pert papillae. But the more they pressed on flesh-colored pads and stuck them down with strong surgical adhesive, the more her nipples seemed to swell, pushing through the material like two acorns.

Dominique felt impatient, hating the whole infuriating performance. She was already in a state of advanced sexual arousal, and having her breasts poked and pushed only encouraged it. She just longed to be back cuddling up to Julian and feeling him inside her again.

Eventually the women were satisfied with their handiwork and Dominique was dismissed. She rushed back to Julian's cabin, where her lover waited, his erection long since deflated. When he saw Dominique's breasts covered with a curious network of masking tape, Band-Aids and flesh-colored silk, looking something like a cubist collage, he threw back his head and roared with laughter.

"What's so funny?"

"Darling heart, I'm sorry but they do look strange—like two perfect little peaches all bandaged up!"

"Not so little, thank you very much—I think you're a very rude man," said Dominique, giving him her most seductive smile. "And now, since you're not allowed to touch them"—she bounded friskily onto the tiny bunk bed—"I'll just have to play with this soft old thing." With that she took some moisturizer from the shelf next to the bed and began massaging the liquid on his slumbering cock. In no time Julian was back at full stand and he groaned ecstatically as she gently lowered her body onto him once again.

Dominique's sensual dance had excited practically all of the male crew members to such an extent that for the next few nights the whorehouses of Acapulco did a roaring trade.

Hubert Croft had found himself tremendously aroused by the girl's erotic dance. Although he had no feelings one way or another about Julian Brooks, thinking him merely a conceited but handsome actor who had just been lucky, Umberto felt angry and jealous that Dominique seemed so crazy about him. His only consolation was that the whore Inès seemed to be getting what she deserved. He knew the bitch was on the verge of a miscarriage, and it pleased him enormously that her fiancé was blatantly two-timing her with a girl young enough to be his own daughter.

The night following Dominique's dance scene, Ramona's small house party dined as usual on her candlelit terrace. Dominique was extremely tired, as well she might be, thought Scrofo, excusing herself soon after dinner to retire to her room.

Half an hour later, Hubert tapped at her door.

"Go away—please," the girl called out sleepily. "I'm asleep."

"I have to talk to you, Dominique," said the producer. "It's extremely urgent."

"Merde," he heard her mutter as she opened the sliding opaque glass doors to her bedroom.

"What do *you* want?" she asked sulkily, loping back into her room to sprawl sleepily on the edge of the bed. She hadn't bothered to put a robe on, and was wearing just a tiny baby-doll nightdress of sheer white cotton edged with *broderie anglaise* and blue ribbon. Umberto could see her matching panties as she looked up at him with bored resignation.

He never felt quite sure of himself in her presence. She seemed to possess the assurance of an adult, and never seemed intimidated by him, unlike so many others on the film.

"I think that your liaison with Julian Brooks must stop," said Hubert stonily, feeling the familiar tingling in his groin.

She laughed contemptuously. "It's none of your business, Mr. Croft. Whatever Julian and I do off the set has *nothing* to do with you."

"But it most certainly has, my dear," he said frostily. "Please *don't* forget that you're still a minor, and as producer of this film *I* am the one responsible for your welfare."

"Agathe is responsible for all that," yawned Dominique, leaning back cross-legged against the zebra-striped headboard, a challenging expression on her sulky face.

"And she doesn't know a thing about your sordid little affair, does she? You've been very clever, Dominique, very clever indeed. But if Agathe had been aboard the ship last night she would certainly have known about it. Everyone else does."

"So what?" said Dominique. "I'm doing nothing wrong."

Umberto's breath started to quicken, and lowering her eyes, Dominique saw to her dismay a small distention in his trousers. She raised her eyes quickly—*merde,* the pig was getting excited. *Quelle horreur.* She uncrossed her long tanned legs and tried unsuccessfully to pull her nightgown down a little more.

"If you told Agathe about it she wouldn't believe you anyway. She thinks I'm a blushing virgin—just like she is."

"And of course you didn't allow her on the ship to watch your dance, did you?" said Umberto ominously. "So she could see your disgusting behavior."

"Well, that was her idea," Dominique shrugged. "She had a migraine or something—she just wanted to go to bed."

How very convenient for Agathe, thought Umberto. She was obviously unable to bear the sight of her idol making love to this minx. "What does she think happens when you go into Mr. Brooks' locked trailer at lunchtime?" Umberto was genuinely curious.

"She thinks we're practicing our lines, of course, or maybe even having lunch," laughed Dominique. "Rehearsing—and that's exactly what does happen," she added defiantly, disconcerted because the fat man's expression had become more intense.

He took a step nearer the bed.

"That's what we were doing last night, Hubie—and you have no proof of anything else."

"Oh, don't I?" sneered Umberto. "What about these?" From behind his back he produced a large manila envelope which he threw on the bed. "Open it."

Slowly Dominique undid the flap, pulling out several black-and-white photographs.

Her hands flew to her mouth. "What are these? Where did you get them?"

"I'm sure you know perfectly well what they are," sneered Scrofo. "They are some photographs of you and Mr. Brooks which I took on the beach the day you were fornicating together in front of anyone who happened to be passing. *Slut*," he hissed. "French slut."

He suddenly felt totally omnipotent, as finally Dominique looked up at him with genuine fear in her eyes.

"What are you going to do with them?"

"That rather depends." Scrofo advanced slowly towards her, his bulk ominous in the semi-darkness of the room. "It depends on how nice you are to me."

"Nice? *Mais, c'est une blague! Non—non!*" Dominique tried to scramble across the huge bed, but despite his size Umberto was too fast for her. He grabbed her ankle and pulled her towards him as she screamed for help.

His huge body pressed her down onto the bed, and he clamped his hand over her mouth. *Merde,* the pig was strong, she thought with mounting panic, as she thrashed around trying to throw him off. To her disgust she became aware that he was trying to unzip his trousers with one hand as he moaned his litany of lust to her.

"Don't scream, Dominique—just be a good girl, a nice girl, you'll like it, I know how much you like it—you'll like it with me too—I'm good—just as good as Brooks." She tried to squirm away from him, but he was so heavy that she was pinned like a butterfly to a specimen board.

"Be a good girl now," he rasped, his mouth close to her ear. "A good nice little girl, and I won't show the photographs of you fucking Julian to your chaperone—because if I *do*"—his hand tightened sadistically over her face—"she will make sure that your parents hear about everything that's happened, and you'll be bundled back to St. Tropez in disgrace, faster than it would take you to unzip Julian's fly."

Dominique tried to scream out, but it was impossible with his clammy hand pressed hard over her mouth. She tried to raise her strong dancer's legs to kick him in the stomach before he could manage to force himself into her, but his sheer weight made it impossible.

Momentarily she lay still, the realization of what could happen paralyzing her. Agathe. Would she report back to Maman and Papa? Surely not—Dominique could twist Agathe around her little finger, the woman was always in such a daze.

Umberto continued to drone on in his horrible rasping voice, his erect penis pressing itself against her bare thigh. "Just be a good girl, Dominique—just be good, my dear, and when I've finished I will tear up all the pictures and you won't have to worry about anything anymore."

"No, get away!" she screamed with a sudden surge of strength, struggling more forcibly as a rough hand grabbed at the elastic around her panties and began to pull them down. The pungent smell of his vile cologne assailed her nostrils, and she threw her head from side to side as his bulbous lips drew closer.

At that moment there was a knock at the door and Agathe's shrill voice called out, "Dominique, are you all right?"

Dominique's eyes widened with relief, and triumphantly she looked into Umberto's bloated face. For a second he froze, then the knock came again.

"Dominique, I said, are you all right? I thought I heard you call out? Answer me, Dominique, otherwise I'll call the guards."

Umberto bent his gross head and whispered, "I'm going to take my hand off your mouth—and you better say you're all right or *I can promise you that you'll regret it*—right? No tricks now."

She nodded and gradually he released his hand. After a deep breath of air, she shouted towards the door, "Agathe, oh Agathe, thank God it's you. I've had such a scary dream—I feel so frightened."

"Let me in, *chérie*," Agathe ordered, worriedly rattling at the locked door. "Right now."

"No, no, don't come in," Dominique called, gloating exultantly at Umberto's face which was grotesquely contorted in anger and panic. "I'll come out to you—I want to sleep in your room tonight, Agathe. I've had such an awful nightmare."

"Of course, *chérie, viens,* hurry up. I'll take care of you."

Triumphantly Dominique rolled away from under the Italian and scampered over to the door, grabbing up a dressing gown and stuffing the photographs into a pocket.

"You haven't heard the last of this," Umberto whispered hoarsely as she glanced over at him from the door. "No one ever gets the better of me, you little slut—no one."

Dominique made no answer as she slid open the glass doors and fell into the security of Agathe's arms.

"Oh, Agathe, it was such a horrible nightmare," she sobbed, tears of relief running down her flushed cheeks.

"Hush, hush, don't cry, *chérie.* I'll take care of you, *ma petite,* come—come with me."

With her arms enfolding the shaking girl, Agathe led Dominique into her room and locked the door behind them.

Umberto Scrofo listened carefully to his telephone caller, blue jowls creasing into a wider and wider smile, as he heard the news which made him so pleased.

"In Paris, you say—you found him in prison?" He listened again and then laughed, "French drunks—I've seen 'em—they're all the same. They'd sell their grandmothers for a glass of absinthe. How much does he want?" He frowned when he heard the reply. "One hundred thousand francs, that's ridiculous—I wouldn't pay him nearly as much. Offer him ten thousand."

The caller continued to jabber on, and Umberto's demeanor became increasingly ebullient. "Tell him to call me himself—no, better not—the poor bastard probably can't afford it. I'll call him. What did you say his name was?" Umberto scribbled down a name and a telephone number in Paris, saying softly to himself as he hung up, "Yves Moray, how very, very interesting."

Julian had been in a turmoil of guilt since his two nights of frenzied sex during the shooting of Dominique's nude scene. He knew only too well that everything he was doing with Dominique was completely and utterly wrong, but his body recently seemed not to belong to him anymore. It was nothing more than a series of raw nerve endings, all connected to his cock, which swelled expectantly each time he found himself near her.

They had made love for hour after hour in the cabin and now he could barely walk. Last night he'd arrived back at the hotel just as the gray fingers of dawn were creeping over the hills.

When he staggered into the bathroom he started thinking of their love-making, and immediately became hard again. He stared at himself in the mirror in shocked self-disgust. He was either Superman or on the way to becoming certifiable, and although this amazing virility which Dominique inspired had enslaved him, he knew that he was in the throes of a selfish obsession which could well destroy his relationship with Inès forever.

He had tried to obtain a copy of the newspaper Croft had mentioned, but no one had it or seemed to have read it, so he dismissed it from his mind, thinking that it was obviously just some cheap ploy to annoy him. Croft was not worth worrying about. He was a low life whom Julian found intensely disagreeable. He knew Inès disliked the Italian too. She had told him so after Ramona's party. Did *anyone* have a good word or kind feelings for Hubert Croft? Obviously not.

In the bedroom Inès awoke from a drug-induced slumber as she heard Julian in the shower. Dr. Langley had sent her pills to help her sleep at night, because she was so inactive with nothing to do all day except read, or stare at the view, that to sleep at night had become more and more difficult.

"Are you all right, darling?" she murmured when Julian quietly slipped into his side of the big double bed. "You've been working so hard lately, such long hours, I've been worried about you."

"I'm fine, just exhausted," he whispered, a painful pang of guilt hitting him like a physical blow. "Please don't concern yourself about me, sweetheart, just worry about yourself and our baby. Goodnight, my darling." He kissed her gently on the forehead and turned over, pretending to sleep.

Inès stared into the darkness of the room. Her finely tuned instincts told her something was wrong. She knew all about Julian's sexual past and the succession of liaisons with every single one of his leading ladies. Surely he wasn't having an affair with a sixteen-year-old girl? Not now, when the two of them were in such harmony together, and she was finally giving him the child that he'd always wanted. Surely he couldn't contemplate doing such a thing—could he?

Although not an analytical man or one to share confidences, Julian felt he had to talk to someone or else go mad. He decided to confide his problem to Nick Stone, whom he believed to be discreet, a man he could trust. The day after the dancing scenes were wrapped, filming finished early. Also

Dominique wasn't around to bat her eyelashes coquettishly and bewitch his cock into a state of perpetual tumescence, so on the way back from location he asked Nick, "Fancy a drink, old chap?"

"Good idea—how about hitting La Perla? We can watch the divers—and I don't know about you, but I feel like diving into several margaritas," said Nick. He was in high spirits about the film, although his hatred for Scrofo was smoldering away just beneath the surface. He tried hard to control it, but Umberto seemed capable of inflaming his anger with only the slightest provocation.

At La Perla, Julian and Nick sat at a corner table, away from the tourists. As soon as they had ordered, Julian began to unburden himself.

"I don't know what the hell to do, Nick," he said. "I'm truly up the proverbial shit creek without a paddle."

Several young muscular Mexican boys were crawling like spiders up the steep rocks behind him as they prepared to perform their famous death-defying dives into the ocean far below, but the two men ignored them.

"I presume you've noticed what's been going on?" said Julian.

Nick smiled ruefully. "Kiddo, you might as well have stood on the Empire State Building and yelled it out," he said. "I guess you mean you and the girl?"

"I certainly do," said Julian glumly. "The girl. I can't get enough of her, Nick. I don't want to do this, but I can't stop myself. Christ, I'm thirty-seven years old, for God's sake—old enough to be her father. I hate myself for it, but she's honestly bewitched me."

Nick listened sympathetically, glad that he didn't suffer similar problems with women—maybe that's what comes of being too handsome, he thought. Julian had always been romantically incontinent, but who could blame him with the way women had always thrown themselves at him? "Do you love Dominique?" he asked.

"Hell, *no*—of *course* I bloody don't. I'm *madly* in love with Inès—at least I think I am—that's why I'm in such a bloody state about Dominique. Every time I'm *near* that little minx, I just have to have her. I think I'm going mad—I think I'm going stark staring bonkers, Nick."

"Of course, you're not," said Nick. "You're not crazy, Julian—you're a man, just like the rest of us."

"A man doesn't behave like this," said Julian bitterly. "A man is faithful to the woman he loves, especially when the woman is as wonderful as Inès, and lying flat on her back all day long to save our baby."

"So why *do* you do it?"

"She's a witch—I've told her as much," breathed Julian. "A siren; a Circe. She's springtime—she's innocence—and she's unbelievably sexy. Sex with her is *incredible,* indescribably amazing. She's *sixteen,* Nick, and she makes love like—like a goddess. I want her whenever I'm near her—she's like a drug and I've become a complete addict."

They ordered more margaritas, and watched as the first of the Mexican divers took off like a swallow from the peak of the high rock, hitting the water at the exact moment when the seventh wave crashed into the shallow gully. As the boy's head appeared triumphantly above the water and the assembled patrons cheered and applauded, Julian leaned forward.

"I want to end it, Nick, but every time I manage to make that decision I see her again and this bloody thing"—he pointed angrily at his crotch—"changes my mind for me, and what's more, so does the rest of me."

Nick laughed. "Then I guess you do have a problem—I can't really help you. I wish I could. I can only say that every man on this film would give his balls to fuck Dominique."

"Even Sir Crispin?" laughed Julian.

Nick smiled. "Perhaps not him, but I've talked to the guys—I've heard what they say about her. It isn't just you, Julian—you're not alone. She's a mantrap, she's like a walking aphrodisiac. Every single guy has got the hots for her, and the more they see her the more they want her—and how they envy you! I think she's just sex appeal personified, it's like some kind of gift."

"That's for damn sure," said Julian ruefully.

"Monroe, Brigitte Bardot, they're gonna have to look to their laurels when our kid hits the screen," said Nick. "I think she'll be the biggest female star that Hollywood's had for years."

"Yes, well, that doesn't exactly solve my problem," said Julian, "which is simply that the woman I love is off games until our baby is born, while I *cannot* stop being self-indulgent and fucking this nymphet. Wherever and whenever I can."

"Listen, Julian," said Nick. "I'm not a man of the world, I'm nowhere in your league—I'm just a simple Greek guy who happens to be happily married and wants very much to stay that way." But let me give you a bit of advice."

"What is it?" said Julian. "For God's sake, I'll do anything that will help me to get out of this mess."

"There's only one way," Nick said simply. "If you really love Inès you've gotta pretend Dominique doesn't exist. You're an actor—you can do that, can't you?"

Julian looked skeptical.

"Cold turkey," said Nick. "It's the only way, Julian, the only way to do it."

Inès sat on the hotel balcony numb with shock. A slim manila envelope, addressed to her, had been placed on her breakfast tray that morning. A wave of nausea had engulfed her when she'd opened it. Blurred black-and-white photographs, taken with a telescopic lens, revealed a couple entwined on a beach.

There was no mistaking Julian's back, just as there was no mistaking the slim, sensual legs and long black hair of Dominique, her body hidden from the camera by Julian's. Inès was aghast as she read the enclosed press clipping from Harrison Carroll's Los Angeles gossip column:

Mr X, the handsome but not yet divorced matinée idol, has been "oh-so-close" with the beautiful but very young Miss Y, while they toil together on a tropical location. This column is concerned as to how attractive Miss Z, the fiancée of the former, must be coping with the situation.

Who could have hated Inès enough to send this disgusting, loathsome piece of gossip, take these perverted photos? She knew the answer only too well. There was just one person in the world odious enough to want to hurt her so much. Umberto Scrofo.

What was Julian doing? One blissful year together, a baby on the way, a wonderfully romantic life, the most fulfilling happiness she had ever known, and Julian had started to cheat on her. Why? What was he getting from Dominique that he could not get from her? She knew the answer to that, if she knew men. Gloomily she stared out of the window. He was getting sex, and plenty of it. But was it just sex, or was it something more?

She mustn't let Julian suspect that she knew of this affair, or behave any differently towards him. Any change of attitude from her would cause him to ask questions that she didn't want to answer. Certainly he had been no less affectionate or considerate towards her in the past few days, even though lovemaking had been forbidden. What did he say about that to Dominique, a girl not quite seventeen? Did he confide in her the truth that his love life with Inès was suddenly nonexistent because of her pregnancy? Or did he lie to her, saying Inès was cold, unaffectionate, did not give him what he wanted? Inès knew that old routine. Her past lovers had often told her how disappointing their wives were in bed.

Her hands cupped her still-flat stomach. Dominique—young, French, beautiful. Maybe she should take some small measure of comfort in the fact that Dominique was so like herself—Julian had remarked on the amazing resemblance between them when they had first met the girl.

It was all because of Scrofo that she had not had enough time to spend with Julian. Scrofo, who had made her so involved in his script problems. Scrofo, who had made her life so miserably stressful recently, and Scrofo, who had abused her so brutally as a girl, causing her to suffer the pain of imminent miscarriage. If only she had succeeded in killing him, none of this would be happening.

Inès fingered her lucky bracelet of amber and silver. That loathsome creature was ruining her life. She had to do something about him. But what? He was the producer of her fiancé's movie, he had power and influence, she was just the girlfriend. But she had survived Scrofo's monstrous humiliation before. She would again—she had to.

Without doubt it was he who had sent her the vile photographs, planted that sickening blind item. Could he also possibly have contacted the dreaded *Confidential* magazine too, telling them of her past? Knowing his sick mind, that would obviously be his next step.

A pair of tropical birds was singing outside her balcony, chasing each other around the lush foliage. Beyond the palm trees Inès could see the hard red tennis court, hear the thwack of ball against catgut, the excited cries of the players.

This is a war, but one neither of you will win, she thought. I've been in plenty of battles before and I have come out of them intact. She smiled grimly to the empty room.

You, Mademoiselle Dominique, even though you are more than a dozen years younger than me, and a little sex bomb to boot, will be quite easy to eliminate. Scrofo, however, would be another problem entirely. Until he was out of her life she would never have the secure future she craved.

17

Ramona Armande's dinner party for Dominique's seventeenth birth-
day was a command performance for all the principals in the cast. Filming
had been going well, and everyone seemed to be in high spirits as they
gathered on the starlit terrace to toast the girl. But Dominique herself was
in a sullen mood. She had been given a horrid shock when Julian arrived
with Inès, who had pleaded with Dr. Langley to allow her to go to this party.
Inès had decided that she must fight fire with fire. Even if that meant a
possible risk to the baby, it was better than losing Julian to that pubescent
Jezebel.

Julian had expressed guilty surprise when Inès told him that the doctor
was allowing her to get up and do a little more, but he was delighted to see
how gorgeous she looked when she was dressed and ready. More ravishing
than ever—more desirable. He knew that sex was still out of bounds for
them but he realized how much he truly loved her.

"I love you, Mrs. Brooks," he whispered as they walked arm in arm into
Ramona's marble-and-crystal palace. "I can't wait to be married to you."

She smiled up at him radiantly as they strode into the room, the two of
them a perfect picture of togetherness. Inès, pale but ravishing in a Balenciaga sheath of apricot chiffon, a color which complemented her luxuriant
champagne-colored hair, Julian, as heart-stoppingly handsome as ever, in a
black voile shirt and white linen trousers.

Dominique drew in her breath sharply and gritted her teeth. Her finger-nails cut deeply into the palms of her hands, and she was flushed with fury. How could Julian show up with *her*? Why hadn't he told her that he was coming to her birthday party with Inès? She was supposed to be bedridden. *Merde*. This would certainly ruin her party. Particularly since the horrible Hubert Croft, who she had tried to keep away from the past several days, kept glaring at her with a secret disgusting smile. She shuddered. She hated that man. He was a sick monster, and she wished he was dead.

As for Hubert Croft, he thought himself quite a *bella figura* tonight in his overly tight black silk trousers and his white frilled Mexican shirt. But he too was also extremely surprised to see Inès. Surprised and angry, even though she'd been doing exactly what he'd instructed her to do. The six or seven times that he'd ordered her to persuade Julian to choose a particular scene, she had always managed to convince him to do it.

Hubert had been delighted that she was ill and no doubt tortured by the possibility of a miscarriage. Serves her right, the murdering whore. He'd put her out of his mind recently, concentrating all his attention on over-seeing the movie and on keeping the studio in Hollywood up-to-date on what was happening.

Now here she was once again, the picture of elegance, dressed up like a fashion plate, hanging on to the arm of her famous fiancé, and smiling as charmingly as if butter wouldn't melt in her slut-mouth. His lips closed in a grim line as he observed Inès' perfect composure across the terrace. Surely she must have received the photographs he'd sent? It was meant to be his little joke, just to make her suffer more as she lay in bed day after day. Obviously the joke had misfired, because here she was looking radiant and carefree, and gazing at Julian as if he were Romeo, and she his Juliet. He'd like to wipe that sweet smile off her face. Oh, how he wanted to hurt this woman who had almost managed to put an end to him. He fingered his scar, which had started to itch again. Well, it wasn't too late—not at all. There was a week left to go on the movie, still time left to give Mademoi-selle Inès Juillard a real taste of what she deserved.

Ramona was also thrown into a tizzy. She had a superstitious dread of thirteen people at her dinner table and Sir Crispin had brought his boy-friend, Tony, who had unexpectedly flown over from London. There was little she could do about it other than cross her fingers, pray to the blessed Virgin and nervously twist her elaborate necklace of gold-and-amber beads. She had placed the guests with her usual care tonight, with some help from Agathe, who had become friendly and helpful to her in so many ways. Ramona was pleased with her natural ability to bring shy people out of their shells.

Ramona drifted off to her winter dining room, where the glittering table for twelve twinkled with crystal and silver. Polished mirror placemats reflected the white lilies and hothouse roses which had been flown in specially on her private plane only that morning from Mexico City. Thirteen for dinner. Damn, damn, damn. She didn't want to make a fuss, but she felt it was a terrible omen. She ordered her butler to set another place, and after a few deft arrangements was satisfied that all would be well, though she hoped that no one else would notice the unlucky number.

Dinner proved a great success, and no one paid much attention to Dominique's barely disguised sulking. The oysters Mornay were delicious—several people asked for more—and the roast partridge, flown in from England, was a triumph.

"I'd like to make a toast," Nick said, raising his glass of vintage Krug. "To our new young star. Happy birthday, Dominique—we all love you, darling." He had been persuaded to come to Ramona's, just this once tonight, by a prettily pouting Dominique. He could hardly refuse.

Inès winced as everyone raised their glasses to Dominique and an enormous pink birthday cake, ablaze with seventeen long sparklers, was wheeled in. Dominique cut the cake prettily, posing flushed and excited for photographers from *Look* and *Photoplay*. She looked over at Julian, who smiled back at her coolly.

Hubert Croft made a pompous speech in his croaking voice, then Sir Crispin said a few amusing and well-chosen words, and finally Julian was cajoled into speaking. He rose, not one person at the table missing the irony of this situation: Julian and his two mistresses, both hanging on his every syllable. After he had finished a brief simple toast, finding it difficult to meet Dominique's wounded stare, there was a sudden silence. To break the tension, Irving Frankovitch decided to stand up and take the limelight.

"To a young actress of charm, talent and grace beyond her years," he began. "We are delighted—" Suddenly, a spasm of pain contorted his face; he weaved slightly and then slumped back into his chair, breathing heavily, his face ashen.

"I'm terribly sorry, but I don't feel at all well," he wheezed as Shirley rushed over to him.

Suddenly Inès too felt a wave of sickness, and she had a terrible feeling that if she did not leave the table at once she might embarrass herself dreadfully.

The baby, oh, the baby, she thought, as she felt the familiar and agonizing empty sensation deep down in the pit of her stomach. She looked towards Julian pleadingly, who was shocked at her pallor. Damn. He had told her he didn't think she could come out, but she had assured him that the doctor had said she could. Now she was the color of chalk and looked on the verge of collapse. He started to help her from the room when there was a piercing scream from Shirley Frankovitch as her husband fell heavily forward onto the table, his bald head smashing down on a Limoges plate of birthday cake with a sickening crash. The entire table was now in an uproar as all the guests started up, their faces greenish white, dashing for the bathrooms, some collapsing onto the floor with groans of pain.

Ramona was in a panic. "What on earth is happening?" she called to her dumbstruck butler, who couldn't seem to move. It was exactly as she had feared. The curse of thirteen at dinner was coming true with a vengeance.

"For God's sake, call a doctor," Nick shouted, unable to control the great tide of sickness which engulfed him. "Get an ambulance."

The stunned butler and waiters all stood rooted to the spot with fear, as if by moving they too might be infected by this terrible plague.

"We've all been poisoned."

Inès had no recollection of collapsing, no memory of the drive to the hospital, the trip in Ramona's private plane to Mexico City, or the long, complicated and dangerous operation which had been performed to save her life.

When she finally regained consciousness, it was several days later. She lay in a narrow white room, tubes and needles connecting her to various drips, and a pale, frantic Julian standing at the foot of her bed.

"Darling, oh, my darling, thank God," he cried softly, covering her arms and face with solicitous kisses. Then he held her face between his warm and reassuring hands, kneeling on the floor next to her bed, gazing at her with wonder, sadness and, most of all, with love.

"I thought I'd lost you, my angel. I thought you'd gone." His tired eyes were tearful, and Inès saw the exhaustion in his face.

"What happened?" She heard her own voice as if from a great distance. "We were at the party, then I can't remember anything. What was it, Julian? What happened?"

"Food poisoning," he said. "We all got it, everyone who was at the dinner. Some had it worse than others. You were one of the unlucky ones, I'm afraid."

"Where am I?" She looked out of the window, expecting to see palm trees and luxuriant foliage, but seeing only the concrete slabs of a city.

"Mexico City, darling—the best hospital in Mexico. Ramona sent us here in her plane. Oh, God, Inès, you nearly *died*. It's made me realize what a total fool I've been, what a bloody, stupid fool. I'm sorry, darling, I'm so sorry." He started to weep tears of both remorse and relief.

"Don't, darling, please don't." She lovingly stroked his hair and touched his tear-stained cheeks. She had never seen him cry before. Then her hands went to her flat stomach.

"The baby?" Her eyes were pleading now, filled with tears. "I've lost the baby, haven't I?"

He nodded sadly.

"Darling, listen." He sat on the bed, holding her close to him, filling his voice with optimism. "Please don't think about the baby—it's tragic, I know, but you're young, you'll have another baby, the doctor said so—many babies." He put a hand to her trembling lips, holding her closer as she started to sob.

"No, Inès, no," he said firmly. "*Stop* it. Please don't feel self-pity. It really could have been so much worse."

"How?" She tried to stop crying, but found she couldn't. "How much worse?"

"Irving Frankovitch is dead."

"Oh, God, no!" Inès' hand flew to her mouth. "How? Why?"

"According to the autopsy it was those bloody oysters Mornay we all ate. Apparently they were flown in from Mexico City the day before, but they were all rotten." He shook his head. "God, darling, you can't believe how sick everyone was. I've *never* seen anything like it, but poor old Irving didn't stand a chance. The old boy sort of crumpled up, collapsed in agony, and just died in front of us before the doctor could even get there. Sir Crispin got it very badly, too, but he's a tough old bird—he seems to have recovered now."

"And Dominique, how is she?" Inès tried to keep her voice expressionless as she watched Julian's reaction carefully.

"About the same as the others, I suppose," Julian replied simply. "I haven't spoken to her." This was the truth. "The only person who didn't get sick was Ramona."

He wanted to stay off the subject of Dominique. He had been burdened with even more guilt and shame ever since the dinner party. He had seen his weakness for what it was: purely and simply the lure of flesh, the lust of a greedy, selfish lecher who cares nothing for anyone or anything other than himself. An aging man making love to a teenager. He felt ridiculous and weak.

He despised himself for his affair with Dominique, for allowing it to get out of hand, for stupidly allowing it to become a subject for common gossip. He now realized that he would hate himself forever if he did anything to hurt Inès. But he *had* hurt her—he could clearly see the pain in her face which she was trying so hard to disguise.

"Why not Ramona?" Inès' voice sounded weak. "Why didn't she get sick?"

"She hates oysters—never eats them at all," Julian told her. "It was a stroke of luck that she didn't—she was able to organize the panicking servants, telephone doctors and arrange the ambulance and the plane for you. God, darling, it was ghastly."

"It must have been." Inès' eyes started to close. She felt so tired, but still clung tightly to Julian's hand. "I don't remember ... I must sleep now, darling. Do you mind?"

He kissed her pale forehead. "Of course not. Sleep tight, angel," he whispered. "I love you, Inès—so much. I'll be right here when you wake up. I'll always be waiting for you, my love. Always."

Dominique had tried continuously to contact Julian. She, like the others, had suffered from the particularly virulent bout of salmonella food poisoning, and it had left her feverish and vomiting for twenty-four hours, frail and listless for several days.

The doctors had advised Hubert Croft that it would be unwise to shoot in the tropical heat while the actors were still in such a weakened state. The insurance company in L.A. had screamed their heads off, but the doctor remained adamant. The only people he would allow to work were Ramona, who had not been affected, and Julian, who had barely touched the oysters so had suffered little. But there were no scenes in *Cortez* which involved Ramona and Julian alone, so the crew and technicians sat idly by in the cafés and on the beaches, drinking beer and tequila punches and playing cards, while the insurance company fumed and Umberto weakly croaked out his instructions and sent long telegrams from his sickbed to the studio.

When Dominique hadn't been able to reach Julian, she had presumed he was just too sick to answer the telephone. But when Agathe reported that he had gone to Mexico City to be with Inès, Dominique was beside herself.

She stayed sobbing for hours in her room, not eating, playing Edith Piaf records of love and betrayal, miserably unhappy that Julian had not contacted her, not even sent her a note, a flower, anything. So this was the pain of rejected love which Piaf sang about. Well, she was certainly experiencing it for herself and she hated it—her heart felt empty and hollow and she had no appetite at all.

Whenever Agathe or Ramona called to see if she was all right, she sent them away, then buried her head in the pillow, weeping until she felt that she had no more tears left. Even Hubert Croft came to visit once, knocking at the door, but she had screamed "Fuck off" to him with such a volley of hysterical fury that he hadn't returned.

She had heard from Ramona about what had happened to Inès, and the thought that Julian was with his fiancée made her sick with jealousy. After discovering the name of the hospital in Mexico City she had instructed Ramona's operator to place a call.

When she heard Julian's voice on the crackling line, her knees started shaking.

"Julian," she whispered. "Oh, Julian, *mon amour,* is that you?"

"Dominique?" His voice was hushed as he stood in the corridor outside Inès' room. "Dominique—how are you?"

"Oh Julian, Julian—how *could* I be? I'm *terrible,*" she cried, starting to weep softly into the telephone. "I've missed you so much, but I didn't hear anything from you—nothing, nothing—oh Julian, what is happening to you—to us?"

There was a long silence before Julian answered.

"Dominique, what I am going to say to you is going to hurt you very much, I know, but I have to say it—I must say it now, otherwise I'm being a coward—and I *am,* Dominique—I've been the most terrible coward and I despise myself for it."

"What do you mean?" she asked, a feeling of panic rising within her.

"We can not go on, Dominique," he said. "We can't—we just can't—it has to end."

"No," she moaned. "No, Julian, you can't mean it—I will *die*—I *swear* it—I'll kill myself."

"Hush, silly little girl, you'll do absolutely no such thing." His voice had a stern authoritative tone—almost fatherly, she thought bitterly.

"I was going to tell you properly, Dominique, when I returned to Acapulco, I was going to tell you face-to-face—not like this on the telephone. But now that you have called, I must confess."

"Confess what?" she whispered. "What, Julian, *mon amour, l'amour de ma vie?*"

"Stop it, Dominique," he said. "Darling child—and you *are* a child, Dominique—I don't want to hurt you, I *never* wanted to hurt you—I loved you—in my fashion."

"I know you did," she breathed. "I know that—when you made love to me I knew how much you loved me."

"But it's not going to *work,* Dominique," he said firmly. "It *can't* and it *won't.*"

"Why?" she asked. "You love me—you said it many times. Why can't it work?"

"Because I'm in love with Inès," he said simply, "and my life, my future is with her. I know that this is hard for you to understand, Dominique—and God knows I feel like a first-rate bastard for telling you like this, but even before the food poisoning I was going to tell you that it was all over between us. Our affair, my darling girl, must end."

"No, Julian, it's not true!" she cried.

"Please, Dominique darling—*please try* to understand. I know you're young. You're a baby. I'm twenty years older than you. You need to be with someone of your own age. It could never work. I don't want to hurt you but this must be the end." He could hear her sobs but he continued, "Please understand, darling girl, please."

"No," she sobbed. "I can't—I won't understand."

"You must," he whispered. "You *will,* my darling child. I know you will. Now be a good girl—go back to bed and tomorrow you'll start forgetting all about me—good-bye, my darling."

"Never," said Dominique, tears running down her face. "I'll never forget you, Julian, how can I?"

But there was nothing more to be heard from Mexico City. The line was dead. Sobbing, Dominique threw herself on the bed, buried her head in her pillow and finally cried herself to sleep.

And some three hundred miles away in a stark hospital room, Inès quietly closed the door, a faint smile on her lips, having listened to all of Julian's conversation.

Dominique eventually decided that weeping over Julian wasn't worth it. Her pragmatic French brand of common sense took over, and she decided that she had been a complete fool to fall in love with a man the same age as her father. Yes, he had been a wonderful lover, he had taught her a great deal about sex, but then so had Gaston. Perhaps now was the time to put their lessons into practice.

Two days after speaking to Julian over the telephone she had recovered, and her natural youthful energy returned. She put on her beach clothes, and knocking on Agathe's door, called that she was heading for Caleta Beach to go water-skiing, did Agathe want to come? The door was slightly ajar so she pushed it open wider and saw, to her surprise, Agathe fast asleep on the bed. She was wearing a man's dirty white shirt, an old rag was bunched up under her chin, and a large album crammed with what looked like press clippings and photographs lay on the floor next to the bed.

"Agathe," Dominique said softly, "want to come skiing with me?" There was a groan from the sleeping woman, so Dominique shrugged, closed the door and skipped off to the beach.

She was seventeen, gorgeous and a budding movie star. The world was hers for the taking. Young men whistled wherever she went, and she smiled back at them. There was nothing for her to feel sad or down about, nothing, not even Julian Brooks. He was a middle-aged man, she was young—young and free and beautiful. She could have her pick of men.

She took one of Ramona's jeeps to drive to the beach. The soft breeze blew her hair across her face, and she could smell the tang of the ocean and the aroma of tacos cooking in the little beach restaurant. As she came nearer she could hear mariachis playing and see teenagers dancing and enjoying the glorious day. She parked the car, conscious of the many eyes watching her. Dominique always enjoyed people staring, and she swung her hips in her snug shorts as she walked.

She quickened her stride as she saw a tall, tanned boy with yellow curls looking at her, smiling invitingly with eyes that were bluer than the sea.

"Hi. Wanna Coke?" he asked as soon as she entered the bar. She nodded. When he brought it over to her, she noted with some interest his strongly muscled arms and sculpted chest. How firm and deeply bronzed they were. In contrast, she noticed that he had tiny golden hairs like down all over his arms. Very pretty indeed, she thought. How exciting to have those arms around me. He was good-looking, too. Not the handsomest man in the world but young and sexy and very virile.

"An' then maybe you an' I can go water-skiing?" He grinned lazily, and Dominique smiled back.

"Would you like that?" he said.

"I love water-skiing," she told him. "I know *just* the place to go." And her eyes strayed down to the bulge in his shorts.

Agathe awoke just when Dominique closed her door. At first she didn't know where she was, and then it all came back to her. In the week since the salmonella outbreak, she had thought of nothing else.

Fool. She was a fool and an idiot. She had failed to do what she had planned so carefully. It had been a faultless scheme—the perfect murder which she had read about long ago in one of her books in the cellar in Paris, but it had backfired badly. Her plot had killed the wrong person. Agathe hadn't really spoken more than a dozen words to Irving Franko- vitch—a nice enough man, now dead because of her ineptitude.

She had bought some oysters at the local market some days before

Dominique's birthday party, and had hidden them in a windowsill just outside her room. The day of the party she had helped Ramona and the servants set the table and had supervised the staff as they brought in the first course of oysters Mornay. Unknown to them, she had inserted an eyedropper into the rotting oysters and dripped a tiny drop of their poison onto each fresh oyster. One of the bad ones, however, as well as some slightly poisoned oysters, she put on the plate intended for Inès. The Mornay sauce, Agathe assumed, would disguise the taste of the rotten oyster, and Inès would die soon after she swallowed it.

But Sir Crispin had unexpectedly brought a friend, and Ramona had not consulted Agathe about changing the place settings. Irving Frankovitch had eaten the oysters meant for Inès. Agathe's *soi-disant* perfect murder was ruined.

She had bungled it badly, very badly indeed. It was Inès who should have died . . . Inès the whore . . . the murderess . . . the traitor . . . the enemy slut. Agathe's hatred for her was so intense that it was almost like a burning coal in her chest. She moaned, clutching Julian's tattered shirt to her lips, sniffing the cotton fabric, trying to find a taste of him, his scent, his essence, his sweat.

Where is he now? she thought. With *her,* in Mexico City, planning their wedding day, the birth of their baby, their life together in London? *No!*

Agathe sat bolt upright in Ramona's silky lime-green-sheeted bed, staring at an enormous painting of some huge butterflies of all shades and varieties. She was trembling violently, both from the aftereffects of the self-inflicted food poisoning and from pure hatred. She looked around the silk-paneled room decorated with every species of butterfly imaginable. Her heart was beating so fast she thought it would burst, and she pounded her fists on the mattress in an uncontrollable fury.

First the woman had been Inès Dessault. Then Inès Juillard and within the next few weeks she would be Inès Brooks—Mrs. Julian Brooks. "No . . . no." Agathe was crooning softly now, feverishly turning her amber rosary around her neck. "It can't be. It can't happen. She will *not* marry him. She cannot. She *will not.*"

Two people now seemed to be in possession of her psyche, each battling for supremacy. There was Agathe Guinzberg the prim chaperone, the spinster ballet teacher—polite, quiet and well-mannered. And then there was Agathe the devil, the woman who slaked her lust for Julian Brooks every night on her bed, in the green onyx bath, on the floor . . . whispering his name, rubbing herself fiercely with his shirt, kissing his photographs, moaning with infatuated madness.

She could not stop herself anymore. Just the thought of him made her until only the rough touch of his shirt could ease the burning between her legs.

Last week, when she had sat on a canvas chair next to Sir Crispin, watching Julian laugh, studying the tiny beads of sweat on his muscled chest, right there in the chair she had felt the waves rise within her. She could almost feel him entering her as she squeezed her thighs together tightly until she reached a plateau of pleasure which had been unknown to her a few weeks ago.

It was as though a dam had burst inside her. She couldn't stop. Six, seven, eight times a day, whispering her love's name, she reached more and more tumultuous orgasms. But once—oh, God, just once—she wanted *him* to make love to her, to fuse that magnificent body with hers. She yearned for that.

Agathe was still technically a virgin and had only a vague idea of what a naked man even looked like, but last week, she had even stolen one of the phallic-shaped candles Ramona kept for her winter dining room, and now this, too, was used to pleasure herself.

Thirty-one years of frigidity exploded into lust as Agathe found herself on a merry-go-round of erotic enslavement without a partner to satisfy her. Julian belonged to her. He was her destiny—her man—she had to win him away from Inès. He had to know how much Agathe loved him—how they were meant to be together.

Despairingly, she did it again now, almost viciously—chafing, hurting herself with the blue shirt which was now not much more than a tattered rag. Afterward, exhausted, she tried to think. She *had* to think, she knew she must try to end this obsession with Julian—his face, his body, his eyes, his cock which she had glimpsed once, outlined by yellow bathing trunks when he was playing ball in the water with some of the crew.

She knew that what she was doing and what was happening to her was a sin, but she was no longer in control of herself.

She rang for some coffee and papaya, and while unsuccessfully trying to read the *Acapulcan News,* she thought again of how her plan had failed. It had been a good plan—an excellent plan, but the next one had to be absolutely foolproof.

18

*T*here were only a few days of shooting left, and Inès began to feel better both physically and emotionally. Although saddened by her miscarriage, she was assured that she could have more children, and there was the consolation that the experience had brought her closer to Julian again. He had confessed his affair with Dominique, apologizing so profusely and so fiercely that Inès forgave him. Now she could visit the set to watch him work again, and she went every day, trying not to be intimidated by Scrofo and his cold, deadly stare.

Much to Scrofo's chagrin, the sexual electricity between Julian and Dominique had fizzled out completely. He had tried to cause a chasm between Inès and Julian by sending her the scandalous photographs he had bribed a local photographer to take the day Julian and Dominique had gone to the island. The pictures were excellent but his ploy hadn't worked, for Inès and Julian were still together. Stupid bitch, she had forgiven him. To take a man back into her bed when she knew he'd been fucking another woman—she didn't deserve to be happy.

Scrofo followed Inès one night when she took a solitary walk along the beach, away from the shooting; then he cornered her.

"You think you're safe now, don't you—whore," he said, his eyes gleaming a sulphurous yellow in the humid darkness as he grabbed her arm, holding it too tightly.

"Let go of me, Scrofo," Inès said calmly, realizing that no one was around to help her.

His grip became more viselike as she repeated, "Please let me go."

"I'll let go of you when I'm good and ready, whore," he hissed. "You got my little present, I presume?"

"If you mean those filthy photographs—yes, I received them. And I tore them up," she said coldly.

"Of course—of course you did. You didn't want to look at snaps of your fiancé making love to his underage paramour, did you?"

"Look, Scrofo, why are you doing this? I did *everything* you asked of me."

In spite of herself Inès felt hot tears stinging her eyelids. Still weak from surgery, she detested this man so much that the mere touch of his hand filled her with loathing.

"*Every* scene that you sent to Julian I persuaded him to do—for weeks I did that, Scrofo. Surely that's enough for you?"

"No—it'll *never* be enough," he croaked. "It's a small price to pay for *this.*"

He pushed his neck closer to reveal in ghastly detail the puckered scar tissue. She could almost see the surgeon's stitches in his flesh.

"*You* did this, bitch, and you must be punished. I need to punish you much, much more—and you will be when the magazine comes out. You certainly will be." He laughed triumphantly. "That will make you squirm."

"What magazine?" she asked.

"Ah, that's *my* little secret," he gloated. "But the whole of America, in fact the whole of the world, will see the pictures of Dominique and your fiancé screwing each other—censored of course," he sneered. "Then the whole world will know about you and your whoring past."

"How will they know? How—what have you done?" cried Inès. "Whatever I did to you . . . whatever happened was *years* ago. Can't you forget it, Scrofo—leave me in peace? Why do you need to do this now? Why?"

"I can *never* forget, slut—never," Scrofo said savagely. "But it isn't just me who's contributing to your downfall. I have an expert witness to your sordid past. One who knows you well. Better than Julian—better than anyone in fact."

"Who?" breathed Inès. "Who is this person?"

"Yves Moray," chortled Scrofo, relishing his moment of victory. "Your ex-pimp. Your ex-lover—the one who deflowered you. My people found him in Paris last week."

"No, it's not possible," whispered Inès. "You couldn't have."

"Oh, but it is, it's very possible. The world is really a very tiny place," sneered Scrofo. "Look at us, Inès my dear—who would ever think that you and I, who met in such unfortunate and squalid circumstances in Paris, would be here together in beautiful Acapulco making a film?"

His brutal hand held her arm so tightly that she could feel the bruises his fingers were making.

"Where did you meet Yves?" she asked, her voice shocked into a thready whisper.

"Oh, I didn't meet him—I didn't even see the man. It all happened quite by accident, a fortuitous coincidence for me. He was arrested in Paris for fencing some stolen jewelry. At the police station he was babbling on in an alcoholic stupor and pleading his innocence—his complete innocence—of the theft, but of course he was such a pathetic drunken bum that no one believed him, so they threw him in a cell. And guess what, Inès?" He bent his face close to hers, leering with vindictive glee. "There was a photograph of you and Julian in a magazine that another prisoner had; poor Yves started bragging that he knew you. In fact he knew you extremely well— because *you worked for him when you were fourteen years old!* He said he was your pimp and you were his little baby whore, and he taught you everything he knew."

"No ..." sighed Inès. "It's a lie."

"Oh, no, my dear—it's no lie," said Scrofo, relishing his power. "One of the prisoners happened to be an old army acquaintance of mine, a Signor Volpi, who knew that I was producing a film with Julian Brooks. He contacted me and told me the whole fascinating story, and then I phoned your old boyfriend Yves. Of course he told me everything. It's amazing what a drunk will do for a few hundred francs," he remarked contemptuously. "Well, the rest, as they say, is history. It makes a wonderful story, Inès—rags to riches, tart to movie star's wife—and then *fini.*" He looked at her pityingly. "Enjoy the short time you have left with your fiancé, Mademoiselle. Because when he reads the truth about your whoring past, your life with Julian Brooks will be finished."

On the way down to the beach from his trailer, Nick was stopped by the harsh sound of Scrofo's raised voice. What was Gouroni doing now? Who was he trying to intimidate? He drew closer into the shadows to watch and listen, silent as stone. Scrofo obviously had some sort of sick hold on Inès. Nick heard the vicious blackmailing threats and his lips tightened in anger. Scrofo was vermin. He didn't deserve to breathe the same air as decent people.

Nick was just about to go over and help Inès when he heard Bluey's voice yelling on the loudspeaker from farther along the beach: "Nick, where the hell are you? We're ready for rehearsal, pal, get your butt down here pronto."

At that the Italian released his grip on Inès' arm, pushing her away from him so violently that she stumbled and fell to the sand.

In Nick's mind Inès suddenly became his mother, cowering on the ground while the monster Gourouni towered over her, ready to kill. The tableau was so real, so terrifyingly graphic that Nick wanted to scream—out at the top of his lungs. Nick was going to kill the murdering slime now. He had to.

As he started to race towards them the tableau suddenly dissolved. Inès had clambered to her feet and run down the beach and Scrofo had turned, laughing, strutting off in the opposite direction. Nick's hand clawed at the knife in his pocket and he started to follow Scrofo.

"Nick! For Christ's sake, where are you? It'll be dawn soon. Hurry up." Bluey's amplified voice brought Nick back to the present. He shook his head as if to clear it as he watched the squat figure of Gourouni disappear into the night, then he walked rapidly down to the set, with more loathing than ever in his heart for Scrofo.

The following evening in the production office at Scheherazade, Scrofo attempted to tell Nick and Bluey that Inès had been a prostitute. Bluey looked at him with disgust.

"That's a helluva thing to say," he spat. "You've got a dirty mind, Hubie baby."

Nick however, suddenly became violently angry.

"Listen, you suet-faced prick," he roared as he gripped the Italian's fleshy shoulders and pushed his face close, "don't you ever, *ever* talk about a lady—*any* lady—like that around me, or in front of *anyone*, do you understand, you motherfucker?"

Suddenly Umberto was genuinely terrified as Nick's hands were now around his neck, his voice hoarse with hatred as he squeezed the adipose, scarred flesh of Scrofo's throat.

"You rotten scum," he bellowed. "You *dare* to talk about whores. *You're* the whore, you lump of shit. What you did to those people. What you did to them . . ." His voice started to crack as his grip tightened, and Scrofo's eyes were beginning to pop out of their sockets, his face turning crimson.

The vision of his mother filled Nick's brain. Her quiet beauty and goodness snuffed out by this bastard. He was going to kill him now, at last. He'd rid the world of this filth.

Nick's eyes were closed and his hands, clamped around Scrofo's neck, began to squeeze even harder.

Bluey could see that Hubert was losing consciousness.

"For Christ's sake, quit it, Nick. He's not worth it," Bluey screamed as he tried to pry his friend off the wilting Italian. The transformation of a man who was usually so controlled in spite of all the difficulties on the set, calm in emergencies, hardly ever losing his cool, was as alarming as what he was actually doing.

"*Stop* it, Nick, for God's sake stop it! You're only hurting yourself," Bluey yelled. "Get hold of yourself, man—you must."

Nick released Scrofo's neck as Bluey's voice penetrated his consciousness and slumped into the chair, his breathing shallow, his face still contorted with rage. Bluey realized that Nick could have killed Umberto if he hadn't intervened—and the Italian thought so too. His pudgy hands gingerly massaged his scarred and now bruised throat where the livid red marks of Nick's fingers were imprinted.

"Jesus, kid. Jesus Christ, slow down," Bluey said and quickly poured him a stiff scotch.

Nick tossed it down, his burning eyes fixed on Scrofo.

"Get out of here, you fucking pig," Nick spat, his voice hoarse and shaking. "I'm making a fucking movie. I'll do what the fucking studio tells me to do on the set but don't *ever* talk about that woman or *any* woman in front of me again or I'll squeeze your fat neck until your eyeballs come out of your head. I mean it, pigface—get out of my sight. *Now.*"

Bluey poured another whiskey as Umberto, badly frightened and quite the opposite of the *bella figura* he fancied himself, nervously slunk out of the office. I will have my revenge, he thought. When these idiots see what comes out in *Confidential* they will realize I am right about the French slut. They'll know she's a murdering whore. That will be my first revenge on her. After that—who knows? His mind boiling with ideas about how to ruin Inès, he limped off through the dark corridor to his room.

"I hate that motherfucker," Nick breathed. "It's only a matter of time before I kill the bastard."

"Hey, hey, kiddo, *quit* it, will ya?" Bluey tried to soothe Nick. "We all know he's a complete asshole—a phony who knows as much about the movie business as my left testicle. Don't let him get to you. You're doin' great. The studio loves the dailies, you're keeping your head above water, and the picture's on schedule and even on budget. We've only got a few days left. You're a whiz kid, so calm down, will ya?"

Nick nodded, the whiskey clearing his head a little. "Gotta get some sleep, Bluey." He pulled his worry beads out of his pocket and swung them morosely while he gazed out of a window at the sliver of new moon palely reflected on the still, black water. Then he picked up his bulky script, and walked decisively to the door. "I'm sorry, Bluey. It's a good thing you stopped me. I was out of control—I was gone, man, gone."

"Get to bed, kiddo," Bluey said. He looked worried. "Big scene tomorrow. You gotta give it your best shot. Forget Hubert, Nick, for God's sake."

"I can't forget him, Bluey—I've seen that face too many times. I've seen it in my dreams and in every fuckin' nightmare I've ever had."

"What are you talkin' about, man?" asked Bluey. "You only met the motherfucker a few months ago."

"Oh, no," Nick said harshly. "He's haunted my life for more than ten years."

"Jesus," Bluey was silent as he stared at Nick's grim face. "What has he done to you, kid? Whatever he did, it couldn't have been that bad."

"He murdered my mother," Nick said simply. "He killed her and I'm going to kill him."

19

Inès had been undecided about whether or not to watch Julian and Dominique shooting their tenderly erotic final love scene. The two actors had not worked together since Dominique's birthday party, and when they saw each other again there had been a noticeable coolness between them. Inès had heard through the gossip grapevine that although she now had a new boyfriend, Dominique was still furious and hurt that Julian had ended the affair. Inès understood how the girl must feel; Julian had not conducted himself at all well.

"Do you want me to come to the set tonight?" she asked casually as she lay back on the bed in the twilight dusk, watching Julian prepare to leave.

"It's entirely up to you, darling." He found it difficult to meet her eyes. Julian was in a quandary. He hadn't spoken to Dominique since he terminated their affair, and felt like a cad because of explaining the situation to her only on the telephone, but the circumstances had never seemed right to face her directly. He had been working hard on the exhausting battle scenes, and in his free time had thrown himself into his reconciliation with Inès. They had been utterly inseparable as he comforted her over the loss of their baby.

He was secretly dreading his lovemaking scene with Dominique. It was tricky enough to have to simulate making passionate love to a girl with whom you had recently ended a blazing real-life affair, but even more galling was knowing that he had not behaved at all like a gentleman towards her, and he was angry with himself.

Now the thought of Inès watching their fervent kisses and caresses embarrassed him.

With her natural intuition, Inès understood completely. "Darling, don't worry," she said, smiling. "I'm expecting a call from the doctor in Los Angeles. The results of those blood tests should be in. I think I'll just stay here, drink margaritas and watch the sun set."

"No, I really think you should come, darling. Yes, yes, really, I want you there," Julian said firmly, moving next to her on the bed, gazing into her glorious eyes. "Please come, darling. I need you. You know it's over between Dominique and me, you do believe me, don't you?"

"Of course I do. All right, I'll come, later tonight," Inès agreed, brushing a strand of hair off his forehead, then kissing him lovingly. "I'm not worried about you and Dominique. And I'll stay well in the background. Don't worry, my darling; I won't make a fool of myself, I promise."

Julian gave her a rueful look as he picked up his script and blew her a kiss.

"I love you, Inès. You're magnificent. I'll see you later."

Inès stared at the closed door for several minutes, trying to analyze how she really felt about watching Julian and Dominique making love. Did she mind? Did it bother her, knowing that the whole crew would be watching her reaction? And the odious Scrofo, who had gone to such pains to blackmail her, gloating—looking at her for any signs of weakness.

She shrugged as she sauntered into the bathroom. It didn't bother her anymore. She believed that Julian was completely over his infatuation. If his verbal assurances were not enough, his passionate declarations of love, even though lovemaking was still forbidden, reassured Inès that he was hers, and hers alone. As far as others were concerned, she really didn't give a damn what people thought. If they chose to gossip and tittle-tattle, she would be above all that. The only person who made her skin crawl, whose very presence in a room made her squirm with loathing, was the sluglike Scrofo. She had to do something to stop this terrible story coming out in the magazine. She had tried hard to talk to Scrofo the day after he'd threatened her, begging him not to print it, but he had merely laughed, telling her, "You have a couple more months of the good life left, Inès. The magazine is holding the story until just before the release of *Cortez*. It will be great publicity for the film—huge coverage. Make it an absolute surefire box-office blockbuster, don't you agree? Those pictures of Julian and Dominique making love—so sexy—so titillating—everyone will race to see the film. We'll be a runaway hit."

Sickened, unable to reply, she had walked away. There was still some time left to stop the story from being published, but it would be common gossip in Hollywood long before that. As soon as Julian heard, he would question her. Of course she could lie, but she would have to tell him the truth, the whole sickening ghastly truth. Inès shuddered.

Next week, as soon as she and Julian arrived in Los Angeles, they were going to be married. The final decree had been issued, and she would be Mrs. Julian Brooks at long last. She had to stop Scrofo from printing the truth about her in that magazine. She had to—but how?

Agathe sat beside Dominique in her small, stuffy trailer by the water's edge. She was going through tonight's dialogue with her, but her heart wasn't in it.

On the sofa was a week-old copy of *The Hollywood Reporter*. The lead item in the gossip column had caught Agathe's eyes the instant she sat down:

> Wedding bells will ring out at last for Julian Brooks and the lovely Inès Juillard. The happy couple will tie the knot next week at the home of Spyros Makopolis after an arduous three-month stint in Acapulco on *Cortez,* the legendary Julian's first American film. Congratulations to the two of them.

A white-hot flame was burning in Agathe's head and she couldn't concentrate on anything Dominique was saying or doing.

Makeup girls and hairdressers bustled around the young star as she sat having pancake makeup applied to her chest and shoulders. She seemed as usual to have no modesty; she was bare to the waist, calmly allowing the body makeup girl to paint her exposed flesh.

She had few words to learn except "I love you" and "My father will never understand." Kisses and burning passion were the main ingredients of the scene tonight as Cortez and the princess would be rolling around naked on the sandy beach in the moonlight. Dominique had been given a flesh-colored body stocking to wear to save the censors' blushes. Her nude dance scene had been approved by the Hays Office but there was still a limit to the amount of licentiousness which they would allow on screen.

Dominique thought about how it would be to make love with Julian again. Always during their scenes together he had wanted her afterward, and their combined passion had rocked the flimsy walls of the trailer. But Inès had never been around then. Now she was on the sidelines watching all the time, never taking her eyes off her fiancé. Dominique sighed. There was little chance of a reconciliation with Julian, she realized. But she had seen the flash of desire in his eyes when they had kissed during rehearsal, though it had gone as quickly as it appeared and he was again the ultimate professional—the actor—coolly removed, pleasant, trading japes and jokes with the crew, polite and considerate towards her. Dominique knew she had lost him, but after all she had Frankie. Her new boyfriend was a member of the crew, American, young, blond, a most attentive suitor and a good lover. Not as good as Julian but certainly younger.

Agathe, her own passion for Julian still raging, couldn't have cared less by now that her young charge was having an affair. Nothing mattered to her anymore. She tried hard to act as normally as possible around the crew, hoping that no one would notice that she was thinking about Julian all the time. No one did.

There was a knock on the door and Frankie loped in, a broad smile on his face.

"Oooh!" Dominique said, pretending to be shy and half-covering her breasts. *"Méchant garçon.* You surprised me—give me a kiss."

They kissed lingeringly, neither noticing that Agathe had slipped out of the trailer as soon as the boy entered it—she needed her fix. A glimpse of Julian, maybe even a word from him, it was all that she lived for these days.

As the new moon slid behind a puff of darkened cloud, a lone figure sped quickly down the hundred or more stone steps that descended at one side of Scheherazade. The guard dogs were silent; the figure knew at exactly what time they were taken on their rounds, and had timed the arrival at the cable car perfectly to avoid the watchdogs and their handlers.

Swiftly the figure squatted by the side of the wooden carriage and, removing a few small tools from a pocket, made some slight adjustments to the machine's gear box. It took only a few minutes; then, with a furtive glance around, ears strained for the slightest sound, the figure disappeared into the thick tropical foliage which surrounded the vast estate.

Now, as the moon reappeared from behind the clouds, it was reflected in the small puddle of amber beads which had been dropped behind the padded seat of the wooden cable car.

They had decided to shoot Dominique and Julian's love scene on Ramona's private beach, well away from the prying eyes of Acapulco tourists. Part of the beach was brilliantly lit by a dozen arc lamps, which were placed around the area on which the stand-ins for Julian and Dominique were lying on the sand entwined in each other's arms.

Nick paced up and down nervously, a cigarette hanging permanently from his lips, talking to his lighting cameraman and to Bluey. Sometimes he glanced over to where Scrofo stood, half concealed behind an arc lamp, as usual speaking to no one but occasionally staring over at Nick with hatred.

Nick stared right back at him. How could this man have become such a monster, he wondered. What in his childhood had created such a sadistic beast? There had to be some reason for his venom, for the evil that seemed to radiate from him. He looked over again, but Scrofo was gone.

Nick shrugged as he went over to where his unit bustled about chatting quietly. They were all thankful that for once the Toad was not hanging around the set to irritate them. All the crew, and most members of the cast, had suffered from Croft's foul mouth during the past few months. All of them despised him, and few made it a secret.

Shirley Frankovitch's reports on his acumen as a line producer had been totally exaggerated. The charm, diplomacy and respect she had glowingly talked of were all sadly lacking. His knowledge of the mechanics of filmmaking was rudimentary, and his alienation of the crew and the actors was remarkable in its totality. Things were always more calm on the set, and certainly Nick was easier to work with, when the fat Italian wasn't around.

Farther down the beach Julian sat in his canvas chair wearing a light seersucker robe over his flesh-colored bathing suit. He flicked through the pages of his dialogue casually, looking up as Inès came to sit beside him, smiling as he put his hand lightly on her shoulder.

The moon shimmered on the flat ocean, with only a slight tide disturbing the shoreline as Inès put her hand on his, and they both stared out at the sea.

One of Ramona's houseboys suddenly appeared and tapped Inès on the shoulder, handing her a scribbled note.

"Excuse me, darling," she said. "The doctor's calling from Los Angeles. I must go up to the main house to take the call."

"I hope the results from the tests are okay," said Julian.

"I'm sure they are," Inès smiled. "I'll be right back, darling."

Julian blew her a kiss and admired her slender body as she walked across the beach to the cable car.

It sat at the base of the jagged rocks, its plain white wooden frame strangely out of place against the splendor of the exotic, sumptuous surroundings.

Inès got in and pressed the third button. With a shuddering creak the ancient contraption started its gradual ascent up the side of the steep rocks to the house. It seemed to be going much slower than usual, Inès thought; it shook and trembled all the way up, and there was an odd sort of rasping sigh from the pulleys as they dragged the groaning machine up to the third level.

The third floor was in complete darkness. Inès stepped from the cable car onto the white marble floor, her flimsy sandals echoing hollowly as she made her way to the main production office.

The room was pitch black. Inès shivered even though it was a humid night. She switched on the light, went over to the telephone and told the operator to put through her call from Los Angeles.

"There's no one on the line for you, *Señora,* the operator said.

"But there must be. I just received a message that my doctor was calling," Inès told her.

"No, I'm sorry. No one has called you at all tonight, Miss Juillard. It must be a mistake."

Puzzled, Inès replaced the receiver and sat thinking for a moment before she went to the door. As she reached it she saw in the hallway the shadow of a horribly familiar squat figure strutting slowly between the marble pillars of the terrace. She stopped. The last person she wanted to see or talk to was Umberto Scrofo. She did not want to be cornered by him again. Not at night, in the empty darkness of the villa.

Suddenly Scrofo stopped in his tracks, turning around swiftly as if he had heard something. He was like an animal, Inès thought, he had the instincts of a beast.

She could smell his cologne, that foul, cheap scent which seemed to hang in the night air like a noxious vapor. Even the odor of his body lingered after him.

After a few seconds Scrofo continued on his way, obviously heading for the cable car. Inès saw him press a button, then heard the familiar loud creaking as the machine began its laborious, strained descent.

The funicular had not gone more than a few feet when there was a harsh rending noise, a cacophony of screeching wires and pulleys exploding out of their sockets, and a hideous animal scream from Scrofo as the white wooden carriage was ripped from its moorings and began to fall down the sheer cliff.

Inès ran to the cable car's top landing and to her horror saw the cable car smashing its way down, down, down to the bottom of the rocks. All the way Scrofo screamed in terror. Inès could see as if in slow motion the hated bullet head, the great yaw of a gargoyle's mouth opened in the agony of his inevitable death as he plummeted to the ground.

Scrofo tried to hang on until the last impact. When his body was thrown twenty feet through the air, it landed on the rocks like a smashed doll. All that he had managed to clutch for support was a small row of broken amber beads, and the tiny crucifix which hung from them.

Epilogue

HOLLYWOOD. ONE YEAR LATER

*F*or over a year the whole of America had been bombarded with hype on MCCP's latest, greatest and soon to be released blockbuster, *The Legend of Cortez*. It was a rare newspaper or magazine indeed which had not featured some story, photograph or article on one or other of the principals in the movie. *Cortez* mania gripped the nation, and MCCP was crossing its corporate fingers that the publicity machine had done its work well enough to guarantee that every box-office register would be working overtime.

Although the new stretch-version Cadillac was fitted with the latest in air-conditioning, the hot California night still made the air hang heavy inside the perfumed darkness of the car. There were six of them in the limousine—Nicholas and Elektra Stone, Dominique with a handsome escort, and Julian and his wife.

She was concerned that the excessive and controversial publicity which he had received might adversely influence the critics. Julian was being hailed as the greatest English actor since Olivier, and his name had become a household word long before most of the American public had even had a glimpse of his talents. Hubert S. Croft's death and the scandal of Ines' past had been universal gossip for months after the incident. The death of the Italian producer was as juicy a piece of news as anyone had heard for years.

Julian held his wife's hand, smiling at her reassuringly. He had seen a rough cut of the movie, and although self-critical to an extreme, he realized that his performance had been electrifying. He had brought to his stereo-typed role a swashbuckling magnetism, combined with a sensitive natural-ism, which had been nurtured and polished on the London stage. The word was out in Hollywood that he was about to become as big a male star as Gable. The stacks of offers which poured into his agent's office ensured him a place in cinematic history, but his thoughts, in fact, were less on tonight's premiere than on his next challenge. He was going back to his roots to star in *Coriolanus* on the West End stage. He felt that he'd already spent enough time on the Hollywood scene, even though the result so far had been just two films, but he had only two more pictures to make for MCCP. When those were finished their baby, David, would be almost three years old, and they had decided to settle down in one place to give the child the security of an ordered life.

"Did David mind that you didn't stay with him until he went to bed?" Julian asked.

"Oh, no, darling. I think he must somehow have realized how important tonight is to his daddy." She thought lovingly of month-old David's beau-tiful smile as she handed him to his nanny after giving him his bottle. Julian was her life, but David ran a close second, and she adored her two men passionately.

She sighed happily. She felt she was a lucky woman.

"Oh, look," Dominique pointed excitedly to a small art-house cinema they were just passing on Sunset Boulevard. *"La Città Perduta*—wasn't that Hubert Croft's Italian film?"

Everyone peered through the tinted windows of the limousine to where the flickering neon sign spelled out the names of the cast and that of Umberto Scrofo as producer.

"Honey, don't remind us of *him*—that's all over and forgotten," Domi-nique's escort told her. "It's yesterday's news."

Nick stared out blankly at the cinema. Hubert S. Croft, Umberto Scrofo. The man whose ghastly image had haunted him for so much of his life. Dead now, but the memory of him would never die. Nick could never forget the horrors of those war years on Hydra, the countless atrocities which Scrofo had committed, culminating in the brutal murder of his mother.

"It's a year ago tonight," Nick said quietly.

"What is?" Dominique asked.

"It's one year exactly since Scrofo died." Nick's voice was so soft that the others had to strain to hear him.

"Oh, my God, so it is, you're absolutely right," breathed Julian. "God, only a year."

"As far as I'm concerned that bastard finally got what he deserved," Nick said harshly.

"Poor Agathe," Dominique muttered. "I wonder what she's doing now."

"Rotting behind bars in some Mexican jail." Julian's voice was uncharacteristically unsympathetic. "She was a madwoman, completely certifiable. If Croft or Scrofo, or whatever his name was, hadn't died that night, it would have been Inès for certain."

"And all for the love of you, Julian," Dominique teased. "All for the love of you." She flashed him her sultry gamine smile as she snuggled closer to her escort.

There had been several men in Dominique's life in the past year. As an eighteen-year-old star with a brilliant future, she was more gloriously sexy than ever and reveled unashamedly in her sorceress ways. She smiled at Julian, who smiled back uncomfortably. They were friendly now, but she knew she would never get over their passionate romance until he belonged to her again. How could she? It had been the ultimate and perfect love for her—and she wanted it to happen all over again. It was a once in a lifetime affair, never to be forgotten.

But something which none of them would ever forget was that night— that terrible night in Acapulco exactly one year ago.

When the Acapulco police arrived at Ramona's villa, Inspector Gomez had begun his slow interrogation of each of them about Hubert Croft's "accident." He strongly believed it to be murder, and questioned everyone with painstaking care. By the time he turned his attention to Agathe, the woman was trembling violently, her face shining with sweat, and she was wringing her hands in a frenzy.

Before the Inspector could question her, she fixed her eyes on Inès and crooned softly, "It's all her fault. She made me do it—didn't you, Inès?" Her eyes seemed to burn into Inès who was suddenly dry-mouthed, unable to speak. "Yes, you did," Agathe spat. "You forced me to do it. I killed Hubert Croft. *I* did," she hissed. "But I didn't mean to. I meant *her* to die. She—*she* should have been the one who ate the poisoned oyster, not Irving." She took a step toward Inès, who stood absolutely still, rooted in shock. "Inès Dessault—Inès Juillard, the *whore*. She should have been in the cable car."

"What? What did you say? Why did you kill him?" said the Inspector, scribbling furiously as the others watched Agathe's transformation in amazement. The mouse was turning into a she-wolf, and it was not a pretty sight.

"Because of *her!*" she screamed, saliva flecking the corners of her lips;

her eyes wild and bloodshot. "The enemy whore—why didn't you die? Why—why? You should have. I planned it so well—so perfectly."

Dry keening sobs racked her emaciated body and her hands became claws as she suddenly tried to pounce on the spellbound Inès. Two burly policemen grabbed her by the arms, trying to hold her as her sobs became heaving cries of pent-up rage and frustration.

"The wrong person died. Hubert wasn't a saint but he didn't deserve to die like that—the filthy slut should have died. I arranged it for *her*. Why didn't she die?"

Julian was stunned. Whore—Inès? Enemy slut? What was this demented woman saying? His arms tightened around Inès, who was staring at Agathe, a faint flicker of recognition dawning in her eyes.

Oh, God, Inès thought. Another one—another creature from the past come to destroy my life. But who was she? Inès desperately racked her brain to try to recall when she had known this woman.

Agathe screamed hysterically, "You didn't know she was a famous Parisian prostitute, did you, Julian? Did you?" She laughed, her face a mask of hatred.

Inès' face paled and she felt the rigid body of Julian moving away from her. Then suddenly she remembered.

"Oh, my God," she whispered. That wispy, strange girl she had seen only once or twice at the cash register of L'Éléphant Rose during the war. She had never even seen the girl's face properly, but now she remembered all the stories they'd told about her. Those years of privation when the Jewish girl was hidden down in the cellar; how her hair had turned completely white; how when she got out she had despised not only the enemy but all the girls who fraternized with them.

Inès took a step towards the babbling woman whose face was a twisted mask of pain and vengeance. She seemed barely human now. "Please stop, Agathe," Inès pleaded. "Don't. I beg you, *don't! Please*. Why are you saying these things? They're lies. You mustn't do this—you *can't*."

"I can—oh, but I can and I *will*." Agathe's smile was vicious, her laugh a crone's cackle. "Now that *he* knows what you were—what you *are*—he won't want to marry you anymore—will you, Julian?"

Suddenly she burst away from the restraining grasp of the two policemen and rushed towards Julian, crooning, *"Mon amour—mon amour."* One skinny arm clamped itself around his neck, while the other yanked feverishly at the knot of his robe, trying to pull it open.

"My God, Agathe, what the hell are you doing? Stop it!" Julian was strong, and he held her at arm's length in a tight grip, staring into her demented eyes.

"Tell me what you meant about Inès," he said, his voice steady and menacing. "Tell me, Agathe."

Inès sank on to a couch, hiding her face in her hands. It was over now. All over. Now the truth would finally be known. To her lover, the man whose child she had carried—whose wife she was going to be. It was finally finished. And ironically not by Scrofo, but by a woman she hardly knew. Her whole life lay in ruins around her. Julian would never forgive her for her past and her deception. How could he?

"Yes, yes, Julian, of course I'll tell you—I want to tell you *everything*." Agathe licked at her dry lips, her eyes darting gleefully between Julian and Inès, reveling in the attention of the whole group who were riveted to her every word with horrified fascination. She was center stage finally, now they would watch *her,* listen to *her,* while the arms of the man she worshiped held her tightly.

"Paris. It was Paris—at the nightclub L'Éléphant Rose during the war— she fucked them—all of them—the Boche, the Gestapo, the SS, the Italian pigs. Soldiers, officers, she didn't care who she did it with. She danced with them—she laughed with them and she let them *all* fuck her. Do anything with her. They gave her money which she threw around, showing off to everyone. She loved the life of a whore, didn't you, Inès?" She glanced over at Inès' slumped figure and, with a contemptuous laugh, continued, "Then one night she went too far. She killed a man with his own razor, she cut his throat. At least she thought she did— didn't you, bitch?" Again, she looked towards Inès huddled on the couch, the humiliation of having her past laid bare rendering her mute and immobile.

"*Who*—who did Inès kill?" Julian's voice sounded hoarse, cold and tired. Inès could tell now as he looked at her that he hated her. Her dream was just another nightmare.

"*SCROFO!*" Agathe screamed. "Umberto Scrofo—the Italian General, the fat one with all the medals. The one who called himself Hubert Croft here. She was his girl—his doxy. He made love to her *many,* many times in Paris. Then she tried to murder him—but you didn't succeed, did you?" She sneered at Inès. "What a pity for you, whore. You didn't succeed just like I didn't succeed in killing you—but maybe I've done something even better. I've *ruined* you, and your precious life with Julian, because he's *mine—MINE!*" With that she lashed a bony hand across her dress, tearing off the buttons to reveal her shriveled breasts.

"Kiss me, Julian! *Mon amour.*" Eyes closed, she tried to squirm closer to him, but Julian held her away from him, an expression of disgust on his face.

"I've been waiting for you, *mon amour,* my Julian," she cried despairingly, her eyes now open and pleading. "Waiting, my love. I know you want me too, it's our destiny to be together."

As Agathe tried to press her writhing body against his, the Inspector signaled to the two policemen, who grabbed her, pulling her away from Julian. Ramona put her shawl over Agathe's half-naked body, her eyes mirroring the pity she felt for this poor wretch, and the rest of them turned away in shocked embarrassment.

Julian stood quite still, his tanned face ashen.

Nick went over to him. Unable to find anything to say, he put his hand comfortingly on Julian's shoulder. Dominique drew closer to the two men, her childlike, inquisitive eyes riveted to Inès, who still hadn't spoken.

Ramona was comforting Shirley, who was weeping quietly. "Irving, my poor, poor Irving. That mad bitch killed him too, that bitch. Oh, Christ."

The rest of the cast and crew stood stiffly like extras in a crowd scene, huddled in the background, staring at Julian, Agathe and Inès in fascination. They sensed that something even more dreadful was about to happen in this frozen tableau. All the principals were silent except for Shirley's muffled sobbing, and the faint sound of waves sighing on the shoreline was the only background noise.

Then Julian spoke in a dark, threatening voice which sent a shudder through Inès. "Is all this true, Inès? Is what Agathe said the truth?"

How could he? How *could* Julian ask her that question in front of everyone? Couldn't he leave her with even a shred of self-respect? Inès had waited to find the man of her dreams for many years. Now he stood before her with dozens of people as witnesses, about to denounce her for what she had been, and for what she had done in what seemed a former lifetime.

Julian asked the question again, his voice even icier than before. The electrified silence of the onlookers intensified his theatrical presence. He was center stage—the leading actor—and all the supporting cast seemed to be waiting with bated breath for the inevitable drama to unfold.

"I asked you if what Agathe has said is true, Inès," he said for the third time, his voice raised. Inès could hear the suppressed rage, see it in his posture, his attitude. His fists were clenched, his eyes narrowed, his regal head proud. The king was demanding obedience from a subject.

"Answer me, Inès!" he roared authoritatively. "Say something."

Inès raised her head to look unflinchingly into Julian's cold eyes, struggling to keep her face impassive. She had too much pride to cry, though her throat ached with pain. The man she loved was demanding a public confession from her, demanding that she reveal her past to him—to all of these people—because of what he considered to be *his* divine right.

Slowly Inès rose to her feet and the crowd held its breath in anticipation. There was silence as Inès stared defiantly at Julian, a slight breeze stirring her dress. He took an angry step towards her, roughly brushing aside Nick's restraining hand.

"I said *answer* me, Inès, I want the truth. *Now.*"

Inès' voice was only slightly louder than the whisper of the breeze. "Julian, oh, Julian, the camera isn't turning. You don't have to perform now."

"How dare you!" The power of his voice caused the sleeping parrots in the trees to awaken and raise a cacophony of screeching. "Don't *preach* to me, Inès. Answer my question. That's all I ask of you."

"Not here—not *now.*" Her eyes never left his face. "No, Julian. No. I can't and I won't."

She turned, light as gossamer, and walked swiftly from the great marble hall into the welcoming darkness of the night, the tears that she had held back almost choking her.

Nick grabbed Julian's arm as he tried to follow her. "No, Julian, no, let her go. She's right. This isn't the time or the place. Leave her alone, you must."

Weeping with despair, Inès began flinging her clothes into suitcases. One of Ramona's drivers waited outside the hotel. She was leaving Acapulco. Leaving Julian. Leaving behind her perfect future. She was going—to where? She didn't know; she knew only that she had to escape. Hastily she pulled off her silk dress, putting on a skirt and jacket. She snapped her suitcases shut, oblivious to the pieces of stray fabric which trailed from their sides, and rang down for a porter.

The door opened suddenly and Julian walked into the room. He had changed out of his robe into trousers and a shirt. His face was pale, his eyes full of pain.

They stared at each other. He looked down at the closed suitcases, at her traveling clothes, at the defiant hurt expression on her beautiful face.

"Why are you leaving me?" he asked.

"Why?" She smiled weakly. "Oh, you know why, Julian. It's true what Agathe said—not all of it—she exaggerated—but I *was* a prostitute in Paris, and I *did* try to kill Scrofo or Croft or whatever he called himself."

"My God." He shook his head and sat down heavily on the bed. "But *why,* Inès? Why in God's name did you never tell me before? You must have known that one day I'd find out?"

"I just hoped that you wouldn't. I suppose I didn't think you could bear to hear the truth. Yes, I was a whore," she said quietly, "but only because of circumstances. You see, my mother had been one, and probably my grandmother before her."

She looked at him but his expression remained enigmatic. She sighed.

"It was an easy, almost normal way of life to me, Julian—I was very young when I started, an adolescent, and I really knew no other life. Perhaps I was too greedy; maybe in London I should have stopped being a prostitute, taken a proper job in a shop or an office, and found a man, any man, to marry. I shouldn't have cared whether I loved him or not. I should have just married him for security and to have him take care of me."

She looked at him, her eyes huge with tears. "That's how it's supposed to be for a woman, isn't it, Julian? No one said you had to be in love to be married—but to me, to marry someone I didn't love was an even worse kind of prostitution."

Julian said nothing, his face still expressionless, as Inès continued, "I loved you so much—I *do* love you so much, that I couldn't run the risk of probably losing you. I know you, Julian. Don't forget that. I know how you think, how most men think. You have double standards regarding men and women. You would have left me if you knew, I know you would. You wouldn't have been able to bear what people would have said, the malicious gossip, the scandal and all the whispering that would have gone on behind your back."

"No, Inès." He took a step towards her and she thought she could see tenderness gradually coming back into his face. "It isn't true. I would have understood, and I would have forgiven you because I *love* you. You are—you always have been, always *will* be, the only woman for me in my whole life. Don't you know that?"

She stared at him uncertainly. "But my past? Doesn't it bother you—surely you must mind?"

"Mind—mind? Of *course* I bloody mind, you silly little goose. But what can I do about it? Nothing. It happened, it's part of what has made you the person you are, the woman I love, the woman I want to marry and spend the rest of my life with. Inès, you forgave me for Dominique—a far worse thing. How could I not forgive you, my darling, how could I not?"

"But you were so angry in front of everyone—it was so humiliating. I was mortified, Julian."

"I'm sorry, my darling. I'm truly, truly sorry. What more can I say? I hate myself for hurting you, Inès. You've been hurt too much in the past."

His arms reached out for her and she found herself wanting to melt into their safe refuge.

"God knows I've been a bastard to you, worse than a bastard."

"It's all right, darling," she murmured. "It's all forgotten."

"None of it really matters to us anymore," he whispered, taking her in his arms, and the breath left her body in a great sigh of abandoned relief. "It's all forgotten, my love. All over now."

"Thank God," Inès breathed. "Thank God, everything's out in the open.

I'm glad you know the truth, Julian. I think our life together would have become impossible if I had always to pretend."

"You're right, my angel." Julian smiled lovingly at her. "You're absolutely right, it's never any good to pretend. That's only for actors."

Long before their limousine arrived at the theater, the occupants could see the dozens of searchlights crisscrossing the thick blackness of the sky and hear the excited shrieks of the eager fans in the bleachers greeting each arriving celebrity with approval.

"Here goes," Nick said, adjusting his black bow tie. "This is what we've all been waiting for. It's sink or swim time, boys and girls."

The women took out their powder compacts to check their perfectly made-up faces for the last time. All of them were silent with their own particular thoughts of what tonight's premiere would mean to each of them.

For Elektra it meant that Nikolas would finally achieve his lifetime's desire: to be acknowledged as an important director in the American cinema. He had expunged the memory of Gourouni from his mind in the past year and was filled with optimism about the future.

Dominique was being hailed as the brightest, most exciting new star in Hollywood, and the studio was considering casting her opposite Julian in his next film.

Inès smoothed the folds of her ice-white velvet gown. Turning her perfect profile away from her husband, she looked out the window into the night, the encroaching cheers of the fans suddenly provoking thoughts of the past. She thought how lucky she was—so, very lucky. Luck had saved her from the vengeance of the Gestapo after the incident with Scrofo. If it hadn't been for luck, she too might have lived those years of torment that Agathe had endured, which had slowly driven her mad. If she had been forced to exist in that cellar, would her life have been any different from Agathe's? Could *she* have remained sane?

Inès really couldn't blame Agathe for what she had tried to do. The ravages of war and evil had created a certain kind of madness in almost everyone who had survived it.

As the white limousine drew up outside the brilliantly lit theater, the crowd's cheers built to a tumultuous crescendo.

"Ready, darling?" Julian gently squeezed Inès' white-gloved hand.

"Ready," she said with a brilliant smile. "Ready for anything, darling."

From the darkness opposite Dominique looked across at them and a sly and secret smile flickered over her beautiful face. One day, she thought, one day soon, Julian, you will be mine again, I know you will. I can feel it in my bones.